By David Sherman and Dan Cragg

Starfist

FIRST TO FIGHT

SCHOOL OF FIRE

STEEL GAUNTLET

BLOOD CONTACT

TECHNOKILL

HANGFIRE

KINGDOM'S SWORD

KINGDOM'S FURY

LAZARUS RISING

A WORLD OF HURT

FLASHFIRE

By David Sherman

The Night Fighters

KNIVES IN THE NIGHT

MAIN FORCE ASSAULT

OUT OF THE FIRE

A ROCK AND A HARD PLACE

A NGHU NIGHT FALLS

CHARLIE DON'T LIVE HERE ANYMORE

THERE I WAS: THE WAR OF CORPORAL HENRY J. MORRIS, USMC

THE SQUAD

Demontech

GULF RUN

ONSLAUGHT

RALLY POINT

By Dan Cragg

Fiction

THE SOLDIER'S PRIZE

Nonfiction

A DICTIONARY OF SOLDIER TALK

GENERALS IN MUDDY BOOTS

INSIDE THE VC AND THE NVA (with Michael Lee Lanning)

TOP SERGEANT (with William G. Bainbridge)

STARFIST
FLASHFIRE

FLASHFIRE

BOOK ELEVEN

DAVID SHERMAN

AND

DAN CRAGG

BALLANTINE BOOKS • NEW YORK

Starfist: Flashfire is a work of fiction. Names, characters, places, and incidents are the products of the authors' imagination or are used fictitiously. Any resemblance to actual events, locales, or persons, living or dead, is entirely coincidental.

Published in the United States by Del Rey Books, an imprint of The Random House Publishing Group, a division of Random House, Inc., New York.

DEL REY is a registered trademark and the Del Rey colophon is a trademark of Random House, Inc.

Cataloging-in-Publication Data is available from the Library of Congress.

ISBN 0-345-46054-5

Printed in the United States of America on acid-free paper

www.delreybooks.com

2 4 6 8 9 7 5 3 1

First Edition

Text design by Julie Schroeder

To:

Sergeant W. D. Ehrhart, USMC
Scout/Sniper, First Battalion, First Marines
RVN, 1967–1968

and World-Class Poet

STARFIST
FLASHFIRE

PROLOGUE

A small, black object arced out from the crowd, described a graceful parabola, and burst into greasy orange flame in the middle of the street. "Steady, men, steady," the lieutenant murmured from behind the thin line of infantrymen facing the mob. To his men he appeared calm and in control; in reality his legs were about to give way on him.

"Shee-it!" one of the infantrymen exclaimed, grasping his lexan shield more tightly and glancing nervously over his shoulder at the sergeant of the guard, who shook his head silently, gesturing that the man should watch the crowd and not him. The troops had only just been called out to face the unexpected mob of irate citizens. Already the area between the Fort Seymour main gate and the demonstrators, a very short stretch of about one hundred meters, was littered with debris that had been thrown at the soldiers. Now a firebomb! Things were getting serious. That firebomb belied the innocuous messages on the signs carried by the demonstrators, GIVE US INDEPENDENCE!, NO TAXES TO THE CONFEDERATION!, CHANG-STURDEVANT DICTATOR!, and others.

Lieutenant Jacob Ios of Alfa Company, 2nd Battalion, 1st Brigade, 3rd Provisional Infantry Division, Confederation Army, was pulling his first tour of duty as officer of the guard at the Fort Seymour depot. Neither he nor his men had received civil-disturbance training, and the only equipment they had for that job were the lexan body shields they were using to protect themselves against thrown objects. Fortunately, none of the crowd's missiles had yet reached them. He wished that

Major General Cazombi's recommendation to keep the contractor guard force—all men recruited on Ravenette—responsible for the installation's security, had been followed, but he'd been overridden by General Sorca the tactical commander with overall authority for security. Still, Ios couldn't help wondering what Cazombi had done to get himself stuck at Fort Seymour.

The sergeant of the guard interrupted his musings. "El Tee, should I have the men unsling their arms?" he whispered.

"Not yet." Ios made a quick estimate of the crowd's size and his stomach plummeted right into his boots. There had to be at least three hundred people in it; his guard force was outnumbered ten-to-one.

"If they start coming at us, Lieutenant, we won't be able to stop them," the sergeant whispered. Surreptitiously, he unfastened the retaining strap on his sidearm holster. As if confirming the sergeant's fears, several men in the crowd ran forward a few paces and tossed more firebombs. They exploded harmlessly in the street but much closer to the soldiers than the last one.

"Confederation soldiers! Go home! We do not want you here! Confederation out!" a woman with a bullhorn began chanting shrilly. Ios couldn't see the woman. That was ominous, someone leading the mob from behind.

"That's okay with me!" One of the soldiers grinned and several of his buddies laughed nervously. More and more people in the crowd took up the chant, *"Confederation out!"* until the slogan swelled to a roar. People banged clubs and iron pipes on the pavement as they chanted, beating a steady *Whang! Whang! Whang!* A chunk of paving sailed out from the mob and skittered across the roadway, coming to rest against the knee-high stone wall that flanked the main entrance to Fort Seymour. That wall was the only shelter the soldiers would have if the mob charged them; the iron gates across the entrance, which had never before been closed, were chained shut and two tactical vehicles were drawn up tight behind them in the event the mob tried to break through.

"Climate Six, this is Post One, over," Ios muttered into the command net, trying very hard to keep his voice even as he spoke. Climate Six was the Fort Seymour staff duty officer's call sign.

"Post One, this is Climate Six, over."

"We need immediate reinforcement, over," Ios said, his voice tensing as more bricks and stones pelted the road. The fires had burned themselves out.

"Ah, Post One, what is your status? I hear shouting but I cannot see your position from here, over."

Ios suppressed an angry response, "Climate Six, several hundred rioters are approaching my position! We are in danger of being overrun! Request immediate reinforcement!" Stones and bricks hurtled toward Ios. Then another bright orange blossom. "Climate Six, we are being firebombed, repeat, firebombed!"

"Casualties? Over."

Ios took a breath to steady himself. "None, so far, Climate Six, but we cannot hold unless reinforced immediately! What the hell am I supposed to do?"

"Ah, Post One, use proper communications procedure. Use your initiative but hold that gate at all costs. You will be reinforced ASAP. Climate Six out." The staff duty officer, Lieutenant Colonel Poultney Maracay, who only a few moments ago was happily contemplating his position on the promotion list for Full Colonel, had begun to perspire. "Just where in the hell am I supposed to get reinforcements?" he muttered.

"All the line troops are out on Bataan," the staff duty NCO replied.

"I know that!" Maracay responded angrily. Both generals Cazombi and Sorca were out at the Peninsula on Pohick Bay, where the division was billeted. The division hadn't been on Ravenette two weeks yet and already the troops, in the infantryman's age-old cynical way, had dubbed the Peninsula "Bataan." It'd take fifteen minutes or more to get a reaction force back to Main Post and by then . . . he left the thought hanging. All he had at Main Post were supply specialists and, since it was Saturday afternoon, most of them would be out in town or otherwise incapacitated.

"Sergeant," he turned to the staff duty NCO, "I'm going down to the main gate and see for myself what that young stud's got himself into. Inform General—" he thought for a moment. Major General Cazombi was the garrison commander and the senior officer at Fort Seymour but Brigadier General Sorca commanded the infantry division. "—General Sorca and request that he send immediate reinforcements to Main Post.

Keep the net open with Lieutenant Ios and keep HQ informed. Jesus, what a mess!" Shaking his head, he strapped on his sidearm as he went through the door. Where'd these people come from? He knew there were tensions between the Confederation Congress and Ravenette and its allies, but that was esoteric, trade-relations crap, not the kind of thing to drive people into the streets, much less motivate them to attack a Confederation military post.

Lieutenant Ios and his men were not at that moment worrying about trade relations. The young officer was so rattled that he couldn't remember if there was a specific command for "unsling arms" so he fell back on the oldest and most reliable method for passing on a command at an officer's disposal: "Sergeant, have the men unsling arms!" he said crisply while unstrapping his own sidearm. As one, the men dropped their shields and unslung their rifles. "Take up firing positions behind the wall!" Ios ordered over the tactical net. "Do not fire unless I give the command! Steady, men, steady! Show them we mean business! Reinforcements are on the way." He said it with a confidence he didn't feel because he knew, as well as the SDO and every man in his tiny guard force, that useful reinforcements were all out on Bataan.

Seeing the soldiers take up firing positions, the mob howled and rushed forward to within fifty meters of the gate. Now rocks, paving stones, bottles, all kinds of junk began raining down on the soldiers. Ios could clearly hear people in the mob shouting for blood. Protected somewhat by their helmets and equipment harnesses, the troops crouched behind the low wall. "Hold on!" Ios shouted into the tactical net, but at that moment a brick smashed into his mouth and he fell to the ground, dazed, spitting teeth and blood.

As he lay there in agony Lieutenant Jacob Ios, "Jake" to his friends, heard only dimly the fatal *zip-craaaak* of a pistol shot.

Panting, out of breath, Lieutenant Colonel Maracay, whose fate it was to be there at that time and in that place merely through the impersonal agency of the post sergeant major's duty roster, gasped in horror at the sight in the street before the main gate.

A driver assigned to one of the blocking vehicles looked up at him, face white, eyes staring. "I-I didn't fire my weapon," he managed at last.

From somewhere off to the right, someone yelled, “Hooo-haaaa!” and began laughing hysterically.

“Open the gates,” the colonel said. He stepped out into the street, his now forgotten sidearm dangling uselessly in one hand, and surveyed the carnage. Scores of mangled bodies lay in pools of blood; wounded men and women, even some children, lay moaning in agony. Directly overhead, spanning the gate, incongruously happy and welcoming, a sign announced, FORT SEYMOUR ARMY SUPPLY DEPOT. YOU CALL, WE HAUL.

“Get—get medics!” Maracay screamed into the command net. “Get the fucking medics!” Dimly, he became aware that someone up the street was pointing something at him and instinctively Colonel Maracay raised his pistol, but it was only a man with a vid camera.

CHAPTER ONE

It wasn't late in the evening, but at high latitude on Thorsfinni's World the sun was long down by the time the liberty bus clattered to a stop next to a vacant lot near the center of Bronnysund, the town outside the main gate of Marine Corps Base Camp Major Pete Ellis. The driver levered the door open and thirty Marines clattered off, whooping and hollering in unrestrained glee at their weekend's freedom from the restrictions on behavior imposed by the Confederation Marine Corps during duty hours.

Well, most of the restrictions. They were required to maintain a certain level of decorum—at least, they were not to commit crimes, or get themselves injured badly enough to miss duty, or go anyplace from which they wouldn't be able to return for morning roll call on the third morning hence. And it was only *most* of them who whooped and hollered; there was a loose knot of eight who were somewhat more restrained. The eight in question were the junior leaders of third platoon, Company L, 34th Fleet Initial Strike Team.

"So where are we going?" Corporal Bohb Taylor, second gun team and most junior of the corporals, asked when the other twenty-two Marines had scattered.

Corporal Tim Kerr, first fire team leader, second squad, and the most senior of the eight, simply snorted and turned to lead the way.

Corporal Bill Barber, first gun team leader and not much junior to Kerr, slapped the back of Taylor's head hard enough to knock his soft cover awry, said, "Taylor, sometimes you're so dumb I don't know how you ever got your second stripe." He turned to follow Kerr.

"Yeah, Taylor. What do you know about the Top that the rest of us don't?" asked Corporal Rachman "Rock" Claypoole, third fire team leader, second squad, and not much senior to Taylor. He followed Barber.

"What do you mean, what do I know about the Top?" Taylor squawked.

"Blackmail!" Corporal Joe Dean, first squad's third fire team leader and also not much senior to Taylor, hooted. "There's no other way you could make corporal!" He laughed raucously.

"Which begs the question of how *you* made corporal," Corporal Raoul Pasquin, first squad's second fire team leader said with a loud laugh.

"Hey!" Dean yelped indignantly.

Corporal Dornhofer, first fire team leader, first squad, not much junior to Kerr, chuckled and shook his head. He and the other corporals fell in with Claypoole.

Taylor had to run a few paces to catch up.

A few blocks and a couple of turns later, Kerr shoved open the door of Big Barb's, the combination bar, restaurant, ships' chandlery, hotel, and bordello that was the unofficial headquarters of third platoon, Company L, 34th Fleet Initial Strike Team during liberty hours.

"Te-e-em!"

Twin shrieks barely preceded two young women, one blond and fair, the other brunette and swarthy, both beautiful by any standard, who flew across the large common room and flung themselves on the big corporal with enough force to stagger him back a couple of steps.

"Hey! Watch where you're going, Kerr!" Corporal Pasquin shouted into the back of Kerr's head. He raised his hands and pushed Kerr off his chest.

Corporal Dean helped keep Kerr upright and moving forward. The press of advancing bodies behind them forced Kerr and the others farther into the room.

Kerr barely noticed the hands and bodies holding him up and forcing him forward, he was too distracted by the four arms clinging to his neck, the four breasts pressed into his chest, the two mouths raining kisses on his face. He wrapped an arm around each waist and lifted, to ease the weight on his neck and shoulders.

"Way to go, Kerr!" Corporal Dean said, slapping Kerr on the back as he squeezed past and began looking for a table that would hold them all—and their girls.

"Some people," Corporal Chan laughed, following Dean.

"Raoul!" shouted another girl, Erika, who sidled through the crowd to take Pasquin's hand.

Another voice boomed out, "Vat's all dis commoti'n oud 'ere?" and Big Barb herself waddled out of the office to the rear of the large room and began plowing through the crowd like an icebreaker through pack ice. Freyda Banak wasn't called "Big Barb" for nothing—she not only weighed more than 150 kilos, she carried her weight lightly when she wanted to move fast. She planted herself in front of Kerr and loudly demanded, "Who you tink you are, Timmy, hogging two a my best girls all t' yersef?"

Their cheeks still pressed against his, Frieda and Gotta stopped kissing Kerr to look back at their employer. Kerr loosened his hold around their waists and they dropped down a couple of centimeters, but not all the way to the floor.

"B-but . . ." he began.

"Vot you mean, 'B-but . . .'? Dere's no 'b-buts' 'ere, Timmy. You led go a dem girls!"

"Big Barb," Frieda said calmly, "you gave him to us."

"And we intend to keep him," Gotta finished just as calmly.

Big Barb glared from one to the other, then planted her hands on her hips and roared out a long, raucous laugh. "You right, girls," she said, tears streaming down her face when her laughter eased enough for her to speak.

"Wha's a madda you, Timmy, lettin' dem two girls dangle like dat? Hol' 'em up like a gennleman! Where you been? All we seen o' Marines fer the pas' few mont's is dem base pogues. Dirty-fort FIS' yust up 'n take off somewhere wid'out sayin' noddin' t' us and we don' know when we see you again, or if we *ever* see you again." She quickly looked around and before Kerr could answer, asked, "Vhere's Chollie Bass? I vant my Chollie!"

"He's probably with Katie," Gotta giggled.

"I don' care no Katie!" Big Barb boomed. "Chollie don' need no skinny voman like Katie, he needs a full-size voman!" She thunked a meaty thumb into the center of her own chest.

"I don't think Charlie thinks Katie is skinny!" Frieda laughed.

"I don' care vhat Chollie t'inks neider! Zomebody go tell him I'm 'ere pinink avay to nodink, vaiting for him!" She turned her attention back to Kerr. "How many a you are dere 'ere donight? I make sure you godda good table. Vell? Answer me!"

Kerr hesitated, unsure which of her many questions to answer first. Claypoole stepped into the breech.

"There are eight of us, Big Barb. The corporals."

"Eight corporals?" She quickly scanned the room. "Vat's de madda vit Corporal Doyle, vhy ain't he 'ere? He gid kilt vhereever it vas you vent?"

"No, no, Big Barb. Doyle's fine. This is just the team leaders," Claypoole quickly assured her.

"Chust da team leaders? 'Ow come Doyle ain't no team leader? He's a corporal. Corporals suppose t' be fire team leaders, gun team leaders, so how come he ain't?"

Claypoole opened his mouth, but couldn't think of how to explain why a corporal was filling a lance corporal's billet. He looked at Kerr. Yeah, Doyle was in Kerr's fire team, let him try to explain it.

"Neber mine," Big Barb said, looking around again. "You Marines make yer own rules, whedder dey makes sense or not. Come, I get you gut table. Give you back room. You," she looked at Kerr, "come vit me. You," she looked at Claypoole, "go gid de oders, bring dem along." She did her icebreaker impersonation again, drawing Kerr and his happy burden in her wake.

Less than an hour later, the eight Marines and nine young women in the back room were seated around a large, round table digging into a medley of reindeer served "family style." The table was filled with platters of reindeer—steaks, cutlets, a roast, chops, sausage, even a steaming bowl of stew. Other bowls held several varieties of potatoes, legumes, grains, squashes, and less easily identifiable foodstuffs, most of which were cooked with sauces or gravies. Spices and condiments were spread about, the full range near to hand for everybody.

For a while, all that was heard inside the room was the chewing, sighs, and belches of contented diners; they ignored the hubbub that came muted through the door. At length, most of the platters and bowls were cleared down to bits and crumbs—Marines fresh back from a combat deployment have prodigious appetites.

Dean belched loudly enough to make Carlala, a skinny, busty girl seated next to him hip to haunch, jump. "Ahhh," he sighed, "that was great."

"A lot better than the reindeer steaks we used to get here," Dornhofer agreed.

"Very much so," Kerr added. "What happened?"

"We have a new cook," Klauda said as she moved from her chair to Dornhofer's lap.

"She's a fancy girl," Erika said, casting a nasty look at Carlala.

"Oh?" Chan said meaningfully. "Then what's she doing in the kitchen?"

"You'll see," Erika said haughtily. "And that's not the kind of 'fancy' I meant." She darted a look at Dean and made a show of shifting onto Pasquin's lap.

The hubbub in the main room suddenly grew in volume.

"Oh, wow, look at that!" Lance Corporal "Wolfman" MacIlargie murmured, then let out a wolf whistle.

Lance Corporal Dave "Hammer" Schultz didn't bother looking to see what had drawn MacIlargie's admiration; he'd seen her as soon as she stepped through the kitchen door. She was a full-bodied woman in a starched white shirt-jacket, closed all the way to the throat, over black pants. The heels of her black shoes were high enough to lift her a bit above average height. A white cap restrained her mass of lustrous chestnut hair. She held her head high, and her aristocratic face turned neither left nor right as she wended her way between the tables filled with eating and drinking—but mostly drinking—Marines. Two kitchen helpers followed her, guiding a covered cart. The woman was old enough to be the underaged mother of the youngest Marines in the room, or the younger aunt—or at least older sister of nearly any of them. But that didn't matter to the Marines.

The woman yelped and spun about with her hand raised to slap whoever had just pinched her bottom. Only to be confronted by four grinning faces, any of which could belong to the offending hand. She dropped her hand, gripped the bottom of her shirt-jacket with both hands, and jerked it down. She flung her head high, spun about, and, as regally as possible, stalked off. Guffaws, whistles, and raucous laughter trailed her.

She was pinched twice more and propositioned four times by the time she reached the door to the room where third platoon's corporals were luxuriating in postprandial bliss, and hustled inside to what she fully expected would be relief from the unseemly harrassment she'd undergone in the common room. She barely remembered to leave the door open long enough for the two kitchen helpers to wheel their cart into the room.

"Hey, baby," Pasquin shouted as soon as he saw her, "come on over here! My lap's big enough for two!" He held out a welcoming arm. Erika knuckled him in the ribs, but that only made him laugh.

The woman's palm tingled, and she began to raise a hand—now she *knew* who to slap—but noticed several faces leering at her, and lowered it without striking.

She again adjusted the fall of her shirt-jacket, held her head regally high, and announced, "I am Einna Orafem, the new chef at Big Barb's—"

"Chef? Did she really say 'chef?' " Dean crowed.

Einna Orafem managed to ignore Dean's boorishness and went on as though he hadn't spoken. "I have been given to believe that you—gentlemen—are special patrons of this dining salon."

"Patrons? Dining salon?" Barber hooted.

Once more, Einna Orafem ignored the rudeness of the remark and went on. "I have come to see if the modest repast I prepared for you met with your satisfaction." She looked at the empty platters and serving bowls. "Judging from the state of the table, I take it it has."

There was a brief pause as the Marines translated for each other: "She wants to know if the chow was any good."

"Hey, babe, that was the best feed I've ever had in this slop chute!" Taylor called out.

"Honey, you can stuff my sausage any day," Chan yelled.

"No, it's *your* sausage that's supposed to stuff her . . ." The rest of whatever Claypoole was saying was cut off by the finger Jente quickly pressed across his lips. Unlike the other young women around the table, Jente wasn't one of "Big Barb's girls." She was from Brystholde, a nearby fishing village from which many young women had come to a blowout party Brigadier Sturgeon threw for his FIST when they returned from a major deployment against Skinks on the Kingdom of Yahweh and His Saints and Their Apostles. First Sergeant Myer had strongly admonished the Marines of Company L that the village women were "nice girls," and were to be treated the way they'd want their sisters treated. Of course, Top's warning could not stop Jente from latching onto Claypoole and behaving just like one of Big Barb's girls—but only with him. Claypoole didn't realize it yet, but Jente saw him as prime husband material.

"Come and join us when Big Barb lets you off kitchen duty!" Pasquin called to Einna Orafem's brilliant red face.

"Here is a dessert I prepared specially for you," the cook managed, waving a wavering hand at the cart.

The helpers opened the cart and joined her in a hasty retreat to the kitchen. But first they had to run the gauntlet of the common room.

"Wazza madda, dolly," someone shouted, "didn't they want what you were offering?"

"Yours ain't good enough for them corporals?" another Marine shouted.

Uproarious laughter broke out at the comments.

"She's the *cook,*" Schultz growled.

Everybody close enough to hear his growl shut up.

Jente was the only one fastidious enough while gobbling the dessert to really notice what it was.

CHAPTER TWO

"Who in the hell is that idiot with his mouth hanging open?" Madam Chang-Sturdevant asked, coming halfway out of her chair as she stared at the image on the vid screen.

"Um, that, Madam President, is ah, the Fort Seymour staff duty officer, that is, the officer who was staff duty officer on the day the ah, 'incident' occurred," Huygens Long, the Attorney General answered, glancing at Marcus Berentus and Admiral Porter for confirmation. "You can see by his badges of rank he's a lieutenant colonel in the army."

"That's correct, ma'am," Porter said. "Mr. Long's investigation is not complete yet, so we don't know all the particulars."

The camera now took in a ragged line of soldiers standing and crouching behind a low stone wall and then panned a long view of the human carnage that lay in the street in front of them. It zoomed in for close-ups of the bodies and Chang-Sturdevant gasped in horror. "Why did we not know about this immediately after it happened?" she asked. Then: "That's enough, Marcus, I don't want to see any more." She put a hand to her face and bowed her head. "Our soldiers did that?" she gestured at the now blank vid screen.

"Yes, ma'am," Long answered. "The entire incident was filmed by a crew the demonstration organizers invited to cover it. Our troops were unprepared for what happened, so we have no visual record of what they saw. Then the government of Ravenette immediately released the vid to every news agency in the Confederation," he shrugged. "Their formal protest did not reach us via diplomatic channels until several days after the film was shown via all the Confederation news outlets. Our military people on Ravenette initiated a preliminary investigation and reported what they found to us through channels. That also took a few days."

"How many casualties?" Chang-Sturdevant asked in a dull voice.

After a brief pause, Berentus answered, "Well, the only figures we have are from the news media reports, which are based on the information given to them by government sources on Ravenette, but it appears seventy-five were killed outright with about another hundred critically wounded, some of whom will no doubt succumb. Infantry small arms at close range kill thoroughly and without discrimination."

Chang-Sturdevant snorted in an exasperation she seldom felt for her old friend. "Marcus, sometimes you old war horses really can't see beyond your toys. There were children among the dead!"

"Yes, ma'am, I am aware of that," Berentus answered evenly, "and they were supposed to be among the casualties. I'm telling you now, it was a setup. Maybe the organizers didn't know how the demonstration was going to end but they were prepared to show what did happen. I'm sure our investigation will show that our troops were provoked."

"What good does that do me now, Marcus? I've got to preside over a full session of the Congress in ten minutes. What am I going to tell them? Summers has requested time to address the Congress and you know what a goddamned rabble-rouser that bastard is!" Preston Summers was the head of the delegation from Ravenette and a firebrand known for his support of the secession movement.

"We are conducting a full investigation, ma'am," Long said. "We'll soon have all the facts and then you can hold a press conference."

"All right. I'll let Summers rave on and tell the other delegations we don't have all the facts yet but will, soon, very soon. I'll make it clear that if our people opened fire on these demonstrators without cause someone'll hang for it. That lieutenant colonel looks like a prime candidate to me right now. Meanwhile, Hugh," she turned to the Attorney General, "you get the chief of the diplomatic service and you, Marcus, Admiral Porter, be here when this session is finished. I want a full briefing on this mess, as far as anyone can give me one at this time, and then I'll call a news conference." She paused and sighed then stood, straightening out her suit jacket. "I am getting too old for this," she smoothed her hair. "Well," she brightened, "I now don the face of the Great Humanitarian with the cares of all Human Space on my thin shoulders, or, as the playwright put it, 'Once more into the breach, dear friends, once more!' " and then she walked proudly to the door that led out onto the floor of the Congress Hall.

It was absolutely silent in the Congress Hall as Representative Preston Summers concluded his Crime Against Ravenette speech. Summers was an accomplished orator. Here, before the Confederation Congress, his words rolled off his tongue in Shakespearean tones, but back home, among his colleagues, he talked like a hick because that's how his colleagues talked; Preston Summers played to his audience. Now he was fully wound up:

"This unprecedented act of mayhem by the Confederation's hirelings, this crime against Ravenette, is but the most heinous of many, aimed by this government and its supporters against the peace-loving people of my home and our allied worlds! I have expressed my outrage against these unfair practices many times in this hallowed hall and will now mention only the many discriminatory tariffs the member worlds have, at the instigation of the President, imposed on us, the unscrupulous business practices this government has tolerated against the citizens of Ravenette, and the introduction of military forces among our people, the only purpose of which is to further oppress us! And now it culminates in this—this horrid act of murder most foul, murder most bloody! *Murder!*"

Summers paused for effect and it was stupendous. Members shouted "Foul! "We demand an accounting!" and directed other words at President Chang-Sturdevant and her government too harsh to repeat. Sped on its way by Beamspace drones, Summers's speech, however, would be repeated in every corner of Human Space.

Summers waited for the delegates to quiet down. "Now," he continued, "our demands! We, the government of Ravenette and our allied worlds, demand the immediate withdrawal of all Confederation armed forces from our territories. Furthermore, we demand the lifting of all trade sanctions imposed by member worlds of this Confederation against the goods and services provided by our peoples. Third, we demand the liquidation of all debts incurred by the member worlds of our Coalition as a result of the unfair tariffs and embargoes imposed on us by the following member worlds: St. Brendan's—"

"Hold on a bloody damned minute there! Madam President! The floor, the floor, please!" Brooks Kennedy, the representative from St. Brendan's World, shouted.

Summers rattled on and then: "Furthermore, Madam President, if these demands are not met, we of the Coalition of Worlds for which Ravenette speaks with the authority of them all, will formally submit an Act of Secession and withdraw from this Confederation!"

"I demand the floor!" Kennedy shouted. "I've heard enough from this blatherskite rogue, Madam President, honorable members! What happened on Ravenette was a tragedy but this damned Coalition Summers is so proud of has been looking for just such an incident for months now! All these people want is an excuse to shirk their just debts. That is just what we've come to expect from these people, the descendants of louts and incompetents of whom the best anyone can say is that they settled so far away from the rest of us! I say if they want to leave this Confederation, good! It'd be worth it to give up their debts to get rid of them all! Good riddance to bad rubbish!"

"Is the honorable member from St. Brendan's World saying that we arranged the massacre of our own people?" Summers asked in a deceptively mild voice.

Brooks Kennedy was so worked up by now that he spoke without thinking. "I so accuse you! A proper investigation will reveal that the so-called 'Crime Against Ravenette' was planned and fomented by radicals who want only to secede from this Confederation and are willing to sacrifice the lives of their own people to achieve that goal!"

Many believed the cane Preston Summers always carried with him was a prop, that there was nothing at all wrong with his left leg that required its use. Now, before anyone could stop him, he demonstrated what the cane was really meant for by leaping across the aisle that separated him from where Congressman Kennedy sat and bringing it down forcefully on the other man's upraised arm, breaking it. The blow was clearly heard throughout the chamber. He struck again, this time fracturing Kennedy's skull and driving him to the floor.

"Sergeant at Arms!" Chang-Sturdevant shouted but already the burly ex-sergeant major of infantry who was the congressional sergeant at arms was bulling his way through the astonished delegates. Grabbing Summers by the collar he threw him to the floor and pinned him there while other members assisted the bleeding Kennedy to his feet. "That's a good gentleman, now," the sergeant at arms whispered, "no more of your violence in this chamber, sir."

"Fuck you—" Summers began but the sergeant at arms finished the sentence with a massive fist to the congressman's jaw. Later a member of the Ravenette delegation who had been standing nearby quietly retrieved Summers' cane. It was returned to him with the following motto inscribed on it: "HIT HIM AGAIN!"

"Order! Order!" Chang-Sturdevant shouted. "Order! Ladies and gentlemen, order, please! This session is now concluded. I will be giving a press conference at sixteen hours." She beckoned to her aides and left the chamber. "Now," she was heard to mutter, "we'll find out just what in the hell's going on."

"I need the most reliable and up-to-date information you can give me on the Ravenette incident and the secession movement in general for this press conference I'm giving in a few hours. Julie, give me a short rundown on the secessionist movement," Chang-Sturdevant turned to Julie Wellington-Humphreys, Chief of the Diplomatic Service since the death of Jon Beerdmens.

"The so-called 'Coalition' formed by the dozen worlds in that sector of which Ravenette is the most prominent do have grievances, Madam President, some of which can be addressed, with time and patience. The members refuse to admit the former because they have none of the latter, so our negotiations with them have led nowhere. The main stumbling block to a relationship with any of these worlds is that the people living on them are utterly disagreeable. They are arrogant, self-centered paranoids who want to believe that the rest of the Confederation is against them. The government of Ravenette has been accepted by the other secessionist worlds as their leader. Those other worlds are," she counted them off on her fingers, "Cabala, Chilianwala, Embata, Hobcaw, Kambula, Lannoy, Mylex, Ruspina, Sagunto, Trinkatat, and Wando."

"Where'd they come up with those names, particularly one like Ravenette?" Admiral Porter, the Chairman of the Combined Chiefs, asked.

Wellington-Humphreys shrugged, "Ravenette takes its name from a native species that somewhat resembles a Terran raven."

" 'Mylex,' " Porter mused, shaking his head, "sounds like a marital aid."

Chang-Sturdevant turned to Huygens Long, her Attorney General. "Hugh, what have you found out about the massacre?"

"That army lieutenant colonel we saw on the vid, Maracay is his name, was not responsible for what happened, ma'am. He was staff duty officer at Fort Seymour and when the vid was shot had only just arrived on the scene, after the shooting had ceased. It was just his unfortunate luck to be caught on film like that."

"He is a supply officer, ma'am," Admiral Porter interjected, "a noncombatant. I dare say, though, after this, um exposure, his career is ruined. He is on the promotion list for Full Colonel, but as everyone in Human Space will soon have seen him in this vid, we cannot afford to alienate public opinion by promoting the man."

"Well, then who the hell was in charge?" Chang-Sturdevant asked.

"The officer of the guard, the ranking man on the scene, was a Lieutenant Ios of the 3rd Provisional Infantry Division, the outfit we sent to Ravenette to reinforce the garrison at Fort Seymour," Long replied. "But he was struck by something the mob threw at the soldiers and unconscious when the firing began. The soldiers agree, however, that up to the moment he was struck he exercised commendable restraint. Had he not been knocked out, this tragedy might've been avoided. We've interviewed the soldiers on the guard force and they all agree that someone in the mob fired a pistol at them and they responded."

Madam Chang-Sturdevant was silent for a moment. "Well they sure 'responded,' didn't they?"

"Ma'am, the government of Ravenette is not cooperating with our investigation at all," Long went on. "They have refused our numerous requests to interview the survivors, and their responses to our queries as to who organized the demonstration have been vague at best. I suggest you emphasize that at your conference. But here's the bottom line:

Thirty of our soldiers, new to duty on Ravenette so they had no way of knowing what was going on, face over three hundred angry demonstrators who are pelting them with junk and tossing firebombs at them. Someone, we think it was someone in the mob, fires a pistol. The guard force, leaderless and each man thinking his own life was in peril, fires back." He shrugged. "That's it."

"Are you sure, Hugh?"

"Well—," Long hesitated, "—my personal opinion at this point is that the soldiers were goaded into firing because the secessionists wanted an incident like this to further justify their secession movement, but I do not advise you mention this until our investigation is complete."

"When will that be?"

"Within days, ma'am. We have people on Ravenette and," Long nodded at Admiral Porter, "the preliminary investigation by the military was thorough and we've had splendid cooperation from them in our own investigation."

Chang-Sturdevant sighed and leaned back in her chair. She glanced at Marcus Berentus and wished they could enjoy a dish of vanilla ice cream together. Later, perhaps. "Admiral Porter, what is the military strength of this Coalition?"

"Considerable, ma'am. Individually, none of the worlds is a match for our forces but intelligence estimates put the combined strength of all twelve worlds as very respectable. And they have good leaders among their officers, all of whom are graduates of our military academies." He permitted himself a quick smile. "If they were to concentrate their forces they would present a very grave threat to us. And I do not need to point out that just now our own forces are very widely dispersed."

"Mmm, yes, and you all know why. We reinforced Fort Seymour, as we have many other posts on the fringes of Human Space, as a tripwire," Chang-Sturdevant said. She did not bother to explain why because they all knew why: Skinks.

"If we were to tell the Coalition why we reinforced Seymour they would not believe us, not now. Moreover, the word about the alien threat would then be out and widespread panic would ensue everywhere," Marcus Berentus offered.

"So here we are," Chang-Sturdevant said. "We must have a garrison on Ravenette, but we can't tell the people who live there the real reason for that—hell's bells, the soldiers themselves out there don't even know why!—and our best efforts to keep the Coalition from declaring secession have so far failed. If we withdraw and leave those worlds in the dark as to the real threat to humanity that lies somewhere beyond their little slice of the galaxy, we leave the door open to invasion. We cannot allow that to happen." She paused for a moment and then asked, "Who's in charge out there at Fort Seymour anyway?"

"Um, the infantry division commander is a Brigadier General Sorca, ma'am, and the garrison commander is a Major General Alistair Cazombi."

"Cazombi, Cazombi. Where have I heard that name before?" Chang-Sturdevant turned to Marcus Berentus.

"He was involved in the Avionian affair."

"Oh, yes, yes. Well, a brigadier has one star and a major general has two. Why isn't Cazombi in charge?" she turned to Admiral Porter.

Porter shifted uncomfortably in his seat. "Well, ma'am, General Cazombi is a personnel specialist, of sorts, and Brigadier Sorca is a combat soldier, so Cazombi is in charge of the fort and Sorca is responsible for tactical matters."

"You sent a 'personnel specialist' and a general officer at that to be in charge of a supply depot?" Chang-Sturdevant glanced questioningly at Porter and then Berentus. The latter made a wry face, which to her indicated there was more to the story than Porter was willing to let on, and they would discuss it later. "Well," she went on quickly, "I'll never understand how you military men arrange these things. Julie," she turned back to Wellington-Humphreys, "I want every possible effort made to appease the Coalition short of withdrawal of our forces from Ravenette. Get their people together with the Ministry of Commerce, with anyone else you feel has a say in relations with these people, and offer them the moon if they want it. I want these negotiations to be conducted at the highest level. You'll lead them but I want the Commerce Minister himself to be in on the negotiations, the initial ones anyway. Do not leave this to underlings. I'll talk to the minister shortly, then you contact him and together assemble a team of experts. I will announce today that we're prepared to offer handsome reparations for the killed and wounded on Ravenette. I want everything done that can be done to keep these people in the Confederation of Human Worlds. But withdrawal of our forces is not negotiable and I want the Coalition to understand that we will fight to keep them there.

"One more thing. Admiral Porter, Mrs. Wellington-Humphreys, I want to know why it took so damned long for me to find out about what happened on Ravenette. Goddamnit, do you realize how embarrassing this has been to me, to find out about this through the news media? Both of you order a top-down review of your reporting procedures and fix them so that this never happens again."

"Ma'am," Admiral Porter leaned forward, "we support you. But if it comes to war with the secessionists, where will we get the forces to fight them?"

Madam Chang-Sturdevant leaned back in her chair and folded her hands. "We'll find them, Admiral; we must. All right, everyone, let's get to it. Marcus, would you stay behind for a moment? I have something to discuss with you."

After the others had left she turned to Berentus. "Marcus, what's the story on this General Cazombi?"

Berentus smiled. "He was punished by the Chiefs, sent to Ravenette to get him out of the way and put an end to his career. It was unjust, it was unfair, but I do not interfere with assignment policy when the Chiefs make it."

"That's as it should be, Marcus. Well, what did he do to get sent to Fort Seymour?"

Berentus shrugged. "He was the C1, the personnel officer for the Combined Chiefs, an assignment that always leads to a third star. You remember the Avionian incident? You may remember the lawsuit brought against a Marine officer for things he and his men did at the time? It was brought by the chief scientist at Avionian Station."

"Yes. She died, I recall."

"Yes. Well, Cazombi volunteered to appear as a witness for the accused, a Captain Conorado of 34th FIST. Cazombi was dead set against ever bringing that officer to trial in the first place and he expressed, in no uncertain terms, his disappointment with the Chiefs for not doing everything they could to avoid it. And he has also been very much against the quarantine we've imposed on 34th FIST. His view is that if we can trust Marines to put their lives on the line for us we should be able to trust them to keep quiet about the Skinks instead of holding them prisoner on Thorsfinni's World. Others agree with him, particularly the Commandant, but their views have been expressed, um, a bit more discreetly than Cazombi's. His nickname, you know, is 'Cazombi the Zombie' because his demeanor is usually ice cold, even in the most desperate situations. He has quite a distinguished combat record. Well, uncharacteristically, more than once he let loose in meetings with the Chiefs, and now he's out of grace with them."

Chang-Sturdevant shook her head. "Marcus, sometimes your military leaders treat good men like shit. I'm so sick of this goddamned Old Boy's Club attitude! Keep your eye on this Cazombi guy, will you? I don't mean that to keep him in line, but he's on the hot seat out there now and that's just where we need officers who aren't afraid to speak their minds." She smiled. "I know it's bad policy for you to interfere with the inner workings of the military services, but by Buddha's hairy backside, if this Cazombi fellow shows initiative out there, I sure as hell will!"

"Ma'am, one more thing. Admiral Porter's question, about where we'll get the forces if the Coalition imposes war on us, is valid. We are stretched thin."

For the first time that day Chang-Sturdevant laughed outright with good humor. "Marcus, I've said it before and I'll say it again: If it positively, absolutely must be destroyed overnight, call in the Marines."

CHAPTER THREE

You had to give Einna Orafem credit for having guts. Sure, she stayed in the kitchen for the next several days, and went to and from work through the back door in order to avoid the Marines in the common room, but the following Sixth Day, when Big Barb told her there was a party that required special care, Einna again braved the common room to personally describe the evening's specials to Big Barb's favored party. Fortunately, it was early enough in the evening that none of the Marines were too drunk, so her passage through the common room was marked by only a few catcalls and whistles.

"Good evening, sir and madam," Einna said when she reached the table and stood erect, head high, one hand laid across the other's up-turned palm. Talulah, one of the girls on serving duty, hovered behind her shoulder. "I am Einna Orafem, the chef . . . here." She couldn't quite bring herself to say "Big Barb's," the very name was a come-down from the *haute cuisine* restaurants in which she had expected to practice her culinary artistry. "Proprietress Banak has requested that I make your dining this evening a truly memorable experience."

Ensign Charlie Bass leaned back in his chair and looked, mouth agape, at Einna. He closed his mouth with an audible *click,* swallowed, and began to say, "You already ha . . ."

But Katie smoothly cut him off. "Thank you—Miss Orafem? I am Katrina Katanya—Katie to my friends—and this is Charlie Bass, Ensign,

Confederation Marine Corps." She placed a loving hand on Bass's forearm. "We are delighted to meet you."

Einna smiled. Finally, a person of breeding. And the man with Katrina, despite his loutish display of surprise when she introduced herself, was an ensign, an officer; therefore, by very definition, a gentleman. It would be a pleasure preparing a fine repast for this lovely couple. She mentally cataloged the ingredients she had on hand—other than those oh-so-proletarian reindeer steaks the enlisted boors ordered in endless succession. Her talents were being wasted there, she knew.

"I can offer you a fine kwangduk Wellington . . ."

Bass interrupted her with, "North or south end?" He exchanged an understanding glance with Talulah, who feigned gagging at the mention of kwangduk.

"I beg your pardon?"

"Pay no attention to Charlie," Katie said soothingly. "He just returned from a deployment where he and most of his Marines were injured in a forest fire. He's not quite himself."

"I am so—"

"Hush, Charlie. Let this nice lady tell us what she can prepare for our dinner."

"No kwangduk. I don't want any damn kwangduk. North *or* south end."

Katie looked apologetically at Einna. "Charlie had a bad experience with kwangduk, let's move on to something else."

Einna looked down her nose at Bass. No kwangduk indeed! Obviously he'd never had kwangduk Wellington, prepared in the manner of Chochet Viet, which was a specialty of hers. Why, once the stench was leeched out of the meat with a proper marinade, it was a positively divine dish! But she managed to not show her feelings as she went on.

"I have a fresh haunch of Xanadu roc, marinated in Schweppes before roasting, seasoned with Aardheim sage, real Earth thyme, and winter savory from New Carnavon, rubbed with Lechter garlic, and garnished with Wolozonoski's World cloves. Also, choice Dominion veal-lamb chops, sauteed with heart of grosspalm before being braised in Katzenwasser, served awash in a crème of Greece soup base, garnished with slices of Ponderosa lemon. All are served with Boradu rice and a vegetable medley." She cocked her head at them, decided that Bass's expression of disbelief required it, and added, "Of course, there are also the regular menu items."

"No, no, not necessary," Katie said. "Your specials sound marvelous. We will have both the Xanadu roc and the Dominion veal-lamb chops. We'll share them, thank you." In her peripheral vision she saw Bass open his mouth to object. She dug her fingernails into his arm—he winced and closed his mouth.

"Good food preparation takes time, but you won't famish before you are served," Einna said with a slight dip of her head. "While you're waiting, can we serve you something from the bar?"

"Do you have Katzenwasser '36?"

For the first time, Einna turned to acknowledge the presence of Big Barb's girl.

"I think we do," Talulah said. "I'll check." She scampered off to do so.

"If we don't, may I recommend the Alhambran retsina? It's on the sharp side, but should pique your appetites quite nicely."

Katie dug her nails into Bass's arm again. "Thank you, we may do that," she said.

With a slight bow, Einna Orafem turned and regally made her way back to the kitchen. She only jumped once from having her bottom slapped along the way.

"Alhambran retsina?" Bass croaked as soon as Katie withdrew her nails from his arm. "*On the sharp side?* That stuff's so raw, it can strip the chameleon paint off a Dragon!"

"Keep your voice down, dear," Katie said, patting his bruised arm.

"Roast haunch of roc? Do you know what a roc is? It's the main predator on Xanadu, that's what! I wouldn't be surprised if the last meal that 'haunch' she's so anxious to feed us had was human! The Dominion veal-lamb chops were the only thing that woman mentioned that qualifies as food fit for human consumption!"

"Now, now, dear, the woman's a *chef*, not the kind of slap-it-on-the-griddle-and-hope-it-doesn't-burn-before-it-dies kind of cook Big Barb usually hires. I'm sure the roc will be quite tasty—and the kwangduk, too, if you'd only give it a chance."

Fortunately, the bartender was able to find a dusty bottle of Katzenwasser '35 hidden in a deep recess under the bar. It wasn't as fine a vintage as the '36, but far better in Bass's view than Alhambran retsina.

When dinner was finally served, he loved the Dominion veal-lamb chops, but refused to even taste the roast roc haunch. Katie found the Xanadu roc a bit gamey, but otherwise quite delicious. They splurged on a cup of Jamaican Blue Mountain coffee with a dessert of Novo Kongor tart.

Katie dragged Bass out of Big Barb's just before Einna Orafem came out of the kitchen again so he missed the fun.

During the course of the meal consumed by Ensign Charlie Bass and his lady, the common room had filled with nearly a hundred Marines, eating and drinking—mostly drinking. And that didn't count the thirty or more Marines who crowded the bar that stood along one wall, or the local fishermen and rowdies who also used Big Barb's as their home away from home. Staff Sergeant Hyakowa was elsewhere, as befitted his rank, but most of the rest of third platoon had filtered in. Nearly every one of them paused briefly to exchange compliments with Bass and Katie. No more than brief compliments. After all, Charlie Bass was no longer a gunnery sergeant, he was a commissioned officer, and therefore looked upon askance by the enlisted men. Besides, he was with his lady, and nobody wanted to take a chance of screwing things up for him for the night; any screwing to be done was up to him. It didn't take much muscle flexing for third platoon to clear a clump of tables midway along the wall opposite the bar, especially when Lance Corporal Schultz pointed at a table and growled, "Mine."

Then Einna Orafem braved her way through the common room to see how Bass and Katie liked their dinner—she found the common room several magnitudes of rowdiness greater than it had been earlier. She groaned silently when she realized the couple had already left, and turned to make her way back to the kitchen. Catcalls and whistles had started as soon as she stepped into the common room, increased as she made her way through, and reached a crescendo when she turned back.

She had made only two steps before a slap to the rear caused her to shriek and jump. The catcalls and whistles changed to laughs and cheers as she tried to run away. But after just two steps, an arm reached out and seized her around the waist. The arm belonged to a lance corporal from the FIST Dragon company, who pulled her onto his lap.

"What's your hurry, honey?" the lance corporal roared. "You're new here, you gotta get with the program and meet the customers, get friendly with us!"

"But I'm the *chef*!" Einna jerked free of his arm and bounded away but was quickly hemmed in by several Marines who left their seats to surround her.

"Come on, baby, where's your spirit?"

"How are you going to make any money if you don't get friendly?"

"Ignore them, I can take you to heaven!"

Einna spun about, in growing panic, her mouth open in silent screams. Suddenly a hole opened in the circle surrounding her, and a huge figure filled it.

Three words, sounding like a small avalanche, rumbled out of that huge figure: "She's the *cook*!"

The catcalls, whistles, laughs, and cheers died.

The Marines who had stood to surround Einna Orafem dropped back into chairs, and weren't very particular about whether they landed in the same ones from which they'd risen—or even if the chairs were already occupied.

"Ain't Big Barb's girl, she's the *cook*! Leave her alone!"

In Einna's eyes, the huge form resolved itself into a very large, copper-skinned Marine. She flung herself at him for protection. His collar with its rank insignia was just above her eye level. She wasn't familiar with the device, but she knew he wasn't an officer, probably not even a corporal. But she didn't care; he'd made the others leave her alone.

"Thank you," she said, sobbing.

"Come," the big Marine rumbled. He gently put an arm around her shoulders and turned her toward the kitchen. The room was silent as the two made their way to the kitchen, the father of all sheepdogs herding a lost lamb through a pack of hungry but frightened wolves. It wasn't until the kitchen door closed behind them that the silence was broken.

"Way to go, Hammer!" Corporal Claypoole shouted.

Inside the kitchen, Schultz lightly lifted Einna Orafem and sat her on a counter. He held out a hand and snapped his fingers. Someone hurriedly shoved an almost-clean towel into it, and he gently daubed it at her cheeks and around her eyes, blotting away the tears, and only incidentally smearing her makeup.

Einna stopped crying, gave one big shudder, hiccuped, and slumped, still; Schultz put a hand on her shoulder to keep her from falling over. Only then did the big Marine look around at the kitchen staff. They stared at him, awed. He returned their stares, and they abruptly made themselves scarce.

"Okay," he said, looking at her again when they were alone. He wasn't asking if she was all right, he was *telling* her she was.

She straightened slightly, glancing at the steadying hand that had remained on her shoulder since he'd wiped her tears away, then looking into his eyes. "Thank you," she murmured. "You saved me."

He grunted. His grunt seemed to say it was no big deal.

"They won't bother me anymore, will they?"

"No." The word seemed to come from deep inside a bottomless cave.

"What's your name?"

"Schultz."

"You're not an officer, are you?"

He just looked at her.

"You're not even a corporal, are you?"

His head barely moved side to side.

She thought, what were the ranks she'd heard the Marines had? "Lance corporal?"

"Yes."

"Well, now, Lance Corporal Schultz," she said briskly, shaking herself and sitting straight, "for as long as I continue to work here, whenever you come in, you get the best meal I can prepare for you. On the house."

He raised an eyebrow.

"I'm the chef, I can do that. You'll probably have to pay for your beer, but your food is free. That's the least I can do for you."

"Okay?" This time it *was* a question.

"Yes, I'm all right now. You can rejoin your friends."

Schultz removed his hand from her shoulder, but before he could turn, she threw her arms around his neck and kissed him full on the lips. Then, as though shocked by her own actions, she jerked back and dropped her hands primly into her lap.

"Thank you," she softly said again, and watched his broad back as he left the kitchen. He was younger than her, almost all of them except that Ensign Bass were, but not by many years.

She shook herself and wondered why she'd thought that.

Schultz didn't have to say anything when he returned to the common room. He didn't even have to look around. Everybody knew that Einna Orafem was now under his protection, and *nobody* wanted to cross Hammer Schultz.

So things went for a couple of weeks more. During the days the Marines of 34th FIST stood minor daily inspections, drilled on their parade grounds, sat through lectures and trids in company classrooms, cleaned their weapons and gear, and engaged in physical fitness routines and hand-to-hand combat training. In the evenings they pulled liberty, did or did not go into Bronnysund, maybe stayed on base and went to fliks, ate in the mess halls or at Pete's Place, the civilian-run restaurant on base, worked on their Marine Corps Institute courses, studied for promotion exams, or read for the sheer pleasure of reading. On weekends, nearly everybody headed for town. True to her word, Einna Orafem made sure Lance Corporal Schultz ate well and for free. Not that she ever left the sanctuary of her kitchen; she had the girls on table duty tell her when he came in. And, of course, Schultz never went into the kitchen.

Then things changed.

Captain Conorado, commander of Company L, looked over his Marines at morning formation on First Day two weeks after Schultz rescued Einna Orafem and announced, "We have an IG one month from today." He ignored the groans from the ranks, there weren't many of them and they weren't loud. Not many of the Marines in the company had been through the grueling experience of an Inspector General's inspection. In a month, the announcement of an IG inspection would set off such a chorus of complaints that he might have to take disciplinary action to quell them.

"You have one week to get everything squared away," Conorado continued. "Next First Day, there will be a platoon commander's pre-IG. You will then have one day to rectify any discrepancies before a company commander's pre-IG. The First Day after that, you will stand a battalion commander's pre-IG, followed a week later by FIST pre-IG.

"After all that, the gods help anybody who isn't ready to ace the IG's inspection.

"Platoon commanders, to the company office. Company Gunnery Sergeant, front and center!"

Gunnery Sergeant Thatcher, Company L's second-ranking enlisted man, advanced from his position at the right front of the formation, came to attention in front of Conorado, and sharply lifted his right hand in salute.

Conorado returned the salute and both Marines dropped their hands. "Gunnery Sergeant, when I release the company to you, you will have the platoon sergeants begin preparing their Marines for the first pre-IG."

"Aye aye, sir!" Thatcher replied.

"Gunnery Sergeant, the company is yours."

Thatcher raised his hand in salute again. "Sir, the company is mine."

Conorado returned the salute, about-faced, and headed into the barracks, followed by the company's other officers.

Thatcher watched the CO until he and all the other officers were inside the barracks, then turned about, shook his head, and looked over the company from one end to the other.

"Most of you don't know what kind of fun and games you're in for. Lucky you. You're not going to think you're very lucky a month from now, though.

"Platoon sergeants, you heard the man. When I dismiss the company, get your people inside and begin preparing them for the IG."

Again, he looked the company over from end to end, then bellowed, "COMP-ney, dis-MISSED!"

The Marines broke ranks and gathered expectantly around their platoon sergeants, many shouting questions.

Staff Sergeant Hyakowa raised his hands and patted the air to silence the questions being thrown at him. When the hubbub reduced he told third platoon, "Think of the toughest junk-on-the-bunk you've ever stood. Magnify it by ten. That's where the IG starts. It gets worse from there. Fire teams, head for your quarters. Fire team leaders, begin inspecting everything your people have in your rooms. Squad leaders, to my quarters. Move it!"

The week was a madness of long hours, normally lasting until almost taps, as the Marines checked to make certain they had every piece of equipment the manual called for, that each piece was in tiptop condition, and was faultlessly clean and fully functional. They carefully went through all of their personal belongings, separating out those things they'd have need for during the coming four weeks, and those they could manage without. The latter, they packed in seabags that were then stowed in the company supply room.

Sergeant Souavi, the supply sergeant, didn't deliberately make them stand long times in line at the entrance to the supply room. But they stood for long waits anyway as he inspected the outside of each seabag brought to him for storage to make sure it was properly labeled with its owner's name and particulars, and properly sealed and secured so no one could be accused of pilferage. Then he had to stow each seabag in such a manner that it wouldn't be crushed by the bags above it, and so any bag could be quickly found and retrieved if it was necessary to remove one from storage.

The Marines organized the items they felt they couldn't live without for the next four weeks so they were ready to hand and easily packed into a valise that would go into the supply room the day before each pre-IG inspection as well as before the big one.

Sergeant Souavi muttered to himself that he'd *really* make them stand in long lines waiting to stow their valises, because that meant he'd have to spend the day before each inspection storing the bags of personal items. But he didn't really mean it; each level of inspection would include the company supply room and he'd be graded by how well the seabags and valises were stowed. He knew that by the time the IG showed up, he'd be able to store everything properly in his sleep.

CHAPTER FOUR

"Wall, Miz Humpfriz, that ain't hardly what we want," Halbred Stutz drawled. The red splotches on his face flared even redder as he spoke and it seemed to Wellington-Humphreys that the thick black hairs protruding from the nostrils of his bulbous nose vibrated with a life of their own. In an earlier age, she reflected sourly, this caricature of a man would have been dressed in sweat-stained shirtsleeves, thumbs hooked into his galluses, and a huge chaw of tobacco stuck in one cheek.

They had been sitting for hours already, had endured a long lecture on the Fort Seymour incident, which Wellington-Humphreys had managed to terminate with assurances of a full investigation, justice, and compensation for the victims. Befitting her long experience and skill as a diplomat, Wellington-Humphreys successfully concealed the disgust and anger that had been boiling inside her. The secessionists had deliberately selected unqualified individuals to represent them at the negotiations, nobodies in fact, while her own government was being represented by its highest officials. Sitting next to her was the Confederation's distinguished Minister of Commerce, Dr. Rafe Pieters. She didn't know what qualifications the ridiculous little man named Stutz had to be leading the Coalition's negotiating team, aside from the fact that on his home world of Hobcaw he owned several million hectares of arable land that he farmed.

"Y'see, we are an ag-ri-cul-tur-al world, us Cob'uns," Stutz emphasized the word "agricultural" as if speaking to ignorant schoolchildren, "and our economy depends on its produce exports."

"We are prepared to offer substantial subsidies, sir," Pieters said.

"Yeah? Wall, that was tried a long time ago, folks, 'n it din work then neither. You pay us for not growing crops we can't export anyhow and before you know it we'll be dependent on yer handouts. No, siree!"

"It would only be for an interim period, Mr. Stutz," Pieters replied. "It will take some time to get the other member worlds to accept your produce and manufactures into their own markets in exchange for things they can provide that you need on Hobcaw and the other worlds in your Coalition."

"We don't have a lot of time, Mr. Minister Pieters," Stutz replied. "Our trade deficit with your member worlds reached twenty trillion last fiscal year and it's gettin' higher the longer we sit on our rumps here banging our chops. And your bankers, their only fix is to loan us more money to pay off our debts at interest rates that only get us deeper into the debt cycle. You gotta remember, even though there's twelve of us in our Coalition, we're still underpopulated, compared to the longer-settled places, and that deficit is holding back our development. Your financiers are strangling us! The way we figure it, if we was totally independent of the trade policies and treaties your government has cooked up we could go at each member world separately and haggle our own agreements."

"Well, Mr. Stutz," Pieters leaned forward as he spoke, "this is merely our preliminary meeting, a session to familiarize ourselves with the problems. Their resolution will take time, sir. Surely your members would agree that if we can settle these issues to their satisfaction the time would be well spent?" Stutz did not reply, only gazed at the Commerce Minister through half-lidded eyes. Frustrated by the lack of response, Pieters tried being conciliatory. "We agree there are disadvantageous imbalances in our trade relations with your worlds and we're here to see if we can eliminate them."

"But you must try to see things from our perspective," Wellington-Humphreys added. "There was the outbreak of 'Mad Tomato Disease' five years ago that severely damaged your truck garden exports and—"

"That was utter hysteria, madam," Stutz interjected, "typical of the paranoia that has always manifested itself in your relations with us." He smiled, revealing jagged, yellowed teeth.

Wellington-Humphreys stared at Stutz in surprise for a moment. The man did not always talk like a bumpkin! She realized then that his folksy manner was assumed and behind that façade worked a facile and astute intelligence. She had underrated the man. She should have known anybody who could have built an agricultural empire such as the one Stutz ruled was no rube. But he had inadvertently given himself away with that outburst. Obviously his own harvests had been most adversely affected by the Mad Tomato virus. A very undiplomatic smile crept across her face.

"You find that amusing?" Stutz asked, not amused.

"Not in the least, sir." Since her smile nettled Stutz, she enlarged it to a grin. She challenged him with it and at the same time let him know she was on to his tactics.

Realizing he'd made a slip, Stutz permitted himself a tight grin and continued in a more affable tone. "Wall, it was all exaggerated and it's behind us now, but don't forget that other worlds have had their problems too. How's about what happened on Atlas just a while back, whose crops were destroyed by a virus imported from one of the Confederation worlds? We ain't the only ones with problems like that."

"We understand that," Pieters replied, "but there is the problem with Mylex and their failure to protect the intellectual properties of the Confederation's member worlds, their massive violations of the copyright laws, and the very profitable trade they have built up selling cut-rate bootlegged books, vids, all kinds of entertainment media that are protected elsewhere in the Confederation. Why, the Mylex representative isn't even with us today!" He glanced at the three negotiators who'd accompanied Stutz, all of whom shook their heads.

"Naw," Stutz grinned, "ol' Jenks Moody. He couldn't make it, had a bit too much of our fine Hobcaw bourbon last night." The members of his delegation guffawed.

Wellington-Humphreys couldn't help but admire the way the negotiators were laying it on, pretending to be a bunch of "cracker-barrel" cronies. She glanced out of the side of her eye at Pieters, who really did think these people were hicks, and winked. "Well, Mr. Stutz, there is also the situation on Embata, with the use of slave labor in the mines there. That sort of practice doesn't sit well with our ideas of human rights."

"Oh, yeah, Miz Wellington-Humpfriz? Those people are felons, ma'am, they don't have no rights. But you ever hear of a place called Darkside, eh? How does your highfalutin' 'human rights' ideas justify that?" Darkside was the highly secret penal colony the Confederation operated for the incarceration of its worst criminals. Often they were sent there without benefit of a trial.

"Touché," Wellington-Humphreys replied.

"I'll 'touché' you sumptin' else, ma'am." Stutz leaned back, narrowing his eyes. In her mind Wellington-Humphreys imagined him snapping his galluses. "You remember a scribbler, someone from Carhart's World, I recall, he visited Embata about a hundred years ago and wrote a book about the place? His name was Oldlaw, Frederic Oldlaw. He became famous as a city planner back in the last century. He wrote about his travels through Embata but he really meant everywhere in our quadrant. He wrote the Embatans they were all a collection of lazy ignorant folks who'd rather hunt and run with dawgs in the woods than work for a living, lived off their pregnant wimmen's labor, ate a diet that'd puke a hound off a gut wagon, 'n got fallin'-down drunk just to relax. He reported a conversation he had with one fella at a roadhouse on a back road somewheres. The man was braggin' about how he was gonna get drunk 'n go home 'n beat up his wife and kids. 'How much do you weigh?' this Oldlaw fella asked. 'Oh, 'bout a hunner fifty kilos,' the guy answered. 'Wall, how much do your kids weigh?' Oldlaw wanted to know. You see where he was drivin' at? 'Nuttin', when they's flyin' thru th' air,' the man replied." Stutz laughed and slapped his palm on the table.

"Now, Miz Humpfriz, Mr. Pieters," Stutz continued, "that's a good ol' story, but it's pure hogwash, pure hogwash. That writer fella was so stupid he never realized that's just how the Embata people get their fun, leadin' strangers on that way. That's what happens when you don't stay someplace long enough to get to know the folks there. Wall, how do you think trash like that set with the folks who read it but never visited Embata themselves? And that attitude is at the bottom of the problems we are having today with your Confederation of Human Worlds. You people think you're so much better'n we are 'n we don't like it, not one damn bit. Our differences have been growin' us apart for two hundred years now and we want out of this Confederation, ma'am."

Wellington-Humphreys suppressed a sigh. She'd had enough for one day. "Mr. Stutz, I think Dr. Pieters would agree, this meeting has been very fruitful. Can we adjourn until tomorrow, say around ten? Perhaps by then your friend from Embata will be feeling up to attending and we can continue this discussion?"

Stutz nodded affably. "Before you go, ma'am, I want to give you somethin'." He produced a large bottle filled with an amber liquid. "This is a bottle of Old Snort, the finest aged bourbon in Human Space and it comes from my own distillery. I want you to sample it tonight and tomorrow you tell me if you ever tasted anything so smooth and delicious in your life. Yes, ma'am," he nodded, "drink it neat or with spring water, 'n you'll see we Cob'uns know our whiskey."

Wellington-Humphreys had engaged rooms in one of Fargo's most exclusive hotels for the negotiations, something she often did when she wanted off-world diplomats to feel comfortable during difficult meetings. She and Rafe Pieters were sitting in their suite, relaxing.

" 'Old Snort,' " Pieters laughed, regarding warily the bourbon Stutz had given Wellington-Humphreys. "Well, let's try some and see if the old boy knows what he's talking about. 'Old Snort,' Julie, where did he come up with a name like that?"

"Same place they came up with a name like Hobcaw." Wellington-Humphreys grinned, holding out her glass. " 'Pokin' fun at strangers' seems to be ingrained in the 'Cob'un' culture. One finger, please. No, make that two! I need something strong after sitting in there with those characters, but I don't trust this stuff not to make me go blind or something. But you know, Rafe, I could actually get to like that old bastard. There's more behind that ugly nose of his than sinuses full of snot."

"Julie!" Pieters shook his head, pretending shock. He poured her whiskey and then himself. He regarded the amber fluid carefully. "We might be taking our lives in our own hands, drinking this stuff. That'd be the ultimate insult, wouldn't it? Send buffoons as negotiators and then have them poison us to boot." He laughed and regarded the label on the whiskey bottle. " 'Old Snort' indeed!" He sniffed the bourbon carefully and raised an eyebrow. "Umm, might just do!" Then: "They're stalling, you know that, don't you? They want to keep us talking while they plan something. We've negotiated with them for years on these very same issues we've been discussing all day, Julie, and always it's been they've done nothing anybody else wouldn't have done, nobody likes us, everybody owes us, blah, blah, blah. They can be the most fractious, disagreeable, one-way people to deal with. I think we need to report that to the President, advise her she'd better get ready for the other shoe to drop."

"You mean the Ordinance of Secession?"

Pieters nodded. "Yes, and her response."

"They really aren't buffoons, Rafe, you know that, don't you?"

"Yep. That's how I figured out they're up to something. Chin-chin, Ho Chi Minh!" He touched his glass to hers.

They sipped the bourbon.

"My God, Rafe!" Wellington-Humphreys gasped, "it goes down like water and burns like fire!" She took another sip. "Ohhhh! Off with the shoes, my toes are on fire!"

"It really is damned good stuff!" Pieters whispered, holding his glass up to the light, admiring the whiskey. "I can see how Jenks Moody might've overindulged last night."

"Rafe, you've dealt with these people before, what are they really like?"

"Well, I've had contact with the 'Cob'uns' as the people from Hobcaw like to call themselves. A long time ago. That was during one of the Silvasian wars, I can't remember which, can't keep them straight anymore. I was a second lieutenant in the infantry in those days, yes," he smiled as Wellington-Humphreys raised her eyebrows, "the old economist, ah, the *distinguished* old economist, who now stands so humbly before you, was a goddamned ground-pounding soldier once." The Old Snort was having its effect on Pieters. Eagerly he poured himself another generous dollop. "We had a regiment of Cob'uns with our brigade and I got to know some of their officers and NCOs pretty well. They were a hospitable and friendly bunch of guys. In many ways they were a lot like that bum in the story Stutz told us, they liked to get drunk, talked all the time about things they'd hunt when they got home, kept a sloppy bivouac. But, Julie, in a fight you couldn't ask for better men to be at your side! Damn, those boys could shoot and maneuver!

If we have to go to war with the Hobcaws it won't be a pushover, take it from me. I suspect some of the other worlds in that Coalition aren't far behind the Cob'uns in their fighting spirit, especially the Embatans and the Wandos."

Wellington-Humphreys held out her glass for a refill. "I hope we're sober enough to make the meeting tomorrow."

"If we keep this up we sure won't be," Pieters laughed, giving her another two fingers of the bourbon. He refilled his own glass but capped the bottle tightly and then set it aside.

"It's going to be war, Rafe, I can see that now. They will secede and we cannot let them do that. How bad will it be?"

Pieters did not answer at once but swirled the whiskey in his glass and sipped before saying, "They had a saying they liked to quote when in their cups. I always thought it was hyperbole for my benefit as an outsider. It went something like, 'Turn peace away, for honor perishes with peace.' What happened at Fort Seymour was the first fatal move, Julie, and we shall never call it back. If we have war with those people it is going to be bad, Julie, very bad, I am afraid."

But Rafe Pieters had no idea how bad it would really be and he was not half as afraid as he should have been.

CHAPTER FIVE

Tommy Lyons lay dying.

"General, the tests are conclusive. Your son does not have pneumonia or any other form of upper-respiratory infection. It's a particularly virulent form of psitticoid tuberculosis that is very deadly in younger children if not treated promptly. And I have to tell you, it has not been."

"Bu-but the other doctors assured us he . . ." General Davis Lyons gestured helplessly at the tiny form on the bed, its chest heaving spasmodically.

The boy's mother, Varina, sat beside him, mopping the perspiration from the child's forehead, occasionally daubing at the blood the intermittent bouts of coughing brought up from his tortured lungs. She glanced imploringly at the doctor. "Can't you do anything?" she asked.

Dr. Ezekiel Vance, Ravenette's foremost specialist in communicable diseases, shook his head sadly. "We could, if we could get the proper medication. This form of TB is very rare in this quadrant of Human Space but it is endemic on other worlds. I've ordered a stasis unit from Mylex. Once it gets here we could stabilize Tommy and keep him alive until I can find the medicine I need. You know how backward we are in medical science, compared to other worlds in the Confederation. And we don't keep supplies of the medicine required to combat this disease on hand although there is a drug that can cure it, but—" he shrugged.

"But what?" Varina Lyons asked.

Ezekie Vance was a small, stoop-shouldered man, and the anxiety of the past hours was clearly etched on his face. As he spoke he twisted the hairs on his long white mustaches, an involuntary response to the frustration he felt at his helplessness in the face of the child's fading life. "But the embargo," he replied, looking at the two, surprise on his face. "Didn't you know that Merrick Pharmaceuticals's products are embargoed, and they are the only source for the drug that can fight this disease?"

"The embargo? That does not apply to the importation of medicines and food and nonmilitary goods, Doctor!" General Lyons replied. Little Tommy began to cough again and for agonizing moments the adults' attention was directed toward the child. White-hot anger surged through the general. Goddamn the embargo! Goddamn the Confederation for imposing it! Goddamn the secessionists!

"Yes, General, the embargo. Merrick products are embargoed because some of them can also be applied to the manufacture of mind-altering drugs that have specific military applications. On Mylex for many decades there was a thriving industry in bootlegged prescription drugs. They used third parties to buy small quantities from companies like Merrick then replicated the ingredients and resold the stuff at vastly reduced prices. Often the stuff they sell is not as effective as the real drugs and people have died using the cut-rate imitations. So, when the Confederation put the embargo in place, Merrick volunteered to apply it to all their products. That's why Tommy can't get the medicine he needs to save him."

General Lyons, commander of Ravenette's military forces, a decorated veteran of many campaigns, had never felt such helpless anger and despair. Only days before, Tommy had been a healthy, active boy of eight, the light of the Lyons's life, the one bright spot the general could always count on to revive his spirits and restore his fading faith in the future of his world. And now—this? "Maybe somebody on Mylex has some of the stuff Tommy needs," he suggested, "it'd be better than nothing, doctor."

"Maybe. I'm trying to locate some of this drug, believe me, General, I'm trying. If we can get a stasis unit in time—and mind you, that might not work in this case because Tommy's condition is so far advanced—if I can find someone in our Coalition who has a supply of the drug, or contacts within the Confederation who can supply it, yes, I might be able to save your son. But time isn't on our side, sir. General, one more thing. We've got to find out how Tommy was exposed to the virus that causes this form of TB. The public health epidemiologists must be advised. They'll want to know what Tommy's been exposed to these last weeks. If this is the first case of an outbreak of the disease, we could be in for a lot of trouble."

"Then, goddamnit, let's get some specialists in from those worlds who can deal with this! I'll make a naval vessel available immediately! She can depart in—"

Almost in tears, Dr. Vance interrupted him. "General we can't! We cannot do that. Since the Ordinance of Secession was issued, the Confederation has also banned all travel to our sector of Human Space. I have already contacted my colleagues on Manazanares, to no avail. They are as devastated as I am, but any violation of the ban will be met with drastic sanctions. We're on our own, General. Let us hope that we can save Tommy and his case is an isolated one—or we could lose not only him but a whole generation of our children."

"And a whole generation of our young men and women," the bitterness in the general's voice was almost palpable, "if this secession movement leads to war with the Confederation. Their goddamned Ordinance of Secession! The goddamned Confederation!" General Lyons had never before put much credence in the commonly held belief of his fellow Ravenites that the Confederation despised them as second-class citizens. But to have imposed the sanctions on their world was inhumane, worse than what the soldiers did at Fort Seymour when they fired on the demonstrators.

Dr. Vance said nothing, but as a physician he also deeply regretted the Coalition Council's decision to issue the Ordinance because it would mean the loss of many lives he was dedicated to saving. But he kept that to himself because speaking against the war fever that had infected the people of Ravenette and their allies could be decidedly unhealthy. General Lyons, a respected hero, could be a bit more outspoken, and Dr. Vance knew he was dead-set against secession, but the doctor was discreet enough not to express his own opinion in the presence of anyone else, not even Varina Lyons.

Lyons took a deep breath and tried to get control of himself.

"Doctor, will you remain here with Tommy and Varina? I've been called before the Coalition Council. Those goddamned politicians are preparing for war."

"Yes, General. As soon as my contacts find what I need, I'll have it rushed here, and I'll keep you informed of our progress," he extended his hand and they shook.

"Thanks for everything, Doctor, I know you have a lot of other patients who need your help."

"I've been alerted for call-up, General. I'm in the reserves, you know. I may soon have the honor of serving with you in uniform."

"I'm the one who'd be honored, but let's hope it never comes to that. Thanks again for everything you're doing for us."

Vance let a wry smile cross his face, "General, we're so backward here on Ravenette that we doctors still think we're obligated to make house calls like this."

General Lyons's Plans and Operations officer, Admiral Porter de Gauss, had been sitting impatiently in a staff car outside the general's home for over an hour, glancing repeatedly at his chronometer. The Council would have already started its deliberations and they weren't even on their way yet! He leaned back in his seat. Well, if his son were seriously ill, he might be late for a meeting too. But—dammit!—this was an important meeting! War was in the air, you could almost taste it! War would mean a command. Maybe he could get out of the headquarters and back into the fleet again!

General Lyons slid into the seat next to him. "Sorry to keep you waiting, Porter. Driver, take us to the Council hall." He put Tommy's sickroom behind him now, confined it to a remote corner of his mind.

"General, they'll have already started," de Gauss reminded him as he inserted a crystal into his reader. "How's Tommy, sir?"

"No change, Porter. Let's see your crystal." First up on the screen were several tables showing the readiness and strength of the military and naval forces available to the Coalition. Next, similar tables reflecting what forces the Confederation had at its disposal. There were many more pages of those figures than for the Coalition's forces. "The Council will just have to wait. Hmm, how reliable are these figures on what the Confederation has?"

"They're the most reliable we have, General, accurate we believe to within one or two percent. Considering how readiness in any military unit fluctuates almost daily, it's impossible for us to know how many ships of the line they have ready for combat at any given period, how many armored vehicles, how many troops and so on. But all the Confederation units listed there are deployed in those places and in the strengths shown there. Personnel and equipment are according to their respective tables of allowances."

"Ummm. What I'm interested in is where they are, what they're doing there, and how quickly they can deploy to our sector if war is declared. I presume everything we have is ready?"

Admiral de Gauss nodded. "Since we'd only be deploying defensively we can concentrate our entire resources wherever they're needed in this quadrant."

"Good. Logistics? How are we on war materiel, production capabilities, spare parts, all the stuff we'll need if we engage in heavy combat?"

"It's all on the crystal, sir, but it'll take us a while to retool our industries for total war. We have planned to sustain material losses of up to ten percent in the initial phase of a war, personnel losses of about the same. Mobilization orders have been issued. Capture of the stores at Fort Seymour and the naval refueling base on Lannoy in the initial phase is crucial."

Lyons scrolled through the pages dealing with the Confederation's manpower status. Pressed, the Confederation could call up overwhelming numbers, but Lyons knew all the secessionists needed to do was defeat the regular forces badly enough to convince the Confederation's politicians that the cost of keeping them in was not worth it. "How'd you get these figures on the Confederation forces?" Lyons asked suddenly, grinning.

"Our intel boys have their sources, sir."

"I see old Joe Porter is Chairman of the Combined Chiefs. Related to you in any way?"

Admiral de Gauss blushed. "Distantly, yes, I think. One of my great-great grandfathers was a Porter."

"I played poker with him en route to planetfall during one of the Silvasian wars. Long, long time ago. All right, I've seen enough. You stay near me and keep this stuff handy when they call for my evaluation."

"What will you advise them, sir?"

"If we attack their garrisons on our worlds we'll throw them out, no question about it. And it'll take time for them to send enough ships and men to retake them. But something's up, Porter, I don't know what. They didn't send that division to Fort Seymour to 'oppress' us! That's nonsense. You've seen the data. Consider some of those more remote stations in your tables. Not so long ago most of them were no more than way stations to support exploration teams, or to protect new colonies from pirates, that sort of thing. But the Confederation's increased the size of some of those garrisons tenfold. Why? Something's up, and if we force them to fight us over our secession, the only thing we have in our favor in the long term is that their forces are so widely dispersed. But not for long."

"But sir, we cannot forget what happened at Fort Seymour!"

"No, no, but Porter, who was the fool who organized that demonstration and let it get so far out of hand? Those troops were green to Ravenette and, as far as we know now, leaderless at the crucial moment. Mary Eddy's dried up old teats, Porter, what would you expect them to do under the circumstances? Some of our own citizens need to swing for what happened that day. The incident alone does not justify war." But, he thought, that incident at Fort Seymour and the embargo sure didn't dispel the hatred most people felt toward the Confederation. He thought of his son lying on his—he dare not even think of the word "deathbed."

"Then you're against any aggressive act against the Confederation of Human Worlds?"

General Lyons hesitated before replying. "Look, they're our own people, all of them! We know them, we've fought beside them, we're related to them, we speak a common language! Sure, we have our differences but the last two hundred years haven't turned us into another species, for God's sakes! Yes," he sighed, "I'm against war." But as he spoke he really did not know if he believed himself.

" 'I went to the animal fair, the birds and the beasts were there,' humdedum dedum." Preston Summers hummed the old ditty under his breath. Yes, they're all here, all right, all the "birds and the beasts," he thought. The hall was full of the delegations from the Coalition's worlds.

They had been in session for days now, trying to form a unified government. Summers had been unanimously elected interim president, to preside over their deliberations. The delegates unanimously agreed Summers had represented them well in the failed negotiations with the Confederation and was the right man to preside over the Congress, perhaps even to lead the Coalition in the war all of them hoped would follow. A tentative cabinet had been decided upon, but they were about to hear from the military, whose testimony would be the final stone in the road to independence.

Tempers were running hot in the great hall. The Ordinance of Secession had been enthusiastically endorsed by everyone present on the first day and the Confederation's response had been immediate: Total embargo and boycott. In the many speeches that had followed, nobody bothered to point out that the Confederation's message announcing these economic measures had been conciliatory, not threatening, leaving the door open for further negotiations, apologizing for what had happened at Fort Seymour, the proximate justification for the Ordinance. The prevailing mood in the hall was for military action to expel the Confederation's garrisons from the Coalition's home worlds and nobody was willing to back down on that. Thus, General Lyons's forthcoming testimony would be crucial. Could they prevail?

"Where the hell is Lyons?" Summers asked an aide for the umpteenth time.

"He is en route, sir. I understand there's sickness in his family and that's why he's been delayed."

"Humpf," was all Summers said. He went back to pretending he was listening to someone from Cabala who was droning on and on about how the Confederation of Human Worlds had persecuted the followers of some religious sect on that world by denying its ministers chaplaincies in its military forces, blah, blah, blah. Everybody had their grievances and over the past days they had all come out, interminably.

Heads turned at a sudden disturbance at the rear of the hall.

"Wall, Gen'rel, welcome!" Summers voice, magnified by the public address system, thundered and the hall went immediately silent. General Lyons, followed by Admiral Porter, walked down the central aisle, nodding here and there to some acquaintances, stopping briefly to shake hands with others. As Lyons approached the podium Summers permitted himself a sly grin. The general's entrance was grand and triumphal. As Lyons mounted the stairs to the podium, delegates rose and began to applaud and instantly everyone in the hall was on their feet and the place resounded with cheers and whistling. "See, the conquerin' hero comes," Summers snorted sotto voce. He shook his head. What was it someone had once said about the general? I studied dramatics under Lyons? The old boy sure knew how to play to his audience. Well, time to get on with the show.

"Remember, thou art mortal," Admiral de Gauss whispered in Lyons's ear and laughed. Lyons began to laugh too and immediately everyone in the hall was laughing. Lyons held up his hands for silence.

"Time's a-wastin'," Summers thundered. "Gen'rel Lyons, have a seat."

Lyons took a seat on Summers's right. Summers's face seemed more florid and blotchy than Lyons remembered from their last meeting. The effects of his Old Snort. Everyone knew Summers for a boozer. "I hope you're well, Preston," he said in a whisper.

"Tolerable, Gen'rel, tolerable," Summers whispered back. "Sorry to hear there's sickness in your fambly."

"Thank you, Preston."

"Wall, Gen'rel, lay it on. Do we or don't we have the muscle to toss these bastards out?" Summers whispered.

For the next twenty minutes General Lyons presented a detailed analysis of the military readiness of the Coalition's forces as opposed to those of the Confederation of Human Worlds. During this time the great hall was completely silent. "In conclusion, ladies and gentlemen, if military force is used against the Confederation's forces in our sector of Human Space we shall achieve initial success, but the possibility of a clear-cut military victory over the Confederation is highly doubtful. The best we could hope for after a very destructive campaign would be a negotiated settlement and, if I am not mistaken, Madam Chang-Sturdevant's message to us clearly offers that initiative as an alternative to war. While I realize it is not within my province to make such a recommendation, I urge you to take her offer. Thank you."

The great hall remained silent for a long moment. "General Lyons!" it was someone from Ruspina. "Sir, if it is the decision of this body to use military force against the Confederation, will you lead it?"

Lyons hesitated for the briefest instant. "No. If you go to war against the Confederation I shall resign. War would be a foolhardy and criminal act we could never justify with victory." That response was based on the undeniable facts he had just reviewed, not on how he felt as a man.

Again, total silence reigned throughout the great hall as the delegates took in these words. "No!" someone shouted at last and that started an uproar of protest.

"Order! Order!" Summers shouted, "The Gen'rel has given us his professional opinion," the way Summers pronounced the word "professional" dripped with sarcasm, " 'n we must consider what he's told us. I hereby adjourn this session. You all have the Gen'rel's remarks, his tables and figgers, return to your rooms, and discuss them among yourselves. We will reconvene for a vote tomorrow morning at eight hours." He turned to General Lyons, "Guess you better be gettin' on home now, Gen'rel, see to your boy. I'll let ya know how the vote goes, 'less you want to be here when we do it tomorrow."

"Very well," Lyons nodded to de Gauss, who gathered up his briefing materials. De Gauss glanced out of the side of his eye at Summers and shook his head slightly. As Lyons walked out of the hall his passage down the central aisle, in contrast to his splendid entrance, met with stony silence from the delegates.

"We're lucky we weren't lynched," de Gauss commented as they climbed into their car.

"I almost wish I had been, Porter," Lyons replied glumly. They sat in silence as the driver headed back to the general's home. The on-board communicator shrilled suddenly, causing de Gauss to start. Lyons picked it up and listened intently. His face betrayed no emotion but he bit the inside of his mouth so hard it drew blood. He hung up without saying a word.

"Good news, I hope?"

"Good news for someone," Lyons replied. "Driver, back to the convention hall."

Lyons caught Summers just as he was leaving the hall. "Preston, does that offer of command still stand?" he demanded.

Summers paused and regarded Lyons speculatively. "Yeah. Why this sudden change of heart, Gen'rel?"

Lyons thrust his face into Summers's. "You want Ragnarok? Then I'll lead you there."

"Wall, I always liked trips with dramatic endings, Gen'rel," Summers answered coolly. "Is that the only reason?" Summers couldn't help noticing a small drop of blood staining one corner of General Lyons's lip. His eyes were drawn to it for some reason.

"My son is dead," Lyons answered.

CHAPTER SIX

"IG?" Lance Corporal Izzy Godenov shouted. "Why do we have to stand an Inspector General's inspection? Don't we have to be ready to go out at a moment's notice to fight the Skinks? How can we do that if we're wasting time on an IG?"

Sergeant Lupo "Rabbit" Ratliff, first squad leader, appeared in the doorway of his third fire team's room. "I heard that, Lance Corporal," he snarled. It was the end of Fifth Day's pre-IG preparations and the Marines were anxiously waiting for liberty call, when they'd be free until eight hours on First Day. "Look at this room," he said; the room was a mess with essential personal items spread about. "Just how long do you think it would take you to put all your shit in order, stow your personal belongings in the company supply room, and get whatever you're taking on a deployment ready to hump?" He stepped into the room and loomed over the seated Godenov. "It'd take so long you'd miss the goddamn Essay to orbit, that's how long!"

"I-I'd be ready in t-time," Godenov stammered.

Ratliff ignored Godenov's protest. "When you stand the IG, your personal shit will already be stowed away and the rest of your gear will be in such condition that you can have it all packed and on your back in less than ten minutes. That's not a waste of time!" He suddenly bent over and pulled Godenov's cargo belt out of his open locker box.

"What's this?" the squad leader asked, closely inspecting the belt. "It's frayed. Lance Corporal, do you intend to deploy with your gear on a cargo belt so frayed it will break and you lose something important that might save your life and the lives of other Marines? Well?"

"Ah, Sergeant, ah . . ."

"You won't have a frayed cargo belt when the IG comes through, Godenov. You *will* go to the supply room and have Sergeant Souavi replace this defective belt. Now."

"LIBERTY CALL, LIBERTY CALL, LIBERTY CALL!" Staff Sergeant Hyakowa bellowed in the squadbay corridor. "Base liberty only!" The squadbay reverberated with the raucous cries and clatter of Marines anxious to get out of the barracks, even if they couldn't leave base.

With Ratliff no longer looming over him, Godenov jumped to his feet and made final adjustments to his liberty clothes before joining everybody else.

"Not so fast, Izzy," Ratliff barked. He slammed the cargo belt into Godenov's chest. "You don't leave on liberty until you see Sergeant Souavi and replace this belt."

"But, Sergeant Ratliff, liberty call's been sounded, he's probably already gone."

"Maybe not; you had best get down there and find out if you want to go on liberty this weekend. And clean up this shithole when you get back!"

"Aye aye, Sergeant!" Clutching the cargo belt, Godenov twisted past Ratliff and bolted through the door.

"And you make sure he's got that cargo belt replaced and this room is shipshape before he goes on liberty," Ratliff added to Corporal Dean. He turned and stalked out of the room. His footsteps thudded loudly in the corridor as he headed for the squad leaders' quarters.

There was a moment's silence in the room before PFC Quick softly asked, "You think he's pissed off about having to stand an IG?"

"I think he's pissed off about having to stand an IG," Dean said, then added, "And I believe you better get out of here before he comes back with a reason to keep *you* from getting out of the barracks."

Godenov and Dean weren't the only members of first squad Sergeant Ratliff found cause to keep in the barracks. Nor was he the only squad leader who took out his displeasure about the pending Inspector

General inspection on his men. Fully a third of the platoon was effectively confined to the barracks—everybody who wasn't fast enough to get out of the barracks in the first couple of minutes after Staff Sergeant Hyakowa sounded liberty call was stuck. The three squad leaders also stayed in, taking the rare opportunity to prepare their own gear for the IG.

At 17 hours, Sergeant Kelly stepped into the quiet corridor and called out, "Third herd, fall in outside the barracks. NOW!" He stalked to the stairway and out back of the barracks. In a minute or so, a dozen members of the platoon were lined up in front of him.

"Chow call," Kelly snarled. "Form in two ranks. Right FACE! Fo-art HARCH!" He marched them to the chow hall, and marched them back when they finished eating.

On their return, the squad leaders saw to it that their Marines were working for the coming First Day's round in the pre-IG inspection cycle. Over the course of the weekend, most of the other Marines of third platoon filtered back in and were also put to work getting ready for the inspection.

"We aced it!" Lance Corporal "Wolfman" MacIlargie crowed. He collapsed back onto his rack, arms flung out to the sides, his face wreathed in a happy, self-satisfied grin.

Corporal Rachman Claypoole, MacIlargie's fire team leader, straightened up from stowing the contents of his shaving kit back into their normal place in his locker and turned an annoyed look on MacIlargie.

"We didn't 'ace' nothing," Claypoole snarled. "That was just the platoon commander's inspection." One long stride brought him into MacIlargie's part of the three-man room where the two of them lived with "Hammer" Schultz, the most experienced man in the fire team. He jerked a half-open drawer in MacIlargie's chest and poked a finger at it. His voice rose. "Didn't you hear the boss? Your skivvies are ten millimeters out of alignment! Tomorrow, the skipper will point out the same infraction in his inspection. Then there's the battalion inspection. Then the brigadier's inspection. If your skivvies aren't straightened out by the time the IG gets here, you'll flunk the inspection so bad you'll get busted back down to private!"

Claypoole reached full roar. "And I'm your fire team leader, so it'll be my responsibility." He jammed his fists into his hips and leaned over MacIlargie. "I'll be lucky if I only get busted to Lance Corporal!"

MacIlargie's grin vanished at Claypoole's first snarl. His posture wilted as his fire team leader's voice rose. By the time Claypoole reached full roar MacIlargie was drawing his limbs in and beginning to curl into a protective ball. He cast an anguished, silent appeal for help toward Schultz.

Schultz, who *had* aced the inspection, finished restowing his gear and sat at his miniscule desk, where he turned on his reader and opened it to the page he'd left off in Phonton's *Confederation Marines in the Second Silvasian War*. Without lifting his eyes from the screen, he growled, "You flunked, Wolfman."

MacIlargie slid onto his side and pulled his arms and legs in. "But . . ." he said weakly.

"No buts!" Claypoole snapped. "You'll get your shit together before the Skipper's inspection tomorrow and ace that inspection, or I'm going to know the reason why."

Before MacIlargie could say anything else, Staff Sergeant Hyakowa's voice boomed out in the squadbay corridor, "Base-liberty call for everyone who passed inspection. And the gods help any swinging dick in this platoon who doesn't pass tomorrow."

MacIlargie bolted to his feet and began stripping off his garrison utilities, to change into his liberty clothes.

"Not so fast, Wolfman," Claypoole shouted. "You flunked, you don't get liberty."

"What?" MacIlargie squawked. "But . . ."

"I said, 'no buts'!" Claypoole roared, jamming his face close to MacIlargie's. "You've got to get ready for tomorrow!"

"But . . ."

Claypoole cut him off with a raised hand and turned to Schultz. "Hammer, you pulling liberty tonight?"

Schultz didn't look away from his reading, his head shake was so slight it was almost imperceptible.

"I'm taking base liberty; get some chow, take in a flik," Claypoole said. "Do me a favor? Keep an eye on the problem child for me while I'm gone."

Schultz slowly turned his head to look blandly at MacIlargie for a moment before his voice rumbled from somewhere deep in his chest, "I hate babysitting." He turned back to his reader.

MacIlargie's eyes and mouth formed a triangle of "O"s as he stared at Schultz. "No-o-o," he mewed, then jerked toward Claypoole. "You can't do that to me!" he pleaded. "Don't leave me here with Schultz. Not with the Hammer in charge."

Claypoole smiled at him sweetly. "Hammer's not in charge," he said in a jaunty tone. "He's a professional lance corporal, he's never in command of anyone."

Schultz grunted, Claypoole decided to accept the noise as agreement with his statement—he was probably right.

"You can leave this room only to go to the head, or to go to chow," Claypoole told MacIlargie as he began to change into his liberty uniform. "You better pass tomorrow."

Corporal Joe Dean poked his head into the room just then. "Rock, I'm taking base liberty tonight. Want to grab some chow? Hammer, Wolfman," he added, politely acknowledging the two junior men.

"I'll be with you as soon as I finish changing."

"Right. I'll see who wants to join us," Dean said. He barely glanced at Schultz, but paused to give MacIlargie a speculative once-over before leaving.

Claypoole followed a minute later with, "See you before taps," to Schultz and MacIlargie.

Schultz merely grunted. MacIlargie looked pained.

An hour later, Schultz abruptly stood and stretched. "Chow," he announced, and crooked a finger at MacIlargie.

MacIlargie stood shakily and followed the big Marine to the mess hall.

Corporals Claypoole, Dean, Kerr, Pasquin, and Chan, along with HM3 Hough, one of the navy medical corpsmen assigned to Company L, sat at a round table in the main dining room of the 45 Club, the on-base club for junior noncommissioned officers. A huge serving bowl that had contained reindeer stew still sat in the middle of the table, surrounded by the pushed-aside serving bowls at each Marine's place and crumbs of the loaves of pumpernickel and rye bread with which they'd sopped up the stew. Kerr, Pasquin, and Hough were nursing steins of Reindeer Ale, the others sipped from steaming mugs of kafe—real coffee was generally beyond the budgets of mere corporals.

Pasquin leaned back, rubbed his belly, and belched loudly. "You know," he said ponderously, "a body could get tired of reindeer after a while. Reindeer steaks in Big Barb's, reindeer stew here in the 45 Club. All that reindeer shit the new cook at Big Barb's fed us that first time." He hoisted his stein. "Reindeer Ale," and took a quaff.

Kerr snorted. "Raoul, the way you slurped down that stew, I think it'll be a long, long time before *you* get tired of reindeer."

Chan chuckled. "Kerr's right. You inhaled three bowls, the rest of us only had two apiece."

"Four," Pasquin said. He saw the others looking at him. "I had *four* bowls of stew. Hey, I never said *I* was getting tired of reindeer. 'Sides, I'm a growing boy, I need to stoke the furnace."

"Growing sideways," Dean snorted.

"Hey!" Pasquin objected heatedly.

Hough decided to defuse any potential fight by changing the subject. "I see the way you're looking at the beer, Rock," he said to Claypoole. "Like it's your girlfriend holding hands with someone else. Go ahead, have a few. I can give you a hangover pill, you'll be fine for the Skipper's inspection in the morning.

Claypoole shook his head. "Thanks, Doc. I would, but I've got more work to do tonight." He looked at his timepiece.

"Wolfman?" Dean asked. "He didn't look real happy when liberty call sounded."

Claypoole nodded. "Ensign Bass noticed that his skivvies were ten millimeters out of alignment on the rack display. I made him stay in the barracks to prepare for the Skipper's inspection."

Kerr, who'd been with the platoon the longest, even though he'd been away for almost two years after being nearly killed on an operation, chuckled. "I still have trouble thinking of Charlie Bass as 'Ensign Bass.' "

"You and me both," Hough said. He'd been with Company L almost as long as Kerr.

Dean returned to his earlier comment. "Missing a night's base liberty doesn't seem like enough to get Wolfman as upset as he looked."

"Well, it is." Claypoole grinned wickedly. "That and the fact that I left Hammer in charge."

"You what!"

"You left *Schultz* in charge?"

"No way you left Schultz in charge! He wouldn't stand for it."

"Were you holding your blaster on him when you told him he was in charge?"

"Well, I didn't exactly tell him he was in *charge.* I just asked him to keep an eye on the problem child for me."

Kerr hooted. He leaned forward and stretched out an arm to clap Claypoole on the shoulder. "Corporal Claypoole, you just earned your stripes. You figured out how to make the most intransigent lance corporal in the Marine Corps do something he flat refuses to do."

"Schultz really didn't put up a fight when you put him in charge of MacIlargie?" Chan asked.

Claypoole blew on his fingernails and buffed them against his shirt front. They could almost see the canary feather sticking out of his grin when he nodded and said, "I surely did. And, no."

"I do believe MacIlargie's skivvies will be in perfect alignment tomorrow," Dean said, giving Claypoole's back a slap that almost shoved his face into his stew bowl.

Mustering what dignity he could after the near miss with the remains of his dinner, Claypoole asked the table at large, "How did your people do?"

"Just the usual minor gigs," Chan replied. "Nothing more serious than skivvies out of alignment."

"When I was in recon, I never understood how come we had to stand Mickey Mouse inspections," Pasquin said. "We weren't show Marines and junk-on-the-bunk inspections didn't have a damn thing to do with what we did. And now . . . We're on constant standby for Skinks. An IG doesn't make sense." The others ignored him, there was a lot the Marine Corps made them do that didn't make sense to them.

"How come you didn't let Wolfman take base liberty if all he had wrong was a minor misalignment of his skivvies?" Dean asked.

"Because he thought we aced the inspection. I wanted to impress on him how tough an IG can be."

Kerr leaned forward. "You did the right thing. The rest of you should have done the same with any of your people who weren't perfect. I've stood an IG before, they're tougher than any of you realize. Matter of fact," he looked at each of the other fire team leaders, "if any of your people weren't outstanding you should have stayed in yourselves and worked with them." He leaned back and took another swig of his ale.

"Your people aced?" Hough asked.

Kerr nodded. "You know it."

"Bullshit!" Claypoole snorted. "You've got Doyle. No way Doyle aced the inspection."

"Right," Pasquin agreed. "Tell Doyle to screw something together and he'll go looking for a hammer."

Kerr shook his head. "Wrong. Doyle made corporal and senior company clerk because he was good at the Mickey Mouse of keeping records. He's also stood an IG before. The IG gave his office an 'outstanding' rating. He knows what he's doing here." He paused to let the others absorb what he'd said, then added, "Doyle told me the junk-on-the-bunk is a piece of cake compared to what his office had to go through preparing for that IG. He had his shit so together that he had time to help Summers get ready."

"No," the others said in disbelief.

"Fact. Doyle was ready before I was." Kerr checked the time. "I told Doyle and Summers to be back in the barracks by twenty-one hours. I better be back before them." He stood to leave.

"Where *is* Doyle?" Hough asked, looking around. "He's a corporal, he can come to the 45 Club. Hell, he could even sit with us if he wanted to." He returned a bland look to the glare Pasquin gave him.

"He took Summers to Pete's Place. Said he wanted to give him the straight scoop on IGs from the perspective of a junior man who's stood one."

Everybody looked at him with shock.

"If I didn't know better, I'd think he was bucking for the next fire team leader opening. I'll see you back at the barracks." With that, Kerr left.

The others looked at each other.

"Doyle, a fire team leader?"

"No way!"

"Never happen!"

"ATTENTION ON DECK!" Staff Sergeant Hyakowa bellowed. "FALL IN!"

Thudding feet echoed off the walls of the corridor that ran the length of third platoon's squadbay, followed seconds later by the loud clicks of room doors latching open. Less than fifteen seconds after the platoon sergeant's orders, the Marines of third platoon were standing at attention against the walls of the corridor, facing across it, each fire team outside its room.

Hyakowa hit the lights; the morning light that filtered into the corridor wasn't bright enough for an inspection. "Squad leaders, REPORT!" he ordered.

The squad leaders could see their men from where they stood together outside their room at one end of the corridor.

"First squad, all present and accounted for!" Sergeant Ratliff reported.

"Second squad, all present and accounted for!" Sergeant Linsman called out.

"Guns, all present and accounted for!" Sergeant Kelly cried.

Hyakowa turned to face the head of the stairs that entered the corridor and stepped back from it. "Sir, third platoon all present and accounted for!" he said loudly as Ensign Charlie Bass stepped into the corridor.

"Very good, Platoon Sergeant," Bass said loudly enough for everyone to hear as he stopped in front of Hyakowa. He briefly stood at attention, then relaxed into a modified parade rest—feet at shoulder width, hands clasped behind his back—and swiveled side to side to look down the corridor in both directions.

"Today is the company commander's inspection," he said looking in one direction. "I hope you are better prepared for inspection than you were yesterday," he said looking the other way. He returned to attention and said to Hyakowa, "Platoon Sergeant, have the men get their weapons and fall in behind the barracks."

"Aye aye, sir!" Hyakowa replied as Bass about-faced and left the squadbay. As soon as Bass reached the foot of the stairs Hyakowa broke his stance and looked at the Marines. "You heard the man, grab your weapons and fall in behind the barracks. Go! Move-move-MOVE!" The Marines of third platoon got their weapons so quickly he barely had time to back against the wall to avoid being buffeted by them as they scrambled past to the stairs.

"What's up?" someone asked nervously. "We were inside for yesterday's junk-on-the-bunk."

"We won't be inside when the IG comes through," Linsman answered. "What's the matter, did you forget to store your skin-trids in the supply room and you're afraid the Skipper will find them? Now move it!"

In a minute, third platoon was in position behind the barracks along with the rest of the company. No officers, no one from the company command element, only the hundred and eleven enlisted Marines from the three blaster platoons and the assault platoon.

Hyakowa, standing in front of third platoon's three ranks, looked to his left and right at the other platoon sergeants and shrugged a question. They all shrugged back; none of them knew just what was going on either.

He about-faced and said just loud enough for his men to hear, "Stand easy."

The Marines of third platoon relaxed from their positions of attention. To their flanks, the other platoons also fell into "at ease" at the commands of their platoon sergeants. They waited. The platoon sergeants stood facing their platoons, and casting frequent glances over their shoulders at the rear door to the barracks, waiting for someone to come out and tell them what to do.

After about five minutes, Gunnery Sergeant Thatcher, Company L's second ranking enlisted man, exited the barracks and marched to a spot midway along the company's front. At his approach, the platoon sergeants called their platoons to attention.

Thatcher came to attention at his spot and bellowed, "Platoon sergeants, REPORT!"

"First platoon, all present and accounted for!" Staff Sergeant DaCosta reported, followed by the other platoon sergeants in order.

"COMP-ny, at EASE!" Thatcher commanded. He stood feet spread, hands clasped behind his back, leaning forward slightly as he looked over the company from one end to the other. Most of the Marines stood at an easy parade rest rather than slouching into a full "at ease." All eyes were on him. Satisfied that he had the Marines' attention, he announced, "The Skipper, the rest of the officers, and First Sergeant Myer are inspecting the squadbays. When they finish the barracks inspection, they'll come outside and inspect *you.*" He ignored the muted protests and expressions of dismay. "The inside inspection will take as long as it takes. In the meanwhile, we will wait out here." There were more vocalizations in the ranks, less muted than before. "Keep it down to a low roar, people."

When the voices lowered, Thatcher made a slight head movement, and the platoon sergeants left their positions to gather in front of him.

Thatcher looked at Hyakowa and shook his head. "Wang, I wish we still had Doyle as chief clerk. Palmer's a good clerk and he tries hard, but he doesn't have the experience Doyle has, and he's not as meticulous. When Lieutenant Humphrey," the company executive officer, "inspected the records yesterday, he found so many minor gigs he damn near flunked the clerks. The Top had them working all night correcting errors." He paused to heave a sigh. "The records *might* be in proper shape by the time battalion conducts its inspection."

The platoon sergeants grimaced. "Was there anything serious?" DaCosta asked.

Thatcher shook his head. "Nothing major. Just piddling little things, like file names out of sequence by a character so it looked like things were missing. The biggest thing was an incomplete inoculation record in one man's file." He smiled wryly. "Fortunately, it was my file, and I was able to get it corrected right away."

The platoon sergeants murmured unkind words about pogues who couldn't get things right.

Hyakowa shook his head and asked, "Does the Top still want Doyle's ass?" On Company L's still-secret deployment to the quarantined world called Avionia, then-chief company clerk Corporal Doyle had forced an issue, making the first sergeant do something he didn't want to do. Top Myer called it insubordination and wanted Doyle court-martialed. However, the army general, a Major General Cazombi, in command of the operation thought Doyle deserved a medal. They compromised; no medal, no court martial, and Doyle was transferred out of 34th FIST. Only to be returned, in the strongest hint that 34th FIST had been secretly removed from the Confederation Marine Corps's normal personnel rotation. There were no billets open for a corporal clerk in the FIST, so then-Gunnery Sergeant Charlie Bass said he'd take Doyle as a blasterman in his platoon. Doyle had once inadvertently been on a patrol deep behind hostile lines with Bass, who believed the corporal could function well enough as an infantryman. So Doyle was kept away from Myer.

"I do believe so, Wang," Thatcher replied disgustedly. "So you've got to keep him."

Hyakowa shrugged one shoulder. "He's not nearly as good a blasterman as he was a clerk, but he'll do."

"How are they doing it in there?" second platoon's Staff Sergeant Chway asked with a nod toward the barracks, changing the subject.

"The Skipper's got yesterday's gig list from the platoon commanders. He's looking to make sure all the deficiencies have been corrected."

"That shouldn't take too long," Gunnery Sergeant Charlo of the assault platoon commented.

"Think again. The Top's royally pissed about the clerical errors. He's looking for gigs that *weren't* in the platoon commander's reports, or new gigs. And you better believe he's going to keep looking until he finds some."

The platoon sergeants stifled groans at that news.

"We're in for a lo-o-ong wait," DaCosta groaned.

"That's for sure. Tell you what. Return to your platoons and inspect them. That'll help pass the time, and maybe give them a chance to correct any deficiencies you find before the the Top lets the Skipper get out here."

"Right," Hyakowa said sourly, but no more sourly than the responses of the other platoon sergeants.

It was another hour before Captain Conorado led the platoon commanders and First Sergeant Myer out of the barracks. All of the officers looked displeased. The men in the ranks could almost see the canary feather sticking out of the corner of Top Myer's mouth.

Much to Top Myer's disgust, Captain Conorado and Lieutenant

Humphrey, who conducted the inspection of the Marines and their weapons, passed all of them. Still, he had a *lengthy* gig list from the junk-on-the-bunk portion of the company commander's inspection. There would be no liberty call until after the battalion commander's inspection—not even base liberty!

CHAPTER SEVEN

"Nacqui all'affanno, al pianto. Soffri tacendo il core . . ." the mezzo-soprano voice soared, filling the room with its power and the beauty of the music. Preston Summers sat transfixed, a half-full glass of bourbon in one hand, a cigar smoldering in the other. Slowly, slowly, he raised the cigar and inhaled the tobacco smoke. He held it in his lungs for long moments and then expelled it in a long, lazy puff through mouth and nose, savoring the rich flavors. Such private moments had always been precious to him, the more so as the events of the past weeks rushed his world headlong into a dubious future.

"Didn't know you were into opera," a voice boomed suddenly behind Summers, causing him to start upright.

"Goldurnit, didn't know you came into rooms without knocking." Then, almost defensively, "I may still have dirt under my fingernails but that don't mean I got dirt between my ears."

"What're you listening to?"

Angrily Summers shut the music off, the mood destroyed, and got out of his chair. "A snort of Snort?" he asked, offering General Davis Lyons a drink of Old Snort.

"No, I never drink when I'm on duty. But I will have one of those cigars, if you please."

"I do please. Yer always on duty, Gen'rel," Summers laughed. "These are Davidoff Anniversario Number Ones, the best they is." Deftly he cut the cigar and handed it to the general. During the last weeks the two had formed an uneasy alliance, a grudging respect for one another. "How's Varina?"

"Tolerable, tolerable," Lyons answered, lighting his cigar. Funny, he thought, how he was beginning to adopt some of Summers's manners of speech. A month before he would have hesitated even to shake the man's hand, now he was visiting him in his home and smoking his cigars.

"It's an opera by a guy named Rossini, *La Cenerentola,* ever hear of it?" Talking like this about one of the secret loves of his life, opera, embarrassed the gritty old politician, like talking about the secrets of his sex life or his religious beliefs, which he believed a man should hold in the utmost privacy.

"No, Preston. What language is that?"

"Italian. 'Cenerentola' is Italian for Cinderella. Everyone knows the story, Gen'rel. Hell, we know it better'n most 'cause that's all we are, a world full of little goddamned Cinderellas. What she's sayin' is, 'I was born to hardship and sorrow, my heart suffered in silence.' Well, we ain't sufferin' in silence no more, are we, Gen'rel Lyons?"

Lyons shook his head, more in wonder than agreement. "There's more to you than meets the eye, isn't there, Preston?"

"Aw, I dunno know 'bout that. I'm a pretty simple type of guy," the red blotches on his face grew darker. "Are we ready, Gen'rel?"

"Yessir, we are ready."

"How will it all end?"

"Badly. I don't need to tell you that."

Summers nodded. "You don't give a damn anymore, do you? Yer gonna ride this dark horse just like me, aren't you?" Summers puffed on his cigar and sipped some bourbon. "I feel we ain't really in charge anymore, Gen'rel, we're being carried forward on a big wave, like. The wave of history, huh?" he laughed. "Ke-rist, am I gonna miss all this," he gestured about the music room that was the heart of his home. "I oughta be in retirement, livin' out the last of my years instead of—" he shrugged. "Anyway, if we lose and we don't get ourselves kilt, they'll come for us, you know that. Gawdam, though, we'll go down swingin'! The bastards'll know they had a fight."

"We can always call it off."

"Nah, too late for that," Summers finished his drink in one gulp and wiped his mouth with the back of his left hand. "Well," he held out his right and they shook. "I'll see you at your headquarters in the morning. How come you military fellas can't ever start a war at a civilized hour?" He paused and then muttered, "God help those poor boys at Fort Seymour."

"God help us, Preston."

"As luck would have it, God's on our side, Gen'rel, didn't you know that?" Summers laughed. "Now, sir, would you leave me alone here until the morning?"

After General Lyons had left Summers let the glorious music fill the room again, but the mood was irretrievably lost and after a short while he shut the music off and turned his attention to finishing the bottle of bourbon.

Charlette Odinloc stretched luxuriously under the sheets. She ran a hand through her short, brown hair, cut to regulation length. "Hand me a cigarillo, would you, Donnie?" she purred. Donnie Caloon shook a cigarillo out of the pack, lighted it, and passed it over to Charlette, propping one hairy arm on her chest as he did. Donnie was stocky, muscular, with a pleasant, boyish face. The thinning hair in the front of his head made him look older than his thirty years. But he was a simple man consumed by a youthful enthusiasm for everything physical. Charlette had actually come to like him in the time they'd been together, something that surprised her somewhat. Professionals weren't supposed to do that.

"I ain't never had a gal as—" he began, but she placed a finger on his lips.

"Don't say it, Donnie," Charlette murmured. "Thanks," she sucked in the smoke and held it in her lungs. The cigarillo was a blend of tobacco and thule and its combined mild narcotic effect was immediate. "Get yer arm off my chest, Donnie, I can't breathe."

"Sorry." Donnie lay back on the pillows. "Y'know what we need right now, Charlette?"

"No, Donnie, what do we need right now?" Since all Donnie thought of when he was with her was sex, she thought that's what he meant. Donnie was impervious to sarcasm, but he was good in bed. And he was good for some other things too. As a courier for a major import-export firm he got around the capital city of Ravenette, saw things, liked to talk about what he saw, and trusted anyone who as much as smiled at him.

"Honeybabe, we need brekfus 'n plenty of it!"

"Yeah, after all those calories we just burned up. But Donnie, we can't go out. It's not wise for me to be out in the daytime since I'm technically AWOL. I've told you that. I can make it back at night okay but I don't want to take a chance on being picked up in broad daylight. I'm puttin' my young ass on the line for you, stud boy!"

Donnie grinned. He liked being called "stud boy." As did most simple men, he fancied himself a great lover. And like men in general he loved having a good-looking woman confirm that for him. "I know, Hon', I know. I'll rustle us up somethin' right here! I got the fixin's! You lay there and smoke a bit and I'll get started!" Completely naked, he got out of bed and without bothering to dress, began banging pots around in the small kitchen.

For weeks Fort Seymour had existed under a state of virtual siege. Only the most essential business authorized military personnel to make trips off post and only under heavy armed escort. Charlette claimed she could get out when she was not needed in her job at the post quartermaster laundry by using an unguarded gate at the back of the post. As he did everything, Donnie took the statement at face value, only briefly wondering if it was very smart of the military, leaving a gate unguarded after there'd been so much trouble at Fort Seymour. Then he shrugged off the thought; that was somebody else's business and if it enabled Charlette to be with him, more power to the unguarded gate.

"How'd things go last night?" Charlette asked from the bed.

"Oh, same old shit. More heavy stuff comin' in, comin' in. Bunch of cars last night, from Mylex, 'n last week we had bulldozers from Sagunto. Well, maybe not bulldozers, cranes, I'd guess. You know, with the long arms stickin' out the cabs? Lotsa 'em, all lined up under canvas out at the port. 'N night before last, whole bunches of people from Cabala come in. Soldiers on vacation."

Charlette suppressed a laugh. Nobody, not even anybody from Cabala would ever take a vacation on Ravenette. All she needed now was to see for herself. "Think they'll be stayin' long, Donnie? Did they bring much baggage with 'em?"

"Baggage? Oh, yeah. Maybe they's here for manures or whatever they call those games. I dunno, but they was scads of 'em out there. You know, I thought maybe about joinin' up? Folks keep sayin' there's gonna be a war? I went to see a recruiter, you know? He tole me to come back later, my job was too important for me to go for a soldier," he said proudly as he cracked eggs into a skillet. Donnie often rattled on like this. That was another thing Charlette liked about the man, all she had to do was punch the right button and he'd launch into a very useful monologue.

"I wouldn't want you to go into the army, Donnie. Who'd cook me up eggs in the morning?" Donnie laughed happily. Charlette rolled onto her side. "Hey, Donnie, suppose I go with you tonight? I'd like to get out and about instead of being cooped up around here."

"Sure? Ain't you afraid of gettin' picked up?" There was genuine concern in Donnie's voice. Then, like the big child he was, he brightened to the idea. "Well, you ride with me and there's no problem! I'll take you as my helper! Anyone asks, I'll say I'm trainin' you for the job! There's room on my bike! But won't they miss you back at the laundry?"

"No, Studly. I'm off until day after tomorrow. But maybe I'll nip back in tonight, after we're done." Actually, the army quartermaster laundry facility at Fort Seymour was overworked, ever since the post exchange operation closed down because General Cazombi had ordered the local civilian personnel employed there off the installation as a security measure.

Charlette Odinloc, Sergeant Charlette Odinloc, Army Intelligence, rubbed her feet together and drew deeply on the cigarillo. Donnie Caloon really was a stud and the smell of the eggs and bacon he was cooking up, mixed with the aroma of strong coffee, made her stomach growl. She'd decide for herself tonight if the "cars" parked at the port were tanks, tank retrievers, or artillery pieces. The "vacationing" military personnel with their "baggage" could only be infantry reinforcements, that was very good to know. That information had to get back to the Division G2 ASAP. Without a string-of-pearls in orbit and the division's recon activities severely limited, a ride in the country might be very productive. But right now—

"Come on, babybug!" Donnie gushed, "Come and get it!" He placed two huge platters heaped with golden scrambled eggs and rashers of bacon on the table. Not even slightly embarrassed standing there buck naked, facing Charlette as she slid nude from under the sheets, he almost pounded his chest with joy. "Honeybun, I ain't had so much fun since the hawgs ate my little brother!" he laughed. He was such a simple boy.

Charlette permitted herself a sly grin as she slipped quickly into a vacant chair. They began eating. Donnie forked masses of eggs into his mouth, slurped from a cup of steaming black coffee, leaned across the table, and whispered conspiratorially, "Honeybun, you got the best rack of tits the Good Lord ever did put on a mortal woman!"

CHAPTER EIGHT

Private Alee Solden, first squad, second platoon, Bravo Company, 2nd Battalion, 1st Brigade, 3rd Provisional Infantry Division, Confederation Army, wiped the condensation off his helmet's faceplate and sighed. "I can see better with this thing up." Standing orders were that during the hours of darkness every man on the perimeter was to keep his eyes glued to his night-vision optics, despite the fact that anti-intrusion devices had been scattered everywhere within a kilometer of Fort Seymour's main gate. But staring through the optics all night long was just impossible to do. Risking possible company punishment, Solden lifted the plate and immediately the dim outlines of the street in front of the gate disappeared, replaced by the dense, white fog. But the air smelled good and fresh and reminded him briefly of the open fields of home on Carhart's World.

"Solden! Stay alert and stop messing with your gear," his squad leader's voice crackled in his ear.

How the hell does Sergeant Carman know I've got this goddamned plate raised? Solden wondered, lowering it into place immediately. Good NCOs had an uncanny ability to know what was going on and Carman was a good squad leader. And he wouldn't report the infraction to the lieutenant, not so close to the end of the company's tour on the perimeter. "This fog ain't natural, Herbie," Solden whispered in reply.

"I can't see shit through these optics," PFC Mort Stuman, complained, wiping the moisture off the M72 Straight Arrow antiarmor rocket the pair had been issued.

"Cut the chatter, you'll wake the other guys up," Sergeant Herb Carman chuckled. Like the other seven men in his squad, he was thinking now of getting back to Bravo Company's bivouac and breakfast. "Another hour to first light and we can get off the line," he reminded his squad. No one needed reminding since everyone was concentrating on his watch now.

"Not that anyone would know when it's first light in this crap," someone muttered over the tactical net.

"Next guy who opens his mouth goes on shit detail when we get off the line, and I mean it," Carman announced. The net went silent.

"All right," Stuman whispered to Solden, "so when the tanks come rolling over us we sit here and don't say nothing and after we're all prisoners they'll ask why we didn't warn anybody and we'll tell them, 'Well, Sergeant Carman told us to shut up or we'd go on shit detail . . .' "

"Shhhhhhh!" Solden hissed. "Do you hear something, Mort? I heard something!" He lowered and adjusted his night-vision optics. Carefully, Stuman switched his Straight Arrow to firing mode.

"You sure? I don't hear or see anything!"

"I don't know," Solden confessed, feeling a bit silly, but his pulse was racing and now he was fully alert. "I thought I heard something like a rumble . . ." Cautiously he eased the safety off his rifle.

For two weeks Bravo Company had been pulling night guard along that section of Fort Seymour's perimeter. The engineers had constructed reinforced firing points and bunkers that were manned around the clock, but for two weeks nothing had happened. They had been warned by G2 that the Coalition forces were massing armor to use against them. To improve their fields of fire, and to the great consternation of the citizens of Ravenette, the engineers had evacuated the nearby buildings and demolished some of them, leaving only one approach route: the main road that led to the gate, called "The Strip" by Fort Seymour's garrison. The entire company was equipped with the Straight Arrow. It would be suicide for armor to approach them down that road. At least, that's what they hoped.

"I wish they'd try it, I truly wish they would," Stuman was muttering half to himself, "I wanna get some so bad I can taste it." Most of the men of the 3rd Provisional Infantry Division, which had been formed on Arsenault, the Confederation's training world, had never seen combat, but they all believed they were ready for it. They also believed, with the certainty of young, unblooded soldiers, that the Coalition rebel forces were not capable of taking them on.

The early morning, fog-shrouded silence enveloped the men of Bravo Company.

Private Solden's eardrums ruptured, so he never heard the air-to-ground rocket detonate on his firing position. The force of the explosion picked him up, flung him backward, and slammed him into the wall of the bunker. He lost consciousness instantly.

Major General Alistair Cazombi was known as "Cazombi the Zombie" for a good reason: he never showed emotion, never even cracked a smile; well, almost never. The one time he did reveal how he really thought about something was the reason he'd been exiled to Fort Seymour on Ravenette. As the Director for Personnel to the Combined Chiefs of Staff, General Cazombi was fully aware of the reason why the Marines of 34th FIST, men he had come to know and respect, were quarantined on Thorsfinni's World. He did not agree with that policy, nor did he agree with the government's policy of keeping the alien threat a secret from the Confederation's member worlds. And he said so in meetings with Admiral Porter, the Chairman of the Combined Chiefs.

"I could have you sent to Darkside for even talking about this!" Porter had raged at last. This time they were meeting alone, but Cazombi had also brought the subject up when other members of the staff were present; he was determined not to let the matter rest.

"Sir, if we trust our Marines to fight the Skinks we can trust them to keep quiet about them too. Confining them like this is tantamount to sending them to Darkside."

"Well, who ever heard of a twenty-three-year-old with a snout full of beer who can keep his mouth shut?" Porter said, echoing a statement his personnel director had made in a previous meeting.

"Sir, that's a good point, we must assume somebody on Thorsfinni's World already knows about the Skinks. And what about the people on

Kingdom? They've seen the Skinks up close and personal. A lot of people other than our Marines know about them, and we can't impose quarantines on whole worlds."

Admiral Porter drummed his fingers on his desk, showing his impatience with Cazombi's pressing this point. "General, nobody on Thorsfinni's World is going to believe the sea stories of a drunken Marine! You know the Marines are the biggest braggarts ever. And the Kingdomites? Hell's bells, General, they're religious fanatics! They're always having 'visions' and 'epiphanies' and all that nonsense! Nobody believes them on principle. And the fact is, the word has not gotten out and it won't, as long as the quarantine keeps those blabbermouth Marines away from the rest of humanity!"

Cazombi took a breath. "Admiral Porter, hasn't anyone in this government figured it out yet? We're trying to keep the biggest secret in history from people who absolutely need to know about the threat."

"That order comes from the President herself, General!" Porter banged his fist on his desk. "Do you realize the panic that would ensue if we let the word out now, without preparation? We're reinforcing our garrisons in the outlying worlds for that very reason. When the people have all the protection we can give them, then they'll be informed as to the reasons why—and not until then! We do not want them thinking we're leaving them on their own. We let the word out now and every world in Human Space will be begging for troops we don't have."

"But they are on their own! We don't have the forces to provide the protection everyone needs. The Skinks can strike anywhere, anytime, and we cannot block all the holes in our defense, not with the available forces. And what happens if we have a major war of our own on our hands? We can't fight on two fronts at the same time." Now Alistair Cazombi finally lost control and blurted out the words that sealed his fate: "I wish sometimes someone would go to the goddamned press with this story and blow the whole thing."

Porter's mouth fell open. "You—you—" was all he could get out at first. "You are a brave and very competent officer," he finally gritted. "You've served with distinction on my staff, and your third star is virtually assured—"

"Admiral, you cannot bribe me—"

"Shut up!" Porter thundered. He took a moment to regain his

composure. "You will end this train of thought immediately! One more mention of the alien threat and I swear by the Holy Martyrs's twisted guts, you are finished here."

"Admiral," Cazombi replied coolly, "you and everyone who supports this stupid policy are a goddamned ass. The farther I can get away from you the better."

And Admiral Porter obliged him.

So Major General Alistair Cazombi found himself sitting quietly in a strategy meeting as Brigadier General Balca Sorca and his staff tried desperately to devise a defensive plan to deal with what everyone knew was coming, a Coalition attack on Fort Seymour. Bitterly, Cazombi reflected that if the Confederation government had let everyone know about the Skinks, the reinforcement of Fort Seymour would have been seen in a different light and they might not now be in this pickle. But he was not at liberty to say that, even if anyone had been willing to listen.

Cazombi had been invited to the planning meeting as a courtesy because he was the ranking officer at Fort Seymour, but he was not expected to participate except insofar as the involvement of his garrison complement was concerned. The meeting had been going on for an hour before Cazombi decided to speak up.

"General," Cazombi said, interrupting Sorca in midsentence, "do you really think a front-line defense is wise? I should think a defense-in-depth would be more effective."

"Yes, General! We put everything up front and stop them cold. If they break through and take the main post we're finished. We can't let them do that."

"Allow me to demonstrate." Cazombi got up and moved to the huge briefing screen. "Give me an installation schematic," he told the console operator. "Gentlemen, I've been here for months now and I know this post like the back of my hand. Observe the main post area here. It's a bewildering jumble of warehouses, barracks, offices. Dead-end streets are the common rule. Get any enemy force in there and they'll slow down."

"Yes, General, but the other side knows how this post is laid out. The civilians who work here no doubt have cooperated fully with the enemy. They know where the dead-end streets are, where the warehouses are situated, everything. You can bet they know the prices of the women's wear and cosmetics in the PX too." Everyone laughed at this remark because the soldiers of the infantry units eagerly bought those items to further their liaisons with the local girls.

"They won't once we get started. We'll block the streets, demolish buildings, dump them into the roadways. I can change the complex of this post in only a few days. What I recommend is delaying forces at the choke points here, here, here, and here. We mine everything and blow the mines as the delaying forces withdraw. When the enemy crosses the open space, about two kilometers deep between main post and the Peninsula, we'll have registered our artillery on every square meter and they'll take heavy casualties before they ever reach our main line of resistance, which we'll have the engineers construct for us. They'll take ten times our casualties just getting through the Main Post area. That should give them pause. In any event, they'll have to withdraw and regroup at that point while we sit snug in our defenses. We can hold out on the Peninsula until reinforced. I can defend that place against ground, air, and seaborne attack. For how long? I don't know, that depends on a lot of factors, but two months at least, long enough to interrupt their timetable and maybe just long enough for a relief force to land and turn the tables."

"No wonder they call the place 'Bataan,' " Sorca said. Several of his staff officers laughed obligingly, but they saw the sense in the argument Cazombi was making. "We're outnumbered, General. We retreat into the Peninsula and we'll be stuck there."

"Yes, General, we're stuck no matter what. Our alternatives are bleak: Either they overrun us in the first few hours or they overrun us in a few days or weeks. But once they attack, time is not on our side. They can bring in a million men if they want to. They may have already, so far as we know. They did bring in armor, your G2 verified that." Cazombi gestured at the lieutenant colonel who was the division G2. He nodded.

" 'Armor,' " Sorca snorted, "you'd think after what happened on Diamunde nobody would invest in that stuff anymore."

"We have some Straight Arrows," Cazombi said, "but not a lot of them. Armor is very effective, if you don't have antitank capability."

"Sir," the Division G2 interjected, "these people decided that for their own purposes armored attack vehicles would be a wise investment.

We have a few dozen Straight Arrows in storage on the Peninsula. After Diamunde the excess production of the weapons was distributed to various posts and this was one of them. I am not sure how many of the enemy's tanks we can knock out. If we run out of the tank killers before they run out of armored vehicles . . ." He shrugged.

"In any event, we will be outnumbered no matter how many men they bring in, but rest assured, General, they'll throw everything they've got at us to take this installation," Cazombi said.

"I'm well aware of that," Sorca answered, losing his patience now. "We have already decided to proceed with a frontline defensive posture."

"Very well, sir," Cazombi nodded, his expression never changing even though he knew this plan was a sure prescription for disaster. "I only ask you to do one thing for me. The Peninsula has a warren of underground storage facilities. It shouldn't take too much effort to convert the complex into a very strong redoubt. Let me take my garrison force to the Peninsula. Loan me your engineer battalion as soon as it's free, and give me one battalion of infantry and two batteries of artillery. I'll build a redoubt out there that can be your fallback position if the enemy breaks through your line. Do that and I'll get out of your hair."

Sorca smirked. "That's a fair price to pay, General. Go ahead, it's your post, after all. Wreck the place if that makes you feel better. Just make sure your operation doesn't get in the way of the deployment of my troops." He addressed his G3, operations officer, "Can we do that without weakening our capabilities?"

"Yessir! No matter how many troops the Coalition might have brought in to use against us, they will not stand up to what we can throw at them," he said with the bravado of the loyal staff officer. "I'll see that General Cazombi's request is honored immediately."

General Cazombi bowed politely to the staff officers and left the room, followed closely by his own operations officer. "Sir," that man asked as they stepped out of the building, "what are our chances?"

Cazombi twitched his lip—which passed for a grin with him. "You know something that Sorca doesn't understand? These people who formed this so-called Coalition really are rubes, through and through, but they can fight. You know who's leading them? Davis Lyons. I played poker with him on the way to fight in one of the Silvasian Wars—that was before your time. He's no fool, and he acquitted himself well in combat. He won't commit any errors when his troops attack us, you can bet on that."

"Yessir. But what are our chances?"

"Well, Colonel, we have three alternatives. One, we hold out until reinforced by the Confederation, and that is what we are going to try our damnedest to do. Two, we go into POW camps. And three?"

"Yessir?"

The General stopped. They were standing in front of the post exchange, which was now shuttered and deserted. The families that had accompanied the garrison soldiers to Ravenette had long ago been evacuated. There was nothing in that post exchange a soldier needed to perform his duties. Cazombi's garrison troopers wore battle dress now, ate in their messes, slept in barracks, and spent their off-duty hours in their units. The fog was lifting but the lights still glowed dimly along the deserted streets. Every surface was slick with moisture. As they stood there droplets of condensation dripped on them from the building's eaves.

"You know, Colonel, whoever named the Peninsula out there Bataan was a goddamned genius. You know about Bataan, when a twentieth-century American army was forced to surrender to the Japanese forces in the Philippine Islands? They held out for two months on this peninsula that jutted out into Manila Bay, Bataan it was called. What happened to those men after they surrendered I hope doesn't happen to us if Alternative Two is our fate." He paused. "Just give me the time I need to fortify Bataan, and I think we can hold out."

"Yessir. And Alternative Three?"

"Alternative Three, Colonel? Alternative Three is quite simple; we all die."

If they are dug in well enough, troops can survive almost any kind of bombardment, and General Sorca's infantry was very well dug in. But the devastation General Davis Lyons unleashed on Fort Seymour the morning the war began, the war that henceforth was to be known as the War of Secession, was terrible.

First, electronic countermeasures were employed to screen the movements of the secessionist forces. As soon as they were initiated,

General Sorca's troops knew an attack was imminent and countermeasures were attempted but the Confederation had seriously underestimated the sophistication of the Coalition's technological capabilities, and Fort Seymour's defenders found themselves essentially blind to what was coming.

Then Crickets, small, light, highly maneuverable flying gun platforms, dashed in under the antiaircraft umbrella hastily thrown up by the 3rd Division's air defense battalion and blasted the fort's perimeter with deadly air-ground missiles and on-board laser cannon. Because the air-defense artillery units' target-acquisition suites were actively searching for threats, the Crickets' missiles homed in on their command and control modules and destroyed them, leaving the firing batteries uncoordinated and ineffective so that the next phase of the attack, from high-speed fighter-bomber aircraft, proceeded almost without opposition. And after the fighters had done their terrible work, Lyons's artillery laid down a terrific barrage under which his armor and infantry began their advance.

Stunned and reeling, what was left of General Sorca's infantry began a fighting withdrawal from their positions at Fort Seymour's Main Post. The only bright spot was the destruction of a small Coalition navy force that attempted to land troops in their rear on the Peninsula from Pohick Bay. General Cazombi had planned for this when he fortified the Peninsula, but his small victory was of little immediate help to the beleaguered infantry at Main Post.

CHAPTER NINE

Sergeant Herb Carman struggled to free himself from the remains of his bunker. The blast that had destroyed his position had blown off his helmet so he was unable to communicate with the other members of his squad, if indeed they were not all dead. All around him was fire and smoke punctuated by the concussions of the heavy shells detonating everywhere along Bravo Company's line in their sector of the perimeter. The concussions of nearby explosions slammed back and forth and pelted him with debris, but as far as he could tell he was not seriously injured. At least he was able to move every part of his body as he scrambled from under the wreckage of his bunker.

A tremendous explosion slammed Carman to the ground, crushing the air from his lungs. Ears ringing, he crawled forward. He was so disoriented he couldn't tell if he was crawling toward the line or away from it; all he knew was that he had to crawl. He was dimly aware of moisture staining the lower part of his body but he couldn't tell if his bowels had involuntarily let loose or if he'd been wounded by a shell fragment. He felt no pain. He was beyond fear, driven only by the instinct for survival.

The shelling stopped suddenly. Carman lay amid the rubble, gasping heavily. He had no weapon, his gear was lost and his clothing shredded; he had no idea if he was the only survivor of the attack. As his lungs labored for oxygen in the deafening silence that followed the roar of the bombardment, a tiny spark of his former noncommissioned self began to glow again deep inside him. He had no idea what had become of his platoon leader or his platoon sergeant or the men of his squad, but he knew his only chance of survival lay in reaching the battalion's second line of defense, held by the men of Charlie Company, some buildings about a hundred meters to the rear of the main gate. He peered over the pile of rubble in front of him. At least he was headed in the right direction! He could see the buildings through the haze and smoke. The ground beneath him began to shake. He staggered to his feet and ran. He knew he didn't have much time to cover the distance because that roaring noise behind him now meant only one thing: Tanks! Other men began emerging from the debris and suddenly Carman was himself again. He called out the names of his men.

Private Alee Solden slowly recovered consciousness. Something was pinning his legs. It was the body of Mort Stuman, or what was left of it. He'd been cut in half at the waist by the rocket that had destroyed their fighting position. The blast had ripped Solden's helmet off and left a deep gash along the top of his head but the bleeding had stopped; from the pain along his left side he realized some ribs had probably been fractured. But he was able to move.

"Sorry, Mortie," he whispered, shoving Stuman's body aside. The torso flopped obscenely; he couldn't see what had become of the rest of Stuman's body. At least the man had died quickly.

The ground began to shake and he heard the unmistakable rumble and squeak of heavy armored vehicles, the very targets he and Stuman had been trained to engage with the Straight Arrows. But where in hell was the goddamned thing? Desperately Solden shifted debris searching for the Straight Arrow. The plan had been that each squad would employ a Straight Arrow and then withdraw to the second line of defense. The enemy must've been wise to the plan, Solden reflected as he looked through the rubble. With a cry of joy at last he pulled the Straight Arrow out from under some junk. The rumbling was heavier by then and the sounds of the advancing behemoths much closer.

He shook the dust off the weapon and examined it. "Jesus's nuts!" he swore. The optics had been ruined, there was no way to use the range finder or magnification to acquire a target or the lock-on device to ensure a hit. But the missile itself was intact and ready to fire. "M72,"

Solden whispered, "I love you!" But with no optics, he'd have to fire it with only the naked eye and he could only hope for a hit if he waited until the monsters were almost on top of him. "Mort," he shouted, "I'm gonna get us one of them fuckers!" He rested the launcher on some rubble and peered down the street. It was hazy with dust and smoke. Fires burned everywhere, causing Solden to cough and sneeze, but way down at the end of the road he could see a vast gray shape emerging from the haze. His heart skipped a beat. How many times had he gone through this in virtual training chambers and on the range?

On the range the missiles were only used to engage targets at a considerable distance. At 500 meters the M72 was designed to rise up to 250 meters and then home in on its target at supersonic speed. But in these circumstances the missile wouldn't have to travel that distance, he'd be firing at point-blank range. If he missed his one shot, he'd be dead. But Private Alee Solden was not going to miss the shot of a lifetime. He did not know that he was the only man left on Bravo Company's line. Even if he'd known, that would not have made any difference to him.

Sergeant Carman stumbled into the building and staggered over the debris littering the floor. The place had been heavily damaged in the bombardments but its walls and most of the roof were still intact. It was crowded with heavily armed infantry. A stocky captain was giving orders to his men, the few who were left of his company, as they emerged from the basement with their weapons. Carman was relieved to see that they were heavily armed with Straight Arrows and infantry assault weapons. He noticed now that the building was the old post exchange and much of the inventory was still on its shelves and racks.

From nearby someone was cursing volubly. He recognized the voice at once. It was his battalion sergeant major! "Top!" he crawled over to where the grizzled old NCO sat in a pool of blood. His left leg had been shot off just below the knee.

He looked up from applying a tourniquet. "Herb?" The sergeant major prided himself on knowing the name of every NCO in his battalion. "Come here and give me a hand."

The part of the post exchange building they were in had once been the women's wear department. The sergeant major had torn a dress into strips and was using them to stanch the flow of blood from his severed leg. "Didn't bring a first-aid kit and I think all our medics are down," he said, leaning back and relaxing as Carman tightened the tourniquet. The sergeant major's face was white from loss of blood and his lips were turning blue. "You got a cigarette on you?" he asked.

"I don't smoke, Sergeant Major. Sorry. Look, you stay here, I'm gonna find a medic."

The old NCO put a hand on Carman's arm, "Don't mind, lad, I've lost too much blood. These boys took a direct hit from a heavy shell, wiped out half the company. You go over there and see the captain. He can use your help more than I can." He closed his eyes.

"Captain! Captain!" Carman yelled.

"Who the hell are you?" the stocky officer demanded.

"Sergeant Carman, Bravo Company, Sir! Sir, the sergeant major needs a medic," he gestured to where the old soldier lay.

The captain only shook his head. "Old fool," he muttered but it was said in the way young men talk about older men they admire, "he should've stayed up at battalion headquarters, but you know him, always out with the troops." He shook his head. "I don't know where the hell my medics are—most of my NCOs and officers for that matter! We got plastered in here, goddamnit! Who'd you say you were again?"

"Sergeant Car—"

"See those men over there setting up the Arrows? That's what's left of my third platoon. Their platoon sergeant and officer are down. You get your ass over there and take charge. Mohammed's toenails, I've got goddamn PFCs acting as squad leaders! You are now Platoon Sergeant—what's your name again, son?"

"Carman, sir."

"—Platoon Sergeant Carman. Bravo Company doesn't exist anymore, Sergeant. You're my man now."

"But the sergeant major, sir!"

"He's dead. Get to work," the captain spun on his heel and gave orders to some other men.

"They're *coming*!" someone shouted. It got very quiet among the men of Charlie Company in the women's wear department of the Fort Seymour post exchange.

* * *

Private Solden struggled to control his breathing. He found that cursing to himself helped. "Come on, come on, you bastard, come on!" he whispered. "I'm going to get you, you bastard, I'm going to get you!" As the lead tank in the column loomed bigger and bigger Solden knew that if he remained calm he could not miss. If he could stop that one tank the others in the column would be blocked and that would give the men in the fallback positions time to bring up more antitank weapons and to reinforce the line against the infantry assault that was sure to follow.

He thought he was familiar with the machine approaching him. It had thick sloped armor plating on the front. To stop it he'd have to get his missile to detonate at the point where the armor plate met the turret, otherwise the missile could bounce harmlessly off the glacis plating. The Straight Arrows could penetrate the thickest armor, but only if they hit straight on, so the shaped charge inside the warhead could burn its way through to explode inside the machine. That would be a very difficult shot under these conditions. He knew the best way he could make it count for sure was to let the monster get almost on top of him before he fired. But he could not let it get out into the small plaza before the main gate, otherwise there'd be room for the rest of the column to drive around it, so he'd have to take his one and only shot at a range of about one hundred meters! Or: run out into the plaza, get close enough to be sure he couldn't miss, and fire the M72—in full view of the tank gunners.

Private Alee Solden picked up his weapon and ran.

The people who lived on the world known as Cabala were very religious. They frequently had epiphanies during which the Spirit of the Lord would be revealed to them in all its stunning glory. Such experiences could come upon the people of Cabala at almost any time. They relished them and honored those who had them and rejoiced in their revelations. Thus the gunner on board the lead tank approaching what was left of Fort Seymour did not see Private Alee Solden running toward him; he saw an Angel of the Lord and unbounded joy seized him, consumed him so thoroughly he never heard his tank commander screaming, "Kill him! Kill him!" in his headset. And then a sunburst enveloped him and lifted him to heaven on fiery wings.

The column was stopped, just as Private Solden hoped it would be and the 3rd Division's artillery slaughtered the infantry behind it. But then the fighter-bombers returned and other columns easily broke through different parts of the unmanned perimeter and began a relentless pounding of the remaining defenders, forcing them inexorably back into Bataan.

Private Alee Solden was never heard of again.

General Alistair Cazombi's face was drawn and pale in the dim light of his command bunker. For three days and nights the enemy had been pounding them relentlessly but infantry and armor had not been able to cross the plain that separated the Main Post from Bataan. Brigadier Sorca had integrated the remains of his division into Cazombi's defenses and he had agreed without argument that as the ranking surviving officer, Cazombi was to command the remaining Confederation forces on Ravenette, and he would serve under his orders. In fact, Major General Cazombi was the senior representative of the Confederation in that whole sector of Human Space because the Confederation consulate had been silent since the attack began. Either the diplomats were prisoners or they had been sent packing; the naval base on Chilianwala likewise had not been heard from so it was assumed that it had also been taken.

On the fourth day, there was a lull in the fighting and an officer bearing a white flag drove toward them in a command car. He was now sitting opposite General Cazombi, his blindfold removed.

"General, General Lyons sends his greetings and wishes you to review the terms he is proposing for your surrender."

"Coffee, Colonel?" Cazombi asked. The emissary shook his head. The terms were written on a sheet of paper, not recorded on a crystal, and that made Cazombi smile. So typical of a throwback like Davis Lyons, he thought. "Return to General Lyons with my compliments, sir, and tell him we shall review these terms and respond within an hour."

The Coalition colonel stood. "Sir, you have put up a splendid defense. Your troops fought valiantly. We wish to end this slaughter. Please consider General Lyons's terms, General. There would be no dishonor in your surrender."

"Thank you. I have to discuss this with my officers."

"These terms are very generous," Brigadier Sorca admitted after he'd scanned the paper. "I think the terms will be observed with punctiliousness. And my men don't have much fight left in them, sir."

General Cazombi could have disagreed with that statement but he chose to say nothing. "Gentlemen?" he looked at the small group of senior officers standing in around him. "A show of hands? Those in favor of surrender, raise a hand." All but one officer—a colonel who'd commanded a brigade, now decimated—raised their hands. "It looks almost unanimous, gentlemen. Colonel, why do you disagree?"

The colonel stepped forward. He was a big, red-faced man and his hands were swathed in bandages. "Because, General, when I swore my oath as an officer, I swore never to surrender my men so long as I had the means to resist. We still have those means, sir, thanks to your foresight," he glanced at Sorca, who shot him a killing look. "To surrender now would dishonor the men who served under me and who sacrificed their lives obedient to orders."

The room had gone silent except for the subdued crackling of the communications systems as outposts reported in. Work had stopped momentarily because everyone in the bunker knew what was going on and they all watched the small knot of officers intently.

"Good point, Colonel. Anybody have anything to add?" Nobody spoke up. Brigadier General Sorca glared at the colonel and the other officers stared at the floor. "All right, gentlemen, we fight on." He held up a hand to forestall any further argument. "Yesterday I dispatched a Doomsday drone outlining our situation and requesting immediate reinforcement. We shall hold out in the hope that reinforcements arrive."

"You *what*—" Sorca blurted. "You—you made up your mind before we had this conference?"

"I just made up my mind, General, now that I've seen Lyons's terms. Now that we've discussed them I reject them."

"But it'll take three weeks before the drone reaches Earth!" Sorca exclaimed. "And who knows how long after that until a relief force can be dispatched much less get here to do us any good! Goddamnit, General, we cannot possibly hold out that long!"

"Three weeks less one day, General," Cazombi replied calmly. "Gentlemen, return to your commands and duties. When and if surrender becomes imminent, we shall dispatch a second drone. Until that becomes our only alternative, I want no more talk of surrender."

He turned and retired behind the curtain that divided his small sleeping cubicle from the rest of the command post. He sighed and sat at his field desk and took a folded piece of paper out of a pocket. He had written a difficult message on it during the night. It was intended for the second drone, if one was ever sent. "Madam President," it began, "it is with head bowed in sorrow but not in shame that I have the sad duty to inform your Excellency that today," the date and time were left blank, "I have arranged for the surrender of the remaining Confederation forces at Fort Seymour on Ravenette . . ." He had not gotten any further. He had wanted to add something about the valor of his troops and commend them for the fight they'd put up, but he felt superstitious about doing that while they still had a chance. He could write something flowery and deathless when the time came. And if he wasn't around to write it, well, somebody else would have the chance to go down in history. He folded the paper and put it back into his pocket.

Now, for the second time in a long while, Major General Alistair Cazombi let his real feelings show as he stepped back out into the command post. *"All right, people!"* he shouted, turning every head in the bunker, "get back to work, goddamnit! We aren't dead yet! These bastards have started a war on us, and as long as I'm in command, we're going to fight them and we're going to win!"

Everyone stood and cheered.

CHAPTER TEN

Madam Chang-Sturdevant's hand dangled loosely at her side; her face, drawn and white, showed clearly the lines of worry etched there. "This means war," she muttered wearily. "War," she repeated.

"We have no other response," Marcus Berentus said bitterly. "This is what they've wanted all along. They have forced this on us."

Chang-Sturdevant cast her eyes back on the screen where the message from General Cazombi glared back at her. She read it again.

> MADAM PRESIDENT. I HAVE THE DUTY TO REPORT TO YOU THAT AT 0631 HOURS LOCAL TIME THE FORCES OF RAVENETTE, REINFORCED BY MILITARY UNITS CONTRIBUTED BY THE OTHER MEMBERS OF THE SO-CALLED SECESSIONIST COALITION, LAUNCHED A CONCERTED AND UNPROVOKED ATTACK ON FORT SEYMOUR. OUR INITIAL CASUALTIES HAVE BEEN HEAVY BUT WE ARE HOLDING A REINFORCED POSITION THAT THE ENEMY, DESPITE BRINGING HEAVY FORCES AGAINST US, HAS NOT YET BEEN ABLE TO PENETRATE.
>
> THIS ATTACK CONSTITUTES AN AGGRESSIVE AND UNPROVOKED ACT OF WAR AGAINST THE CONFEDERATION OF HUMAN WORLDS.
>
> THE STATUS OF OUR DEFENDING FORCE IS INCLUDED AS AN ATTACHMENT TO THIS MESSAGE ALONG WITH OUR ESTIMATE OF THE ENEMY'S STRENGTH AND CAPABILITIES AND HIS ORDER OF BATTLE. WE ARE COMPLETELY SURROUNDED IN OUR POSITION AND THERE IS NO HOPE OF A BREAKOUT OF ANY KIND.

WE HAVE BEEN OUT OF CONTACT WITH THE CONFEDERATION CONSULATE ON RAVENETTE AS WELL AS THE NAVAL BASE ON CHILIANWALA AND MUST ASSUME THEY ARE BOTH TAKEN AND OUR PERSONNEL THERE INTERNED BY THE ENEMY. THEREFORE, AS THE SENIOR CONFEDERATION REPRESENTATIVE IN THIS QUADRANT OF HUMAN SPACE, AS WELL AS THE RANKING MILITARY OFFICER PRESENT, I HAVE TAKEN CHARGE OF THE FORCES STILL INTACT AT FORT SEYMOUR. IT IS MY INTENTION TO HOLD THIS POSITION UNTIL REINFORCED. I ESTIMATE THAT AT OUR PRESENT LEVEL OF COMBAT WE MAY SUCCEED IN HOLDING THIS PLACE FROM SIX TO EIGHT WEEKS. YOU WILL NOTE BY THE ATTACHMENT THAT WE ARE VASTLY OUTNUMBERED IN MEN, WEAPONS, AND MATERIEL, BUT NEVER IN FIGHTING SPIRIT, COURAGE, AND SACRIFICE IN OUR SWORN DUTY TO RESIST THIS NAKED AGGRESSION.

I RESPECTFULLY REQUEST IMMEDIATE REINFORCEMENT.

GOD BLESS OUR TROOPS,
CAZOMBI, MG

"This was sent three weeks ago?"

"Yes, ma'am."

"So we don't even know if General Cazombi and his men are still holding out or are prisoners by now, do we?"

"No, but General Cazombi has quite a reputation as a fighter. He meant what he said in that message. We have no choice, barring another message announcing his surrender, except to send a relief force. And if Cazombi is forced to surrender, well, either we send a field army or two and a fleet to back it up, or we negotiate."

" 'God bless our troops,' " Chang-Sturdevant repeated. "At least this officer knows who really counts in our armed forces. Marcus, where do we get the troops and the vessels to send a force large enough to help these poor, brave—" her voice caught and she shook her head silently, sadly. "Well, dammit, Marcus, we are not going to negotiate with these people! I tried—we tried—every way we could to work out our differences, offered them every concession they asked for, and now this?" She gestured angrily at the message on her screen. "They didn't even have the courtesy to let us know in advance that they would attack. A sneak attack!" The color rushed back into her face. "Well, they're sure as hell going to know when we responded to this—this outrage!"

"The Combined Chiefs are on their way here now."

"Good! I want that Marine, Aguinaldo, in on this, Marcus, I want him here more than anybody else." Chang-Sturdevant sighed. "I shall summon the rest of my cabinet and we shall agree on how to respond. Then I'll go before the Congress and read them General Cazombi's message. I'll inform them that I'm going to issue an Executive Order authorizing the deployment of troops to Ravenette to respond to a threat to the Confederation. I have that authority as President under the War Powers Section of our Constitution. Our Congress is like all democratic deliberative bodies, Marcus; its members divided in their opinions, overly cautious, and slow to act. I'll get the votes for a war resolution, but not right now, not even with this," she gestured at Cazombi's message. "They've been in session debating our response since the Ordinance of Secession was issued. This should change everything but it'll take time. We can have only one response now.

"Now, Marcus, would you leave me alone for a while? When everyone gets here we'll meet in the secure conference room. My aides will let me know when you're ready." Berentus nodded and walked to the door. "Marcus? One more thing? Thanks for sticking by me. Stay close by until this is over, would you?"

"Good heavens, Admiral, it'll take that long to raise an effective force to relieve those poor devils?" Attorney General Huygens Long exclaimed.

"I'm afraid so, AG," Admiral Porter answered, glancing apologetically at the President. The other members of the Combined Chiefs nodded their assent. "We have to assume that once our force gets there they'll need to engage the enemy's fleet before a landing can be attempted and as the CIO has just informed us," he nodded at Clements Barksdale, the newly appointed Director of the Central Intelligence Organization, "and our own analysts agree, the secessionists' combined naval strength is potent. We'll also need time to organize the ground forces necessary to obtain a foothold on Ravenette if Fort Seymour is taken by the time they get there or to relieve the garrison if they've managed to hold out that long. That is the best we can do."

"So it is agreed. I will go before the Congress in a few moments and announce the attack on Fort Seymour. I shall not ask for a formal declaration of war, gentlemen, because I won't get it and I'm not going to show these people how divided we are. But I can order full mobilization of each member world's reserve forces. Admiral, the Chiefs shall coordinate the integration of those forces into our regular components and work out the deployment schedule. All this will be done with the greatest possible speed. Send a drone to General Cazombi, let him know we're coming, no details, of course, in case it falls into enemy hands. But we owe him and his troops that much. Admiral, you may proceed to the Congress now and meet me there in fifteen minutes. I want everyone else to go back to their offices and evaluate the impact this war will have upon our government's operations. We'll all meet here again, in full cabinet session, tomorrow morning. General Aguinaldo, Marcus, come with me for a moment."

The Minister of War and Marine Commandant followed Chang-Sturdevant into her private office. "General, this Cazombi, tell me what you know about him. I know he was the ranking officer at Fort Seymour but he was not responsible for the installation's defense? How did that come about? And Marcus says he had some dealings with your Marines."

"Yes, ma'am, it was over the Avionia affair. One of my officers, the company commander who was actually present at Avionia Station, was sued by the chief scientist there for making a decision that countermanded her orders about the treatment of captive Avionians. She later sued him personally. General Cazombi, who was also there at the time, appeared as a witness in his defense. The chief scientist died before the trial had proceeded very far and the whole thing was dropped. General Cazombi was the Director of Personnel for the Chiefs and I knew him as an honorable man and a courageous officer.

"I might also say, since he expressed this opinion to me, that he was very upset with the Chairman for not doing everything he could to squelch that trial, which we all believed was frivolous to begin with. Ma'am, may I add something? I think if anybody can hold out at Fort Seymour, it's Alistair Cazombi."

Chang-Sturdevant smiled. "Thank you, General. Now, Marcus, shall we?" She held out her arm, which Berentus took, and they left the room. "Marcus, I am afraid," she whispered.

"Don't be! We'll win."

"I know that. That's not what scares me. Oh, I'm sad about all our people who'll die in this war, the secessionists are our people too. But I'm afraid of the real threat that's out there somewhere, Marcus. It was a mistake, our keeping its presence a secret, I see that now."

"If they come back we'll deal with them just like we did on Kingdom."

She squeezed Marcus's hand. "Thanks, thanks very much. Okay. Now, we step into the arena and deal with the real threat to this Confederation!" Marcus did not know if she meant the Coalition or the Confederation Congress.

Representative Haggl Kutmoi, from Bulon, a portly gentleman known for his long-winded speeches and sarcasm, read from the Ordinance of Secession: " 'Whereas, in addition to the well-founded causes of complaint set forth by this Convention, in resolutions adopted against the party now in power on Earth, headed by Cynthia Chang-Sturdevant, who has, through the use of unwarranted military force slaughtered innocent citizens of Ravenette, we therefore resolve no longer to submit to such rule or remain in the Confederation of Human Worlds, which would be disgraceful and ruinous to the interests of the worlds whose representatives to this Convention have thus signed this Ordinance. Therefore, we do hereby declare and ordain that we resume to ourselves all rights and powers heretofore delegated to the government of the Confederation of Human Worlds . . .' and on and on honorable members, balderdash ad infinitum."

Representative Kutmoi drew himself up to his full shortness and glared at his fellows, most of whom were dozing at their places. For several days the Congress had been debating the Confederation's response to the Ordinance, and tempers were growing short. Given the late hour, they would all have been home in bed except that the President had asked them to remain in session for a little while longer, to hear an announcement. Suddenly there was a stirring at the rear of the chamber. All heads turned as Admiral Porter and the Combined Chiefs filed in and quietly took seats in the rows before the podium where the President of the Congress waited impatiently to give the floor to Chang-Sturdevant.

"The dirty bastards have gone and done it!" Kutmoi shouted, guessing immediately the import of Chang-Sturdevant's presence.

"I would remind the honorable gentleman from Bulon that such language is not appropriate in this august body," the President of the Congress intoned. But nobody was listening because the arrival of the Chiefs had stirred them all awake and all eyes were focused down the aisle at the main entrance to the chamber. "Ladies and gentlemen!" the president shouted, rising to his feet, "Madam Chang-Sturdevant!" Suddenly everyone was on their feet, clapping and shouting. Chang-Sturdevant, nodding and smiling, followed closely by Marcus Berentus, slowly walked down the aisle. Marcus took a seat with the Chiefs and she mounted the podium, shook hands with the President of the Congress, and turned to face the members.

"Ladies and gentlemen, as of oh-six-thirty-one Ravenette time, on the sixth day of the third month of this year, a state of war has existed between this Confederation and those worlds aligned with Ravenette in the so-called Coalition of Worlds—the Secessionist Coalition as it has also come to be known."

Outraged shouts and screams filled the chamber and it was some time before the sergeant at arms could restore order. When the delegates had finally settled down, a deathly quiet had fallen over them as they hung on her every word. Chang-Sturdevant read General Cazombi's message. When she was done many of the delegates were openly weeping at their desks. "Our casualties have been heavy," she announced. "As of the time this message was sent, of the more than eighteen thousand men and women who composed the garrison at Fort Seymour, only eight thousand were fit for duty. We do not know what has happened since." She paused. "The garrison may have fallen by now. I hope and I believe that the brave soldiers under General Cazombi are still fighting, fighting on in the belief that we shall not abandon them"—delegates shouted "No! No! No!" over and over again. "Therefore, I come before you now to inform you that I have issued an executive order for the mobilization of all the armed forces at our disposal, and my military chiefs are already organizing a force to dispatch to Ravenette with all possible speed to relieve the garrison at Fort Seymour. Ladies and gentlemen, thank you for attending me. I shall keep you fully informed as events unfold."

Few in the Congress of Worlds slept that night.

General Davis Lyons sat impatiently before the newly formed Committee on the Conduct of the War. The committee had been created by the Secessionist Congress shortly after commencement of hostilities, its membership composed of representatives of the Secessionist Coalition worlds, none of whom knew anything about the conduct of war. But General Davis was honor bound to appear before them and show them the respect due the members of the Coalition's ruling body.

"These were very generous surrender terms you offered General Cazombia, sir," the chairman intoned.

"I believe his name is Cazombi, sir. Yes, the terms are generous because the man and his soldiers deserve to be treated humanely."

"But General, here you offered to repatriate them! Return them to a Confederation world so they could fight again? You offered the same terms to the naval personnel and the diplomats."

"Yessir. In the case of the latter, it has been the custom since time immemorial to repatriate diplomatic personnel at the outbreak of hostilities between the warring powers. For the military personnel, I did not want to be bothered with the care, feeding, and guarding of thousands of prisoners. We are not set up for that."

"We could have sent them to Sagunto, General, where there would've been plenty of room for them and they would not have required a large contingent of guards to keep an eye on them."

General Davis controlled his temper with effort. He had more important business to attend to than to sit before the committee, which he had been doing, patiently, for more than an hour. "Sir, Sagunto is hardly yet a settled world, fit for our own citizens. Interning thousands of prisoners of war there would be tantamount to a death sentence for them."

"We are not concerned with the welfare of our enemies, General," the chairman responded.

"Well, I am, sir!"

"General," it was a member from Ruspina, Davis could not

remember his name, "when do you expect to conquer the remaining forces at Fort Seymour?"

"I do not expect to do that, sir."

The committee members looked at one another in astonishment. "You do not? But you have the forces! Are you just going to leave them there?"

"Yes. They are no threat to us because they aren't going anywhere and besides, I've lost enough of my men already. I will not sacrifice more in further attacks on a very well fortified position such as General Cazombi has built on Pohick Bay."

"But—but . . . !"

"Gentlemen, those men out there are our hostages. As long as they are there the Confederation is obliged to relieve them. The main battle of this war will be fought right here, gentlemen. I am preparing for *that* battle, not wasting my time and the lives of our troops reducing that fortress. The Confederation must attempt to relieve that garrison. Given the current dispersion of its forces and the short period of time they have to effect a relief, they can only do that piecemeal and I shall defeat their forces in detail. I have recommended to the president, and he has accepted that recommendation, that the government be moved to a safer location and the city evacuated in anticipation of the heavy fighting that shall eventually occur here."

"General, that is why this committee is sitting here now," the chairman shot back.

"Sir, that is why this committee will not be sitting here much longer!"

"General Lyons," the chairman's face had gone brick red, "you have been an arrogant and uncooperative witness before this committee! We are considering recommending to President Summers that he relieve you of your command!"

"I serve at his pleasure, sir. Now, if you will excuse me, I have important matters to attend to."

"General Lyons, one more thing! One more thing, please," the chairman insisted. "The next time you offer surrender terms they will have been composed by the members of this committee! I'll be damned if we're going to coddle these people! That is all."

"Sir, we're damned if we don't."

* * *

Charlette Odinloc had returned to Donnie Caloon's apartment the night before the war started and now she was stuck there.

"Geez, Hon, they're really dusting it up out there!" Donnie exclaimed.

"Yeah, Donnie, I couldn't help hearing." Sergeant Odinloc tried to hide her distress. The fighting had started and she was trapped in the city. She mentally kicked herself for coming back, but she had desperately wanted that ride in the country to learn about the enemy's troop dispositions and the G2 had agreed. But her place was back at Fort Seymour, with her comrades, not holed up in Donnie's apartment. She'd been trapped there for five days now.

"Folks are sayin' they're evacuatin' the city, movin' us all out somewheres! What do you make of all this?" There was real concern in Donnie's voice. "I wish I could join up," he added, pensively, hands thrust deep into his pockets.

"Donnie, if anybody finds out who I really am, I'll be arrested. I can't get back to the fort. You're the only hope I have to stay free. You don't want me to spend the rest of my life in a POW camp, do you?"

"Oh, no, Hon, no! Gee, yeah, that would be bad news, wouldn't it?"

"Donnie, since your company has closed down and they're evacuating the city, why don't we go back to your hometown?"

"Ya mean it?" he brightened. "Gee, yeah! Mom'd love to meet you!" But just as quickly Donnie's face fell. "I don't have no money, Hon! How we gonna get home? It's halfway around the world! I spent all my money on this place!" He was almost in tears.

"I have money." Charlette had generous funds for expenses. She fumbled in her clothes and withdrew a large wad of bills that she handed to Donnie.

"Geez! I din' know they paid you soldiers so well!" he exclaimed, counting the money, his eyes widening as each bill turned over in his hands.

"I saved it up. Where'd you say you live?"

"Cuylerville, over in Loudon County," Donnie answered, still counting. "Holy chickenshit, babybugs, we are rich! This is enough to get us there and back twice!"

"Where, exactly, is Cuylerville, Donnie?"

"Ah, about ten thousand kilometers east of here. You don't get seasick, do ya? We'll have to take a boat. But with this much money we can have us a room to ourselves and, y'know, fuck our way across the ocean!" he laughed and waved the bills in the air. "We can leave tonight!"

"I'm looking forward to that," she said, dryly. "We need a cover story to explain who I am, Donnie, while we're traveling, you know? In case anybody asks? I don't have any papers, any ID, anything like that, you know."

"Yep. You'll be my sister. I don't have any of that ID stuff either, so who's to know?"

"Well, Donnie, that might not work so well. We'll be on that ship a while and you know what we'll be doing, things a guy doesn't usually do with his sister?"

"Oh, sheeyit, you're right!" Donnie slapped his forehead and laughed. "Well, we're engaged, then. You used to work for my company. I'll tell you all about it before we leave. Think that'd work?"

"Might just do, Donnie, might just. Ah, one more thing? Before we leave?"

"Why sure, good-looking lady with the big jugs!" Donnie laughed, tossing the roll of bills on the table and jumping into the bed.

"I think you ought to know I missed my period."

CHAPTER ELEVEN

In the weeks since the survivors of the Fort Seymour garrison had been surrounded on the Pohick Bay Peninsula, General Cazombi's engineers had deepened and strengthened the fortifications and his command post had been moved even deeper inside the complex. Not that Cazombi ever stayed there very long. He spent most of his waking hours out touring the fighting positions, encouraging his troops, making eye contact with them.

Now the same enemy colonel who'd brought Lyons's first surrender terms was back again with another offer. For this meeting Cazombi had ordered the emissary brought to the CP to give him some idea of how well dug in his force was and to show him that morale was high without revealing anything about the complex defenses.

"You're looking fit, General," the colonel said, blinking his eyes as the blindfold was taken off. The command post was a hub of activity and to the enemy officer the soldiers there actually seemed to be enjoying themselves. They were; General Cazombi had ordered sandwiches for everyone to give the impression they were feeding well.

"We meet again, Colonel," Cazombi held out his hand. From inside a tunic pocket the colonel produced a crystal and handed it to him. "So you've agreed to surrender, have you?" Cazombi permitted himself a slight twitch along the right side of his face, which for him passed as a grin.

"Not quite, sir," the colonel smiled grimly.

"So General Davis has now stepped into the twenty-fifth century," Cazombi remarked. He hefted the tiny crystal speculatively. "Writing on paper has its advantages. Wait here, Colonel, until I find a scanner and we'll talk some more."

In an isolated cubicle Cazombi, his chief of staff, and several other officers read the contents of the crystal. "We can never agree to something like this!" The others, reading over the general's shoulder nodded their concurrence. "Anybody know where Sorca is right now?" Since Cazombi had pulled rank on the brigadier and taken charge of the survivors, Sorca had been making himself scarce in the command post. "Go find him," he told his operations officer. "I want him and his officers to see this. I don't think Lyons himself wrote this—this—garbage, but note one thing? They've called for a cease-fire while we consider these demands. That's time, gentlemen, and time is what we need."

"A big Wanderjahr Canfil tomato is what I need right now," Cazombi's operations officer laughed.

"I think that's what the guy who wrote these terms needs," Cazombi replied, referring to the well-known laxative effect the Canfil tomato had on people not used to it. He didn't need reminding either that the first signs of dysentery had already made their appearance among the defenders. "No talk about food, Colonel. Go find Sorca, that'll take your mind off eating."

When Brigadier General Sorca finally arrived in the command post he looked sleek, well-groomed, and rested. Obviously, Cazombi noted, he was not suffering the same degree of deprivation as his men. He was accompanied by two of his officers, his operations officer and his supply officer. The latter appeared extremely well fed.

"I don't consider these terms that unfavorable, General," Sorca said after he'd read them. "We'll be well treated," he added, meaning the officers.

"They want to separate us into three camps, general, officers, NCOs, and enlisted ranks and on three separate worlds within their Coalition."

"Well, it's accepted doctrine on the handling of prisoners of war, General, to separate the leaders, to keep order in the camps."

"Yes, I know that, General Sorca and I also know it's against every convention of warfare to demand that POWs sign oaths not to take up arms against their captors if they're released. I know we have to go into three separate camps but I will not accept any arrangement where I can't personally visit and inspect the conditions in the camps maintained for my NCOs and enlisted people. I've led them here and I'm going to lead them in captivity as well, if it comes to that. Not negotiable."

"I think you should reconsider, sir."

"Not negotiable, General. And surrender is not an option either. We're too close to being relieved."

"We do not know that, sir," Sorca's face colored. "And we both know that when relief forces do arrive, if they do, they'll most likely be fed in piecemeal and all that'll mean is more prisoners for the Coalition to boast about."

"Gentlemen," Cazombi addressed all the officers standing around him, "we know this place is going to be the set-piece battle of this war. It'll be decided here, among the fleets in orbit and here on the ground. We must keep this foothold open! General Sorca's probably right, the Confederation will only be able at first—at first—to feed in reinforcements piecemeal. But if we hold out long enough, the preponderance of force will swing in our favor. I intend to accept the cease-fire offered, to gain every minute of time we can until decisive reinforcements can be landed, and then we shall break out of this hole and engage the enemy and defeat him. I charge all of you now with the responsibility of ensuring that our forces do not adopt a defensive mentality. I've been to every fighting position and, despite everything, morale is high. You all know the age-old prescription for battlefield victory: Morale is to firepower as three is to one, and we have that advantage! We must not lose it. So we cannot accept these terms."

"If that's the case, General, then why did you bother to call us here to 'discuss' these terms in the first place?" Sorca asked.

Cazombi did not let his face show what he really thought of the natty, white-haired brigadier general standing before him, his chest thrust out and one hand on his hip. "I wanted you to know what the terms were, General and I wanted you above all to know what my orders are. Now, gentlemen, to your posts."

"General?" Cazombi's operations officer took him aside for a moment. "What are our chances, really, sir? You've always leveled with me and you know I don't shoot my mouth off."

"Hank, they're grim, very grim. But if we can hold this place, that'll give the Confederation a foot in the door and I think the war will be decided here. What we have to pray for is front-line combat soldiers—Marines, Hank! That's who we need here and soon!"

Brigadier Balca Sorca took his operations officer aside. "I don't want our G4 in on this, the man's a blubbering idiot, a box kicker. You I can trust. That Cazombi, the man's a glory hound!" he whispered. "Any reasonable officer would have accepted the original surrender terms!"

"Don't you think the Coalition'd reneged on them by now, sir?"

"Sure. But once we're out of this hole we could maneuver, position ourselves to advantage, Colonel. As it is, Cazombi is going to get us all killed."

"What can we do about it, sir? Every man jack in what's left of our division is ready to fight, despite the reduced rations and the living conditions."

"There's always something that can be done, Colonel." Sorca smiled and patted the colonel on his shoulder. "You just stick with me."

Two huge explosions shook the bunker. "There goes Nine O'Clock Nina again," Corporal Barry ("The Liver") Livny muttered. Barry was famous in the company for his drinking ability, when drink was available, which it had not been since they'd left home months ago. "Hard to tell what time it is outside unless she drops in on us." He grinned and rubbed the nonregulation beard stubble on his chin. He wasn't old enough to grow a regular beard but the fuzz had lengthened noticeably over the past weeks. He tolerated very well the snide comments from his buddies, "Hey, Liver, you didn't shave this morning, did you?" because shaving was a luxury: The water ration had been cut again. There were only two electric razors in the whole company and Corporal Livny maintained he would not take sloppy seconds on a shave. As a Guardsman he could get away with it; a regular would've long ago taken a bayonet to his whiskers.

"This crap is bad enough to puke a dog off a gut wagon," PFC Harry ("Whimper") Quimper complained, spooning the viscous mass that was his breakfast out of his mess kit. He ran a filthy forefinger around the inside of the tin and stuck it into his mouth, sucking up the last bit of juice.

"You'd bitch if they hung you with a new rope, Whimper. That is real fancy 'kwe-zeen,' as the French say," Private Ennis ("Shovel") Shovell muttered. "I believe you are actually gaining weight on these rations," he added, finishing his ersatz coffee. Ennis was forty and married and no one in his platoon could figure out why he'd ever volunteered for the infantry. Whenever the subject came up, which it did frequently, all he'd say was, "Well, take my wife. Please." In civilian life, he'd been an accountant with an insurance firm, earning more money than either of his bunker mates had ever imagined having in their own pockets. Why he hadn't joined the finance corps was also a mystery to them and when frequently asked about his choice of arms inevitably he'd say, "I'm Jewish. I refuse to be cast as a stereotype." Shovell stood over two meters and was well built for a man who'd led a sedentary life. He never complained when it was his turn to use a shovel on the frequent repair details or to clean out their bunker.

"Nah, I lost three kilos this past month," Quimper said. "What're we getting, fifteen hundred calories a day now? Man, how I long for the old days, when we got twenty-five hundred a day." The "old days" for these men of the New Geneseean National Guard had been when they were first inserted on Ravenette. They'd brought their own rations with them. General Cazombi's troops were already by that time reduced to living on a thousand calories a day. Nobody could now agree on what they needed more, food or reinforcements.

"Isn't it pronounced 'koo-zine,' Ennis?" Livny asked.

"Nah, 'kwe-zeen', I studied French once. Before you children were born. I love dead languages, you see?"

"Then why study them, if they're dead?" Quimper asked. He looked genuinely puzzled.

"Wimpy," Ennis replied patiently, as if talking to a child, "I may need to know it when I die, which if our rations don't improve and their aim does, might be fairly soon."

"I been thinking, maybe we could eat them ratlike things, those 'slimies'?" Quimper suggested. "I'm hungry enough for some fresh meat, but ugh, a guy'd have to really be starvin' to chow down on one o' them things!"

"There ain't that many of 'em, Wimpy, hardly worth the effort to catch one."

"Oh, you'll see more of them, if we stay in here long enough," Shovell said. "They're scavengers and the longer we're here the more of them'll be attracted by the waste and—and—you know, the bodies." He shuddered.

Almost on cue, several heavy explosions shook the bunker. The men scrambled to their positions but nothing moved in the no-man's-land between them and the rubble that had once been Fort Seymour.

"I wish they'd come," Quimper sighed, "get me some action." Since these men had been on Ravenette, the Coalition forces had not mounted a single ground attack against them, just this intermittent pounding with artillery, missiles, and bombs. Their landing had been tough and their division, composed of regiments hastily gathered from several different worlds, had taken very heavy casualties.

"Be careful what you wish for, Wimpy," Ennis advised.

"I wish I was with Napoleon at Thermopylae, Shovel, at least I'd have a chance to actually fight someone," Wimpy retorted. Wimpy fancied himself a military historian but he could never understand why the Greeks at Thermopylae didn't use their cannon to better advantage.

"You are at Thermopylae, my child," Ennis replied. "Do I need to remind you how that one ended?"

Quimper's stomach growled audibly. "Man, I used to eat some good shit at home, you know?"

"You get hungry enough you can eat anything," Shovell replied, dryly.

"Bacon, eggs, sherobies for breakfast every goddamned day! Hey, Shovel, we go into a POW camp like some of the guys are saying, will they feed us better? Man," he sighed, changing the subject abruptly, "what I wouldn't give to exchange one of you guys for a woman right now."

"Wimpy, sometimes you really don't make much sense," Shovell replied. "A real man would exchange us for two women."

"Nah, Shovel, I'd only exchange you, so Liver could have somethin' to watch," Quimper laughed. Quimper's laugh was very disturbing to most people, a high-pitched braying sound, but his bunker mates had gotten used to it.

"I was up to the battalion S3 a couple of days ago," Livny offered, "and the word is out that more reinforcements are on the way. Marines. They're sending the goddamned hard-assed jarheads here!"

"And then what? Well, then, all our problems will be over," Shovell snorted.

"Hey!" Quimper shouted, sitting up straight, "maybe the Marines will bring some good-looking wimmen with 'em!"

"Women, my ass," Livny snorted, "I hope they bring some extra field rations."

CHAPTER TWELVE

"Mr. President! Mr. President! Would the honorable gentleman from Bulon kindly yield the floor? His time is up! Mr. President!" The representative from Novo Kongor, Ubsa Nor, was shouting. He had been trying for several minutes now to get the long-winded Haggl Kutmoi to yield so he could speak.

"Mr. Kutmoi, please yield to the honorable gentleman from, er," the President of the Confederation Congress had to consult his roster to remember the Novo Kongor representative's name and where he came from, "the Honorable Ubsa Nor from Novo Kongor?"

Kutmoi glared at Nor, who was striding purposefully toward the rostrum. Squat, dark, powerful, Ubsa Nor had spent his youth in the mines on his home world and was not a man to be trifled with. "I yield to the honorable gentleman from Novo Kongor, Mr. President, but I will continue my remarks at a later time!" Kutmoi deliberately jostled Nor as they passed but the man from Novo Kongor merely whispered, "There's no glory in tangling with a little shrimp like you," and mounted the platform. He adjusted his reading glasses. "Mr. President, honorable members," he began in a powerful voice that almost needed no amplification, "we of Novo Kongor stand in complete opposition to the headlong rush to war that Madam Chang-Sturdevant, the honorable member from Bulon, and their supporters are urging upon this august body."

"You ought to join the rebels then!" a female voice shouted.

"Order!" the president intoned.

Ubsa Nor paused, glaring at the representative who'd interrupted him. "The idea that we Kongoreans would break with this Confederation and go to war against it is unfair and also personally disgusting. But that's not all that's disgusting. The way this government has treated the people of the secessionist worlds is disgusting and I remind all the honorable members of this Congress that it was our troops who slaughtered the citizens of Ravenette, not the other way around, so it was us and not them who committed the first act of war." A tumult arose, and delegates shouted for Nor to be seated, accusing him of disloyalty and cowardice. But a few voices expressed support for what he had said.

The president called for order.

"I know how those people out there feel," Nor continued when the delegates had finally quieted. "Many of you here consider us Kongoreans no better than hairy animals who burrow in the earth and live among the ice and cold because we don't know any better and because nobody else would have us. You make fun of the way we talk when we're among you and I've heard all the jokes you love to tell about us, 'How does a boy from Novo Kongor know when his hut is on a level? When his dog drools out both sides of his mouth at the same time,' and on and on and on." No one laughed at that joke but it was an oft-repeated slur against the people of Novo Kongor that many people found amusing. The delegates were shamed by it into a temporary silence.

"You need the ores we mine from the unforgiving crust of our world." Nor went on, his voice rising. "Ores that my people risk their lives and health to extract in an environment so harsh none of you here, *none* of you, can even imagine from the comfort and luxury of your homes, but when we ask for a fair price from your refineries you accuse us of gouging and you pass laws to protect your own industries because you say we undercut them. Do you think we're so stupid we can't see the inconsistency there?" His voice rose a full octave on the last word. "No, no, no," he waved a forefinger at the assembled delegates, "the people of those worlds in rebellion have legitimate grievances and since this government does not wish to settle them through negotiation, we of Novo Kongor say, 'Let them go their own way!' We reject Madam

Chang-Sturdevant's call for troops and shall remain neutral in this war." He paused, removed his spectacles, bowed slightly saying, "Thank you, Mr. President, honorable members," and left the podium.

Haggl Kutmoi was on his feet immediately, addressing his remarks directly from his seat. "I remind everyone, this government bent over backward to find ways to keep the rebels in our Confederation and it failed. Why? Because they wanted war from the beginning! And one more thing, honorable members! The gentleman from Novo Kongor forgot to inform you that the worlds now in rebellion against this Confederation are Novo Kongor's best trading partners! The embargo against trade with them has hurt the Kongoreans' pocketbooks! And I have evidence, which I shall submit at the proper time, that Novo Kongor has been ignoring the trade sanctions imposed against the rebels and is now carrying on a clandestine trade with them!"

The chamber burst into an uproar. "That is a damned lie!" Ubsa Nor shouted. He and the other members of the Novo Kongor delegation got up from their seats and marched out of the chamber.

The president called for order.

"So forget all this palaver about how badly they've been treated," Kutmoi continued in a whining falsetto when the noise had finally died away, "Novo Kongor's opposition to sending troops to help the rest of us has to do with money, that's all, money! And I say this, I say this to you now, people of Novo Kongor," Kutmoi raised a hand over his head and thundered at the retreating backs of the Novo Kongor delegates, "If you aren't with us, you're against us! Novo Kongor, take your ores and shove them up—"

The president called for order.

"Preston! Preston!" the representative from Hobcaw shouted over the tumult in the Coalition's senate chamber.

"Yes, Halbred," President Summers, who was presiding, acknowledged Halbred Stutz, who then stood forward to speak. "The rest of you, pipe down so Stutz can say his piece!" It was Summers's responsibility as president of the Secessionist Coalition to preside over the meetings, but he did so reluctantly and with frequent snorts of bourbon. In his view, the business of government was settled in committee and backrooms, not by full sessions of the senate, which more often than not ended in shouting matches. He was finding that getting a dozen disaffected and fiercely independent worlds to agree on even the most routine matters was difficult and that government by presidential fiat, when he could get away with it, was much more effective than the democratic process. The one thing they did agree on was their willingness to fight, often among themselves.

"Preston, we agreed to movin' the guvmint way the hell and gone out here, so Gen'rel Lyons could wreck the capital city," Halbred said, to the amusement of his fellow representatives, many of whom were not entirely sober themselves. "But gawdammit, sir—"

"Watch yer language, Halbred!" Summers shouted.

"Yessir! But Preston, gawdammit, all he's done these past weeks is sit on his hindquarters back there at his headquarters," this pun elicited a roar of approving laughter from the other delegates, " 'n exchange pleasantries with this Gen'rel Zombie! I mean, people are callin' Gen'rel Lyons 'granny,' the way he moves so damn slow! Well, I call 'im the 'King of Spades,' Preston, the way he's diggin' all those fortifications!" More roars of laughter and catcalls from the delegates. Halbred's little pot belly shook with joy at the attention he was getting and his greasy red ringlets hung down around his collar, jiggling every time he shook his head. "Now I wanna know why you ain't yet removed him, like the Committee on the Construct—Conduct—of the War has recommended."

"Halbred, I haven't removed General Lyons because I am the commander in chief and I do not wish to remove him," Summers said, carefully pronouncing every word. Some people, when they are excited, revert to the language or the idiom of their home regions, although they otherwise use Standard English to communicate. Just the opposite was true of Preston Summers. Several of the representatives shouted "Hear! Hear!" but others booed their disagreement. "Pipe down, gawdammit!" Summers shouted. "Gen'rel Lyons has got a strategy—"

"My ass has got a strategy, which at least I can find with both hands!" Stutz shouted to the vast amusement of his cronies.

"Halbred," Summers replied carefully, "I don't have my cane with me today, but if you will permit, I'll go home 'n fetch 'im and do a job on your thick skull that you won't soon fergit!" The reference to the caning Summers had given to the Confederation representative from St. Brendan's World elicited roars of laughter, applause, and ribald comments throughout the chamber. On the verge of a desperate war, the outcome of which was severely in doubt, the representatives were enjoying the lively debate. It was a pleasant distraction from the deadly boring business of running a vast enterprise such as their Coalition. In the early stages of their rebellion, the senate had resounded with flowery speeches and the delegates threw themselves body and soul into creating a new, unified, government to conduct their mutual affairs. But that spirit of cooperation and enterprise had soon cooled amid the minutiae of running a government and the vicissitudes of war.

"You sumbitch!" Stutz roared, "yew manage to hobble yer old bones outta that comfortable chair of yers 'n I'll oblige by puttin' another hole in yer head!" and to emphasize the remark, he drew a pistol from his pocket, which he waved triumphantly over his head, grinning lopsidedly up at Summers.

"Fire a round!" someone shouted.

Stutz, grinning broadly now, turned to the chamber, bowed slightly, and pocketed the weapon. He turned back to Summers. "Mr. President, I believe we would dearly love to hear what that 'strategy' might be."

"Gentlemen, it's very simple, as are all good plans," Summers began in a tired voice, because it had all been explained in detail before. "Admiral de Gauss maintains his fleet in orbit around Ravenette. General Lyons, who now has an army of over a million men at his disposal, draws the Confederation reinforcements in to Fort Seymour—if they can get through the blockade, which will be costly to do—where he defeats them with his superior firepower. The Confederation's military forces are stretched very thin, gentlemen, and it will have to rely on levies, not the very best front-line troops. You know who those levies will be, city boys mostly, part-time soldiers, well-fed, well-bred boys who have no real stake in this war. They'll be up against our men, who know how to carry a gun. When the people of the Confederation start to see those long casualty lists, this war is over, gentlemen."

The chamber erupted again into shouting and applause.

"So that, Halbred, is why good ol' Gen'rel Lyons has laid siege to Fort Seymour and is in no hurry to take it, which he could do in five minutes flat. It's a magnet, it'll draw 'em in and he'll squash 'em."

"Well, that sounds mighty fine, Preston," Stutz shouted, "but ain't you forgot somethin'? Ain't you forgot them hard-assed Marines the Confederation's got jist waitin' to get in here, to kick our doors wide open? They done it before in plenty o' other wars."

"I have not forgotten, Halbred." Summers took another surreptitious sip of whiskey. The question of Lyons's relief had been settled, for now, and it was time to move on to another matter. "Halbred, kindly yield to the Minister of Public Health, who is going to give us an update on the war on disease."

Summers leaned back and closed his eyes as the Minister of Public Health took the floor. No, neither Summers nor General Lyons had "forgotten" about the Confederation Marines. Preston Summers did not know which he feared worse, Marines or the plague. But the Old Snort he was sipping had left a very pleasant aftertaste in his mouth and as it warmed its way through his vitals, the sharp edge of the affairs of state dulled and he started to see things more clearly. "Yep," he whispered, "all things considered, I'd rather fight the plague."

"Mr. President, I have the most important news! I had to bring it in person," General Davis Lyons stood in Preston Summers's study, breathing heavily.

"Relax, Gen'rel, have a seat. I have news for you too," Summers said from where he'd been sitting. He had been drinking this evening, as he'd been doing almost every evening since the war began.

"Sir, this cannot wait—"

"Lemme tell you my news first," Summers smiled, "and then you tell me yours." He gestured at an empty chair but Lyons remained standing.

"Preston, this cannot wait!"

"It'll have to. Gen'rel, the Committee on the Conduct of the War has formally asked me to dismiss you as the commander in chief of our armed forces. And the senate is forming a resolution to that effect."

"Politics!" Lyons sneered. He sat down heavily in the chair Summers had offered. "If these asses on the committee don't stop interfering with me we'll lose any chance we ever had of winning this war. Who'd you replace me with?"

"Admiral de Gauss."

Lyons laughed outright. "Politicians," he shook his head. "Those surrender terms they forced me to offer Cazombi, and you endorsed them, would've insulted a guttersnipe."

"Yep. Politicians," Summers shrugged. "You know I support you, one hundred percent, but even I gotta bow to the reality of political life." He leaned forward and offered some bourbon to Lyons, who summarily waved the whiskey away. Summers shrugged and splashed a finger of the rich brown fluid into his own glass.

"Preston, you've got to cut down on that stuff."

"Gen'rel, yer sittin' there, complaining about politicians messing in your business, kindly refrain from telling me how to cope with my own problems." He held up his whiskey glass and regarded it in the light. "Down the hatch!" He threw the whiskey back and shuddered.

"I've never understood how some men can regard alcohol so reverently. If it makes you shudder like that, Preston, why drink the stuff?"

"Ahhhh," Preston wiped his mouth with the back of one hand, "it does taste like lubricant outta one of yer tanks, but good, but good! Now, Gen'rel, we are a democracy, this Coalition of ours. We have a constitution that establishes powers and responsibilities and tells us who's got 'em and who don't."

"I know all that."

"Well, jist bear with me. I am bound by that constitution to consider the advice of the senate committees when rendered and that applies to the Committee on the Conduct of the War. Sure, what they say don't make a lot of sense to a military man like yourself. But it's a quid pro quo situation, Gen'rel. They 'advise' me, Do This or You Don't Get That, 'n that's the reality. Two senators sittin' on that committee, Halbred Stutz from Hobcaw and Jenks Moody, from Mylex, flat tole me, issue the rewritten surrender terms or no more military support from their home worlds. And I don't need to tell you how much we're relyin' on the support Mylex has given us. They think yer too slow to reduce that fort and they think you're mollycoddlin' our enemies. They want me to replace you with de Gauss or someone else."

"I serve at your pleasure," Lyons answered stiffly.

Summers snorted. "Dammit, man, I ain't gonna replace you! I understand what you're doin'! You just gotta bear with these asses. Look, the longer we can draw this out the better it is because we got allies in the Confederation who don't want no part of a fight with us. That's why ol' Chang-Sturdevant ain't gone to the Confederation Congress and asked for a formal declaration of war! She don't have the votes and if she put it to a vote and lost, her whole administration would look bad. So you pin 'em down out there on Pohick Bay, chew up them replacements as they're fed in, and sooner or later the Confederation's gonna ask to negotiate and then we've got what we want."

"You must support me, Preston."

"I have, I am, and I will. But you have just gotta give a little. Why the hell raise sand over these surrender terms? You don't even want no prisoners."

"Because it is not right to offer dishonorable terms to a valiant enemy. Preston, I knew Cazombi would not accept the original terms, but there's a protocol that should be followed."

"Gen'rel," Summers held up a hand, "I will never understand you military men. You kill each other one minute and then worry about 'honor' and 'protocol' the next."

"And I will never understand you politicians, Preston," Lyons responded softly. "You scream for war, but you want to wage it through compromise and negotiation."

"Wall," Summers laughed, "so long as we both don't understand each other—" He offered the whiskey bottle again and this time Lyons accepted. They sipped in silence and then Summers said, "Gen'rel, I like these talks with you. They're good for the both of us. You know what yer doin', so you keep doin' it 'n I'll watch yer back for you in the senate. Agreed?"

Lyons smiled, "Yessir. Say, Preston, may I trouble you for one of your cigars?"

Summers took a cigar from the humidor, clipped one end, and handed it to Lyons. "Gen'rel," he offered a light, "I got some other news for you, off the subject, but somethin' you should know."

Lyons, head wreathed in cigar smoke, nodded.

"That galloping form of TB that carried off your Tommy—Gen'rel, it's showed up in some other kids. We might jist have an epidemic on our hands."

Lyons went cold. Their children were dying on the battlefield and in the nursery. And the killing had only just begun. "Preston, I guess in view of what you've just told me my news isn't all that important after all. I just thought you should know that Admiral de Gauss reports his ships have detected the Confederation fleet."

CHAPTER THIRTEEN

The bridge of the heavy cruiser CNSS *Kiowa* was quiet, with only the soft *pings* of monitors, the metallic *tings* of settling metal, and the muted voices of officers giving commands and crew responding. Just the normal sounds of a navy ship approaching hostile forces. The tension, though high, wasn't palpable; what could be felt was more along the lines of violent-action-in-waiting.

The tensest, though outwardly one of the calmest, person on the bridge was Commander Inap Solwara, the ship's captain. The main reason for Captain Solwara's tension was in the command chair mounted next to his; Rear Admiral Hoi Yueng, commander of Task Force 79, then only a few hours away from engaging the Coalition navy cordon around Ravenette, to clear the way for the Amphibious Battle Group following TF79. Admiral Hoi had selected the *Kiowa* as his flagship for the hastily thrown together task force. While Solwara had been in battle before as skipper of a destroyer, it would be his first time on the bridge of a flagship going into battle. Sitting next to the admiral, he found, was quite different from being the senior man on his own ship.

"Relax, Captain," Admiral Hoi said softly. Solwara was pleased that he didn't jerk at the unexpected words. "I'll be heading for my CIC shortly, you won't have me looking over your shoulder during action."

"Sir, I . . ."

"Nonsense, Inap. A captain is always nervous the first time his ship is the flagship. I wouldn't have planted my flag on the *Kiowa* if I didn't have full confidence in you. When the battle begins, fight your ship the same as you would if I was on another ship."

"Yessir." That shouldn't be difficult. Once the admiral was in his Combat Information Center, directing the entire task force, Solwara should have no more awareness of him than he would if the admiral weren't on the *Kiowa* at all.

Should. But the captain knew that some things were more difficult than they should be, and forgetting the presence of an admiral was one of the more difficult ones.

Hoi studied the trid schematic displayed on the big screen on the bulkhead in front of the helmsman and found it odd. The same three destroyers orbited Ravenette in equatorial orbits just below geosync. The same three medium and two heavy cruisers circled the planets in lower orbits, only two of them in circumpolar orbits. The four fast frigates moved constantly among the other warships.

Why were they concentrating on equatorial?

Starships reentering Space-3 from Beamspace almost always made the transition several days' inertial flight above or below the plane of the ecliptic in order to reduce the odds of occupying the same space as a piece of space debris, with possibly catastrophic results. Task Force 79 had entered Space-3 along the plane, less than half the normal distance from the objective planet, and used its transition momentum and simple gravity to move its starships toward Ravenette. That admittedly risky tactic, combined with the stealth capabilities of the task force's starships, should have allowed TF79 to approach within a standard day of orbit before it was spotted by the planetary defense system, which would normally be oriented to approaches from above and below the ecliptic.

Task Force 79 was now only a few hours from orbit, yet Ravenette's guardian fleet was in the same defensive formation it had held when the *Kiowa*'s sensors first detected them—they weren't responding to the task force's presence.

Rear Admiral Hoi felt there was something very, very wrong. At a simple glance, it appeared that Task Force 79 had the advantage of surprise. Even though the Confederation task force's seven starships were outnumbered by the defenders, they were stronger in both weaponry and defensive measures; on the face of it, TF79 should have relatively little trouble knocking a large enough hole in the defensive cordon to allow the follow-on amphibious task force carrying the army's 27th Division to make planetfall relatively unmolested.

On the face of it.

Or did the Coalition have a surprise of their own hidden somewhere?

"What's the latest data on the moon's farside?" the admiral abruptly asked.

Solwara touched controls on the arm of his command chair and a screen to the left of the main display showed the side of Ravenette's major satellite opposite the task force. Lights showed on the moon's surface, but they were in the locations of known mining and research operations. The drones sent adrift to check out that particular blind spot in the task force's approach detected no sign of starships, space ships, or defensive weapons systems. None of the task force's surveillance drones had detected anything that even remotely resembled a hidden surprise on the moon's far side.

At the last jump point before arriving in Ravenette's space, Hoi had assembled his captains for a final briefing. They knew the operational plan he drew up was based on the most recent intelligence. Each captain also had a copy of the contingency plans in the event the naval situation had changed in the interim—Hoi's operations staff had drawn several contingency plans, each assuming a different change or changes in the tactics. Depending on what they found on reentry to Space-3, the *Kiowa* would tight-beam a four-word code to each of the ships in the TF, instructing the captains which of the contingency plans to follow.

There were no tight-beam transmissions; Hoi hadn't had to switch to a contingency plan.

That was very, very wrong—*all* plans were subject to last-minute changes. Surely the Coalition had spies scattered through the Confederation of Human Worlds, and at least one of them would have learned, if not of the actual plans for Task Force 79, at least of unusual activity indicating the preparation of a task force to strike the cordoning forces. Even if they didn't, the Coalition had to know the Confederation would send a task force to break the cordon.

Or was the Coalition leadership so naïve it believed the Confederation wouldn't react with force to the attack on its garrison at Fort Seymour? That didn't seem likely.

Hoi abruptly stood. "I'm going to my CIC now," he told Solwara. "Watch for company coming from the direction of L1."

"The admiral has left the bridge," the officer of the deck announced as soon as Hoi ducked through the hatch.

The direction of L1? Solwara wondered. What did Admiral Hoi mean by—Of course! The admiral must have been thinking the same thing he had; it was too strange that the Coalition task force around Ravenette wasn't reacting to their presence. Lagrange point 1—the balance point between Ravenette and its sun, a place where an object could park in a stable orbit. Except that L1 was an unstable position, and anything parked there would have to periodically adjust its position.

Solwara toggled his horn to the Surveillance section. "I want a thorough data search for any emanations from sunward of Ravenette," he told the division commander. "I want to know if any ships are hiding at L1." He signed off. It wasn't likely there would be any sign; anything parked at the L1 would only have to adjust position once every three, three-and-a-half weeks standard, and TF79 had only been in Space-3 for four days. Still, if Surveillance was looking, and there was someone there, they could get some warning if that someone began to maneuver.

Task Force 79 continued its drift toward Ravenette. The seven Confederation starships weren't in good formation, they hadn't risked showing themselves by making any course or attitude adjustments on their return to Space-3. They were only an hour from battle orbit and the Coalition task force still didn't show any indication they had been discovered. That was entirely too strange—TF79 was close enough to be detected visually with minimal magnification.

Rear Admiral Hoi sent tight-beam orders to his starships: "Visually aim missile batteries at assigned targets. Do NOT use electronic locks until so ordered. Stand by to lock and launch on my order."

The *Kiowa,* the largest starship in the task force, pointed one of her missile batteries at a heavy cruiser and another at a medium; he held his third battery in reserve. Five of the task force's other starships each pointed their missile batteries at a different enemy vessel, as assigned by the primary attack plan. The other four defending starships were out of sight, eclipsed by the planet.

Something sparked on one of *Kiowa*'s targets. Solwara swore to himself just as Surveillance reported, "Target Alpha has thrown alfa-chaff." A second later, "Target Beta has thrown alfa-chaff." Alfa-chaff, large sheets of reflective materials designed to decoy missile guidance systems away from their target, similar to the way atmospheric craft used thin strips of reflective material to decoy fire-and-forget munitions.

"Acquisition radar is locking on us," Radar reported.

"All starships, lock and launch," Admiral Hoi tight-beamed the order. "Use inertial guidance where possible. Power up and maneuver independently until further orders."

Inertial guidance was possible, but only by delaying missile launch. Solwara ordered each of his aimed missile batteries to lock and launch half of their missiles and use inertial guidance on the other half, using a generous spread. The generous spread was necessary, as the target starships were already firing their thrusters to change orbit.

"Engines, fire main thrusters as soon as first salvo is launched," Solwara ordered. He followed up with, "Sound general quarters."

A carefully modulated female voice sounded throughout the starship, "General quarters. Prepare for sudden maneuvering. I say again, general quarters. Prepare for sudden maneuvering."

Before the message was complete, a shudder went through the *Kiowa* as two batteries launched half of their missiles.

"Multiple emanations coming from the limb of the planet," Surveillance reported.

"Details," Solwara said.

"One is medium cruiser Charlie, one is destroyer Alpha," Surveillance identified two of the known ships currently eclipsed by Ravenette. "The other five are unknown, possible cruisers."

Task Force 79 had seven starships engaging twelve enemy starships, and now another five possible enemy vessels were joining the battle? Solwara didn't like the odds. The army's 27th Division, crammed into a lightly armed, ten-starship gator task force, was only half a day behind; TF79 *had* to clear the way for the gators before they arrived.

Solwara forwarded the information to the admiral's CIC as another, greater, shudder wracked the starship—the main thrusters firing. It was quickly followed by another shudder rippling through the starship as one of the batteries launched the other half of its missiles under inertial guidance.

Solwara watched the main monitor with its schematics now showing the icons for more than a hundred missiles from both sides converging on the icons for the starships of both task forces. "Helm, two points up and starboard," he ordered. Attitude jets fired and the *Kiowa* began a slow, ponderous turn. "Release alfa-chaff," he ordered, and sheets of shiny aluminum shot forward in a wide swath around the starship's course, followed closely by brilliantly burning magnesium flares that mimicked the firing of the starship's main thrusters.

The main display showed all the starships of both flotillas firing main thrusters. Curved, dotted lines delineating cones gave projected trajectories of each starship. Colors in the cones blended one into another, showing the optimal places for the starship to fire its attitude thrusters to leave orbit, gain orbit, or plunge toward the planet below. Simple dotted lines showed the projected trajectories of each missile. Most of the missile projections stopped where they intersected a starship cone, indicating likely hits. Six of the enemy missile paths intersected the *Kiowa*'s cone. The missile paths were numbered.

"Torpedoes, fire killer decoys down the paths of bogies one, four, and five," Solwara ordered. "Display, close in." The display on the main screen altered to focus on the *Kiowa* and the missiles approaching her.

A moment later, three new dotted lines appeared, radiating directly from the *Kiowa*'s icon to three of the missile icons terminating in her cone. Not visible on the display were the wires that trailed from the torpedoes to the starship, along which guidance commands were sent to keep them on the proper course for intercepting. The missiles were approaching each other at a combined velocity that danced on the edge of relativistic.

Closing missile three veered off course by a few degrees, homing on one of the magnesium decoys. Confused by signals returned from the reflective chaff, missile six began zigging and zagging. Only missile two continued, unimpeded, on course to strike the starship. Solwara focused on the colors in his ship's cone. The *Kiowa* was already feeling the tug of the planet's gravity well; he needed to make another course adjustment soon to avoid being pulled into orbital altitude. But changing just then would move the heavy cruiser into earlier contact with missile two.

"Reverse thrusters," he ordered, to delay when he'd have to alter vector to avoid plunging into the atmosphere.

The starship shuddered, pings and creaks echoed throughout as the main thrusters cut off and the bow thrusters began blasting. With the abrupt change in velocity anybody not strapped in, and everything not secured in place, would be thrown forward. Solwara knew some breakage was inevitable from the sudden maneuver, but he trusted that his crew was well enough disciplined that there wouldn't be any injuries and nothing important would be broken.

Slowly, slowly, the *Kiowa*'s plunge toward the planet slowed. Solwara looked at the display; missile two was still closing, but not quite as rapidly as before.

"Close-in Fire Control," he said into his comm, "do you have a solution for missile two yet?"

"Yessir," close-in Fire Control replied.

"Probability?"

"Eighty-five percent."

"How long for ninety-nine percent?"

"One hundred and thirty seconds for ninety-nine."

"How long 'til closing?"

"Two hundred and twenty seconds." Ninety seconds between the time there would be a ninety-nine percent chance of hitting the missile and the time it would be close enough to detonate and damage—perhaps kill—the *Kiowa*. Solwara could order the close-in batteries to fire now, but it would take them longer than ninety seconds to reload and reacquire their target if they missed. He glanced at the display; he had more than ninety seconds before he could adjust vector. "Keep on it and kill it when you have ninety-nine," he ordered.

"Aye aye, sir."

"Keep me apprised of the situation." Solwara returned his attention to the display and ordered it enlarged again to show the entire battle.

The numerous icons representing the missiles fired by the starships of both sides were more scattered, and there weren't as many, perhaps a hundred. Most of them had been successfully decoyed by defensive chaff or flares; confused by the chaff and flares, a few jittered about erratically. Some dotted lines ended in pulsing Xs, indicating missiles that had been killed by defensive fire. Only a quarter of the dotted lines still showed probable intercept with starships.

There were two pulsing circles in the display, one red and one blue. The red one was labeled "medium cruiser Gamma," a Coalition starship that a missile had put out of commission, perhaps killed. The pulsing blue circle made Solwara's breath catch in his throat; it was labeled *Everett Fulbright,* a Confederation Navy destroyer. He had friends, former shipmates, on the *Everett Fulbright.*

But Inap Solwara was a navy warship captain, he had a battle to fight. There would be time for mourning later, when his crew's lives didn't depend on his paying attention to the job at hand. He focused on the icons indicating the missiles fired by the *Kiowa.* All the missiles in the first salvo had been decoyed or destroyed, and half of the manually guided missiles had gone astray or been killed. Six of the remaining ten looked like they would do no better than minor surface damage to their targets. The last four would probably do more substantial damage, perhaps even kill their targets.

He looked at the limb of the planet and saw icons emerging from behind it. Two of them were labeled "medium cruiser Charlie" and "destroyer Alpha." Labels on the other four flickered until Surveillance identified them. One of them resolved to a frigate, two others to destroyers. Solwara was startled when the fourth was identified: "dreadnought Alpha."

He forwarded the information to Admiral Hoi's CIC. The task force CIC probably already knew about the four new starships—and that one was a dreadnought—but it was better to be certain than to assume.

The CIC was aware of the dreadnought, as Admiral Hoi proved by almost immediately tight-beaming orders to the *Kiowa* and two light cruisers to prepare to volley missiles at it.

"Batteries, status," Solwara said into his comm.

"Battery one, rearmed."

"Battery two, rearmed," came the responses.

Solwara glanced at the display to see how close the *Kiowa*'s guided missiles were to detonation, then tapped out a new target—target Charlie, the dreadnought. "Prepare to launch two salvos at target Charlie, one locked, the other under inertial guidance. We are coordinating with *Broward* and *Pawnee*. Launch on my order."

"Sir, what about targets Alpha and Beta? The inertial missiles haven't reached them yet."

"Keep guiding those missiles, but be prepared to cut them loose if I order firing at target Charlie before they close."

"Aye aye, sir."

"Let me know when the inertials reach targets Alpha and Beta."

Close-in Fire Control came on, "We have reached ninety-nine. Four. Three. Two. One. Fire."

Solwara imagined he could feel the firing of the defensive guns through the deckplates. He looked at the display, where he could see the enemy missile still closing on the *Kiowa*. In seconds, the missile ran into the cloud of half-gram pellets thrown out by the guns, and it detonated. Seconds later, he heard light pinging as debris from the explosion impacted the *Kiowa*'s hull. He allowed himself a curt nod, certain that his ship had suffered no damage beyond chipped paint.

On the display, the remaining missiles of the *Kiowa*'s first salvo continued to close on their targets. One by one they flared and turned to Xs. Target Alpha's icon changed to a pulsing red circle, target Beta's trajectory cone began slowly moving away from Task Force 79—it was damaged as well. A muted cheer rose on the bridge.

"Battery three, solution found and ready to fire," Main Fire Control reported.

"Acknowledged," Solwara said.

New icons appeared on the display as other starships rearmed and fired at new targets; more Coalition starships fired than Confederation. Eight missiles were headed toward the *Kiowa*.

"Helm," Solwara said, "hold steady until main batteries fire, then change course three points down, two starboard."

"Hold course until the main batteries fire, then change course three points down, two starboard, aye," the helmsman replied.

"Battery two, solution found and ready to fire," Main Fire Control reported, followed immediately by battery one.

Outwardly calm, Solwara waited, watching the enemy missiles on the display. He let them close half the distance, then ordered, "Torpedoes, fire killer decoys," and watched as eight torpedoes launched and headed for the missiles locked on the *Kiowa*. At almost the same moment, he saw a spray of missiles launch from the *Broward*, headed toward the dreadnought.

"*Kiowa*, launch main batteries at dreadnought Alpha," Admiral Hoi ordered.

"Launch main batteries at dreadnought Alpha, aye," Solwara replied, then into his comm, "Main batteries, launch all."

The *Kiowa* shuddered almost as violently when the thirty missiles launched toward the dreadnought as she had when he ordered thrust reversed. *Pawnee* launched shortly after.

The enemy powerhouse was in for a hard time with sixty-eight missiles heading at her and arriving at the same time. Solwara expected the dreadnought to survive, but she'd be effectively out of the fight until she dodged, destroyed, or absorbed damage from the volley on its way to her.

The *Kiowa* shuddered again as maneuvering jets on her top and port side fired.

"Flank speed," Solwara ordered. There was a moment of seeming silence when the forward thrusters cut off, then the starship was jolted by the firing off of the main thrusters. The view in the main display began to shift up and right, and moved more quickly than before as the *Kiowa* began to move and increase speed.

Solwara checked the positions of the killer decoys and the missiles they were aiming at. Five of the torpedoes, possibly more, would successfully intercept their targets. Near Ravenette's limb, he saw the three destroyers break formation and begin moving to shield the dreadnought from the incoming Confederation missile volley. *Good.* If they were extremely lucky, the three destroyers might be able to successfully divert or destroy half of the oncoming missiles, but they probably wouldn't get that many. The main thing was that they, along with the dreadnought, were out of the fight until the volley completed its run. It was also probable that one or more of them would be totally knocked out of the fight.

Before Solwara could select his next targets, Admiral Hoi came on again and designated targets Delta and Eta, a heavy cruiser and a fast frigate. "One battery on each," Hoi told him, "keep one battery in reserve. Let me know when you're ready to launch at Delta," the heavy cruiser. "I'm going to coordinate your launch with *Broward.* Launch at Eta when ready."

"Aye aye," Solwara replied. Then, "Main batteries, status."

"One minute to rearmed," Main Fire Control reported.

"Here are your targets, one battery at each." He tapped buttons on his console to transmit the target data. "Let me know when you've got solutions."

"Aye aye."

On the display, several missile icons turned to Xs, including three of the missiles headed toward the *Kiowa.* Others changed course, chasing chaff or flares. Solwara checked the positions of target Delta and the *Broward;* when they launched at the heavy cruiser, their missiles would come at her from different directions, making it very difficult for the heavy cruiser to defend. By the time Main Fire Control reported the batteries were rearmed, only three missiles were still on course to intercept the *Kiowa,* and the icon for one of the Coalition fast frigates had changed to a pulsing red circle.

Solwara reported readiness to fire to the admiral's CIC.

"Stand by," the admiral's CIC said. Solwara waited, never taking his eyes from the main display. The destroyers screening the dreadnought released chaff and fired off flares. A missile from the *Broward* began moving erratically and one from the *Pawnee* veered off, decoyed by a flare. The others continued on course. Another of the missile icons heading for the *Kiowa* terminated in an X. Only two still threatened her.

"*Kiowa,* launch at target Delta. Ready your reserve battery to repeat on Delta."

"Launch at target Delta, ready my reserve battery to repeat on Delta, aye," Solwara replied, then ordered Main Fire Control to launch at target Delta and find a solution for the third battery to launch at the same target. Moments later he saw the icons of *Broward*'s launch. It would be a couple of minutes before the heavy cruiser would react to the launches, so he looked back at the dreadnought.

More missiles in the volley had veered off or were juking about confusedly, but four of them were homing directly on the three destroyers. Forty were still headed for the dreadnought.

Solwara looked back at the two missiles homing in on the *Kiowa;* they had both gotten past the torpedoes. Inertially guided? Possibly.

"Release chaff and flares," he ordered. The *Kiowa* continued turning up and right, and increasing velocity.

At least twenty missiles were past the destroyers screening the dreadnought. One of the destroyers showed as a pulsing circle, and another had turned away, apparently too badly damaged to continue screening. The dreadnought released chaff and flares, sending some of the missiles awry. More missiles passed the destroyer screen.

Closer, the chaff and flares weren't decoying the missiles closing in on the *Kiowa.*

"Close-in Fire Control. Do you have a solution on the two bogies coming at us?" Solwara asked into his comm.

"That's an affirmative. Ninety-four percent probability. Nearest approach in one hundred forty seconds."

Two and a third minutes. He could wait until they were closer, to increase the probability of a first strike hit, but ninety-four was a very high percentage—the "book" said to fire when probability reached ninety-five percent, Solwara had been very conservative when he'd held fire for ninety-nine percent.

"Fire when probability reaches ninety-five, then prepare for another shot."

"Fire at ninety-five and prepare for a second shot, aye."

Target Delta was throwing chaff and flares, and trying to maneuver out of the way of the missiles from the *Kiowa* and *Broward,* but three missiles were ignoring the decoys and closing rapidly. One of their icons suddenly became an X, struck by close-in fire, but the other two continued to close.

A small cloud appeared on the display representing the *Kiowa*'s close-in fire. One of the bogies Xed out, but the other kept coming at the starship.

"Close-in, can you get it?" Solwara's calm voice showed nothing of the sudden anxiety he felt when the last Coalition missile made it through the fire from the close-in defensive guns.

"Working on a solution," close-in Fire Control replied.

"Fire when ready."

"Firing," close-in Fire Control reported seconds later. Solwara felt the tremors sent through the ship by the firing of the close-in guns. On the display, he saw the cloud indicating the defensive pellets rapidly approaching the missile icon—and pass by it without the icon X-ing out.

"Stand by for impact!" the captain said sharply, and made sure he was properly strapped into his command chair.

Throughout the *Kiowa,* klaxons blared a warning, then the same female voice that earlier had announced general quarters began a countdown to impact. The main display whited out when the missile hit, and the warship staggered. Reports immediately began coming in from Damage Control.

The missile hit on the aft port quarter. Initial reports indicated that the inner hull wasn't breeched, though several bulkheads were buckled. Well-drilled Damage Control teams immediately headed to deal with the damage.

"Sir," the officer of the deck reported, "steering has been affected. The aft port vernier isn't responding to the helm."

"Do we have any steerage?" Solwara asked.

"Yessir. The other steering jets don't seem to be affected. We can compensate, but turns won't be as sharp as usual."

"Understood." Solwara returned his attention to the main display while he waited for the chief-of-ship to report with details of the damage to the aft port quarter.

The icon for Target Delta had changed to a pulsing red circle.

Admiral Hoi's CIC again came on, first with a request for a damage report, then instructions to engage Target Eta when ready. Solwara transmitted the damage assessment data he had and instructed that updates be copied to the Admiral's CIC, then asked if Main Fire Control had a solution for Target Eta.

"Yessir, battery three is ready to fire."

"Fire battery three. Acquire solution for battery one on Target Eta."

"Fire battery three, aye. Acquire solution to fire battery one on Target Eta, aye," Main Fire Control replied.

"Skipper, I have a damage assessment," Chief-of-Ship Groene came on.

"Give it to me, Chief."

"We've got five panels of the outer hull blown out." The chief transmitted the detailed data to the captain's console. "Aft port vernier is totally missing. Inner hull is badly buckled next to engine room three. A Damage Control team is working to shore it up, but the bulkhead could bust free at any minute. Request permission to order the engines shut down and the compartment evacuated."

Shutting down the engine would reduce the *Kiowa*'s maximum velocity, but not evacuating the engine room would jeopardize the lives of crewmen in it. On the other hand, losing the power from engine room three, combined with the reduced maneuverability from the loss of the steering jet could jeopardize the entire ship and all hands.

Solwara delayed making a decision by asking, "How long to replace the vernier?"

"Well, we have to replace four struts before there's a firm base for the jet, and run tubing and cables from the nearest junctions. I've got a good crew on each of those jobs now. About twenty, twenty-five minutes to complete those jobs. Then another twenty to mount a new jet—longer if we have to wait for the replacement to arrive. That's assuming the inner hull doesn't blow."

"You'll have the vernier in time. How long to shore up that bulkhead?"

"That's harder to tell. Every time we get one part secured, a bulge opens somewhere else on the inner hull. I'm thinking an hour before we can begin to breathe easy and just pay attention to repairing the damage."

Solwara thought hard for a few seconds, then told Chief Groene, "I'll have the engine room crew get into vacuum suits and evacuate the atmosphere."

"Sir, you realize the engine room crew can't work as well in vacuum suits. And the vacuum might damage some components of the engine."

"I know that, Chief. But reduced function and the possibility of future damage are preferable to losing the engine altogether in the middle of a battle. Do your best, Chief. That's why you make the big creds."

"Aye aye, sir."

Solwara breathed a bit easier, the damage was not as bad as he'd feared. The missile that hit the *Kiowa* must have been damaged by the close-in gunfire; it should have been able to penetrate the outer hull and maybe the inner before it detonated, but its warhead had exploded just inside the outer hull. A big portion of the outer hull was destroyed, and steering was damaged, but the inner hull wasn't breached—yet. He got on his tube to the chief engineer and told him to suit up the crew in engine room three and pump the air out. The chief engineer didn't like it any more than the chief-of-ship had, but agreed with the captain's reasoning.

That emergency dealt with, Solwara returned his attention to the battle. The dreadnought had taken four hits and was slowly turning away without engaging any of the starships in Task Force 79. A task force destroyer, the *Jerseymann,* was dead. So were two of the Coalition's fast frigates and another of its cruisers. The other ships of the Coalition fleet were turning about and heading north or south, presumably to where they could jump into Beamspace.

The 27th Division landed without opposition. Like the Confederation Marines, they made a combat assault landing—straight down from orbit. Unlike the Marines, they made planetfall on land. Major General Cazombi greeted them with considerable relief, and quickly integrated them into his defensive scheme.

CHAPTER FOURTEEN

The company didn't ace the battalion commander's inspection, though they came close. But then Commander van Winkle and his staff weren't as tough as First Sergeant Myer had been in the company commander's inspection. The clerical section almost passed, so Top Myer didn't have enough reason to convince Captain Conorado to cancel liberty for everybody for the entire week until the FIST pre-IG.

In fact, the Top was highly chagrined when the only gig given during the FIST pre-IG was to the command section, when Captain Tamara, the assistant F2, FIST intelligence, found a forgotten, half-smoked stogie in a drawer of the first sergeant's desk. There were only two other gigs in the rest of the company, gigs minor enough that the IG inspectors might pass over them.

The Marines were given base liberty the rest of the week, and shore liberty from the end of Fifth Day to eight hours on Seventh Day, when they had to be back to take care of last-minute details.

Lieutenant General Himan Xintoe, Inspector General of the Confederation Marine Corps, arrived on a navy VIP corsair, the CNSS *Thresher,* and made planetfall directly onto Camp Major Pete Ellis's Boynton Field four days before his scheduled inspection of the FIST units. After a brief meeting with Brigadier Sturgeon, he paid a courtesy call on Rear Admiral Blankenvoort, the commander of the navy supply depot that had been the initial reason for the presence of Marines on Thorsfinni's World. Xintoe and Blankenvoort were entertained that evening by Brigadier Sturgeon in the FIST commander's home. Xintoe and his staff commenced their inspection of the FIST headquarters the next morning.

Another navy starship arrived early on General Xintoe's third full day planetside, bearing a full colonel carrying an urgent message for Brigadier Sturgeon. Sturgeon read the message through once, then handed it to Xintoe. Xintoe read it, then handed it back without comment.

Sturgeon gave the orders to his chief of staff, Colonel Ramadan, and said, "Read this, then assemble the major element commanders, their XOs and sergeants major, along with my major staff, and the Whiskey Company commander. Don't tell anybody why I want to see them."

Ramadan quickly skimmed the document and caught his breath before replying, "Aye aye, sir. Is twenty minutes soon enough?"

"Yes."

Whiskey Company, a catch-unit normally pieced together under dire circumstances in the field, also often called "cooks and bakers," was comprised of clerks, truck drivers and mechanics, and other noncombat personnel. Except that 34th FIST's Whiskey Company wasn't a catch-unit. Following 34th FIST's return from the Kingdom Campaign, then-Assistant Commandant of the Marine Corps Anders Aguinaldo pulled some highly unofficial strings to assign an additional 118 Marines to 34th FIST to serve as on-hand replacements when it had heavy action and consequent losses.

Thirty-fourth FIST had a *lot* of deployments, and suffered heavier casualties than any other expeditionary unit in the Corps.

Lieutenant General Xintoe looked on expressionlessly. When Ramadan left to summon the major element commanders and other people to the meeting, he asked somberly, "May I attend your meeting?"

An hour later, all the company commanders and first sergeants of the infantry battalion and other major elements were summoned to commander's meetings at their own headquarters. An hour after that, Marines throughout the FIST were surprised to be called to company formations.

The Marines of Company L stood at silent attention in their ranks behind the barracks. They all had the same thought on their minds: "What's this about? We know what's happening tomorrow. A formation now is only wasting time we should be spending on final prep for the IG."

When Top Myer came out of the barracks with Captain Conorado and the other company officers, many of the Marines got a sinking feeling in their guts—the first sergeant *never* attended a company formation unless it was something big, really big.

Captain Conorado looked somber when he took his position in front of the company. His eyes swept the company quickly, then he said in a strong voice, "There's been a change of plans. There will not be an IG inspection tomorrow. Instead, we will be boarding the SAT *Lance Corporal Keith Lopez,* which is in orbit now. We have a deployment. The brigadier has granted shore liberty to the entire FIST until eight hours tomorrow morning. At that time I will brief you on what I have been able to find out."

Conorado looked over his company, drew in a chestful of air, and called out, "That is all. COMP-ney, dis-MISSED!"

He stood in place, watching his Marines racing back into the barracks to change into their liberty clothes.

"I wonder how many holes we'll have in the formation when we next assemble here," he said quietly when his Marines were inside.

"I don't know," Myer replied, just as quietly.

Gunnery Sergeant Thatcher merely shook his head. He'd already been briefed on where they were going, and didn't like it at all. Like the other two, he'd noted the expressions of concern on the faces of some of the Marines. A one-day notice for a deployment was highly unusual, and shore liberty the night before was virtually unheard of. The more experienced Marines, those with the most concerned expressions, realized they were in for something *very* big.

General Xintoe had quietly approved of Brigadier Sturgeon's decision to sound liberty call for his Marines. Xintoe understood that it would be a long time before any of them had another opportunity—for some of them, it would be their last opportunity.

"What is this bullshit?" Lance Corporal MacIlargie yelled once third platoon was back in its squadbay. "I busted my hump for this IG, and now it's been called off?" He wasn't experienced enough to understand the significance of a last-minute cancellation of an inspector general's inspection.

"Dumb guy," Corporal Claypoole snarled, whapping the back of MacIlargie's head. He didn't fully understand the significance either, but he could make an educated guess.

It was the kind of dumb question Lance Corporal Schultz would normally let pass with nothing more than a quick you're-too-dumb-to-live look. But Schultz was experienced enough to know *exactly* what the cancellation meant. He whapped MacIlargie upside the head much harder than Claypoole had and sent the other man sprawling.

"Hey!" MacIlargie shouted as he bounded back to his feet. He swung his fist before he realized who he was swinging at and was horrified when he saw he was about to hit. He twisted violently to avoid hitting Schultz and crashed back to the floor.

Schultz briefly looked down at MacIlargie with a quick you're-too-dumb-to-live look, then disappeared into the fire team room.

The squad leaders paused above MacIlargie's sprawled form and looked disdainfully down on him. Sergeant Linsman shook his head and said, "Wolfman, you really *are* too dumb to live," then led Sergeants Ratliff and Kelly to the room they shared.

MacIlargie looked around at the Marines in the corridor; many of them weren't very successful at hiding their snickers at his situation.

"What'd I do that's so damn dumb?" he demanded, then, with as much dignity as he could muster, climbed to his feet and walked to his fire team's room. Claypoole made a show of ignoring him. Schultz behaved as though nothing was amiss, so much so that MacIlargie felt he may as well not have come into the room.

On their last night before deploying, the Marines of second squad occupied a corner table in the main room at Big Barb's—and they weren't alone. Frieda and Gotta were in their usual positions, bookending Corporal Kerr. Corporal Claypoole still didn't get the significance of the way Jente kept looking at him from where she sat pressed against his side. Kone, a new girl, flirted outrageously with Corporal Chan and giggled at everything he said.

When she finished serving a round of steins of Reindeer Ale,

Talulah plopped herself on Sergeant Linsman's knee and announced, "Somebody else can take the food orders, I'm with the squad's boss tonight!"

"What do you mean? You've got floor duty!" Skoge objected—she simply *wasn't* going to leave the side of Lance Corporal Zumwald.

"I mean I'm with the boss, so I'm exempt," Talulah said with a haughty toss of her head.

"Now, now, ladies," Linsman said before Skoge or any of the others could interrupt. "This is our last night before we deploy. I think the fairest thing might be for you to take turns being waitress for us. After all, none of us wants his girl to be too busy to keep him company tonight."

Eight of the nine women at the table—it was a very *big* table—gave Talulah dirty looks, but none of them objected.

Ten Marines and nine women, of whom Kerr had two. Only Corporal Doyle and Lance Corporal Schultz were unattended.

"How come you didn't tell us you were leaving earlier?" Frieda asked. "I thought you were having some kind of big inspection."

"And you just got back from a deployment!" Jente added.

"We didn't tell you because we didn't know ourselves until just a couple of hours ago," Linsman replied.

"That's not fair!" Gotta cried.

Kerr almost dislodged her when he shrugged. "Nobody ever said the Marine Corps is fair."

"Not the way it treats us peons," PFC Fisher agreed.

"You're lucky my hands are occupied," Chan said, "or I'd put you on the deck like Hammer did to Wolfman." He hefted the stein he held in one hand—the other was wrapped around Kone's waist.

MacIlargie didn't say anything, but his face turned bright red.

"What did that nasty Hammer do to you, Wolfie?" Meisge asked, gently kissing MacIlargie's scarlet cheek.

"Didn't do nothing," MacIlargie croaked with a curt shake of his head. He shot an if-looks-could-kill at Chan. Fortunately, nobody else wanted to explain why Schultz had whapped MacIlargie upside the head hard enough to send him sprawling; it was something they didn't want to think about that night.

After a bit, Gotta took everybody's dinner order and got up to take the order slip to the kitchen.

She was almost through the kitchen door on her way back when she was nearly trampled by Einna Orafem, who stormed out behind her.

Einna ignored the hoots and catcalls aimed at her, and the questing hands that reached to pat or pinch her nether regions as she headed for the corner table. Hands tightly clenched, red spots on her cheeks so dark they were almost purple, she stomped to a halt and loomed over Schultz.

"You were going to leave on a deployment without saying good-bye, or even telling me?" Her voice got more shrill with each word.

Schultz stared up at her, dumbfounded.

Silence fell over the table and the surrounding tables—nobody had ever seen Schultz look so shocked and lost.

"I—I . . ." Schultz had no idea what came after "I."

"That's all you can say, 'I'?" The corner of Einna's eye glistened, then a tear oozed out to slide down her cheek.

Hesitantly, Schultz raised a hand and, with a gentler touch than any of the watching Marines could have imagined, brushed the tear away.

"I didn't know—I didn't think . . ."

"That's right, you didn't think," she said huskily.

He went to lower his hand, but she grasped it and held it against her cheek.

"You're the only one who hasn't treated me like some floozy, the only one who's treated me with respect. Don't you *dare* go away without saying good-bye."

She released his hand and started to leave, then turned back and half whispered, "I get off work in two hours. Come to the kitchen then. And don't be drunk."

Unlike her furious rush from the kitchen, Einna returned in a stately march. A well of utter silence surrounded her—*nobody* had anticipated what had just happened but *everybody* knew that they risked the wrath of Hammer Schultz if they said or did anything to Einna Orafem.

When the kitchen door closed behind Big Barb's chef, heads slowly swiveled and all eyes focused on Schultz. But nobody dared say anything for a long, uncomfortable moment.

Finally, Kerr cleared his throat and said softly, "Looks like Hammer's got himself a girlfriend."

Half the Marines of second squad slowly turned their heads to look at Kerr, aghast at his temerity. About as many of the girls with them also looked at Kerr. Everybody else kept wary watch on Schultz, and did their best to unobtrusively ease out of his way. But Schultz's only visible reaction was involuntary—the bronze of his face grew darker.

After another silent moment, Gotta, who had made it back to the table while Einna was confronting Schultz but hadn't resumed her position next to Kerr, said, "That's nice for Hammer. But *her*?"

She jumped and scampered to the presumed protection of Kerr's side when Schultz growled, "Drop it."

It took a little while for tensions at second squad's table to ease, but when they did, merriment reigned once more, fueled by plentiful ale and food—with a special dish for Schultz.

At the end of the appointed two hours, Schultz stood without a word and marched to the kitchen. He wasn't seen again until the next morning, when he was the last man to make formation. He came straight from town and didn't have time to change into a fresh uniform; nobody had seen him so rumpled in garrison before. His face, as usual, bore no expression, but there was something very satisfied in his attitude.

Nobody asked him any questions about where he'd gone or what had happened after he disappeared into the kitchen.

Captain Conorado sat in his office, the door closed. He wasn't looking forward to the conversation he'd have that evening with his wife. He knew Marta would take the news of another deployment with philosophical resignation. She'd been through enough of them, not enough to be used to her husband going off to war, but enough to be inured to the inevitable separations marriage to an officer of Marines imposed on her.

All Marines must be prepared for instantaneous deployment, gear packed, personal affairs in order, and girlfriends, families, creditors, etc., fully aware that Marines had less notice of a deployment order than firemen that someone's house was ablaze, and Marines had to react just as quickly.

When a deployment was called, families were notified after the fact by an officer–NCO team, Marines staying behind for nondisciplinary reasons. It was hard duty because often families, especially young spouses and their children, did not take the news lightly; it was hard on the notifiers too, because it meant they had to stay behind while their comrades went off in harm's way. Deployment notification duty was considered the second worst in the Corps, the worst being casualty notification.

Conorado's heart sank as he thought that, once again, someone Marta didn't know would come knocking on her door to tell her she would be alone. After that, she'd be in constant dread of another knock on the door, one with a chaplain on the other side. As he was contemplating that and other morose thoughts, Owen the Woo hopped lightly onto the edge of Conorado's desk. "You are sad, Skipper," the creature remarked.

"Oh, Owen, old buddy!" Conorado laughed and held out a finger. Owen sat there, his huge, bulbous eyes staring unblinkingly at Conorado, like some old man staring at him through oversized spectacles. The cilia on the top of the Woo's head waved back and forth slightly, like the few remaining strands of hair on a bald man's pate in a gentle breeze. Owen took Conorado's fingers between his talons and squeezed gently. "Yeah, another deployment," the captain answered. "We leave in a few minutes. I was just in here making sure I had everything . . ." he gestured at his equipment, leaving the sentence unfinished.

"I thought as much. You've gone on too many deployments since I've been with you. I suppose this will be another difficult one and I shall stay behind this time?"

"I'm afraid so, old friend. Now don't you go around telling everybody before we get underway," Conorado smiled weakly. That Owen could communicate with humans was a secret Conorado had kept well; he'd never forget that scientist on Avionia Station who had wanted to dissect the creature.

"Of course not. I know the regs." Owen wobbled on the edge of the desk, shimmering a light blue.

"You don't look too good," Conorado remarked, concern in his voice, "are we feeding you properly?"

"Yes, Skipper. The soil here agrees with me. The best thing that ever happened to me is when the boys brought me back from Diamunde. But I feel unwell and fear I am growing old."

Conorado had never considered that Woos might grow old. "I guess we all are," Conorado sighed.

"I was old when the men found me. Will this deployment last long?"

"Yes, probably."

"Then I shall not be here when you return, Skipper."

Conorado glanced sharply at the Woo. He had never noticed before that the creature had a sense of humor, so what did he mean. "Are you being reassigned? Strange, Owen, I haven't seen any orders from Fleet," Conorado said lightly, but something began gnawing at the pit of his stomach.

"I shall most likely pass for what you call dead by then, Skipper."

"Wh—?"

"We Woos do not live long in comparison to the human lifespan, ten to fifteen of your years and as I said, I was old when your men found me. I'm about seventeen of your years now, very old for one of my kind."

"Why didn't you say something?"

"You never asked, and we Woos, unlike you humans, bow to the inevitabilities of our nature. There's no use complaining because it never does any good. I have lived a long and interesting life and I have been very fortunate and I shall die contented."

"Well—" Conorado didn't quite know what to say now. "Do you believe in an afterlife, Owen?"

"No. We go where the energy from the light in this office goes when it's turned off—dissipated, never to regenerate. I know many of you humans believe something of your 'spirit' survives after death, and you've invented many philosophical and theological systems to prove those beliefs. I've heard your men arguing endlessly about them. We Woos do not feel this subject is worthy of speculation. If it is so, we shall find out, otherwise such contemplations get in the way of living."

Top Myer knocked on the door. "Ready to mount out, Skipper," the first sergeant said.

"It's time, Owen," Conorado rose and picked up his gear. "Well, good-bye, old friend." He held out a finger.

The Woo took the finger between his talons. He began to glow, the sign of emotion for Woos, and in a few seconds the office was filled with a bright, golden light. "Good-bye, Skipper, and good luck. If I am here when you get back, good; if not, then I will have reached the limit of my usefulness in this life."

Conorado turned the lights out and left the door ajar behind him as he left so that Owen could get out if he wanted. Gradually Owen's light began to fade until it was a very dim blue and then even that disappeared. Owen sat there in the dark for an eternity.

Captain Conorado came out of the barracks, followed by the other officers, along with First Sergeant Myer, and accepted the formation from Gunnery Sergeant Thatcher. He stood there for a moment, looking over his Marines, before briefing them on 34th FIST's upcoming mission.

"A coalition of worlds, led by the government of Ravenette, has seceded from the Confederation of Human Worlds. The secession began with an attack on the Confederation army base on Ravenette. The rebels overran the base and the remnants of the garrison withdrew to a fortified peninsula where they've been trying to hold on. The garrison has been reinforced by the 27th Division, but the armed forces of ten worlds are arrayed against them and they're having trouble holding on. The Confederation Army is mounting a full field army to go in and deal with the situation, but it takes time to mount a field army, more time than the defenders on Ravenette have.

"That's where we come in. Thirty-fourth FIST is the ready-to-deploy unit nearest to Ravenette. We have been ordered to deploy immediately and hold the line until the field army arrives." He paused to let the implications sink in. It didn't take long; two army divisions, perhaps thirty thousand soldiers, were being overwhelmed and somebody expected a thousand Marines to save their bacon. It sounded like a suicide mission, but Conorado didn't give his Marines time to dwell on that.

"This isn't the first time the army has found itself in a dire situation, and Marines have had to go to their rescue. We've always succeeded, we'll succeed again this time. Other FISTs will join us, but we're going to be the first FIST in.

"I'm not going to stand here and lie to you, we're in for a fight as tough as the one we had on Diamunde or the one on Kingdom. I can't tell you anything about the current tactical situation—." Behind him, Ensign Charlie Bass choked back a snicker; Ravenette was a week away in Beamspace and the most recent intelligence they had was more than two weeks old. "—All I can say is, be prepared for a tough fight as soon as we make planetfall.

"One more thing. The Secessionist Coalition had a cordon around Ravenette. The navy broke through it, so the last we heard, the way was clear. Which doesn't mean making planetfall will be easy. We won't know until we get there if the cordon is still broken, or whether the rebel forces have better antishuttle defenses than they did when the 27th Division went in."

Conorado looked over his company one more time, then said, "That is everything I have to tell you for now. When I dismiss you, return to the barracks and saddle up. We move out as soon as hoppers arrive to transport us to Boynton Field. COMP-ney, dis-MISSED!"

Less than an hour later, Company L dismounted from the FIST's hoppers at Boynton Field, Camp Ellis's shuttle field, and boarded Dragons from the Starship Assault, Troop CNSS *Lance Corporal Keith Lopez,* in orbit around Thorsfinni's World. Mike Company, mounted on 34th FIST's own Dragons, was already boarding Essays from the starship. The hoppers returned to the barracks area to pick up Kilo Company, which would launch in the second wave, along with the infantry battalion's headquarters company, the artillery battery, and the composite squadron. FIST headquarters had gone into orbit at dawn.

"I have a bad feeling about this," Corporal Dean said when the petty officer third who herded third platoon's first squad on a guideline through the Null-G starship to its compartment left them to guide another squad to its compartment. He bent to stow his gear in one of the miniscule lockers in the row below the bunks.

"And why might that be, Dean-o?" Corporal Dornhofer asked.

"It wasn't this compartment," Dean said slowly, "but I've been on the *Keith Lopez* before."

Lance Corporal Godenov punched his fire team leader in the

shoulder. "All that means is you've been in this man's Marine Corps so long you're rotating through the gator fleet again."

Dean looked up from his stowing and grabbed a handhold to keep from drifting away. "Maybe," he agreed. "But the *Keith Lopez* is the starship that took me from Earth to Arsenault."

Corporal Pasquin doubled over with laughter. He laughed so hard that he was out of reach of the handholds by the time he regained control of himself. It didn't bother him, he'd been in that position before.

Dean looked at him, offended. "That's not funny, Pasquin. I had a good job on Earth. Then I got onboard this starship, and ever since I've been going places where people shoot at me!"

Pasquin laughed again, but it was less raucous. He relaxed into a semifetal position and grinned at Dean. "And just who held a handblaster to your head and forced you to board the *Keith Lopez*?"

Dean looked away and muttered, "Nobody." Then, "You two!" he snapped at Godenov and PFC Quick, "Stop standing there playing switch and get your gear stowed!"

Godenov looked at his thumbs; neither was in his mouth nor stuck up his rectum. "I'm not playing switch. Are you playing switch, Quick?"

Quick glanced at his own thumbs. "I don't believe so," he answered.

"Got you there, Rock," Dornhofer laughed.

Pasquin laughed again, then turned to Dornhofer with a mock-serious expression on his face. "You know, Dorny, we're setting a bad example, making jokes at another fire team leader in front of the peons."

"Peons!" Lance Corporal Zumwald exclaimed. "I'm almost at the end of my enlistment, I ain't no peon."

Pasquin chuckled and asked, "How many stripes you got, peon?"

Dornhofer asked, "Are you sure you're almost at the end of your enlistment?"

Just that fast, the atmosphere in first squad's compartment turned somber. Until the threat of the Skinks was removed, or their existence was made public, everyone in 34th FIST was in "for the duration." All offworld leaves, ends of active service, and retirements were canceled.

That was even more unpleasant than going into harm's way. Other Marines knew that no matter how many times they went into battle, eventually, if they survived, they'd get out. For the Marines of 34th FIST, the only way out was death or injury so severe the doctors couldn't patch them up well enough to return to duty.

"You would have to bring that up," Pasquin said sourly after a moment. He uncoiled from his semifetal position and swam to a handhold.

CHAPTER FIFTEEN

Ashburtonville, the primary population center on Ravenette, now host to the secessionist coalition's government, had been founded 250 years earlier by Franklin Ashburton. Ashburton had been a determined and ruthless entrepreneur, cast in the mold common to most early explorers and adventurers of every age, willing to risk everything to stake out new worlds. The city that took his name had developed into the cultural and economic center of Ravenette, with a population of well over five hundred thousand before most of it was evacuated as a military necessity at the beginning of the war.

The early settlers on Ravenette were pleased to discover that it was a world hospitable to human life, and many of the animal and plant species native to Earth thrived there. Although the world had its own diverse evolved and flourishing biosphere, the native fauna and flora proved surprisingly compatible to human needs. In fact, the world took its very name from a native species of birdlike viviparous creatures dubbed *Corvus corvidae* because of their striking resemblance to crows or ravens of Earth. The animals were smaller than their Terran namesakes, seldom growing over twenty centimeters in length. They carried a large, heavy proboscis; a long, wedge-shaped tail; and were covered with smooth, glossy scales, usually bluish-black in color. The name "Ravenette" caught on in the early days but eventually the people of Ravenette just started calling them "blackbirds," naturally. Those early colonists found them to be intelligent creatures perfectly adaptable to life among humans. In fact, over the generations, for many families the blackbirds readily assumed the roles normally performed by dogs.

Ashburtonville evolved into a comfortable and gracious metropolis with grand tree-lined boulevards and Earth-style homes constructed of native woods and stone, where the inhabitants raised large and vivacious families. Although Ravenette's economy depended mostly on agriculture, the people of Ashburtonville did not have dirt under their fingernails all the time, and the lifestyle they developed was diverse and stimulating, drawing to its great advantage on a thousand years of mankind's struggle to make life better for itself.

When the order to evacuate the city came, the people, united in their desire for independence, complied willingly enough. Most moved without complaint into the far hinterlands to avoid the destruction that was coming. Some, remarkably independent souls even for an independent race like the people of Ravenette, just refused to move, a few others stayed because they were curious, and some remained behind because they would not leave their homes. But for the most part the once gracious city now lay in ruins, its broad boulevards, once fragrant with trees and shrubs, reduced to rubble-clogged pathways enveloped in the choking smoke of fires and the air everywhere reeking of high explosive. Burrowed deep into the ruins of the once magnificent dwellings the stay-behinds crouched timorously, praying for safe exit from the doomed city. But there was none.

And everywhere were the soldiers, digging, burrowing, constructing, manning fighting points, tending to the monstrous machines of destruction, soldiers in their thousands, from every world of the Coalition, all waiting eagerly for one word: ATTACK!

In the lulls between bombardments, only the blackbirds moved aboveground, soaring on the thermals of the fires, looking for carrion. They had learned to feed on the dead.

A major military headquarters during a battle is a cauldron of organized chaos. Nothing in a battle headquarters can be done there today, all must have been done yesterday and if not, there is always that time between retreat and reveille when tasks left undone can be completed, because nobody there ever sleeps.

General Davis Lyons established his headquarters on the far side of

Ashburtonville in an abandoned school building. Not that he spent much time there. Lyons was the type of commander who believed that in order to manage a battle he had to be at the front, so he spent most of his time out with the troops, touring their fighting positions, talking to them, buoying morale, and conferring with his subordinate commanders. The sobriquet "Granny" that had been applied to him, mostly by politicians and people who did not know Lyons personally, was not the nickname his soldiers had for him: They called him "general."

The all-important tasks of managing an army's sinews, its supplies, its food, clothing, equipment, ammunition, spare parts, fuels, and a myriad personnel matters, Lyons left to the experts on his staff. But late into the nights he read their daily reports, noted deficiencies to be corrected, actions that deserved commendation, and made decisions on a bewildering variety of problems ranging from what to do with civilians found hiding in the ruins to the decisions of courts-martial boards. To add to the complexity of his mission, Lyons also had to coordinate the activities of the Coalition fleet in orbit around Ravenette as well as a small naval contingent in the Ocean Sea just off Pohick Bay. And frequently he was called back to the new capital city of the Coalition government, Gilbert's Corners, a small town 150 kilometers from Ashburtonville, in an area supposed to be safe from attack, to render in person justification for the way he was running the war. Those politicians were becoming very impatient with him.

The initial anger Lyons had felt over the proximate cause of his son Tommy's death had subsided as he became more and more involved in commanding his army. Now, instead of going out of his life on a wave of fire and destruction, Lyons concentrated on fighting the Confederation to the best of his considerable ability. Acts of self-destruction were just not in the nature of General Davis Lyons.

Lyons knew as well as the politicians bugging him from the safety of their new senate chambers that the longer he kept his army idle in front of Cazombi's fortified positions the worse it would be for morale as his men slowly slipped into a defensive mentality. He also knew that if the Confederation was successful in adequately reinforcing Cazombi the tide could well turn against him despite the numerical superiority of his army. So he found himself on the horns of a dilemma. He was certain a massive attack by his forces would crack Cazombi's defenses and lead to the fall of his fortress, but if he did that then his grand strategy of luring the Confederation's piecemeal reinforcements to their destruction would have to be revised. Time was not on his side. The longer the stalemate endured, the more opportunity the Confederation would have to mass first-class fighting forces. Once they got a toehold on Ravenette, they would commence a war of maneuver. Then, if Cazombi's forces were well-led, and Lyons knew him to be a first-class tactical commander, his own superiority in numbers might not be sufficient to ensure victory.

Well, General Davis Lyons had a few tricks up his sleeve, but first he had to know what was happening inside Cazombi's lines.

During the weeks since the capture of Fort Seymour, Lyons's engineers and sappers had gradually closed the distance between them and General Cazombi's fortifications on the Peninsula by extending a network of trenches and tunnels into the intervening no man's land. Using these, Lyons's troops had been able to advance protected in some places to within one hundred meters of Cazombi's defenses.

Trench warfare is an old tactic of static positional warfare. But the construction methods for Lyons's entrenchments were very different than those used in commercial excavations. Compressed-air and rotary-percussion drilling equipment, blasting and heavy excavation machinery could not be used because they drew fire. Instead, military technicians had developed a special miniaturized laser that vaporized rock and soil at a very rapid rate and a ventilation system that expelled the gases from the excavations soundlessly and dissipated them into the surrounding environment. The laser drill also eliminated the problem of haulage and disposition of detritus. While this equipment was in operation the men using it had to wear protective gear. The connecting tunnels were short enough they did not require special ventilation systems. One had been successfully constructed to come up inside Cazombi's defenses and thus far its existence had not been discovered.

Lyons was meeting with a brigade commander and his officers in one sector of his lines to discuss a raid into Cazombi's fortifications through this tunnel. Because of frequent power outages so close to the enemy lines, they were using paper maps and charts. "I want you to conduct two diversionary raids of battalion strength here and here,"

Lyons told them, jabbing a forefinger at a map of the enemy positions, "while you send a small team through this tunnel to get inside."

"I'll pick my best men," the brigade commander replied. He looked at his three regimental commanders and selected two to provide the diversionary battalions. "I'll hold the rest of my brigade in reserve to exploit the breakthrough. We can be ready in the morning."

Lyons shook his head vigorously. "No, Colonel, this raid is to get prisoners and information only. We shall not exploit the tunnel breakthrough. I want just a small detachment of lightly armed men to get inside, raise hell, and get out. Blow the tunnel behind them. I need to know what the state of affairs is inside there. I'm going to draw him out to us, but only in my good time. That's why I need to know what's going on in there. Colonel, any questions?"

"Nossir."

"What time will they be able to jump off?" Lyons asked.

"It's thirteen hours now, we can be ready at zero three hours tomorrow. My men will be forming up in the tunnel not later than zero one hours. I'll order a barrage to cover the explosion when the engineers blow the tunnel. The demolition charges will be set off by the last man of the assault force out."

"Very well. Colonel, if the raid fails, blow the tunnels so the enemy can't use them to get into our positions." Lyons looked up at each of the assembled officers and they nodded. "I'll see you back here at zero one hours tomorrow. I want to talk to your men before they go in." Lyons shook hands with both officers and left.

Private Amitus Sparks's pulse raced, but outwardly he remained calm. This would not be his first assault but the conditions this time were much different than in any of the other actions he'd seen so far in this war. Still, he was with his friends, men he knew he could rely on even if they were a bit peculiar in a noncombat environment. "Wellers, stop spitting that tobacco juice all over the gawdam floor," he whispered to Private Wellford Brack, the second man in his three-man fire team.

"Shee-it, Amie, what difference does it make where I spit?" he nodded at the solid rock all around them in the tunnel where they were crouching, waiting for the engineers to give them the signal to move forward. "This whole place is gonna go up in smoke before sunrise anyway." The platoon had formed up just inside the tunnel mouth. The tunnel was four meters wide and four high, just wide enough to permit a single-file column of infantrymen with scaling equipment to move forward and leave enough room for the engineers to pass them. Dim fluorescent lamps strung along the ceiling at ten-meter intervals gave them just enough light to see by. At the far end of the tunnel they could just make out the figures of the engineers planting the charges that would blow out an exit at the height of the barrage.

"Well, it's a gawdam dirty habit, Wellers. Ya should of brought your bottle along."

"Yeah? Lug a spit bottle into combat? Sometimes I don't know about you, boy. Anyways, when you make PFC you kin order me around." He nudged their fire team leader, PFC Suey Ruston, who was crouching just in front of him. Brack had been a police officer on Mylex, and like all cops, he'd gotten into the habit of chewing tobacco.

"They's gonna blow up this tunnel, Amie, so who cares if Wellford spits tobacco juice in here? What I want to be assured of is he don't let none of them killer farts of his."

"Hope it don't blow while we're still in here," Brack whispered, spitting a brown stream across the tunnel. It splattered on the opposite wall. In the dim light, he grinned ferociously at Sparks, revealing the discolored stumps of his front teeth.

"Cut it out!" a soldier behind them whispered. Brack turned and gave the man a rigid middle finger.

"Well, if he swallows that chaw in the excitement, we're gonna have to carry him out."

"Shut up!" their platoon leader whispered as he walked down the line of crouching infantrymen. "Noise discipline! Gen'rel Lyons is gonna be here in a minute. He wants to talk to us."

"Hee, hee, hee, somebody give the old boy a bullhorn!" Brack stage-whispered. The lieutenant glared at him as he passed on down the line and Brack self-consciously lapsed into silence.

"Gawdam," someone muttered, "the Gen'rel comin' in here to talk to us? Man, that's bad luck." Someone else cursed the man into silence.

These men were eager for the attack to begin. They had practiced it intensively over the last hours, studied the maps of the fortress, memorized every detail, each knew his assignment. Brack's team was to break through into a specific bunker, if they could, and kill or capture the men in there; if time—ten minutes inside at the most, and then back into the tunnel—and circumstances permitted, they would infiltrate neighboring positions through the communications tunnels the engineers assumed branched off from every bunker, connecting them all into an integrated defensive system. It was really a very simple operation with the exception that they would have to run all the way back through the tunnel with their prisoners—if they got any—and wounded, which they definitely would have.

Brack had never seen General Davis Lyons up close. That morning the general passed within inches of where they crouched, speaking quiet words of encouragement to each man, shaking hands with some, pausing to talk in whispers briefly with others. "I'm counting on you," he said directly to Brack and making eye contact. He passed on, then turned around and came back. "Is that a chaw in your cheek, soldier?" he asked.

"Um, yessir," Brack mumbled, his lips stained dark with tobacco juice that was visible even in the poor light. He began to get to his feet to assume the position of attention but Lyons motioned for him to stay down.

Lyons shook his head as Brack's platoon commander, who was following the general, began to say something. "Well, soldier, make sure you don't swallow the damn thing," Lyons said and, still shaking his head, passed on down the line. Brack gave Sparks a huge, vindicated grin and spit carefully but victoriously, onto the wall behind him. On his way out General Lyons paused before Brack again, laid a hand on his shoulder and squeezed it gently. Brack was astonished and enormously flattered that the general remembered him, but most invigorating of all, he realized, he had just had his brush with history and if he lived through this war, he'd have a story to tell the rest of his life.

A few minutes later the lieutenant came back down the line whispering, "Forward! Forward! The engineers are ready!"

"My name is Andantina Metzger," the interrogator introduced herself, taking the chair opposite Ennis Shovell. "Smoke?" she asked, offering an open pack of cigarettes to Shovell, who shook his head. She shrugged.

"You don't mind if I have one then?" She lighted up, leaned back, and smiled. "So, Private Shovel, how's things?"

Ennis Shovell's head was still bandaged from the blow that had knocked him unconscious and saved his life. He did not know what happened to his companions, Livny and Quimper, whom he presumed were killed in the raid. "I've been worse," Shovell answered. He sized up Metzger warily, the way she sucked the smoke into her lungs and expelled it to one side, to avoid blowing it into his face; her posture in the chair; the way she looked at him; her hair, the bones in her face. She did not look at all threatening. He estimated her age as several years younger than himself, but no spring chicken. Ordinarily she might have been rather attractive to him but under these circumstances Shovell had other things to think about. "When do you start pulling out my fingernails?" he asked.

"Oh, dear boy, don't be so crude!" Metzger smiled slightly, revealing a set of good teeth, "we do so much hate crudity. Ah, hum," she was silent for a moment, regarding Shovell in her turn. She knew something about him from the information contained in the standard-issue army ID bracelet he'd been wearing when captured. She saw a well-built man in his forties, probably, one side of his head covered with a field dressing, his tunic bloodstained. Her training was as a psychologist. In civilian life she conducted interviews with criminal suspects for the police and was considered good at obtaining confessions. "You're from New Genesee? I've never been there. What's it like? What'd you do there? How's your family?"

"At its worst, it's much nicer than this place," Shovell answered.

"Ah, yes," Metzger smiled. She wouldn't get much from this man, she knew, at least not the standard information like troop strength, defensive dispositions, that sort of thing. She nodded. "I come from a place called Trinkatat, ever heard of it?"

"Yeah," Shovell responded, "all the women there are whores, I hear."

"Ennis, be nice. You don't mind if I call you Ennis, do you? How long have you been in the army?"

"All my life."

"Do you like it?"

"Are you fucking crazy?" Shovell almost shouted.

Metzger nodded. "Sorry. Dumb question, Ennis. I'd like to be home myself, drinking a beer right now. Would you like a beer, Ennis?"

Shovell shook his head. "You married?" Shovell asked. He did not see any rings on her fingers. Her nails were cut short but they were clean, he observed.

Metzger smiled. "Please. I ask the questions here, okay?" She leaned forward and lowered her voice. "Look, Ennis, let's cut the crap and get down to cases. I need to know some things about your army, nothing vital, because you don't know anything vital, you're only an infantry private. But tell me about your unit, what you know about the other units in your army, how things are out there. That's not important information. You won't be betraying your comrades! Other guys we captured during that raid have told us a lot, so you wouldn't be the only one to cooperate. Come on, you cooperate with me," she shrugged, "and in a little while you'll be in a comfortable bed or, if you like, way in the rear, sucking on a beer. Ennis, this war is over for you. Make your stay with us easy on yourself."

"Why don't you make things easy on me? Let's fuck." Private Ennis Shovell, New Genesee National Guard, now a prisoner of war, instantly regretted making that remark and his face reddened. Metzger only smiled, as if used to such comments, and this increased Shovell's embarrassment so he rushed on, "All right, all right, I do have some vital information that you need to know."

Metzger nodded, the smile still on her face, but she said nothing.

"You can't crack us, the Marines are on their way, and when they get here, we are going to kick your motherfucking asses into next year."

Metzger had what she wanted.

CHAPTER SIXTEEN

Lieutenant General Jason Billie, Director of Operations for the Confederation Combined Chiefs of Staff, had risen far, thanks to his abilities as the consummate staff officer and a schemer. At the military academy his fellow cadets had dubbed him "Jason the Janus"; they realized even then Billie's aptitude for duplicity. The name had stuck throughout his career.

General Billie never attacked anyone directly, always through insinuation. A master of innuendo and irony, he demolished his enemies and competitors over time by dropping casual remarks about their shortcomings in the presence of their superiors. He did this in the utmost good humor, pretending an innocent joke at the other person's expense. And when those superiors would defend the person Billie was attacking, he would chuckle and instantly agree with them, in fact deny that he bore them any ill will, but the remarks so casually dropped had a tendency to stick.

So in a meeting where Major General Alistair Cazombi suggested maybe the quarantine on the transfer of Marines of 34th FIST might be removed, Billie had immediately replied, "Alistair, have you ever known a twenty-three-year-old with a snout full of beer to keep his mouth shut?" Admiral Porter, the Chairman of the Combined Chiefs, laughed along with the other officers in that meeting, but Billie had inserted a seed in the admiral's mind that eventually grew into the confrontation between him and Cazombi that had resulted in the latter's transfer to

Ravenette. That's how Billie got Cazombi out of the way for good, or so he thought. He hated the plainspoken, laconic Cazombi because behind that stoic facade that had earned him the nickname "Cazombi the Zombie," dwelt a superior intelligence that saw right through Jason Billie.

But not even two-faced Lieutenant General Billie could have anticipated the role Fate was to play in regard to Alistair Cazombi when it thrust him into the position of defending the besieged garrison at Fort Seymour and subsequently brought him to the attention of the President herself, who compared him with the heroic Jonathan Wainwright of Corregidor fame. That was the sort of attention that did Cazombi no harm. Billie either, because Admiral Porter had to take the heat for transferring Cazombi, once the word got out how that brilliant and brave officer had been treated by the Chairman of the Combined Chiefs of Staff. That was how ingeniously Billie planned his moves. But Cazombi's fame did not help Jason Billie, who was hankering badly for his next star. It was the army's turn next to contribute a general officer to be Chairman, since that position rotated among the services periodically. Another star for Billie and the new Chairman could very well be—Full General Jason Billie. And that fourth star could not be denied him if he could get command of the field army the Confederation was raising to go to the relief of Cazombi.

So Lieutenant General Jason Billie broached the subject with Admiral Porter in private after a meeting of the full staff. That meeting had been held to update Porter on Billie's plan to deploy the troops needed for the field army. As usual, Billie had handled the planning brilliantly. He'd dubbed it "Operation MacArthur."

"What's on your mind, Jason?" Porter leaned back comfortably and regarded his operations director frankly, almost affectionately. He was very satisfied with the way the meeting had gone and was thinking ahead to the briefing he would soon give the President. He anticipated a very successful briefing that would restore his luminescence among the civilians. He had moved quickly and decisively, in large part due to Billie's expertise as a planner and organizer. But the President would never know anything about Jason Billie's role in Operation MacArthur, only that Admiral Joseph K. C. B. Porter was responsible for it.

"I want command of that field army, sir."

Porter sat up quickly, clearly surprised. "Ah?" was all he could say at first. "Jason, would you have a cigar?" he offered, to give him time to think of a reply. He already had someone in mind for that command, someone he wanted to get rid of but someone whose selection was sure to please the President.

"Sir, let me be frank."

"Please do." Porter lighted the cigar for Billie.

"I personally organized the force you will dispatch to Ravenette. I know it from the top down, except there's nobody at the top just now. Who better to command it than the man who designed it?"

"Well, ahem," Porter was dithering, as Billie knew very well he would. He even knew who it was Porter had in mind for the command. He would have picked the same officer, were he the chairman, to please the President and get rid of a pain in the ass. But Billie would demolish that officer in a few moments. "I can hardly spare you here, Jason—" Porter gestured vaguely.

"Sir, my deputy can take over as Director. She's fully competent and more than ready for a three-star slot. I never stand in the way of competent subordinates, as you know. But let me point out something. Your sending Cazombi to Ravenette was a brilliant decision! He is just the man for a delaying action, even though we didn't know at the time that this role would fall to him. But the situation on Ravenette was in turmoil when he was sent there. You needed a man with rank and experience on the scene in case the situation deteriorated—"

Porter nodded and grunted; he hadn't thought of that explanation.

"Rumors have been flying around in high places, mostly inspired by the Marine Commandant, Aguinaldo, that Cazombi was sent there by you to settle a grudge you had against him." He made a dismissive gesture, as if he, Billie, didn't believe that was the reason, which he knew full well it was. "In fact, Cazombi is your Horatius at the Bridge, you might say, sir, holding off the hordes. But to win this war you need someone with far greater organizational ability and insight. You need a Caesar. I am that Caesar, sir, you know it, so does everyone. Give me that command and you will have to your credit two brilliant decisions and victory in this war. You can point all this out when you nominate me for the job."

Billie hated General Aguinaldo, the bluff, straight-talking Marine commandant. He had tried never to let this hatred show, always treating Aguinaldo with cool courtesy and deference at meetings, but their relationship had never been warmer than frosty because Aguinaldo saw through Billie as clearly as Cazombi did, and knew him for the sinuous schemer that he really was. Billie knew very well that Aguinaldo despised him and had supported Cazombi's arguments for lifting the quarantine on 34th FIST, and he also knew about Cazombi's longstanding friendliness toward the Marines, which he considered downright disloyalty to the army. Now Cazombi's balls were in a vise and he had called for Marines, an insult to every self-respecting soldier. That had to be corrected and he, Jason Billie, was the man to restore order in the world of military affairs.

"Well—" Porter was impressed. So it was Aguinaldo who told the President about his falling out with Cazombi. And to think he had been going to propose that very same Aguinaldo for command of the army! So far he had only gotten icy stares from Chang-Sturdevant when the subject of Cazombi had come up but he'd not been asked outright to explain why he was on Ravenette to begin with. Now he had that explanation. A brilliant face-saver. Oh, he might have to embellish the facts a bit, not tell an outright lie to make the explanation go down smoothly, but every military man who had to deal with politicians knew how to do that as second nature. "Well, well." Porter relaxed and sat back in his chair. "General," he gestured at a side table, "would you join me in a bourbon?"

"Thank you, General, for coming to see me on such short notice," Chang-Sturdevant said. "I am sending your name to the Congress to confirm your promotion to Full General," Lieutenant General Billie permitted himself a slight nod at this information, "but I wanted to hear from you personally regarding your plan for conducting the war against the Secessionists. I don't mean to interfere with your plans, General, you know far more about these things than I do, but I wanted this meeting because once you leave to command your army, we will not be able to have another session like this."

They sat in Chang-Sturdevant's private office, Billie, Admiral Porter, and Marcus Berentus, the Minister of War.

"Ma'am, I appreciate that and I am delighted we could have this meeting," Billie responded. He spoke in well-modulated tones and was careful to show deference to Chang-Sturdevant whom he privately regarded as a stupid, meddling bitch.

"Uh, you're calling this relief expedition 'Operation MacArthur,' General? That's brilliant!" Chang-Sturdevant smiled and nodded at Berentus. "Who thought of that name?"

"Well, I did, ma'am," Billie replied, his voice dripping with modesty he did not feel. "I thought, under the circumstances, you know, it would be appropriate," he smiled. Things were off to a good start!

"Marcus," Chang-Sturdevant turned to Berentus, "maybe we should introduce legislation to reinstate the rank of General of the Army, and give General Billie here a fifth star? Have you ever thought along those lines, gentlemen?" she asked Porter and Billie. There was a twinkle in her eye. She was joking, sparring with her military advisers.

" 'Grand Admiral'?" Porter laughed, trying out the title, shaking his head. He was rising to the joke.

"Ah, no, no, ma'am," Billie rushed on, "but now that you bring it up . . ." he laughed, but he was not joking. Who better to be the next five-star general after Douglas MacArthur than Jason Billie—after he'd suppressed the rebellion, of course.

Chang-Sturdevant got back to business. "We are all concerned, General, about the amount of time it will take for you to gather and deploy your forces. Our troops on Ravenette have their backs to the sea and even the reinforcements we're sending in will not do more than bolster General Cazombi's position. By the way, I've also recommended him for promotion. You will both have one more star before you leave here and I'd appreciate it if you would be the one to inform General Cazombi of his promotion when you get to Ravenette."

Billie smiled, careful not to show his real feelings at the news. "He is a valiant soldier, ma'am, and I will be honored to pin on his third star when I get to Fort Seymour. He was sent to Ravenette because it was a known hotspot that required a steady hand and Alistair has provided that hand. He will prove a great asset to me when I arrive there to take command."

"But we must move with all deliberate speed, General. General Cazombi is faced with overwhelming forces and he could be wiped out at any time."

"I appreciate that, Madam President," Billie responded. He glanced sideways at Admiral Porter, who nodded that he should proceed. "Ma'am, it is my opinion, the opinion of us all on the staff, that General Lyons, who commands the Secessionist forces, is planning on a set-piece battle to take place in the vicinity of Ashburtonville. His plan is to draw us in to the relief of General Cazombi, whose army is being held hostage, and inflict enormous casualties on us in the hope that our will to pursue this war will weaken and we shall negotiate a peace favorable to the Secessionist Coalition's goal of independence. It is not my place to get into politics, ma'am, but even I can see that popular opinion can shift on this war since the people we're fighting are not the minions of an evil dictator but citizens of a democracy—our own people in fact. This is a civil war and it must be ended as quickly as possible. General Lyons wants a set-piece battle and I am going to give him that and I'm going to win it."

Chang-Sturdevant glanced over at Marcus Berentus, who nodded his agreement with Billie's assessment. "That makes sense," she admitted, "long casualty lists and military disasters will definitely weaken the will of our side to continue the fight." She paused. "Admiral Porter has shown me an outline of your plan, General, but tell me again how you plan to muster your troops and deploy them. I'm an old lady, General, and I need to have these military details explained to me." She smiled.

Billie grinned affably. "Old age runs in my family too, ma'am," he responded, and everyone laughed, but he knew very well that she understood perfectly what his plan was. She was just sizing him up. "Madam President, we all know that, in the end, soldiers pick up their weapons and attack their enemies but there is much that must happen before they get to that point. At least there is much that should take place if the battles are to be won." Chang-Sturdevant nodded that he should continue. "I cannot commence a massive combat operation like this without first integrating all the elements of this army, which will consist of regulars and reserve-component forces. As you know, the reserve and guard units are made up of willing men and women but not all are ready, not as ready as the regular components. We must ensure that any deficiencies in equipment and materiel are corrected before the guard units are sent into battle, especially since they will compose about two-thirds of my total combat force. And we must be sure, too, that the regulars are ready, up to strength in both personnel and materiel."

He called up a chart on the President's vidscreen that gave a detailed breakout of the forces he proposed for his army. "I will command an army of three infantry corps of about sixty thousand men each. One corps I scraped together from various regular troops stationed within the core of Human Space. I did that, ma'am, in order to leave the far-flung garrisons intact. The other two corps will be made up of guardsmen and reservists culled from those worlds that have agreed to support the war and who have troops ready for deployment. Other worlds will contribute forces when they are ready and as required. We cannot organize an army of this size in the face of the enemy. And I emphasize that none of these units has ever fought together under a coordinated battle plan. My commanders must be aware of that plan as well as the capabilities of the other units involved. We will have time en route to Ravenette to work out command-and-control problems. But all the bugs must be worked out before we arrive in orbit around Ravenette. That is why I am marshaling my forces on Arsenault, our training world. It is centrally located in Human Space, can accommodate an army of this size, and is a convenient jumping-off place for onward deployment. I must arrive at Ravenette with my army well organized, fully equipped, and all of my commanders fully cognizant of the role they will play in the battles to come."

"I must also add, Madam President," Admiral Porter spoke up for the first time, "that the same applies to the starships that will make up the fleet that will support General Billie's command. Many of the starships and crews come from the naval militias of the worlds that have agreed to contribute men and materiel, very few of which have ever undertaken actual wartime maneuvers. He is going to Ravenette with a powerful but basically untested weapon of war."

Chang-Sturdevant nodded. "Please continue, General."

"Then there are the logistics of an operation this size. Even if every unit arrives on Arsenault with its full combat load and its personnel complements fully manned, we must arrange for resupply and reinforcement because the level of combat we will encounter on Ravenette will be intense and will consume men and materiel at a very high rate. And we must also acknowledge that the enemy can reinforce his army on

Ravenette over well protected and relatively short distances while everything we need will have to go with us or come to us over the vast reaches of space."

"How long, do you estimate, between the time your forces assemble on Arsenault and your arrival in orbit around Ravenette?"

"Madam, transit time will be two weeks, that's a given. The troops are already on their way to Arsenault and I shall depart for there tomorrow and be on the ground in five days, so a week to assemble the forces and then a week to ten days to do the shakedown. Since Arsenault is also a military stores depot, we can make up any shortages while there. So I estimate one month from now we'll be ready to go into battle."

"One month," Chang-Sturdevant echoed. "Well, if your estimate of General Lyons's plan is correct, our garrison at Fort Seymour should still be intact," she sighed. "And frankly," she added, "I don't see a better plan than the one you have, General Billie."

"What is your estimate of casualties?" Marcus Berentus asked.

This was the one question Billie dreaded but he decided to be frank. "A minimum of ten percent in maneuver elements, sir, quite possibly higher than that in individual units engaged. When we succeed in breaking out of the defenses General Cazombi has established we will be attacking a well-fortified enemy and should anticipate a high rate of attrition. I apologize, ma'am," he nodded to Chang-Sturdevant, "for the necessity of speaking about casualties in such a callous manner and I assure you, the lives of my soldiers are as precious to me as they are to their own mothers."

"I appreciate that, but as a predecessor of yours said famously, any general who can't look dry-eyed upon a battlefield will wind up causing more casualties. Isn't that right?" Chang-Sturdevant asked.

Billie did not show his surprise. He was very familiar with Napoleon's axiom, which he never expected to hear from a person like Chang-Sturdevant. The old broad was sharper than he'd realized.

"I don't see any plans for including our Marines in your army, General."

The question caught Billie off guard. "Well, ma'am, they will be employed as available."

"And how will you employ them, General?" she asked.

"As fire brigades and as battering rams, Madam President, which is their traditional role in military operations of this size. When we mount the breakout Marines will be used to lead the effort. I leave it to Admiral Porter and the Commandant to arrange for follow-on forces, which no doubt will consist of Marine units."

"And their casualties, General?"

"Very high, ma'am."

Chang-Sturdevant was silent for a long moment. "Gentlemen," she addressed them all, "General Billie's plan is sound and I concur that he is the man to command this army," she nodded at Billie. "I commend you, General Billie, on your excellent work. Now as commander in chief of all our forces, I charge you with putting this army together and executing your mission with all deliberate speed." She stood up and the others immediately got to their feet too. "Keep me informed. Good day, gentlemen, and good luck."

"One thing, Madam President?" Billie asked. Chang-Sturdevant nodded. "On the ground with General Cazombi is a Brigadier General Sorca. He commanded the infantry division originally deployed to Fort Seymour. May I ask Your Excellency to recommend him for promotion to Major General? I know him and he will be a valuable assistant to me."

Chang-Sturdevant glanced at Marcus Berentus who shrugged. "General," she said after a brief pause, "if promoting your dog to major general will help win this war, I'd do it. Sure, you give me this officer's particulars and I'll add his name to yours and send them both up for confirmation. I guarantee you'll have your stars before you leave Arsenault. Marcus, stay with me for a while, would you?"

After Porter and Billie had left Chang-Sturdevant turned to Berentus and said, "Marcus, I like that guy. I think he's just the man to win this war for us."

"They call him 'Jason the Janus,' " Berentus said, shrugging. "I think we're in for a long war."

It took Chang-Sturdevant a moment to connect the nickname with the Roman solar deity, heaven's doorkeeper with two faces, one for the morning and one for the evening, and the patron of the beginning and end of things. His temple had always been open during war but closed during peacetime. She looked up sharply at her Minister of War, shaking her head to ward off the cold knot of doubt that had begun to form in the pit of her stomach.

* * *

In over thirty years as an army officer, General Jason Billie had never made a combat assault landing in an Essay. There is a first time for everything and that time was now, from Billie's flagship, the CNSS *Mindanao*. Granted, ground fire from the Coalition forces besieging General Cazombi's position was sporadic, but the admiral commanding the fleet was taking no chances with his starry passenger. The coxswain of Billie's Essay had warned him and his staff that the landing would be rough.

As soon as they were safely on the ground the Essay's coxswain surveyed the passenger compartment and cursed, "Goddamned army lubbers." He would have to clean up the mess they had left behind. Those worthies, on legs like rubber, staggered out of the machine into the sally port. General Billie emerged wearing his breakfast all down the front of his immaculate battle dress uniform.

Major General Alistair Cazombi and his aide, accompanied by Brigadier General Sorca, came to rigid attention and saluted as their new commander stumbled toward where they were standing. "My God, Cazombi, you've lost weight!" Billie exclaimed.

"Yessir, about fifteen kilos. It's Cazombi's New Rapid Weight Loss Program. Absolutely Guaranteed to Work or All Your Fat Will be Refunded: No sleep, lots of worry, and a strict diet of reduced field rations. Welcome to Bataan, sir."

Billie's eyebrows shot up at the associations the nickname brought to mind, but he shook hands with the three officers and rapidly introduced his staff. "What in the world is that smell, Alistair?" he exclaimed. "Is there an open latrine nearby?"

"We hardly notice it anymore, sir. It's ten thousand plus men with no water for washing and a sewage system that's overloaded. It'll be years before they can swim in Pohick Bay again. But I have to admit, sir, there is a certain, uh, 'freshness' to that smell I didn't notice before—" he tactfully left the sentence unfinished.

"Before we got here?" Billie looked around at his aide, Captain Chester Woo, who was standing there red-faced, a sickly grin on his face. "My Gawd, boy, change your drawers!" Billie exclaimed, self-consciously daubing at the puke on his own uniform. "Disgusting," he muttered.

"Well," he brightened, "gentlemen," he nodded at both Cazombi and Sorca, "I have good news for both of you!" He fumbled inside a pocket and fished out two small packages. "I have something here for you two that will add a few grams to your weight," he chuckled, "but they'll boost your morale considerably." He unwrapped the first package and handed Cazombi two sets of lieutenant general's stars. "The President got these approved for you before I left Earth. Congratulations." They shook hands. Then he handed Sorca a set of major general's stars. "Old friend, wear these with pride!"

"Gentlemen," Billie continued, "let us proceed to your command post." He draped his arms around the shoulders of his newly promoted officers. "In your new ranks I want you, Alistair, to be my deputy commander and you, Balca, to be my chief of staff! I need to keep you two close by, so I've got the best brains in this army accessible to me at all times!"

Cazombi said nothing, but the fact that Billie wanted him, a three-star general, to be his deputy and not to command troops spoke volumes. He'd be as useless as a vice president in that role. He was being put out to pasture. Sorca, as chief of staff, would have the real power at headquarters. Well, he promised himself, we'll just see about that.

"This way, sir," Cazombi gestured toward a tunnel. His words were punctuated by several heavy explosions that shook the ground. The arrivals glanced around apprehensively. "Oh, don't let that worry you, gentlemen," he told them, "it's just General Lyons's way of sending you greetings. No doubt he already knows the names of your company commanders."

So, Cazombi thought, Sorca and Billie are old friends? Lieutenant General Alistair Cazombi would never think of abandoning the soldiers who had fought for him here, no matter what, but the thought did occur to him now that he couldn't blame anybody else for resigning his commission immediately and getting the hell out of Bataan.

CHAPTER SEVENTEEN

The CNSS *Lance Corporal Keith Lopez* broke orbit hours after the last Marines of 34th FIST boarded and entered Beamspace two days later. After six days, with only one navigation-adjustment jump, she reentered Space-3, three days from Ravenette. Captain Bhofi called Brigadier Sturgeon to the comm shack as soon as communications were established with the headquarters of the besieged garrison at Pohick Bay.

"I believe you've had dealings with some of my Marines in the past, General," Brigadier Sturgeon said when he realized to whom he was talking planetside.

"On a mission I believe you aren't supposed to know much about, Brigadier," Major General Cazombi said in response. It wasn't possible to tell for sure through the attempted jamming by the Coalition forces, but his laconic tone sounded like he didn't necessarily agree with the decision to keep the commander of 34th FIST in ignorance of exactly what it was Company L had done on Avionia, a mission on which he was the commander and his only ground combat forces consisted of one Marine infantry company.

Then Cazombi turned all business and, once he determined exactly how much power was on its way to his aid, gave Sturgeon a thorough briefing on the current tactical situation.

"I'll work up plans, General," Sturgeon said when the briefing was finished. "We'll be prepared to come in hot."

"If your entire FIST is the same quality as Company L, I believe the forces opposing us are in for a very unpleasant surprise when you make planetfall. Cazombi out."

Sturgeon spent a few seconds staring at the tight-beam radio he'd been talking on as though it might shed light on what he should do, then handed the headset to the chief petty officer who ran the comm suite and thanked him for keeping the channel open despite the best efforts of the rebels to jam it.

"No problem, sir," the chief said. "I've a good crew. We pride ourselves on defeating all attempts to interfere with our beaming." He said it calmly, but his pride still showed through.

Sturgeon palmed the crystal on which he'd recorded the briefing, and headed for his shipboard operations center to brief his staff and begin making plans for the landing.

An hour before 34th FIST began to disembark from the *Lance Corporal Keith Lopez,* Brigadier Sturgeon called his top people together for a final briefing on the situation planetside and what they could expect when they landed.

He concluded with, "Gentlemen, you know your Marine Corps history as well as I do. Whenever the Marines work with the army, it's either to kick a door open for them to advance through or to rescue their sorry asses from whatever mess they've gotten themselves into. The army has gotten itself into a real mess this time, and we're the only thing between them and utter destruction. So we are making planetfall in the highest tradition of the Confederation Marine Corps and its predecessors. Marines have never lost a battle. Thirty-fourth FIST will *not* be the first Marine unit to do otherwise.

"Dismissed."

The Marines of Company L filed into the troop mess and, squad by squad, took seats at the tables. They weren't there for a meal, so the squad and fire team leaders sat with their men instead of segregating themselves at the NCO tables. Gunny Thatcher and the platoon sergeants came in after the junior NCOs and junior men and took station behind the tables near the entrance to the mess. The muted clangs, bangs, and shouts of cooks and messmen could be heard through the drawn shutters behind the serving counters; the voices of the seated Marines were even subdued.

After a couple of minutes, First Sergeant Myer entered from a side entrance and marched to the center of the serving counters. He faced the company, standing at attention, and slowly looked them over. Without visibly taking in a breath, he bellowed, "COMP-ney, a-ten-HUT!"

Throughout the mess, the Marines lurched to their feet and stood at attention. Top Myer looked back at the entrance through which he'd come. Captain Conorado marched in, followed by the company's other officers.

Conorado strode to Myer, who announced, "Sir, Company L all present and accounted for!"

"Thank you, First Sergeant," Conorado said formally.

Myer backed off and stood with the officers, midway between the entrance and the company commander, facing the men.

Conorado stood at ease, looking at his Marines. "Seats!" he ordered, and gave them a moment to get settled. "I don't have to tell you about war," he began. "Most of you remember Diamunde, which was the fiercest war I've served in. Most of you who weren't on Diamunde were on Kingdom, and the only difference between that campaign and a real war was the scale.

"On Kingdom, we were two FISTs against a division-size force of Skinks. Diamunde was bigger, there six FISTs kicked open the door for an army corps, and then fought alongside that corps against a planetary force armed with tanks—those of you who joined us after Diamunde and don't know what a tank is, ask your squadmates after you're dismissed.

"In a couple of days we will make planetfall on Ravenette, where we will join two badly mauled Confederation Army divisions in a holding action against the combined ground forces of a dozen worlds." He paused to let that sink in. "Those two army divisions have one major thing going for them, probably the only thing that's kept them fighting for as long as they have—their commander. Most of us have served under him before, and know how good he is. Major General Alistair Cazombi."

Conorado was interrupted by expressions of recognition and

surprise among his Marines. He patted the air to quiet them down. "That's right, the same 'Cazombi the Zombie' who was in command on Avionia, a man many of you think is good enough that he should be a Marine. Thirty-fourth FIST will be under his command. Make that, Thirty-fourth FIST will be a component unit under his overall command.

"Other Confederation forces, including a couple more FISTs, are on their way to help with the holding action. Our first job will be to help those two divisions hold until those reinforcements arrive. Then we will all hold on until a field army that is being organized arrives. Don't ask how long that will take, Confederation forces have been widely dispersed and divisions and brigades have to be drawn from widely separated locations to form the field army."

While Conorado was speaking, a navy yeoman slipped into the mess and handed a flimsy to the nearest officer, who happened to be Lieutenant Humphrey, the company executive officer. Humphrey signed for the flimsy and glanced at it while the yeoman slipped out as silently as he'd slipped in. Humphrey had no expression as he quietly slipped behind the other officers to hand the flimsy to Captain Conorado.

Conorado glanced at the message while he continued to deliver his briefing. "I said a moment ago that the two divisions already on Ravenette have an advantage. We have an advantage as well. Marines have a long history of going into situations where larger army units are pressed to the point of defeat, and rescuing them.

"I have just been handed an update on the planetside situation. During the short time since the *Lance Corporal Keith Lopez* returned to Space-3, there has been a change of command in the Confederation forces on Ravenette. Major General Cazombi isn't going to be in command much longer. An army general by the name of Jason Billie is en route and will take over on his arrival. Major General Cazombi will be the deputy commander of Confederation Forces, Ravenette."

He smiled grimly. "It doesn't matter who's in command in the theater of operations. We are Marines, and we're going to save the army's asses again. Expect to go in hot. That is all." Conorado abruptly turned and exited the mess, with the other officers tailing him.

"A-ten-HUT!" Top Myer roared. The footfalls of the officers were drowned out by the scraping of chairs as the Marines snapped to their feet. Myer watched until the door closed behind the officers, then turned and nodded at Gunny Thatcher, who marched to that side entrance and dogged it down. Staff Sergeant DaCosta, first platoon sergeant, dogged the main entrance and stood in front of it, mirroring Thatcher with arms folded across his chest.

Myer stood front and center, arms akimbo, glowering at the Marines for a long moment before snarling, "Siddown and listen up." He began pacing, looking into a distance somewhere beyond the surrounding walls, uncertain what to say in his unofficial briefing. He stopped when growing rustles of restlessness broke into his reverie and slowly turned to face the Marines again. The rustling stopped.

"You heard the Skipper: we're going to war," he began. "But this isn't just a war, it's a *civil* war. I'm sure all of you know enough history to know that civil wars are more vicious than any other kind of war. No matter what rationale they cloak themselves in—freedom, equality, religion, ideology, what have you—civil wars are almost always two or more factions fighting over who gets the biggest chunk of the pie, who gets the wealth and privilege.

"This isn't that kind of civil war, it's a war of secession."

Myer's brow furrowed. What could he say about wars of secession to tune his Marines up, to make them more alert and likely to survive the abattoir they were about to plunge into? Maybe if he came at it from the side—

"Civil wars are so bloody because each side is afraid of reprisals if they lose; it gives a different twist on 'fighting to the death.' And the fear of reprisals is realistic; history is filled with examples of the victorious side in a civil war slaughtering the losers. Few have ended without reprisals, whether death, imprisonment, or 'reeducation' of the losers—'reeducation' is a euphemism for imprisonment and forced indoctrination. In a war of secession, if the rebels win their independence from the larger body politic, reprisals are commonly carried out on those in the newly independent territory who opposed the rebellion, or merely didn't even participate. If they lose, they are subject to the most horrendous penalties, including penalties that go beyond the law. So the rebels fight fiercely, not only because they are convinced of the righteousness of their cause, but from fear of the consequences of failure."

Myer stopped and leaned forward, slowly sweeping the room with his gaze so that every Marine thought the first sergeant looked him directly in the eyes.

"You're Marines," he said slowly, "the best, toughest, winningest warriors humanity has ever known. But that doesn't mean that you can cakewalk when we make planetfall, just because we're up against a coalition of planetary forces. *Remember Diamunde!* That was just a planetary force, and we suffered heavy casualties. Ravenette is going to be tougher, because we're outnumbered even worse than on Diamunde. Diamunde was fought because of one man's megalomania and greed. *This* war is being fought by people who believe they are oppressed and want freedom. They think they are second-class citizens, that the Confederation of Human Worlds takes unfair advantage of them, that they are deliberately kept out of the mainstream and are denied their fair share of the wealth of the Confederation. They believe the only way they can correct the inequities committed against them is to rise up and overthrow what they see as a dictatorship.

"They're going to fight harder than anybody you've ever been up against."

The first sergeant glared over the Marines of Company L for a moment, then decided he needed to add a comment about the unexpected change in command planetside.

"Like most of you, I remember Major General Cazombi. Good man, good commander. Could have made a decent Marine brigadier. Every Marine I know who's ever dealt with him says the same thing. And you know Marines, if they say anything good about an army general, he's got to be someone special. As for General Billie, I've never met the man, never served under him. But when you get right down to it, it doesn't matter who the theater commander is. We are Marines. We will do what Marines always do: fight our battles aggressively, and win them."

He straightened to attention, gave his Marines another quick look over, then turned and marched to the door that Gunny Thatcher hastily undogged to allow him out. He hoped nobody noticed that he hadn't said he didn't know anybody who'd met or served under General Billie. He did know such Marines. Not a one of them had a good word for him. And the bad words they had went far beyond simple interservice rivalry.

* * *

The Marines lined up in the passageways outside their compartments. A casual passerby might have been forgiven for thinking the passageways were empty. Of course, if the passerby had tried to turn into the empty passageway, he'd collide with something he couldn't see—and hear the laughter of men he couldn't see. But the sailors of the *Lance Corporal Keith Lopez* knew the Marines were assembling prior to planetfall and those without an official need to visit wisely kept their distance from the troop areas of the starship.

The Marines wore combat chameleons, uniforms that picked up the color and visual texture of whatever was nearest and were therefore effectively suits of invisiblity.

Ensign Charlie Bass, followed closely by Staff Sergeant Hyakowa and a bosun's mate third class, stepped into the passageway that ran along the compartments his platoon was billeted in. Unlike their Marines, Bass and Hyakowa were visible. Their heads at least; they carried their helmets under their arms.

"Uncover!" Bass barked.

In a moment, thirty heads hovered at man-height along the sides of the corridor.

"Keep your damn helmets off until I tell you to put them on," Bass snarled. "I don't want to have to put mine on to find you." His look could have been interpreted as, "Who's the wiseass who told you to put your helmets on?" The Marines wisely chose not to answer the unspoken question.

"Let me hear you," Bass said. The disembodied heads bounced up and down; the only sound was the soft thudding of boot heels as the Marines came down from their bounces. Bass nodded, satisfied—noises made by unsecured equipment could give away an invisible Marine and at least partially negate the advantage his chameleon uniform gave him. "Everybody have everything?" he asked.

"Yessir," the Marines chorused. The loudest voices, almost solos in their volume, were those of the squad leaders; they'd already inspected their men and knew they had all their combat gear.

"Then nobody will mind if I check." Bass slipped off his chameleon gloves and began moving between the two rows of Marines. He touched here and there below the floating heads, not thoroughly inspecting anyone, but checking for one or another item on each Marine.

Finished, he stood at one end of the two lines and looked down them. "I wish I had an update for you," he said, "but I don't. All I can do is tell you what I think. Those poor doggies down there are getting beat to hell. The Coalition forces still haven't shown any sign of having weapons that can knock down an Essay making a combat assault landing, but that doesn't mean they don't. So Captain Bhofi is dropping us *two* hundred klicks offshore. That gives us just that much more time to fret over what kind of shit we'll hit when we cross the beach." He grinned. "Or that much more time to sleep while we can. Either way, we need to be ready to return fire as soon as the ramps on our Dragons drop.

"Now if this nice sailor behind me will lead the way, we'll go to the well deck." Bass turned around and had to laugh at the expression on the face of the junior petty officer who thought he hadn't been noticed by the eerie Marine officer he'd followed to the passageway. Bass gestured with a still-ungloved hand.

"Ah, y-yessir," the petty officer said. "If you'll follow me, please, sir."

Bass followed the sailor, third platoon followed Bass like ducklings. Hyakowa brought up the rear.

Twelve minutes and many turnings later, third platoon emptied into the well deck, where fifteen Essays hulked with their ramps open under the low overhead, exposing the three Dragons each held. The rest of Company L arrived at the same time. The ramps on four of the Dragons were closed; Kilo Company had already boarded. A chief petty officer shouted commands to junior petty officers and ratings, who ushered the Marines into the waiting Essays, where the platoon sergeants herded them into the encapsuled Dragons.

Inside the Dragons, the squad leaders took over, getting their men into the webbing that would secure them during the powered drop from orbit to winged flight. It didn't matter how many times they'd made planetfall, there was always somebody who needed help with the webbing straps. The platoon sergeants came through and made sure the squad leaders were properly secured, then took their own places, where they and the platoon commanders were checked by the Dragon crew chiefs. As the Marines on each Dragon were checked, the Dragon raised its ramp. The Essays' ramps remained down until every one was filled with its full complement of Marines.

Loud clicks reverberated across the well deck and penetrated into the Dragons as grappling hooks latched onto the Essays and lifted them into contact with the magnets on the overhead. A warning tone sounded, and a carefully modulated, female voice announced, "Preparing to evacuate atmosphere from the well deck. All hands, vacate the well deck. I say again, all hands, vacate the well deck. You have forty-five seconds to leave the well deck." There was a pause, then the voice spoke again, "All hands, vacate the well deck. You have thirty seconds to leave the well deck." The message repeated at twenty seconds, then counted down from ten. Even inside the hermetically sealed Essays, ears popped when the air was sucked out of the well deck.

A bosun's whistle sounded throughout the starship, and the female voice announced, "All hands, now hear this. Secure for null-G. I say again, all hands secure for null-G. Null-G will commence in thirty seconds." The seconds ticked by, with another warning at twenty seconds and a countdown from ten. The entire universe seemed to jerk when the *Lance Corporal Keith Lopez*'s artificial gravity was turned off.

A moment later, a subsonic rumble was felt as the well deck's floor was rolled out of the way, exposing the interior to space. The magnets and grapples holding the Essays released and plungers in the overhead gave the shuttles a downward push. The Essays floated gently out of the well deck, and the coxswains fired vernier jets to control attitude and maintain formation. In their slowly decreasing orbits, the Essays moved ahead of their mother ship. Once they were clear, the landing officer gave the launch command, and the coxswains fired their thrusters, shooting the Essays ahead of the *Keith Lopez* and into a higher orbit until the coxswains fired vernier jets on the Essays' topsides to point them planetward.

The landing officer's command and the manipulations of the coxswains weren't necessary, the launch was controlled by computers, but the command was given and buttons pushed anyway, just in case something went wrong with a computer. Just minutes after being nudged from the well deck, the fifteen Essays were diving under power, directly at the surface of Ravenette.

Most orbit-to-surface shuttles spiraled down, taking as many as three orbits to reach planetfall. But Marines didn't make planetfall gently, even when they weren't expecting trouble when they reached the ground. Instead, Marines always made a combat assault landing—powered flight, straight down until it seemed inevitable that they would make catastrophic contact with the surface, before breaking out of the plunge to spin into a tight, velocity-eating spiral and popping drogue chutes, then ultimately gently setting down on the sea. Everybody but the Marines thought they were crazy for *always* making combat assault landings, but 34th FIST *was* expecting a hostile reception, so this time nobody thought the Marines were odd at all. Which didn't stop the sailors aboard the *Lance Corporal Keith Lopez* from thinking the Marines were crazy for being willing to dive headlong into combat.

At first, the atmosphere was negligible, and all that disturbed the Marines in the Dragons was the shaking of the Essays caused by the firing of the thrusters. Then the density of the atmosphere grew to tenuous, and the Essays began rattling like poorly-sprung landcars speeding on a gravel road; the webbing began to adjust to the tossing and pitching of the Essays. From there on, the atmosphere steadily thickened, and the landcar's road became potholed, and the potholes steadily grew in size and depth. The Marines had good reason for calling their method of planetfall, "High speed on a rocky road."

There wasn't a Marine in 34th FIST who hadn't made at least three planetfalls; many of them had long before quit counting the times they'd gone at high speed on that rocky road. Still, at least one Marine on at least one Dragon in nearly every Essay gave in to the roiling of his stomach and had to use the suction hose that hovered over each man's face. A couple didn't manage to get the cup to their mouths in time, and escaped globules of stomach gunk flitted about the interior of their Dragons, to the severe discomfort of their companions.

When the Essays cut their thrusters and their wings swung open, the bottom suddenly fell out of the powered dive. They leveled off to swoop into velocity-eating spirals. The Essays jerked when their drogue chutes popped open, further slowing their speed and rate of descent.

The Essays, still in formation, splashed down with unexpected gentleness after their violent plunge through the atmosphere and pointed their noses at the shoreline, two hundred kilometers beyond the horizon. Their front ramps lowered into the oceanic swells and the Dragons rumbled off, into the water, and began the swim to the distant shore. As soon as the Dragons were clear, the Essays launched back to mate with their mother ship.

At about the same time the Essays carrying the Dragons touched down, the Essays of the second wave, which had begun spiraling earlier, dipped their noses and opened their ramps to the air. The Raptors and hoppers of 34th FIST slid out then dropped a thousand meters before the Raptors' engines lit off and they formed up and sped toward land. The hoppers took nearly as much altitude for their engines to light, and almost as much time to gain formation and head landward; they rocked when the air turbulence of the passing Raptors buffeted them.

The *Lance Corporal Keith Lopez* relayed communications between General Cazombi and Brigadier Sturgeon, who was approaching the Bataan Peninsula via hopper. Sturgeon drew up hasty plans and issued orders to his battalion and squadron commanders. There was a hole in the defensive dike that his Marines had to plug as soon as they reached the beach. Drive the enemy away and hold position.

CHAPTER EIGHTEEN

The twenty-four Dragons of 34th FIST's transportation company hit the beach in two waves. The twenty Dragons carrying the blaster companies of the infantry battalion headed inland in three columns, led by the two command Dragons. The two maintenance Dragons pulled into a prepared laager to set up shop. The FIST's Raptors were flying endless sorties to hammer a rebel brigade that had broken a hole in the defenders' main line of resistance. The second line was barely holding on.

It was that hole that the infantry battalion was headed for.

"Off, off, off!" the platoon sergeants roared when the Dragons pulled up behind a rise and dropped their rear-facing ramps.

"Out, out, out!" the squad leaders bellowed.

The fire team leaders hustled their men out of the Dragons and aimed them at the squad leaders, who stood holding a bare arm high to be seen.

"On me!" the platoon commanders shouted, and looked out of their open helmets so their Marines could see them.

Heavy fire sounded from not too far beyond the rise, piercing the rumble and clank of combat vehicles; the louder booms of plasma fire from the cannons of diving Raptors punctuated the battle din.

"You know what to do," Captain Conorado told his platoon commanders on his helmet comm's command circuit. "Do it!"

"Third platoon, follow this soldier!" Ensign Charlie Bass said into his all-hands circuit. The soldier designated as third platoon's guide didn't flinch from the invisible hand that gripped his shoulder; he was too shaken by the violence with which his position had been overrun for the mere invisibility of reinforcements to faze him. Bass gave the soldier a push, and the man trotted in a staggering gait behind the rise to a trench he led third platoon through.

The battle din crescendoed on the other side of the rise. The guide led the Marines through a maze of trenches until they reached a series of bunkers set into a two-and-a-half-meter-deep trenchline facing the enemy assault.

"Positions!" Bass said into his all-hands circuit. Even with the ears on the helmets of his Marines turned down to damp the battle noise, he had to shout to be heard over it. He transmitted a quickly drawn map to the squad leaders, showing the squads where to take position.

Sergeant Linsman looked at his surroundings to orient himself with the map, then took a quick look over the lip of the trench to check on the disposition of the enemy. He saw direct fire guns moving into position.

"Stay out of the bunkers!" Linsman ordered second squad. "Use the fire step, fire over the trench."

"You heard the man," Corporal Claypoole shouted. "Fire over the lip."

His last words were drowned out by the *crack sizzle* of Lance Corporal Schultz's first shot at the soldiers of the Coalition brigade that was advancing by fire and maneuver. An enemy soldier fell and didn't get back up.

Lance Corporal MacIlargie hopped onto the seventy-centimeter-high firing step six meters from where he'd seen Schultz's shot, and rose up just high enough to see where he was shooting. Claypoole mounted the step between his men.

Seventy-five meters to second squad's right, Sergeant Ratliff saw the same situation Linsman saw and knew the direct fire guns would first rain their fire on the bunkers—making the bunkers death traps when the guns opened up—and ordered his men to set up on the trench's fire step as well.

Corporal Dean positioned Lance Corporal Godenov and PFC Quick and took his own position just in time to see a company or more rise up from a trench less than fifty meters in front of him and charge at third platoon, screaming and laying down fire as they ran.

"Take them down!" Dean screamed. He started snapping shots off, shifting his point of aim with each press of his blaster's firing lever. To his sides, he heard Godenov and Quick also firing rapidly, but was so intent on what he and his men were doing that he wasn't even aware of the heavy fire coming from the rest of the platoon. Most of the bolts from the Marines' blasters hit enemy soldiers—there were too many of them for level shots to miss—but there were so many of them, and they were so close, that most of them reached the trench.

Dean thrust his blaster between the legs of a soldier just as the man began to jump into the trench, he barely had time to see the look of surprise on the rebel's face at not seeing anybody in the trench when his expression changed to horror at his abrupt loss of balance. The soldier fell forward, flipping over, and hit the bottom of the trench face first with a sickening *snap*.

But Dean didn't have any time to deal with the fallen soldier; another jumping body clipped his back, jolting him and knocking him into the face of the trench. Dean spun around to his right and slammed the butt of his blaster into the back of the head of the rebel, who was off-balance from clipping someone he hadn't seen. The man flew forward into the other side of the trench.

Confused by not finding anybody in the trench, terrified at being struck by invisible forces, yelling and gesticulating rebels milled about. Many of them began firing wildly—but the Marines held their fire at such close quarters so they wouldn't accidentally shoot each other. Instead, the Marines used their blasters as quarterstaffs, the way they'd been taught in Boot Camp but most had never had to do in combat. Some dropped their blasters in favor of their knives.

Before the last of the rebel soldiers reached the trench, their officers and sergeants realized that instead of the disorganized and demoralized soldiers they expected to close with, they were up against Confederation Marines in chameleon uniforms. They began to shout orders, changing the assault tactics and easing their troops back from the edge of panic. The soldiers stopped their wild fire and paired off, standing back to back, using their rifles in the same manner the Marines were using theirs—they too had trained with pugil sticks.

But the Marines could see their targets, the Coalition troops could only see an occasional splotch of blood or gob of mud bobbing or twisting in the air—and their numbers had been severely reduced during the long minutes before their officers and soldiers began to restore order.

Dean held his blaster with his left hand behind the handgrip and the right on the forestock. Two soldiers jumped back to back before him, neither facing him directly. Dean leveled his blaster and threw his entire weight into a thrust, striking one soldier in the middle of his face, between nose and cheek, with the muzzle of his blaster. He followed through by swinging the butt of the blaster around to slam into the side of the second man's head, just behind and below the ear, under the edge of his helmet. Both men dropped hard, and Dean ignored them to viciously slam another soldier off his feet.

Two meters away, Godenov ducked under an undirected cross-butt stroke and dug the point of his knife up under the man's sternum, through his diaphram, and into his heart. Godenov jerked the blade out as the soldier fell away, slashing up and to the side at the neck of the man's partner, who was turning to see why they'd lost contact. That soldier dropped his weapon and gurgled as his hands tried to stanch the blood spurting from his opened throat.

In the opposite direction from Godenov, Quick was staggered and knocked over by a wild swing from a rebel behind him. Quick turned his fall into a somersault and rolled to the side when he came out of it, just in time to miss three rifle butts that slammed into the floor of the trench where he'd just been. He jumped to his feet, but he'd lost his blaster. He hopped back from the three rifle butts that were swinging wildly in hope of hitting him, drew his knife, and dove under the three soldiers, thrusting up. One of the soldiers shrieked and fell away as the knife tore into his groin, but the force of his fall tore the knife from Quick's hand. Quick rolled hard, away from the wounded man and into the legs of one of the others, spilling him onto his face. But his uniform picked up enough dust from the trench floor to make him hazily visible. The third soldier saw the spectral image and hammered the butt of his rifle into it. Quick screamed when his right humerus shattered under the blow. The soldier flipped his rifle around and pointed the muzzle down, to shoot the fallen Marine—

But Dean heard Quick's scream, saw what was happening, and shot first. The rebel soldier folded over with a hole burned through his chest.

"Izzy, to me!" Dean called on his comm. "Use your infra." He reached Quick in two strides and stood over him, his blaster held ready to strike with either end, or to fire if he had a good target.

"Here I am," Godenov said an instant before his back made contact with Dean's.

The two fended off other rebel soldiers, who spotted Quick's ghostly, writhing body and thought he would be an easy kill.

But it had taken the attackers too long to realize who they were fighting and adjust their tactics, and the fight was already winding down. It was only a couple of minutes more before the surviving rebel soldiers threw down their weapons and surrendered to the men they couldn't see.

First squad's fight in the trench was over, but the battle still raged. After trussing their prisoners with wrist ties, they returned their attention to the soldiers advancing by fire and maneuver, now not much more than a hundred meters distant. The first of the direct fire guns reached position and opened fire.

Seventy-five meters to the left, second squad's fire changed from individual shots at targets of opportunity to volley fire directed by Sergeant Linsman.

"Grazing fire, ninety meters," Linsman calmly ordered. "Fire!"

Ten blasters *crack-sizzled* and ten bolts of plasma skimmed low over the ground to strike ninety meters downrange. The angle at which they hit glanced them upward to chest-height at a hundred meters, and the impact itself dispersed them, widening their hitting areas, so that instead of ten tiny bits of killing star-stuff, they were ten scythes of murderous plasma—their casualty-producing range was increased from points along a thirty-meter-wide swath to cover half of the swath, a better than fifty-fifty chance of hitting anyone standing along the line.

"Shift left ten meters, the same," Linsman ordered. "Fire!" The Marines fired again, their aiming points ten meters left of where they'd fired the first volley.

"Right, twenty meters, the same," Linsman called. "Fire!" The third volley hit beginning ten meters to the right of the first.

Then the direct fire guns opened up and the ground shook with the impact of their high-explosive rounds. Debris showered down on the Marines, and dust clouds enveloped them.

"Casualties, report!" Linsman ordered.

"Hammer, Wolfman, sound off!" Corporal Claypoole shouted.

Lance Corporal Schultz grunted, and fired off a bolt to show he was all right.

"I'm okay," MacIlargie answered. "I think."

"What do you mean, you think?" Claypoole demanded.

"A lot of shit just landed on me, that's what I mean," MacIlargie snapped back.

"Are you hurt?" Claypoole barked.

"No."

"Dumbass, that's what I asked." Claypoole reported, "Third fire team, no one's hurt." First and second fire teams had already reported; second squad had no casualties.

"Count off from the left," Linsman said. "Even numbers, use light gatherers, odds use infras. Count now."

"One," PFC Summers counted.

"Two," Corporal Kerr said.

"Th-three," Corporal Doyle stammered.

"Four," from Lance Corporal Fisher. And so on, through Lance Corporal Schultz at ten.

"Individual fire," Linsman ordered, "pick your targets." Until the dust cleared, they wouldn't be able to see an aiming line for effective volley fire. Second squad's fire picked up, and became much heavier when the gun squad's second team joined them, spewing out hundred-bolt bursts from side to side. But the fire wasn't equal from all blasters.

Schultz swore under his breath; he was number ten, using his light-gathering screen. The light gatherer did a poor job of penetrating the dust clouds and he couldn't pick out targets to fire at as effectively as he'd like. He slipped his infra into place and began picking off the red blotches that appeared in his view. After four bolts, he switched back to the light gatherer. The dust clouds were thinning, and he was able to see maneuvering soldiers—and shoot them.

Then the direct fire guns fired again. More debris rained into the trench and more dust clouds billowed up. With a roar of tortured, snapping metal, the bunker a few meters to Schultz's right exploded. An inch-thick sheet of fractured plasteel armor plate was wrenched off its foundation and crashed onto Schultz.

The impact of the armor plate and debris it threw out battered Claypoole and almost knocked him over. "Hammer, sound off," he shouted.

Silence from that side.

"Come on, Hammer. Grunt or something. Let me know you're all right!"

Still no reply.

"Hammer!" Claypoole sidled to Schultz's position. Through his infra, he saw a hand splayed out from under the plasteel. He grabbed it and gave it a tug. "Hammer, speak to me!"

No response.

Claypoole gripped the edge of the sheet of armor and heaved. It *cracked* and bent ominously in the middle.

"Oh, shit," Claypoole murmured and eased the plasteel back into place—the place the sheet bent was right where he thought Schultz's back was; if it broke there the jagged edge might tear into Schultz's spine, and he might die before he could be extracted.

If he wasn't dead already.

"Corpsman up!" Claypoole called on the fire team leaders' circuit. Then to Linsman, "Hammer's pinned under a sheet of plasteel. I can't move it without it breaking on him."

"Get back to your position, I'll check it out," Linsman said. "Doc, you on your way?"

"I'm almost there," Hospital Mate Third Class Hough replied. "I see you."

"Help's coming, Hammer. Hang in there." Reluctantly, Claypoole backed away from Schultz and resumed his position on the firing step. He swore when he looked over the lip of the trench, the maneuvering enemy soldiers were only seventy-five meters away. He resumed fire.

Doc Hough reached Schultz right after Linsman did. The squad leader was examining the plasteel armor that held Schultz pinned to the wall of the trench. It was definitely too heavy for him to move by himself, because of the crack in its middle, probably too heavy for even two men to move without risk of the jagged edge of the fracture doing severe damage to the man under it.

He told that to Hough while the corpsman snaked his telltales under the sheet's edge. Hough merely grunted, and focused on his display. After a few seconds, graph lines juttered up and down on the display. Hough grunted.

"He's alive but unconscious. There's nothing immediately life threatening, but we have to get that armor off him—it's compressing his chest and he isn't able to breathe freely." Hough lifted his chameleon screen so Linsman could see his face. Linsman did the same.

Screaming overhead made them look up—a division of Raptors was diving for the ground.

"Shit!" Hough swore. "Grab the other side and hold it in place."

Linsman swore and scuttled to the far side of Schultz. The two gripped the sheet firmly, one hand above and the other below the fracture. The air shook with the sonic boom from the four aircraft, almost wrenching the armor from their grip. The sheet fractured farther, but held.

Then the Raptors fired their cannons, and the ground bucked from plasma strikes.

The ground slammed upward on the plasteel and the air pushed back on the sheet's top. The armor plate snapped.

"Away!" Hough shouted, and pushed both halves of the now broken plasteel plate away from Schultz. Linsman did the same. The bottom half fell away, but the top half was too heavy, and slid down the inner face of the bottom; its ragged top tore along Schultz's back.

Schultz's body arched and a *huff* of agony burst from his mouth. The back of his chameleons began turning red.

Hough didn't hesitate, he shoved an arm under Schultz's chest and grabbed him under the arms to lower him face down to the floor of the trench. The big man's weight staggered him and his grip began to slip. Then it eased when Linsman reached in and helped. Together, they lay Schultz on his stomach. The corpsman tore the back of Schultz's shirt, but couldn't examine the wounds because the blood was flowing too copiously. He quickly stuffed packing where the blood seemed to be heaviest, then applied synthskin over Schultz's entire back.

"I'm not sure this'll stop the bleeding," Hough told Linsman. "I need to do something more radical." He reached into his medkit as he talked and pulled out a black block. He opened it and shook it out; it was a stasis bag. With the squad leader's help, he rolled Schultz into the bag and closed it. The bag's whirring was almost inaudible when he turned it on. In seconds, the stasis bag would put Schultz into a state of suspended animation that would maintain him in his current condition until he reached a hospital.

"Gotta go," Hough said, closing his medkit and rising to his feet. "Got another call." He ran toward first platoon's position, saying, "Tell me what to expect," into his comm.

Corporal Dean injected a nerve blocker into PFC Quick's right shoulder as soon as the surviving Coalition soldiers surrendered. The blocker did its job quickly, and Quick stopped whimpering.

"Corpsman up," Dean called. "Quick's down with a broken arm," he said when Doc Hough ran up. "I've got him settled, but his arm needs attention before the broken bones start cutting tissue and blood vessels."

"Any sign of bleeding?" Hough asked.

"Not external. At least his chameleons aren't turning red."

"What did you use on him?"

"Nerve blocker in his shoulder."

"Where's the break?"

"Upper arm."

"Cut through the material from shoulder to elbow. Let me see your arm."

Dean reached for his knife with one hand and held the other high over his head to let the sleeve slide down, exposing his arm.

"I see you."

Dean had almost finished cutting Quick's sleeve open when Hough dropped down next to him.

"Out of my way," the corpsman said and gave the injury a quick visual examination before gently probing it with his fingertips. Quick's arm was deeply bruised and swollen from elbow to shoulder, and bone fragments moved freely under Hough's gentle probing. He turned to open his medkit. "Don't you have a firefight to deal with?" he asked, and pulled out a fracture stabilizing kit.

"Ah, yeah," Dean said. For a moment he'd forgotten about the battle raging around them. "Is he going to be all right?"

"Barring complications, he'll be back to duty in a week. Won't you, Quick?" He finished applying the stabilizer and peeled Quick's eyelids back, checking for signs of shock.

Quick gave a weak chuckle. "I'm a badass Marine, Doc. Maybe sooner."

"Sure you will."

More Raptors screamed overhead. Hough looked up to see two pairs of Raptors plummeting straight down. He watched as they fired their cannons then bounced almost 180 degrees to climb back to altitude. He put his hands on Quick's arm above and below the fracture to keep it stable when the shockwaves from the plasma bolts reached them.

"What's happening out there?" Hough asked.

"They're running!" Dean shouted. "We did it, we stopped them!"

"Us and a Raptor squadron," Hough said softly.

CHAPTER NINETEEN

The Coalition's badly battered soldiers fell back all across the line they'd nearly broken through; 34th FIST had suffered relatively few casualties in throwing them back. The recently inserted Force Recon units had succeeded in disabling enough of the Coalition's ground-based mobile antisatellite guns for the navy to lay a string-of-pearls.

Commander van Winkle, the FIST's infantry battalion commander, bent over, studying his situation maps and plots and nearly salivated. The real-time images downloaded from the navy's string-of-pearls clearly showed the beaten soldiers running in a disorganized rout.

"It's easier to beg forgiveness than to get permission," he muttered.

"Sir? You said something?" Captain Uhara, his executive officer, said.

"Hum? Oh, nothing. Just thinking out loud." He abruptly stood erect. "I have a new order for the company commanders," he told Uhara. "Prepare to move out. We are going to pursue. Stand by to conference."

"Prepare to move out, we will pursue, stand by to conference. Aye aye, sir." Uhara gave van Winkle an odd look before he turned to his comm to pass the order to the company commanders. He'd heard the orders Brigadier Sturgeon gave during planetfall, and knew the orders from Ravenette defense HQ was to drive the enemy away and then hold the line. Still, he knew, Marines didn't hold, they advanced.

Van Winkle ordered Captain Rhu-Anh, his intelligence officer, to launch the UAV platoon's spy-eyes, and Captain Likau, the logistics officer, to get as many logistics carriers as possible in fifteen minutes loaded with blaster and assault gun batteries, water, medical supplies, and rations—in that order. He turned to Uhara and asked, "Are they ready?"

"Standing by, sir."

Van Winkle held his hand out, Uhara slapped the comm into it. "Company commanders," van Winkle said into the comm, "the enemy has been driven back and is in full flight. We are going to keep them in flight. Move out!" He handed the comm back to Uhara, who nervously cleared his throat.

"Sir, when are we going to inform the brigadier?"

Van Winkle graced him with a feral grin. "When we make contact again."

"Now hear this," Captain Conorado said into his all-hands circuit. "The enemy we have just thrown back is in full retreat. We are going to pursue. Our casualties are already at the battalion aid station, or en route to it, so they're in good hands, and we don't need to worry about them. We go over the top and move out in one minute.

"That is all."

Conorado toggled the all-hands circuit off and looked at Lieutenant Humphrey, Company L's executive officer. His shrug went unseen in his chameleons. "This is what we call a 'fluid situation,' " he said. "All orders are subject to change without notice." Both of them also knew the orders Brigadier Sturgeon had received from General Billie's headquarters.

"What is this happy horseshit?" Corporal Claypoole gasped when he heard Captain Conorado's order. He was more shaken than he could have imagined by the loss of Lance Corporal Schultz.

Lance Corporal Godenov looked open-mouthed in Claypoole's direction and mutely shook his head. His head shake went unseen by his equally invisible fire team leader.

"Cut the crap, Claypoole," Sergeant Linsman snapped. "We're taking the battle to the enemy. Get ready to go over the top."

"Kick them while they're down," Corporal Kerr added. "If we kick them hard enough, they won't get back up."

Nobody had time to add anything more; the order came and

Company L surged over the lip of the trench and moved forward at a trot in pursuit of the enemy.

It didn't take them long to catch up.

Brigadier Sturgeon's mouth pursed as he looked at the movement on his real-time situation map, downloaded from the string-of-pearls in orbit around Ravenette. *What's going on there?* he wondered, but before he could speak, Captain Shadeh, his F1, handed him the comm.

"Incoming from Infantry, sir," Shadeh said.

"FIST Actual," Sturgeon said into the comm. "Over."

"FIST Actual, Infantry Six Actual," Commander van Winkle's voice came over the comm. "We have pursued the enemy and have them pinned at the foot of a hill."

"Can you overrun them?" Sturgeon asked. He didn't mention that the infantry was supposed to have held in place when they drove the Coalition forces away from their breakthrough.

"Not quickly, FIST Actual. At the moment, all we can do is hold them in place. There is another battalion of them dug in on top of the hill and they've started calling for artillery. All we can do right now is hold them in place. Over."

"Wait one." Sturgeon turned to Colonel Ramadan. "Contact Commander Wolfe, I want him to put his entire squadron on that hill to knock out a dug-in infantry battalion. And my compliments to Lieutenant General Cazombi, I'd appreciate it if he would have his artillery put some counterbattery fire on the artillery firing at my infantrymen."

"Right away, sir," Ramadan said, turning away to issue the order to the FIST's composite squadron and make the request to the army. He permitted himself a slight smile. Going direct to Cazombi would get the FIST's infantry the artillery support it needed; going to General Billie's HQ would probably only get an order to have the infantry immediately break contact and withdraw.

"Infantry Actual," Sturgeon returned to his comm, "air support is on its way, and I've requested counterbattery fire. How exposed are you?" The sitmap showed a webbery of narrow trenches spidering their way out from the hill; tiny blips indicated that the Marines were in the trenches.

"Artillery is light so far, and no reports of casualties. We're moving forward; I want to get so close to the enemy positions at the foot of the hill that their artillery will risk hitting their own people if they keep firing at us."

"Do it. FIST Actual out."

Sturgeon looked reflective as he put the comm down. General Billie's orders had been quite clear—and he'd been just as clear in passing them on: Thirty-fourth FIST was to remain in place after driving the enemy out. He, Sturgeon, hadn't countermanded those orders; therefore van Winkle had acted on his own initiative in pursuing the enemy.

Sturgeon allowed a smile to flicker across his face. Marines only defend when they have to, they prefer attacking. Van Winkle had acted in the highest traditions of the Marine Corps. Besides, when you've got the bastards by the short and curlies, you don't let go. If you knock them out now, they just might not come back later. That means you win. And in war, winning is the only thing that matters.

He heard aircraft overhead and looked out the gunport of the bunker where he'd established his temporary headquarters. High up he saw the six Raptors of the composite squadron arrowing in formation toward the hill the infantry battalion was attacking. Trailing lower were the eleven hoppers of the squadron's hopper section. Without being told, he knew that each of the hoppers was loaded with guns and rockets, even though normally no more than two of the tactical transport aircraft were so armed. At a distance, echoing so he couldn't tell exactly where they were firing from, he heard the first salvos of the army's counterbattery fire.

This time, he didn't allow his smile to only flicker.

Corporal Joe Dean was so perturbed he didn't know whether to mutter his displeasure to any gods who might be listening, or loudly swear at them for the predicament he found himself in. So he compromised, and swore under his breath. Normally in a movement like this, Lance Corporal Schultz would be on the platoon point—or the point of whichever squad was most likely to make first contact. But Schultz was out of action for who knew how long. Which was why Dean and Lance Corporal Isadore "Izzy" Godenov were leading first squad along one of the narrow trenches that led to the foot of the hill the remnants of the Coalition attackers were pinned against.

Now, there wasn't any doubt about it, Izzy *was* good enough. But PFC Quick was also out of action, which left only the two of them in the fire team, and Dean really didn't think the two of them were enough to hold the most vulnerable position in the platoon. He felt a sudden jolt—maybe Rabbit, Sergeant Ratliff, thought he and Izzy *were* just as good as the Hammer. Then he almost doubled over with a different kind of jolt when he thought maybe Rabbit thought he and Izzy were expendable.

Dean ducked lower in the trench and tried to pay even closer attention to his surroundings. Not that he could see much from below the lip of the zig-zagging trench. The trench turned every ten meters or so, sometimes almost doubling back on itself. None of its straights were in line of sight of the hill or the Marines would have been in line of sight of the defenders' trench lines. So the enemy on the hilltop couldn't fire into a trench at the advancing Marines except at its corners and bends. So far, none of the artillery rounds impacting in the area had hit inside any of the trenches—at least not as far as Dean knew—though he'd been spattered a couple of times by dirt and debris kicked up by near misses.

So just about all he could see was the stretch of trench in front of him and the sky above. He had to keep flipping his infra screen into place to see Godenov in front of him. It was around the next corner that he—and Godenov—*needed* to be able to see.

Godenov had just stopped to cautiously peer around another corner when a shrieking in the sky made Dean look up. He didn't see the source of the bone-piercing noise immediately, but when he did he let out a whoop. It was the FIST's six Raptors diving on the hill. Their cannons opened up, ripping pulses of plasma groundward in such a rapid stream they looked like a solid line of star-stuff. The Raptors reached the bottom of their dives then bounced skyward, their plasma streams battering the hilltop and setting off secondary explosions. Then the hilltop just erupted, and there was a rapidly expanding cloud of dirt racing skyward in which larger objects could be seen twisting and tumbling.

The shockwave of the eruption almost knocked Dean off his feet, even though he was low enough in the trench. His helmet's ears, which he'd had turned up to detect the sounds of soldiers who might be in the trench ahead of him, struggled to damp out the noise of the explosion.

Then the shockwave struck before he regained his balance, and he thudded to the bottom of the trench, the breath squeezed from his body. Gasping, he pushed himself up to hands and knees, one hand automatically groping for his blaster.

"Izzy!" he croaked into the fire team circuit. His ears were ringing and he barely heard his own voice, so he called again, louder.

"I think I've got all my parts," Godenov replied, but his voice wasn't strong. "I'm not sure they all work, but I'm pretty sure they're still here."

Dean slid his infra into place and looked toward Godenov. He saw a man-shaped red blur on the trench's floor. "Can you stand?" he asked, rising to a crouch himself. The red blur humped up and part of it detached from the ground.

"On my feet," Godenov said.

Dean started to say something more, but stopped when Ensign Bass's voice came over the platoon circuit.

"If that knocked *us* down, how do you think it made the bad guys feel? Move out, fast, before they can recover." To Dean, Bass sounded as bad as he felt.

"You heard the man, Izzy," Dean said into the squad circuit. "Let's move."

Just then, the hoppers whooshed by overhead. Their guns and rockets blasting the foot of the hill weren't as loud as the Raptors' plasma barrage nor did they start a shockwave to rock the Marines in the trenches—but when the Marines reached the foot of the hill, the surviving rebel soldiers surrendered without firing a shot.

Commander van Winkle checked his sitmaps and ordered his companies to advance to the next Coalition position, six kilometers farther out. General Cazombi's counterbattery fire had been effective at silencing the rebel artillery firing at the Marines, so Brigadier Sturgeon asked him to have his artillery fire on the infantry's next objective.

Brigadier Sturgeon ignored the sussuration of voices in his temporary command center; they were the background a commander lived in. If anybody had something important that he needed to act on, they'd get his attention. His people knew what to do, and once he gave them their orders, he got out of their way and let them do their jobs. The squadron was busy refueling, rearming, and relaunching its aircraft so the Raptors would be in position to strike the next hilltop as soon as the infantry was in position and the hoppers could give direct support to the infantry assault. Intelligence was keeping tabs on enemy movement and analyzing the data being beamed down from the string-of-pearls satellites, as well as intercepting and attempting to decode enemy radio messages broadcast rather than tight-beamed. Logistics was readying pallets of the three Bs—"Bullets, Beans, and Bandages" was what they used to be called—and speeding them off to catch up with the infantry so they'd be close at hand when the Marines needed them. The medical section was dealing with the casualties from the initial fight and preparing to patch up casualties from the next fight. Operations was keeping close track of everything everybody else was doing, so they could draw or revise battle plans as needed or on Sturgeon's order.

All Sturgeon had to do was sit back and watch—and be prepared for the next time he had to make a decision or give an order. That was the atmosphere into which an officious voice intruded.

"What's going on here?"

The background of voices paused as the Marines glanced at the entrance of the bunker, then resumed almost immediately.

Sturgeon looked up more casually; he recognized the voice from having heard it before. He stood.

"General," he said, and politely gestured General Billie into the bunker. If he was surprised by Billie's well-groomed and tailored appearance in the middle of a battle, he didn't show it. Nor did he react to Billie's expression of supercilious superiority.

Billie strode into the command bunker and haughtily looked around at the busy staff before bestowing his imperial gaze on the Marine commander. His eyes widened slightly and his nostrils flared when he saw Sturgeon's back—the FIST commander had returned his attention to his sitmaps.

"If the general would look at this, I'll bring you up to date, sir," Sturgeon said without looking back at Billie.

Billie rigidly stepped to Sturgeon's side. Who did this mere *Marine* think he was, turning his back on the Supreme Commander like that?

"Sir, as you can see," Sturgeon said, pointing from place to place on the sitmap as he briefed Billie, "my Marines successfully threw the rebels back from their breakthrough. They have maintained contact with the Coalition forces and taken Hill 140, from which the attack was launched. They are continuing to pursue the enemy, and will shortly assault their position on Hill 161. Given our experience on Hill 140," he finally looked from the sitmap to the commanding general, "I fully expect them to move on and take Hill 521 shortly after they deal with 161. Then," he looked back at the map, "depending on the situation, they may continue to pursue the enemy and drive him completely off the Bataan Peninsula."

Billie cleared his throat to give himself a few seconds to recover from the shock of what he'd just heard. He needed to wrest control of the situation or the Marines would make him look bad and ineffectual.

"That's all very interesting—and impressive—Brigadier. But what about this?" He pointed at a beach on Pohick Bay on the west side of the peninsula, just below Hill 140.

"Yessir, I saw that beach on my way planetside. Had we come ashore there, we would have met resistance from prepared positions and likely suffered an unacceptable level of casualties. Moreover, we wouldn't have been able to provide immediate relief in the area of the breakthrough, and the Coalition brigade that broke through would have been able to raise havoc in your outer positions, perhaps even your inner defenses, before I was able to turn my FIST to deal with them." He kept his expression neutral while stating the obvious.

Billie tilted his head so back he could look down his nose at Sturgeon. "Sir, you miss my point!" He jabbed a finger at the rejected landing beach. "Of course, you would have met with disastrous results had you made your landing there. Hasn't it occurred to you that the *enemy* could make an unopposed landing on that beach and cut your Marines off from assistance from my overstretched forces?"

Sturgeon gave Billie a steady look that, had General Billie been capable of interpreting it, would have thrown the army general into an apopletic fit, then calmly said, "Sir, that potential threat can be dealt with easily enough. One of your battalions, properly led, could successfully defend Hill 140 against a multiregimental landing by the Coalition forces."

Billie's face flushed. "And stretch my resources even farther than they already are? Then what do I do if the rebels attempt a breakthrough someplace else on the perimeter if I've weakened my defenses by manning that hill and your Marines are off gallivanting all around the base of the Peninsula?"

"With all due respect, sir," Sturgeon said with a great deal more patience than he felt. "If my Marines are 'gallivanting all around the base of the Peninsula,' as you put it, the Coalition forces will be too busy attempting to stop them to mount an assault anywhere on your perimeter."

Billie's already red face turned even darker. "*Brigadier,* you *don't* know what capabilities the rebel commanders have. You just *got* here, man! I *cannot* afford to spare any of my too-few forces outside the perimeter. You will break contact with the rebels *now* and bring your Marines back inside the perimeter. Is that understood, *Brigadier*?"

"Yessir," Sturgeon said, stone-faced. He turned to his chief of staff, who had been listening intently from his own station, only a couple of meters away. "Colonel Ramadan, you heard the general's orders. Instruct Commander van Winkle to disengage immediately and return to the perimeter."

"Aye aye, sir. And air?"

Sturgeon paused for half a beat to decide, then said, "The aircraft that are already airborne are to discharge their munitions on Hill 161 and any nearby ground forces, then return to base. Aircraft currently on the ground will launch and provide air cover for the infantry as they withdraw."

"Aye aye, sir." Ramadan turned to his station and transmitted Sturgeon's orders to van Winkle. He took his time about contacting Commander Wolfe with the new orders for the squadron; he knew the squadron's aircraft were all on the ground, and wanted to give them time to launch again before giving the new order to the squadron commander. By the time he turned to report to his commander that the orders had been given, General Billie had left the bunker.

"I've heard 'hurry up and wait' so many times it seems like 'hurry up' *means* 'wait,' " Lance Corporal MacIlargie grumbled. "And I've had to dig a hole and fill it up again so many times that I know that a hole is only temporary, no matter how important it was to dig it in the first place. But break contact and withdraw? When we were doing some serious ass-kicking? I ask you, Rock, what fucking sense does that make?"

MacIlargie may have been disgruntled about having to trudge back to the trench-and-tunnel complex on Bataan, but he wasn't so upset that he didn't make sure his complaining was on the fire team circuit, where only Corporal Claypoole could hear him.

"Damned if I know, Wolfman," Claypoole grumbled back. "I'm just a fire team leader, I don't even know how everybody else in the squad was doing. For all I know, the rest of the battalion was getting *its* ass kicked. Or maybe the bad guys are breaking through the perimeter someplace else and we have to go and plug another hole in the line."

They went on for several more paces while Claypoole thought over what he'd just said, then he picked it up again. "Nah. If they needed us to close another breakthrough, they'd be hustling us, maybe even send the Dragons to pick us up. And no way do I believe the rest of the battalion was getting its ass kicked."

"So why'd we have to break contact and pull back to the trenches?"

"You'll have to ask the Brigadier that one."

"When we get back, I think I'll look him up and do just that," MacIlargie said. He snorted. "Right, just drop in on him, 'Hey, Ted, ole buddy, howcome-for-why you made us pull back when we were putting a serious hurting on them rebels? If you'd let us go, we could of ended this war by morning chow tomorrow.' Yeah, sure I will."

Claypoole grunted. He didn't think they were as close to winning the war as MacIlargie said, but he *did* believe that they were seriously screwing up the Coalition army's plans—until they got called back, that is.

"Aargh!" MacIlargie growled. "This war was all army until we showed up. The Brigadier has to report to that doggie general, what's his name. You know how the army is. They get in a jam, the Marines go in to save their sorry asses, and they get their noses all out of joint about us making them look bad."

"Don't think so," Claypoole said back. "The doggie general in command here is that Cazombi guy, you know, the one who ran the operation on Avionia, the one where we had to catch the smugglers with the birdmen. He's the kind of general who's wasted on the doggies; he's good enough to be a Marine."

Claypoole and MacIlargie only thought their conversation was private; they'd forgotten that squad leaders could listen in on their fire teams' circuits and break into anything that was being said on them—this was to aid the squad leaders in monitoring and controlling their fire teams. Sergeant Linsman *had* been listening in, and he chose this point to break in.

"You're wrong, Rock," he said, making both Claypoole and MacIlargie jump. "General Cazombi's here, but I guess you were sleeping at the end of the Skipper's briefing. Cazombi's not in command anymore. The Combined Chiefs sent a general from the Heptagon to take command of this operation."

"From the Heptagon?" Claypoole squawked. "What did he do there?"

"What I heard was, he was a staff officer."

"What about before?" MacIlargie asked with a note of uncertainty in his voice.

"A staff officer someplace else."

"His entire career?" Claypoole asked, unbelievingly.

"That's what I heard." Claypoole and MacIlargie could hear the shrug in Linsman's voice.

"Buddha's blue balls!" Claypoole swore. "A fucking pogue in charge of a war? Wolfman, I've got this real bad feeling that we're in deep shit now."

CHAPTER TWENTY

Years before the war broke out on Ravenette, that area of Fort Seymour known as the Peninsula had been used as a storage depot. Engineers had constructed deep bunkers connected by tunnels that General Cazombi was easily able to convert into troop and headquarters complexes; power and sewage treatment facilities were upgraded by the engineer battalion General Sorca had loaned him and they also built fighting positions and bunkers to protect the underground facilities. By the time it became necessary for General Sorca's troops to retreat onto the Peninsula it was fully ready to withstand a prolonged siege.

Barring the use of thermonuclear devices, the Coalition forces did not have weapons powerful enough to penetrate into the heart of the underground complex, some of which was as much as forty meters deep.

There were certain drawbacks to the defensive positions, however. Those portions of the redoubt closest to Pohick Bay, which surrounded the Peninsula, were subject to water seepage through the porous rock and soil, making drainage a problem. Even worse, after troops moved into the redoubt it became a source of food and shelter for a certain bipedal rodent-like creature native to Ravenette, *Castor cleaverii.* These were noisome creatures something like a sewer rat mated with a snake. With their strong forelegs and powerful jaws, they could eat or burrow through almost any natural substance and it did not take long for them to construct burrows in the complex. They fed off the troops' food supplies, unattended dead, raw sewage, and one another. Those that survived on such provender grew fat and sassy.

The troops called the creatures "slimies" because the fine scales that covered their reptilian bodies resembled the pelts of wet sewer rats. Exhausted by long watches and short rations, it was not uncommon for a man to awaken from a deep sleep to discover a slimy gnawing away some body part. The bigger slimies could grow to twenty centimeters and weigh up to two kilos, and a pack of them could kill a helpless man. So the troops conducted "slimy hunts" when there was a lull in the fighting, and units vied with one another to see which could kill the most.

But as rations grew very short, the slimies became a badly needed source of protein. "If you can get past the smell," the men joked about eating slimy meat, "it don't taste so bad."

Platoon Sergeant Herb Carman's third platoon, Charlie Company, which was down to only fifteen effectives by the time it reached the Peninsula, drew one of the least desirable posts in the redoubt, a series of two-man observation posts situated in the southwest extreme of the complex, overlooking the bay. Because of their proximity to the water that area was not subjected to as many bombardments and probes as the more landward positions, but the positions were always damp and cold—and infested by slimies.

Carman's mission was to observe the waters of the bay around the clock, apprise his battalion command post of any attempted landings, and engage any infantry assault units. The shoreline below his observation posts was honeycombed with mines and obstacles designed to impale or destroy landing craft. In the event of an actual assault, Carman's men would oppose the enemy long enough to give the garrison commander a chance to shift forces to the threatened sector, and then, if they could, retreat into the bunkers and tunnels to join the defending forces.

Sergeant Carman constantly worked his way through communications trenches that connected the observation posts, making sure his men were alert and that they rotated into the underground bunkers at four-hour intervals to take advantage of the warmth and security. During the hours of darkness he required everyone to be on their toes, but during daylight he allowed men to sleep in shifts right in their positions. Carman slept when he could. And if a slimy crawling across a man's face wasn't enough to make sleep in the posts difficult, a Coalition corvette stationed just on the horizon frequently bombarded the shore with harassing fire. General Cazombi did not have the ammunition or the guns to spare for return fire, but so far none of Carman's observation posts had been hit by the naval gunfire.

"Ahhhh," PFC Raglan "Rags" Mesola exulted, hoisting the squirming slimy on his fighting knife, "lunch!" The slimy squealed piteously, clawing at the knife blade stuck into its guts. Mesola laughed. "Shut up, lunchie," he admonished the creature.

"Unggh," Private Haran "Happy" Hannover snorted, but his stomach rumbled at the thought of roasted slimy meat.

"This sucker must weigh a kilo, Happy." Mesola chuckled as he deftly broke the animal's neck. He sliced off its head, limbs and tail, skinned it expertly, and gutted the carcass. He tossed the offal out through a firing slit, then wiped his hands on his battle dress trousers. The stench of the slimy's insides mixed with the miasma of unwashed bodies, fecal matter (the men relieved themselves into tin cans and tossed the effluvia onto the beach through the firing slits), and dead fish, producing a fetid atmosphere nobody noticed anymore; the air was only a little less disgusting back in the underground bunkers.

"Shall we boil him or roast him?" Mesola asked as he boned the carcass. When he was done he had a respectable pile of white, stringy meat.

"Boil."

"Okay, you know the drill."

Mesola produced a two-liter fruit can, long, long, ago emptied of its delicious contents, and urinated into it. He passed the can to Hannover, who did the same, shaking it to see if there was enough fluid to bring to a respectable boil. Judiciously, he added a little precious drinking water from his canteen to "cut" the liquid. From a pocket he withdrew a little packet of salt, which he emptied into the can.

Hannover groaned. "I never thought I'd live long enough to live like this," he said.

"You call this living?" Mesola chuckled. He put the can on a makeshift grill, produced a whitish lump of material from a cargo pocket, stuck it under the grill and lighted it. The material instantly flared into a bright, white flame that brought the concoction almost immediately to a boil.

Hannover stirred the contents with his knife. "Ready in a minute. Too bad we don't have no bread or crackers to go with it."

"We'll get all the crackers we want when we reenlist," Mesola grunted. They both laughed.

"And just what in the hell is going on in here?" Sergeant Carman's voice boomed from the entrance.

"Mary's knockers!" Mesola exclaimed, almost knocking over the fruit can, "you scared the living daylights out of me!"

Carman ducked through the entrance and nodded at the fire. "Tell me that's not semiprytex you're using to cook that shit."

"No! No!" both men exclaimed. Semiprytex was the explosive used to detonate antipersonnel mines. In small amounts it could also serve as an excellent source of heat to cook rations. Dismantling mines and stealing semiprytex was easy, but if a man took too much of the stuff the charge left in the mine would be too small to set off the mine's main charge.

"That is a court-martial offense," Carman said. He sat wearily on the observation step.

"Well, there's millions of those mines out there, Sarge," Hannover protested, "and we only took one."

"I don't suppose you fellows have had any time today to watch things out in the bay, have you?"

"We was just breaking for lunch, Sarge," Mesola said. "Besides, sunshiny day like this, nothing's going on out there."

"Have you guys heard the news?"

"No, Sarge, what is it? The war's been declared illegal?" Hannover chuckled.

"Better than that. Our new CG has just arrived, a genuine four-star named, uh, I forget his name right now, but he's brought big reinforcements."

"I hope he brought some crackers," Mesola grunted, stirring the contents of the fruit can. He lifted a steaming fragment of meat on his knife blade. "Crackers and slimy—haute cuisine."

"You got enough for three in there?" Carman asked.

The bunker that served as Charlie Company's headquarters and billets was a good twenty meters beneath the ground. It was reached by a complex of communications trenches and tunnels and relatively safe from the enemy's gunfire, not that the men of Charlie Company were allowed to spend much time in there. At least in the observation posts there was a constant flow of fresh air; in the bunker the overworked ventilation system did little to dispel the stench of dozens of unwashed bodies in such a confined space. The one latrine available, a hastily constructed affair, was constantly in use and only contributed to the disgusting smell that pervaded the place. The water used to flush the thing was piped in from Pohick Bay and carried with it the distinctive aroma of dead sealife. But the men of Charlie Company worked and slept there, took their meals there, such as they were, and over time came to accept the conditions as normal.

When Sergeant Carman slept, which was neither very often nor for very long, he slept like a dead man, the dreamless unconsciousness of the extremely exhausted. But on that particular day he was dreaming of home. More important, he was dreaming of Quettana, the love of his life, as remote from him then as the chance he would be promoted to the rank of General.

"Herb! Herb! Get up, goddamnit!" Someone was shaking him, none too gently either. Carman pried his eyes open with effort. It was Captain Jasper Walker, Charlie Company's commander. "Come on, shake a leg, Sarge, we've got visitors."

Carman swung his legs to the floor and stood up. "Visitors?"

An enlisted man stuck his head in from the tunnel and whispered, "Here they come!"

"Ten-HUT!" Captain Walker commanded as General Billie, followed by Lieutenant General Cazombi, Major General Sorca, and Lieutenant Colonel Radford Epperly, Walker's battalion commander, ducked through the doorway. Captain Chester Woo, Billie's aide-de-camp, clipboard importantly in hand, brought up the rear.

"At ease," Billie ordered, wrinkling his nose. "By Allah's pointed teeth, Alistair, this place smells like an open latrine! Chester, make a note we've got to do something about ventilation in this complex!"

"Not much that can be done, sir," Cazombi interjected, "the system is overloaded as it is, and when your reinforcements arrive it'll get even worse."

"Well, General," Billie grinned slightly, "all the more reason to break out and maneuver against the enemy, eh?" Billie casually returned Captain Walker's salute as he reported Charlie Company ready for inspection. "No inspection, Captain, I just want to see what conditions you and your men are operating under. How many men do you have in Charlie Company?"

"Seventy-three, sir. One sergeant and the rest all junior enlisted men. I'm the only officer left."

Billie raised his eyebrows and glanced at Sorca, "No officers, man? How do you run a company, even reduced in numbers, without any officers?"

"I use my noncom, sir, and when he and I are not around, the men know what to do."

"We don't have any other choice, sir," Colonel Epperly said, "and as it is, the system works well. These men have done a fine job, sir, and I've recommended many of them for commendations."

Billie shook his head and put a handkerchief over his nose. "Enlisted men running a company!" he snorted. "How in the hell does anyone survive in this stink? Don't these people ever wash?" he asked Cazombi.

"You get used to it, sir," Captain Walker volunteered, grinning slightly. "We don't have enough water to drink, sir, much less wash ourselves. And the reason I have to use EM to help me run my company is because all my officers are dead, as are most of the men who came to this shithole with me in the first place." Billie frowned and in that instant Walker sensed his days as a company commander were numbered.

Walker silently regarded the officers. Cazombi and Colonel Epperly, haggard, hollow-cheeked skeletons, their uniforms hanging on their bodies like rags, resembled Walker himself. Even Major General Sorca, who had thus far kept himself well out of harm's way, looked the worse for wear, but Billie stood there before him, uniform immaculate, four silver stars gleaming on his collars, a snow-white handkerchief fastidiously held to his nose. The ubiquitous Captain Woo, overweight, skin smooth and face well-shaved, nose wrinkled in disgust, stood self-importantly surveying the men, ready to take down his master's orders. Those men, badly fed, unshaven, unwashed, their uniforms in rags, interrupted by this visit during the only rest they ever got in this sewer, stood respectfully at attention. It occurred to Walker that what he was experiencing now was the height of military insanity. No fighting man deserved to be commanded by such a popinjay.

Walker glanced surreptitiously over at Cazombi, who nodded slightly and in that simple gesture transmitted between them the thousand-year old wisdom of battle-hardened veterans. The age-old disdain that the frontline officer felt toward the staff officer secure in his headquarters began to coalesce into actual hatred for this new commanding general.

"Carry on, Captain," Billie said abruptly, spinning on his heel and striding back into the communication tunnel. Captain Woo scrambled to follow right behind him.

Cazombi grinned at Walker as he turned to go, tossing him a small packet. "Pin these on your man, Jasper."

Walker's men continued to stand at attention, waiting for him to dismiss them. The sotto voce comments he heard about the visitors, however, were not very complimentary. "No talking in ranks, men," he ordered facetiously. "Sergeant Carman, front and center."

Carman emerged from the knot of enlisted men and stood before his commander at stiff attention. "Normally I'd have some beer to wet these down," Walker announced. "You're now Second Lieutenant Carman," Walker handed Carman the pips of his new rank. "Your orders and pay will catch up with you, someday, maybe. All right, men, you may now come forward and kiss your new executive officer." Later, after the handshaking and back pounding were over, Walker said, "I need a sergeant to replace you, Herb. Who do you recommend?"

"Mesola, sir."

Walker raised an eyebrow. "Isn't he a bit of a, um, well, wiseass, Herb?"

"Yessir, but he's very resourceful. He'll make a good junior noncom."

"Very well, Mesola it is," he laid a hand on Carman's shoulder.

"Herb, years from now when we tell our grandchildren we met in the women's wear department of the Fort Seymour post exchange, will they believe us?"

"Depends what we'll be wearing at the time, sir," Carman laughed, "but first we've got to live through this hell."

CHAPTER TWENTY-ONE

In the time Charlette Odinloc had been on Ravenette she hadn't studied the planet's geography in much detail, so she never properly gauged the full extent of the "Ocean Sea"—it had never been given any other name—on the other side of which was Donnie Caloon's home. Likewise, a trip of a mere ten thousand kilometers on any of the settled planets in the Confederation of Worlds was a mere jaunt, at the most no more than a week or ten days even by oceangoing vessel. But not on Ravenette. On Ravenette many things had reverted to the nineteenth century.

Donnie had booked them passage on a *very* slow freighter that took *two months* to cross the ocean, traveling in a huge arc from north to south to north that added thousands of kilometers to a voyage that Charlette thought would've taken them straight across the water to Cuylerville, which was one of the few settlements on a continent about the size of Africa on Earth. And it stopped at every port along the way, even the tiniest inhabited islands, discharging and embarking passengers and cargo. As the captain explained to them on their first night at sea, his ship, the *Figaro,* made this trip twice a year and was the only contact many people along its route had with the rest of the world. "Ve brings dem der supplies and newses, picks up da peoples, drops off da peoples, brings evertings dey needs," the captain, Ermelo Putten, told them in his expansive manner, pulling constantly at his huge black beard as he talked. But the *Fig,* as everyone called the vessel, was a tightly run ship, the crew polite and competent, and the food plentiful and good.

"And vot you do, young lady Miz Charlette?" Captain Putten asked one night at his table. It was obvious to everyone on board that Charlette was not from Ravenette. Her Standard English was perfectly understandable to all on board, but her accent was not of their world. Neither was Captain Putten's or that of most of his crew. Putten explained airily that he came from Earth originally, a place he called "Neederlan," somewhere in Old Europe.

Charlette had anticipated questions like this. She was careful not to answer too quickly. "I was in the army, stationed at Fort Seymour, sir. I met Donnie and we became engaged. I took my discharge when my enlistment was up and now we're going to Donnie's home to get married." As she spoke she felt a sinking feeling in her stomach, like she had stepped into quicksand and was sucked ever downward into it. *Goddamnit, I don't want to get married!* she screamed to herself. Where was this adventure taking her anyway?

Captain Putten slammed a massive fist on the table, causing the silverware to jump, and shouted, "Och, *marry,* you two *marry*? Wunnerful! I, as de captain of dis vessel, I can do the marriages, all legal! Why not you let ol' Ermelo do the marriages for you? Den, ven Donnie he gets himself home, aha! dere you is, *married*! Hooked up for the rest of your lives! Saves a lot of money, do it on board de *Fig,*" he added winking. The other passengers and the ship's officers at the table applauded and heartily congratulated the pair.

Captain Putten's table, Charlette discovered, always offered alcohol in plenty. By the time the talk had gotten around to her and Donnie, everyone had had a lot to drink, including Donnie, who *whoop*ed loudly and slammed his mug on the table. Charlette smiled, hoping she looked enthusiastic, and thought even quicker than before. *This* she had not expected.

"But Donnie, don't you remember?" she stammered. "We were so much hoping your parents would be at the wedding? If we let the good captain marry us here, now, aren't we going to disappoint your folks, ain't they—*aren't* they?" She corrected herself automatically but she had been picking up lots of Donnie's mannerisms lately.

"We were?" Donnie asked, not remembering discussing that at all and looking at the other passengers as if for confirmation. Then he shook his head to clear it. "Well, Captain, we don't want to disappoint my folks."

"Och, of course not! Cap'n Ermelo, he unnerstan! But I tell you what: Vile you on my ship you gets de 'bridal suite'," he roared with laughter. "I gifs you cabin wit single big bed and own head! Ahhahaha, how you likes dat, eh? Ahhahahaha! And," he added, slamming his fist on the table again, "you dines wit me *every* evenink dis whole voyage!"

Both Donnie and Charlette admitted it was a wonderful gesture on the captain's part. When they finally excused themselves from the table everyone was so drunk nobody noticed the gray sickly cast to Charlette's face.

The days passed slowly but too quickly for Charlette. The matter of her impending marriage to someone she liked but would prefer not to spend the rest of her life wedded to boded badly for her future, but something else was worrying her even more. She could now be classified as an army deserter! Sure, she was caught in town when the war began, not her fault. She was on a mission. That's why she was in Donnie's apartment to begin with, and the intelligence she had developed through her relationship with him had proved useful to the troops at the fort. And she couldn't have gotten back to the fort after the shooting started because crossing the lines would've been suicidal. And everyone was forced by government decree to evacuate the city. She dreamed vividly one night of the dialogue she'd have with the prosecutor, a major in the Judge Advocate Corps, at her trial for desertion:

"And so, Sergeant Odinloc, the thought never occurred to you to turn yourself in at the consulate, where you'd have been protected and repatriated to friendly hands? How far was it from this Donnie Caloon's apartment to the consulate?" The way he pronounced Donnie's last name made it sound like an insult. "Tell the panel, Sergeant! How far was it? A block? Two blocks? You broke your leg, maybe?"

"Um, ah, well, sir . . ."

"You were on an intelligence-gathering mission, Sergeant! How could you have gone into the city without knowing the landmarks? I'll tell you how far it was, Sergeant! It was *five blocks*! Five blocks to safety and instead, what did you do? You chose to flee on a ship into the boundless oceans of Ravenette and disappear like a criminal into Hicksville somewhere, and to secure your cover, you *married* this, Donnie *Caloon* fellow—here he actually smirked, gesturing at Donnie, smiling like an idiot, who sat in the vast, hostile audience that had been invited to the trial, which was also being covered by all the news services—"until you were found and arrested! Gentlemen," he said, turning to the court-martial panel, "I think it is plain this, this *traitor* deliberately deserted her post and her comrades in the face of the enemy to save her own skin, and that you should find her guilty of all specifications and charges!"

"We don't need to go any farther!" the judge, a full colonel, shouted, "Guilty, by Amphion's unstrung lyre! Sergeant Odinloc, I hereby sentence you to life imprisonment and a fine of *one million credits* payable to Mr. Donnie Caloon in compensation for the way you used that poor boy to facilitate your traitorous escape!" The crowd roared its approval.

The roaring proved to be Donnie's snoring. Charlette lay there breathing heavily, a very sick feeling in the pit of her stomach. God, God, God, what have I gotten myself into? she asked. The chronometer indicated it was 3 a.m., wherever they were, somewhere at sea. The ocean was dead calm and the only noise was the subdued humming of the ship's reactor-powered turbines. Charlette quietly dressed, took a pack of Donnie's cigarettes, and found her way on to the fantail of the *Figaro*. There was no one there at this hour. She lit the cigarette and drew the *thule*-laced nicotine into her lungs, holding it there for seconds before expelling it into the soft night breeze. Ravenette's moon was full and it cast a bright luminescence over the wake trailing behind the ship. Under normal circumstances this would have been a very romantic moment for a young lady like Charlette Odinloc.

The news that night had been full of war now raging around Fort Seymour where apparently survivors of the 3rd Division were successfully holding out in fortified positions that were under continuous attack and anticipated to fall momentarily to the forces of the secessionist coalition. She discounted everything else in the report as enemy propaganda except the simple fact that her old outfit was still fighting! For a moment a hot bolt of pride lanced through her, but that was followed by despair. She really *was* deserting! She was sitting here on the deck on a moonlit night smoking dope while her friends and comrades were . . . she flipped the butt over the stern, buried her head between her knees, and let the hot tears flow.

"You all right, Hon?" Donnie sat beside her. "OK?" he put his arm around her. "I figured you'd gone for a walk out here, so I come after you," he explained.

Without waiting to think twice, Charlette blurted out the truth about herself.

"Aw, hell," Donnie responded when she was done, "I knew you was a spy all along!"

"You *whaaaat*?"

"Yeah," Donnie shrugged. He took the pack of cigarettes and lighted one. "I mean, lookit yer hands, girl! You ain't never done no work in a laundry! And besides, I figured you was a snoop, that's why you was always so curious about the things I saw, 'n the police tol' me to—"

"The *police*? Donnie you told the *police* on me?"

"Yeah. You're a spy, ainja? They tol' me to lead you along."

"You—you—Donnie! How come they didn't arrest me, then?"

"Well I guess they was goin' to, sometime. Guess when the war started they had other things to think about. Glad they did, tell the truth. Aw, Hon, don't look so, so, damned—"

"Stricken?"

"Yeah! I din' tell'em where we was going! Nobody knows where we are! I just figured it was my duty, ya' know, to make a report, but hell's bells, honeybun, I wasn't gonna let 'em get ya! Gawdam, no, I wasn't!"

Charlette had difficulty getting her breath. It was as if someone had kicked her in the chest, this revelation. It was almost funny. Here she, the sophisticated offworld army intelligence agent, was stringing this yokel along and all the time . . .

"You was only tellin' yer people stuff they already knew or could figure out for themselves," Donnie said. "I din' really see you as a bad spy, Charlette, honest! See, honey, I know I look stupid to most folks, and act stupid too, but I know one thing, you are the best thing that's ever come into my life! Yer smartern' everybody in Cuylerville, maybe, but by Gawd, yer my girl! We get along good together and I know you ain't lyin' when you scratch the livin' shit outta my back in bed! And

I know with my good looks 'n your brains, why that baby of ours is gonna be one good-lookin' smart sumbitch! So what I mean, Charlette, is I want you to give things a chance. We got us a *opportunity* here, you know? 'N I love you enuff, girl, that if you don't wanna stick with me, I won't hold you to it. 'N whatever you done against yer laws 'n regulations 'n so on, we'll worry about that later. But right now nobody knows where we are, nobody can touch us, 'n I bet nobody'd even give a hoot if they knew. So let's see what's waitin' fer us 'n just roll along with the waves."

Donnie drew Charlette close to him and she rested her head on his shoulder and the turbines of the *Figaro* sang on into the night.

CHAPTER TWENTY-TWO

Sergeant Charlette Odinloc received two surprises when she and Donnie Caloon at last arrived in Loudon County on the opposite shore of the Ocean Sea. The first was that Donnie's father was not the one who ruled the roost in the Caloon household. This fact was the source of instant friction. And the second was Cuylerville, when they eventually got there.

"Whar'd you pick her up?" were Aceta Caloon's words upon seeing Charlette for the first time. Donnie's mother stood at dockside, one arm on a bony hip, glaring at her son. Then she shifted a baleful, appraising glance at Charlette. "How long ya been pregnant, girl?" were the first words she spoke directly to Charlette. She turned to Donnie before Charlette could answer and said, "Boy, yer skinny as a rail! Les' git on home and git some food into yer guts!"

Donnie's father, Timor, a bluff, thick-chested man with powerful arms stood by silently, a shy smile on his face. He tentatively but gently took Charlette's hands in his big paws and squeezed them lightly, then, breaking into a huge grin, he pounded his son on the back and shook hands with him vigorously but said nothing by way of greeting.

"We don't got no conveniences here like you do over in the capital, girl," Aceta said to Charlette, "so ya better be wearin' yer walkin' shoes!" Without further word she spun around and began trudging up the road toward the distant hills.

Bringing up the rear of the procession, Donnie's father put a big hand on each of their backs and gently propelled his son and his fiancée after Aceta.

"Momma, Charlette and me et pretty good," Donnie protested to his mother's quickly receding back. She only shook her head and forged onward. "Cuylerville's two kilometers down this road," Donnie whispered to Charlette.

As they trudged down the road Charlette studied the Caloons. Aceta was a thin, bony woman, her steel-gray hair tied into a bun at the back of her head. Her face was long and seamed with wrinkles and dominated by piercing blue eyes. She looked to be in her nineties, but couldn't have been beyond her sixties—old age for backwoods people. Her clothes appeared to be homemade, from some kind of cottonlike fabric, and they hung loosely on her spare frame. She walked at a steady, even pace. After a short while Charlette found it difficult to keep up with her and gradually she and Donnie began to fall back.

"Can't keep up with yer ma? Ya been livin' too soft in that city, Donnie, boy!" she called back over her shoulder but she never slowed a step to let them catch up.

Donnie's father also appeared to be in his nineties but it was hard to judge because hard labor was etched into every feature. He marched along steadily, easily keeping up with his children, and as she watched him Charlette realized he could easily match his wife's stride, but was only hanging back to keep them company. His face and neck were burned brown from years of exposure to the sun and his big hands were thickly callused from work. Donnie had told her his father was a farmer but he'd been vague about just what it was he cultivated on his spread. Whatever kind of farm Timor Caloon worked, it was painfully obvious to Charlette that he used mostly manual labor and he'd been doing it all his life.

At every step along the dusty, unpaved road Sergeant Charlette Odinloc had the eerie feeling she was trudging steadily back into the past of human history. She had no idea such primitive people still existed in Human Space. But what really troubled her was that with every step toward Cuylerville she was slipping inexorably further and further into the status of a deserter.

* * *

The ramshackle collection of homes that made up the village of Cuylerville straggled up both sides of a narrow valley through which ran a sluggish river. The Caloons lived high up along the east side of the valley along a steep road from the lowlands. The fields they passed by were freshly harvested, so Charlette couldn't tell what crops had been grown there. Long warehouses lined each field and there hung about the pastures an odor she couldn't place immediately. "Donnie, that smell. It smells like—like—" she glanced questioningly at Donnie.

"Yep. That's thule you smell," Donnie whispered back. "They store the harvest in them warehouses temporarily 'fore shipping the crops off. Daddy and the other folks hereabouts used to grow grains but the work was hard and there's more money in thule, and it's lots easier to grow. All we got to do is harvest the plants and buyers come out from Bibbsville, the county seat, where they got processing plants and a system to distribute the stuff."

"But, Donnie, it's illegal to grow the stuff without a license. Do you have a license?"

"Nope. Somebody smuggled some of them plants off Wanderjahr and they grow real good in our climate here. In fact they grow better. I been told the two-delta-ten quadrahydrothuminol isomer in our plants is twicet as strong, more 'n six percent, as in them plants they grow on Wanderjahr," he said proudly. "Them cigarettes we smoked back in Ashburtonville and on the *Figaro?* They was manufactured right here in Bibbsville. Why, hell, you import that stuff from Wanderjahr, and the price of a pack is ten times what it cost me in Ashburtonville and here we smoke the stuff for nuttin'. So . . ." he shrugged.

"Quadra—?" Donnie had pronounced that long chemical name like he'd grown up with it. He grinned at her, as if to say, There's more to me than you suspected. Charlette glanced back at Donnie's father, who'd heard every word, but all he did was smile and nod his head. Not only was she an army deserter but she was now in among a den of smugglers and God only knew what else.

"Geez, Donnie, you ever think maybe one reason people don't like you folks so much is because you break the laws all the time and cheat people out of their profits?"

"We all gotta make a living, hon." Donnie grinned. "Ennyway, you was there when they shot all those people at Fort Seymour. The penalty for a little pirating and smuggling ain't death, don't ya know?"

As they passed houses on the way to the Caloon home, people came out into their yards and porches and hollered greetings at them. "Thas a mighty good-lookin' girl ya got there, Aceta," one crone cackled as they passed by. Aceta, still far ahead of them, grimaced but Timor gave the woman a grin and a friendly wave.

"Hey, Donnie!" a young man about Donnie's age shouted, "ya look like a city man!" Donnie's face reddened.

"Git them two married, Aceta," a big man sitting on his porch yelled down at them, "we cain't have young folks livin' in sin around here!" he roared with laughter. Charlette's face reddened at the remark but she seriously doubted that the concept of sin was well-known among these people.

"Don't people work around here?" Charlette asked Donnie.

"In the season," he answered, "but this ain't the season. The harvest is in, it was a good crop, and folks got money in their pockets. You come at a good time of the year, honeybun."

The wedding was a strange affair conducted by a man named Bud Clabber, a sort of mayor, justice of the peace, postmaster, and newspaper publisher all rolled into one. He was the latter by default because he was the only person in Cuylerville who owned a radio, so he was the first to receive news from the outside world. He posted the news, printed in big capital letters on plain sheets of paper that he tacked to the wall inside the rundown wooden structure that served as the Cuylerville community center. It looked to Charlette to have been a church a very long time ago. The "service" was civil, short, and to the point.

"Sign these here papers," Clabber ordered. Perspiration stood out on his inflamed forehead. He hadn't shaved in days and there were enormous perspiration stains under the armpits of his dirty shirt, which was missing two of its buttons. His hands were dirty but not from manual labor. He had Donnie and Charlette sign four sets of elaborately printed marriage certificates. Then he signed. Then two witnesses were called up from the fifty or so people who'd found the time and energy to attend the ceremony, and they signed. "Okay, you two are legally hitched," Clabber grunted. "Now, Donnie, kiss yer new wife then get home and do what married folks do, which I know you been doin' all along anyway." Everyone present broke into raucous laughter. "You each get a copy of this here certificate," Clabber shouted above the noise of the laughter and congratulations. "I keep one, and the fourth one goes to the county seat, next time I get up there." It occurred to Charlette that Clabber was probably the go-between with the people who bought their thule crop.

"We'll have us a little party tonight, hon, up at the house," Donnie muttered as he escorted Charlette outside, "but it's too damn hot to have a shindig right now."

Outside in the broiling sun people gathered around the couple and offered their best wishes. Nobody offered them any presents, but everyone promised to gather at the Caloon house that night with special dishes for the reception.

"Hold on there!" Clabber shouted, elbowing his way through the crowd. He waved a sheet of paper in his hand. "You, there, Charlette, look here! I was gonna post this on the wall but forgot in all the wedding business. I want you to read this." He handed her the paper on which was written in large capital letters:

"BIG BATTLES IN ORBIT. CASUALTIES HEAVY. ENEMY FLEET LANDS LARGE REINFORCEMENTS AT FT. SEYMOUR. PRESIDENT CONFIDENT OF OLTIMATE VICTORY." She noted he'd misspelled "ultimate," but instead of pointing it out to Mr. Clabber, her heart sank and she let the paper dangle in her hand. The expression on her face made her distress obvious to everyone who crowded around to gape at the news.

"Donnie tol' us you was an offworlder. Why in hell did you folks start this goddamned war in the first place, girl?" Clabber shouted.

"We . . ." Charlette began.

"Aw, hell, Bud, lay off!" an older man in the crowd said, "this war ain't no business of ours!" and several other men murmured their agreement.

"Come on, Charlette," Timor Caloon said, putting his arm around his new daughter-in-law, "let us go home." As they trudged back up the road, Timor turned to yell back at Clabber, "Bud, you gonna be our newspaper man, ya oughter learn how to spell."

* * *

"You gotta start pullin' yer own weight around here, girl," Aceta Caloon told Charlette one day. "You said you worked in a laundry? Well, girl, yew kin start by helpin' me do my washin' today."

"Mother," Charlette answered, "my name is 'Charlette.' How'd you like it if I went around here calling you 'woman' all day long?"

Aceta was not used to anyone talking back to her and for a moment she was speechless. "I kin see by those hands o' yers that you never did a bit of housework in yer life. That 'laundry' yew worked in musta had all them machines, 'cause you ain't never had yer hands in a washtub."

"I'm not washing anyone's dirty clothes," Charlette answered. "You dirtied them, you clean them."

At first Aceta said nothing, just regarded Charlette speculatively, as if she were deciding whether to hit her or let the insubordination go. Then she took Charlette by the elbow and gently guided her toward the back of the house, saying, "First time through I'll show you how it's done 'n we kin do the clothes together. But Charlette, you live in my house, you gotta help me with the work, until you get too big. After the baby you 'n Donnie gonna go off to live by yourselfs 'n you gotta know by then how to run a house proper. I'll teach you somethin' about cookin' too. Donnie will need feeding."

Charlette discovered that the housework kept her occupied and her mind off what was really beginning to worry her more and more with each passing day. And her nails chipped and her hands got red and cracked.

Charlette also found that the people of Cuylerville were a gregarious, hospitable community. Each family had its own garden and livestock, which provided plenty of nourishment for everyone. Apparently the thule harvest that season had been very good because there was plenty of money to buy amenities, such as alcohol to fuel the continuous parties and gatherings that were life in the village between harvest and planting times, and fuel for running the generators and machinery and other things the people wanted to improve the quality of their simple lives. They accepted Charlette with friendly curiosity. They seemed not to care there was a war on or that their government had declared its independence from the Confederation of Human Worlds or for anything else that took place outside the limits of Cuylerville. No one held it against Charlette that she was an off-worlder and a member of the Confederation army. No one, that is, except Bud Clabber.

One day Clabber visited the Caloons. His face was red and he was perspiring heavily from the walk up the valley. He sat panting on the veranda of their house as the four Caloons—Charlette counted as one of them by then—took chairs out there with him. Sitting on their porches, drinking, smoking thule, and gossiping were the favorite pastimes in Cuylerville after the harvest.

"Harvest was pretty good this year," Clabber remarked, accepting a cool drink from Aceta as he took a chair next to Timor.

"I'm thinkin' of goin' back to growin' grains, Bud," Timor said, matter-of-factly.

Clabber started in surprise. "You cain't do that, Timor!"

"Why cain't I?" he winked at Charlette. Apparently Timor had threatened to do it more than once, just to nettle Clabber in his prosperous self-confidence.

"Well, well . . ."

" 'Cause ol' Bud'll lose his commissions," Aceta volunteered.

"Well, Aceta, that ain't the only reason!" Clabber protested. "We all depend on the money we're gettin' for growin' thule. Besides, they won't be happy about it, Timor," he cast a dark look at Timor Caloon.

"Who're 'they'?" Charlette asked innocently.

Nobody answered for a long moment and finally Donnie said, "The men in the county seat who make the real money off our crops. Mr. Clabber set the deal up with them so he gets a good commission, but what we get is the leavings. It's like I tol' Daddy, and it's the reason I left here and went to Ashburtonville. You get in bed with them people and they own you."

"We're all prospering from those crops, Donnie!" Clabber's voice rose. It was obvious to Charlette that the joke had gone too far. "Them fellas won't take too kindly, you do somethin' stupid like this, Timor!"

"Ah," Timor shrugged, "I was in the army and now we got Charlette who was a soldier, 'n Donnie, he's always bin pretty good with a rifle. We kin take care of ourselves, Bud. Yep, I might just switch this year."

Clabber snorted and shook his head and was silent for a while.

Once he'd gotten control of himself he changed the subject. "Donnie tol' us, Missus Charlette, that you was a soldier in the Confederation Army. Thet true?"

Aceta Caloon shot an angry glare at her son. "Everybody knows that, Bud. Why you puttin' the mouth on my Donnie?" she said.

Clabber smiled and nodded his head. "But is it true? 'Cause if it is, I should report you to the authorities up at the county seat. You is an 'enemy alien,' I think it's called. Donnie sez," he glanced apologetically at Aceta, "that you worked in the quartermaster laundry at Fort Seymour. Thet true? See, folks, since I'm the gov'mint official in Cuylerville, I got certain responsibilities for the security of the folks in this village and havin' an enemy soldier—no offense, Missus Charlette—livin' here should be reported."

"Yew know damn well, Bud, that girl ain't no threat to nobody in Cuylerville," Timor snorted.

"Well—"

"Yessir, I did work there," Charlette answered quickly, very relieved that Donnie hadn't been able to tell anyone what she was really doing in Ashburtonville. She gave him the cover story they had devised. Aceta, who knew very well the part about Charlette being a laundress was not true, kept silent. "So you see, Mr. Clabber, I'm actually a deserter from the army," she concluded. That word was bitter in her mouth but she spit it out anyway.

"Well. Well, I see," Clabber said. He was silent for a moment, nodding his head. Then he slapped the arm of his chair with a hand and said, "But I gotta report you, Missus Charlette, yew unnerstand?"

"Well, report away, then," Aceta said.

"O' course," Clabber waved a hand, "we might work sumptin' out, jist between the five o' us."

" 'N what might that be?" Timor asked, his voice tinged with suspicion. He knew what was coming.

"Well," Clabber sat forward in his chair and rested his hands on his knees, "you did very good this last harvest, Timor. We all did. We did 'cause I got the connections to get y'all good prices on your thule. Now suppose you jist give me two percent more of what I'm a gonna git you fer next season's harvest—"

So that was the reason he'd come visiting. Timor Caloon shot to his feet. "Bud Clabber, I known you all yer goddamned miserable life, but if yew don't get yer goddamned ass off this here porch right goddamned now, I am gonna kick it all the way back down the valley! 'N you send any goddamned 'report' on my daughter-in-law to those goddamn crooks up at the seat, this here village is gonna get a new middle-man right goddamned quick! And I am gonna switch crops this year! You tell them people if they want grains they kin get 'em from me direct, otherwise they better keep their asses up at the seat! Now git outta here!"

Clabber's face went white and he wasted no time scrambling off the porch. Safely on the road back down the valley he shook his fist at the Caloons and shouted, "Yew are a goddamned fool, Timor Caloon! You are gonna mess up the best thing this village has ever had goin' for it! Yew all's gonna regret this, I swear and be damned, you are!"

Charlette was truly amazed at Timor's outburst. She had never heard him talk so much since she'd come to Cuylerville. Aceta began to laugh. "Old Timor don't ever say much, Charlette, but when he do, oh, Lord, hope yer on the other side of the world!" and she began laughing. It was the first laugh Charlette had heard out of her. Then they all began laughing. Far down the road Clabber heard the laughter and he turned and shook his fist at the Caloons again.

"Donnie," Timor Caloon said to his son after they had laughed themselves out, "that man is trouble for you and Charlette. I think I'm a-gonna have to kill him before this is over. Maybe some other folks too. Those bastards up at the seat he deals with are all crooks, Donnie, 'n they'd slit a man's throat soon as look at him. You was right, son, we never shoulda got involved with 'em. I think next season I really am goin' back to growin' grain and vegetables. Thet'll really piss 'em off."

"I don't want you to do anything on my account that might bring trouble on your family," Charlette said. She was alarmed. This is getting worse and worse, she thought despairingly. And then something that had been growing on her for a while now suddenly gelled—she was becoming attached to the Caloons!

"Don't ya worry," Aceta said, "we kin take good care of ourselfs. But Timor, what you think about these children here?"

"I think you need to put some distance between yourselfs and Cuylerville. When will the *Figaro* be back?"

Donnie Caloon shrugged. "Four, five months, if she makes it back at all, with the war on and all."

"Well," his father answered, "we better jist be on our toes until then. Mebbe it'll all blow over. But fer right now, break out the rifles, son. We better see if we remember how to shoot. You come along too, Charlette. You was in the army. Ya oughter know a sight picture from a mess kit."

The Caloons owned two old-fashioned projectile firearms, shoulder weapons that Timor called "rifles." They had been designed primarily for hunting and Timor used them mainly for keeping blackbirds and other pests away from his crops.

"Each one of these will hold five of these twenty-millimeter ca'tridges in the tube magazine and one in the breach," Donnie explained to Charlette. "You operate this one by working the slide back and forth to eject the spent ca'tridge and put another in the breach. The other, Daddy's favorite, is semiautomatic. The gas from the ca'tridges works the action for ya, so alls ya gotta do is pull the trigger six times and she shoots six times. But this rifle is a light gun and if ya fire heavy loads it kin get away from you mighty quick."

Charlette had qualified as an expert with the various types of handheld weapons that were standard issue in the Confederation Army, but she had only attained Marksman status, the lowest needed to qualify in arms, with the standard individual infantry weapon. But she was not afraid of guns.

"Normally we use real light shot for blackbirds, but we have heavier loads for bigger game. If you wanna bring a man down, you use these," he held up two cartridges about seventy-five millimeters in length, one blue, the other red. "This red one has nine nine-millimeter balls in it and this blue one has one twenty-millimeter slug. Either one of these at close range will bring a man down, but watch out for the blue one because she kicks real bad."

"How 'close' is close?"

"Well, the slugs are good out beyond one hundred meters, if you aim right. The balls spread out twenty-five millimeters for every meter so at three meters, about across the size of our living room, they'd hit your target with a spread of seventy-five millimeters, knock him right through the front door. Now, let's practice a bit out back of the house."

Charlette found that she could fire the rifles with accuracy, but for the next week her right shoulder was sore and black and blue from the recoil. Her right cheek hurt a bit too from absorbing the guns' recoil, but that was only from the first five shots. After that, Donnie had shown her how to hold the weapons properly.

"Daddy says until we're sure there won't be any trouble we keep them full loaded with the safeties on, one in each of our bedrooms at night, close by during the daytime. Just remember, when you fire, press the safety stud to the left to take it off and *never* put your finger on the trigger until yer ready to shoot."

As prepared as they were for violence, when the night visitors finally did come the Caloons slept right through it because the raiders struck not at them but at the Pickens family who lived some two hundred meters farther up the valley. There were three raiders, heavily armed. They cut Amelia Pickens's throat and told her husband if he didn't want his three daughters murdered as well, the thule crop next season had better be a good one. Then they disappeared into the night.

Timor Caloon emerged from the Pickens's home, his face white with suppressed rage. "Wait here," Timor Caloon told the horrified villagers standing around outside. He returned in a few minutes with Bud Clabber and five other men, all armed with rifles. Clabber moaned and protested his innocence but his pleas fell on deaf ears. "Ol' Bud here, he's volunteered to take us to visit these gent'men in Bibbsville. Donnie, go git yer gun, we're leavin' in a few minutes."

"I want to come along," Charlette said.

Timor Caloon looked to his wife, and then Donnie, who both nodded slightly. He fixed Charlette with an appraising look, turned to the crowd and asked, "Ennybody here got a spare rifle they kin loan my daughter-in-law?"

CHAPTER TWENTY-THREE

Trenches and tunnels. Lieutenant General Cazombi had wanted to turn the warren of storage tunnels on the Bataan Peninsula into a warren of strongpoint-studded combat tunnels and trenches. The 3rd Provisional Division's engineers worked valiantly, and gave Cazombi what he wanted. Those trenches and tunnels were how Cazombi's understrength force had managed to hold out long enough for the 27th Division and then the Marines to arrive. When General Billie arrived, he made it clear that he wanted everybody in the tunnels and trenches. And he wanted the Marines in a tunnel that had strongpoints facing across a no-man's-land without trenches. What a general wants, he gets.

Which doesn't necessarily mean everybody else is happy.

"I hate tunnels," Corporal Kerr muttered as he led his fire team to a strongpoint. Each Marine carried three Straight Arrow antitank weapons in addition to his blaster.

"But these are *our* tunnels," Corporal Doyle protested.

"I wasn't talking to you, Doyle," Kerr growled.

Doyle looked at him indignantly.

PFC Summers studiously avoided looking at either of their bobbing heads; they carried their helmets so they could see each other in the tunnel. Why did *he* have to be the one stuck in a fire team with two corporals?

"You were on Waygone, you were on Kingdom," Kerr said sourly. "Don't tunnels remind you of anything?"

Doyle opened his mouth to say something, sucked his words back, and reconsidered. "Yeah, well. But they aren't here."

Kerr's jaw clenched. He didn't care whether Skinks were around or not; he had fought Skinks in tunnels on two operations, tunnels reminded him of the implacable aliens.

Summers couldn't help himself, he looked from one corporal to the other despite not wanting to look at either. He had joined 34th FIST after the Kingdom campaign and hadn't yet encountered the hostile aliens the Marines called Skinks. He hadn't even *heard* of them until he reported to Camp Ellis for duty. FIST Sergeant Major Shiro had briefed the replacements on the Skinks. Until then, Summers had believed that all stories of alien sentiences—especially hostile alien sentiences—were fiction, mindless entertainments. The sergeant major's briefing hadn't emphasized tunnels, yet Corporal Kerr was seriously disturbed by tunnels because of the Skinks. Thirty-fourth FIST had encountered the Skinks twice, or at least Company L's third platoon—the platoon Summers was in—had. They were the first humans to do so—at least, the first humans who lived to tell the tale.

Except that they weren't allowed to tell anyone; 34th FIST was permanently quarantined to make sure nobody told. A shiver ran up Summers's spine. He didn't know whether the shiver was because of the Skinks, or because of the quarantine—he never intended to make a career of the Marines, just one adventurous enlistment, but apparently assignment to 34th FIST was for life.

Assignment to 34th FIST had proved to be more adventurous than anything Summers had ever imagined.

"Here we are." Kerr's voice broke into Summers's thoughts. The fire team leader ducked into an unoccupied bunker and turned on the lights.

Summers followed Doyle into the cramped room and automatically threw a hand over his nose and mouth—the place owned a stench that would gag a kwangduk.

"Damn doggies," Kerr swore, and kicked a piece of litter at the wall. It squelched. Clearly it was "organic." "Look at this crud and corruption. I've seen kwangduk nests that were cleaner than this!"

The bunker was indeed filthy. The walls and ceiling were stained from things Summers didn't even want to guess at. The floor probably was, too, but it was covered with so much garbage, he couldn't see it to tell. Some of the debris was obviously organic—bone chips and globules of slimy. The fearsome odor rising from a two-liter can in one corner was evidence of its use as a latrine. And the yellowish-brown goop on the bottom of the firing slit said dumping the can through the firing slit was the flushing system.

A sudden noise sounded from some crushed cans. Summers and Doyle both jumped and pointed their blasters in that direction. A small, sharp-muzzled face peeked out from under the debris. Kerr moved fast to stomp the beast, but it was faster, skittering from its hiding place and slithering into a narrow crack in the wall of the bunker.

"The doggies *eat* those things," Kerr snorted. "And they say Marines are animals."

"If you'd lived here under these conditions, you'd eat them, too."

The three turned to the new voice. Sergeant Linsman's head hovered in the entrance to the bunker, his helmet tucked under his arm. All three of the Marines were used to seeing disembodied heads hovering in midair, none were surprised at his appearance, though both Doyle and Summers had jumped at his unexpected voice.

Linsman crinkled his nose. "I wish I could give you a high pressure hose to clean this shithole out," he said, "but water is in short supply." He shook his head at the mess left by the last soldiers to use the bunker. "I'll get you some supplies to clean it up. Make it livable, I don't know how long we'll be stuck here." He turned to leave, then turned back.

"Tim," he directed his words at Kerr, "doggies say a lot of things about us. Let them. They're just pissed off because they weren't smart enough to join the Marines so they got stuck in the damn army." He finished turning and vanished almost as thoroughly as if he'd put his helmet on.

Summers wondered whether Linsman was joking or if he meant it.

Kerr didn't wait for the promised cleaning supplies; a well-worn broom with a cracked handle leaned in a corner of the bunker. He ordered Summers to use it to shove the debris into a pile and Corporal Doyle to supervise while he himself went in search of a container to haul the detritus away. Two hours later, the floor was cleared and the worst of the mess stuck to the walls, floor, and ceiling was cleaned off. But it would be some time before the stench was gone.

A twinge in his stomach made Summers think of food, but the thought of eating amid such rank odors made him gag.

"I hope they send armor," Kerr said quietly; he was watching through the firing slit.

"Why?" Doyle's voice squeaked on the question. He'd still been the chief clerk during the Diamunde campaign, but he remembered the tanks Marston St. Cyr's army used, and he was smart enough to be afraid of them.

"Because we'll have to get out of here to fight them."

"Oh."

"Wh-why?" Unlike Doyle, Summers didn't understand.

"Explain it to him."

"Ah, right." Doyle turned to Summers. "Because we can't use the Straight Arrows in here, and they're the only weapons we have to use against tanks."

Summers looked blank.

Corporal Doyle took a deep breath and assumed a lecturing tone. "The Straight Arrows are rocket powered, they can't be safely used in an enclosed environment." He cocked his head and looked for an indication that Summers got the implication—he didn't. "They're extremely loud, the bunker walls will contain the sound and maybe burst our eardrums, even with our helmet ears turned all the way down. And the rockets have a backblast. We'll probably get fried if we fire one without space behind us for the backblast to go."

Now Summers got it. He blanched and swallowed. Suddenly, the bunker didn't smell too bad to eat in.

A few hours later, Summers was nearly as badly shaken as Corporal Doyle was when Kerr got his wish.

Corporal Pasquin was jolted out of an exhausted sleep when Sergeant Ratliff's voice crackled in his helmet comm, "Second squad, up and at 'em! The bears are prowling, and we're going hunting. Assemble on my position. Bring your elephant guns. Team leaders acknowledge. *Now!*"

"First fire team, we're on our way," Corporal Dornhofer said immediately.

"Second fire team, be right with you," Pasquin reported. "We'll race you," he added to Dornhofer. He scrambled to his feet, popped his helmet on his head, slung his blaster, and scooped up three of his fire team's Straight Arrows. He saw PFC Shoup's disembodied head looking a question at him—Lance Corporal Longfellow was already standing and armed, waiting impatiently by the entrance to their bunker.

Pasquin flipped up his helmet screens to expose his face, and said, "Grab your weapons, Shoup, we're going out to fight tanks." He headed for Longfellow. Shoup grabbed his helmet and weapons and followed Pasquin into the tunnel.

"Third fire team, see you right away," Corporal Dean said. "Let's go," he added to Godenov.

The three fire teams reached Sergeant Ratliff almost simultaneously. The squad leader was standing on a logistics retriever vehicle. He held up a bare hand, signaling his men to wait, while he listened intently to the instructions coming over his helmet comm.

"There's a breakthrough," Ratliff said, all business, lowering his hand when he had the orders. "We're going to plunge out the influx and plug the hole until relieved. Dragons are waiting for us. Let's do it." Second squad scrambled onto the retrieval vehicle and grabbed whatever handholds they could. The retriever hummed and began rolling, picking up speed. In seconds, faster than a man could trot, it was moving through connecting tunnels to a winding, baffled exit tunnel, where the Marines dismounted. Staff Sergeant Hyakowa met them and directed them into a waiting Dragon. Corporal Taylor and second gun team were already in the Dragon. Hyakowa followed them up the Dragon's ramp. The amphibious vehicle rose onto its air cushion and sped off, trailing another Dragon with Ensign Bass, second squad, and the platoon's other gun team. Hyakowa picked up the comm that allowed him to communicate with the Dragon crew and plugged it into his helmet.

Minutes later, the Dragon swerved to an abrupt stop and began backing up, firing plasma cannons as it went. It slewed around and its ramp dropped with a clank.

"They're on our right," Hyakowa said into first squad's circuit. "Two hundred meters plus. Pick your targets; we don't have firepower to waste."

The Dragon had backed into defilade behind a coral outcropping.

The top of the outcropping was jagged, vaguely resembling the crenellations of a medieval castle wall. First squad scrambled up the rocky face and found positions where they could look over it without exposing any more of themselves than they had to. A hundred meters to their right, second squad was doing the same in a field of broken boulders. The gun teams stayed behind; their assault guns wouldn't be much good against tanks. If the tanks had infantry support, though, the guns would move into position to take them on.

Pasquin swore when he looked between two small peaks on the top of the coral outcropping. Unless Ensign Bass had managed to come up with more Straight Arrows, third platoon had fewer than sixty of the tank killers. It looked like there were more tanks than that chugging through the gap they'd blown in the defensive works two hundred meters away. He slid the magnifier screen into place and swore again—what looked like an entire battalion of infantry was moving among the tanks and leading them.

"Choose your targets and start picking them off," Ratliff's voice said in his earpieces.

Pasquin sighted in on a tank moving across his front at a slight angle. "Watch my hit," he said on the fire team circuit. "Longfellow, take out the one to my left, Shoup, get the one to my right." Satisfied with his sight picture, he fired. The Straight Arrow roared and an instant later fire enveloped one of the tanks. It shuddered to a stop, hatches flew open, and burning crewmen struggled out. One man rolled on the ground to put out the flames that enveloped him, another ran like a human torch until he dropped, the third didn't move after he hit the ground.

Longfellow and Shoup fired simultaneously. Pasquin swore for the third time since looking over the coral outcropping; Longfellow's aim was low and his Straight Arrow erupted in the treads of the vehicle he'd fired at. At least the tank couldn't maneuver. It was a sitting duck for anyone who wanted to fire at it. Shoup yelled in frustration, his rocket lodged between the barrel and forward armor of his tank and fell off unexploded when the tank swiveled its turret toward them.

"Down!" Pasquin shouted, and slid back several meters. The tank's first shot struck the forward slope of the outcropping between his position and Shoup's. It exploded, throwing rock shards all over, some impacted behind the ridge and Pasquin felt them pepper the backs of his legs and glance off his helmet. He didn't have time to think about whether any of the shards tore through his chameleons and into his flesh, because more cannon rounds exploded against the forward face and rained more shards and chips onto the Marines.

"Get your fire going!" Ratliff shouted into the squad circuit. "Hit enough of them and they'll break off. They aren't suicidal."

I hope not, Pasquin thought. *If they are, we can't kill all of them, and the ones we don't will do for us.* Out loud, he said, "Let's get back up there and kill some bad guys." He scrambled to a position a few meters to the left of where he'd originally fired from. On the way, he reminded Longfellow and Shoup to shift their positions as well; it sounded like the tanks were concentrating their fire on the spots from which they'd already fired. Next round, all three of them got kills.

Corporal Kerr did his best not to think about the boulder field second squad was in. The boulders were good protection against the infantry weapons they were facing, but a tank barrage could shatter the boulders and send sharp rocky shrapnel flying thick enough to wipe out the entire squad. He had positioned Corporal Doyle and PFC Summers before finding a spot for himself behind a large, slab-sided stone. Or he'd positioned Summers. Corporal Doyle had picked a spot that Kerr wished he had himself: closely hemmed in on all sides, it provided cover from most hits that weren't directly on him, while giving him two good directions in which to fire and three easy routes out if he had to leave in a hurry, and he had space for the backblast to diffuse without bouncing back on him.

Kerr looked around the side of his boulder. A tank had advanced to within a hundred and fifty meters of second squad. A boulder to Kerr's front partly obstructed his view of the tank, but he had a clear view of its turret. He aimed his first Straight Arrow to barely skim the top of the obstructing boulder and fired. The rocket cleared the boulder by centimeters before dropping out of his view. Then it hit, stopping the tank and rocking it backward. After a few seconds, secondary explosions threw the turret into the air, where it crashed upside down onto the tank.

To the left of his kill, where Kerr couldn't see, there was another explosion, from Corporal Doyle's shot; Kerr's kill clanged when fragments of jagged armor pelted it.

"I hit the gun!" Summers shouted excitedly a second after another explosion to the right of Kerr's kill.

Kerr risked rising up to take a look. Twenty meters from his dead tank, another lumbered backward with its cannon jutting out of the turret at an odd angle—that one needed its barrel, and maybe its entire turret, replaced before it could return to duty.

A flash of light made Kerr drop back down—the infantry supporting the tanks was beginning to fire at the Marines. *Where are our guns?* Kerr wondered.

Sergeant Kelly positioned his guns, first gun team in the middle of first squad on the coral outcropping, second gun team on the right flank of first squad in the boulder field. He didn't like the position of either gun, but there was no place he could position them where they wouldn't be too exposed to return fire from both the infantry and the tanks. But he had confidence in Corporals Barber and Taylor; they'd keep their guns from getting killed too easily.

Corporal Taylor didn't like second gun team's position any better than Kelly did. There was no way he could bring his gun to bear on the rebel infantry without rising above the boulders. Not for the first time in his career as a gunner, he wished for a gun capable of indirect fire. But plasma guns were strictly line-of-sight. The boulders were aggregate, mixes of coral and sandstone. If he'd had the time, he could have used the gun to slag boulders and provide firing lines that didn't force his gun to rise above all cover, but the enemy was too close, and he didn't have the time.

He peeked around the side of a boulder and saw a squad of infantrymen crowded close to a tank! He grabbed one of his team's Straight Arrows, took quick aim, and fired. His years of spotting for his gun, and being gunner before that, paid off—his aim was true.

The Straight Arrow slammed into the front of a tread, shattering it and the wheels behind it, throwing out killing shrapnel. The tank made a half turn in the direction of the broken tread before the driver stopped it, but not before it ran over two soldiers knocked down by the shrapnel, and banged hard into three more who were still on their feet. Immobile, that tank was easy picking, and its crowded, supporting squad was almost wiped out.

"Kindrachuk," Taylor said to his gunner, "here, you've got a shot now." He looked to his left front and described an arc of fire to his gunner.

Lance Corporal Kindrachuk followed Taylor's instructions and opened up on the infantry supporting a tank platoon that was approaching the gap between the platoon's two blaster squads. He fired controlled bursts into the infantrymen, sending them to ground.

Taylor grabbed another Straight Arrow and killed a second tank before he had Kindrachuk drop back into cover. In little more than a minute of fighting, second gun team had accounted for two tanks and more than a platoon of infantry.

Corporal Barber and his first gun team had a less exposed position than second gun team. At least, the gun was able to send enfilading fire into the infantry to its left without being directly exposed to fire from its front. Barber positioned himself a few meters to the right of the gun where he could direct its fire while keeping a lookout to the front and left for good targets as well as danger from those directions. He saw a tank swivel its gun to fire on the gun's position and hefted a Straight Arrow to his shoulder, simultaneously ordering Lance Corporal Tischler and PFC Yi, the assistant gunner, to take cover. Barber aimed more deliberately than Taylor had, and scored a killing hit on the tank's side before the beast could get off a second shot at the gun team's position. Secondary explosions from the tank's ammunition shattered the armored vehicle.

"Get back up there!" Barber ordered after a quick scan failed to show any other tanks taking aim on their position. First gun team resumed fire.

"Shit-shit-shit!" Corporal Claypoole repeated as if the word were a mantra. He'd never wanted Schultz in his fire team to begin with—he was afraid of the man. But now that the Hammer wasn't there, he wished he was. Claypoole was a good Marine, he knew that, and he knew that Lance Corporal MacIlargie was a good Marine, too. At least they were as fighters, even if both of them lacked something as garrison Marines. But both of them combined weren't as good at fighting as Schultz was all by himself. Shit-shit-*shit*! but Claypoole felt vulnerable without the steadying presence of Schultz.

Claypoole fired off Straight Arrows, shifting his position from boulder to boulder with each shot, while MacIlargie used his blaster to protect his fire team leader from the infantry advancing with the tanks.

But one lousy platoon of Marines against an entire tank battalion supported by an entire infantry battalion? Was somebody crazy somewhere? Where was the rest of the company? Maybe if the entire company was defending they'd have a chance of slowing the attackers long enough for enough blasters and tank killers to arrive to drive them off. But one lousy platoon?

Claypoole didn't know that the rest of the company was there, facing an entire armored regiment supported by an infantry regiment.

Claypoole thought the situation was like that time on Kingdom, when he and Wolfman were sent out to patrol with a platoon of Kingdomite soldiers. Then he wanted to know why he and MacIlargie were being sent on a suicide mission. Well, they survived that patrol, but only because they didn't run into as many Skinks as he'd been afraid they would. But here, he didn't have to imagine how many enemy third platoon was up against—he could see them.

A whole fucking armor battalion and a whole goddamn infantry battalion.

And third platoon wasn't even whole, they were short four men, casualties from the previous day's fighting.

Right, the previous day's fighting. The company had air cover yesterday. Yesterday it was the whole company up against infantry without a tank to be seen. Today they've got tanks, so where the hell is air?

Claypoole fired another Straight Arrow and scooted to a new position without sticking around to see if he'd hit his target.

He reached over his shoulder for another Straight Arrow. He groped over his shoulder for another. He twisted around and *looked* over his shoulder. *He didn't have another Straight Arrow!* Manically, he looked around, he must have dropped a few of them somewhere. He asked MacIlargie for his.

MacIlargie looked at him oddly. "You already fired mine," he said, then turned back and shot another rebel rifleman.

Claypoole scrambled back the way he'd come, searching for dropped tank killers. He couldn't find any. Had he fired all of them?

He risked a quick pop up to look over the boulder he was behind. The quick pop up lasted longer than he'd meant it to: Spread out in front of second squad's boulder field was more than a company's worth of smoldering tanks. He had to have killed some of those tanks himself. But *six* of them? Tanks were still advancing and firing at them, but nowhere near as many as when the fight started. And the infantry wasn't just marching along in support of the tanks, the soldiers were advancing by fire and maneuver—and a lot of them were just lying there, neither firing nor maneuvering.

Three lines of brilliant light flickered past Claypoole's peripheral vision almost too fast to register, and he suddenly remembered he was exposing himself to enemy fire. He ducked back into cover and shifted position, closer to MacIlargie.

"Wolfman, how are you holding out?" he called.

"I'm okay, oh great-killer-of-tanks," MacIlargie called back. "Too bad you don't have any more of those rockets."

Great-killer-of-tanks? Had Claypoole really fired six Straight Arrows and gotten six kills? He unslung his blaster and looked around the side of his boulder. An infantryman jumped up to advance another few meters and Claypoole snapped off a shot. The infantryman went back down and didn't move.

"Shit, is Hammer back with us?" MacIlargie asked. "That was a Schultz shot!"

A Schultz shot? Claypoole looked for another target and another infantryman fell to his shot.

But there were still too damn many tanks.

Corporal Dean didn't take all of his fire team's Straight Arrows for himself, he kept his own three and left Godenov with his three. The two fired their blasters, or set them aside in favor of the tank killers when they had a good shot. Between them they killed five tanks and damaged another. Dean had no idea how many soldiers they'd accounted for. But there were so *many* of the rebels coming at them. It was impossible for one platoon to hold out for very long against the combined force they were facing. Even if they'd had enough Straight Arrows to kill the entire tank battalion, the enemy had too short a distance to cover when the battle began for the Marines to win the fight.

Well, Dean, for one, was going to sell his life dearly. He ignored the cries of "Corpsman Up" and snapped off another bolt; yet another rebel would never rise again.

An unexpected aerial screaming made him duck into a fetal ball before he realized what it was. He looked up and couldn't hold back a scream of glee.

Sunlight glinted off four dots high above and growing fast as they dropped—Raptors! Marine air finally showed up! The Raptors began firing plasma cannons while they were still high. The ground in front of third platoon gouted and erupted with the plasma strikes. Infantrymen where the bolts hit were incinerated, out a few meters from the strikes, their uniforms ignited into torches. Tanks that were hit erupted massively. Tanks a few meters behind a strike rolled into the steaming craters blasted out by the bolt, and not all of them climbed back out.

By the time the Raptors reached the bottom of their dives and bounced back, the infantry was in full rout, and the surviving tanks were turning to run as well. The Marines of third platoon stood up and fired their remaining Straight Arrows, then used their blasters on the running soldiers until Ensign Bass ordered them to cease fire. They'd won.

But how high was the butcher's bill?

CHAPTER TWENTY-FOUR

The corpsmen patched up the casualties and loaded them all onto one Dragon, which sped them back into the tunnel system, where the wounded were transferred to a logistics truck, which trundled them off to the battalion aid station.

"Damn, I hope I'm not making a habit of this," Corporal Pasquin grumbled. He was on a gurney at the battalion aid station while HM1 Horner tweezed bits of shrapnel out of the back of his body from shoulder to calf.

"What habit is that?" Horner asked, twisting a fifteen-millimeter fragment that resisted simple plucking.

Pasquin gasped, then gritted his teeth and said, "Getting wounded. This is the second consecutive deployment I've been wounded on."

The shard clinked when Horner dropped it into the pan he was collecting the fragments in. "Stop your complaining, Marine," he said as he daubed at the blood oozing from the wound and applied a touch of synthskin to the cut, "or I'll write you up for a wound stripe for every one of these booboos."

"Please don't do that, Doc! I've got enough dumb-stripes on my sleeve now." The movement of the tweezers changed as Horner shrugged, sending a spasm through Pasquin's back.

"Then how about if I write you up only for the ones in your ass?"

"You wouldn't!"

"Why not? You're not the first Marine who got shot in the ass . . ."

he paused while he did a quick count of the wounds in Pasquin's posterior, ". . . twenty times." He paused again, then amended, "Or maybe you are. I think the current record for ass-wound-stripes is seventeen, held by some staff sergeant in 11th FIST who pissed off the corpsman who was cleaning shrapnel out of his ass."

"Doc, don't do that to me. I promise, I'll be a model patient. What do you want me to do?"

"Just lie quietly and let me do my job. And if we ever find ourselves in the same card game, let me win a hand or two."

"You got it, Doc."

Corporal Pasquin wasn't the only casualty in third platoon. Fortunately, none of the Marines were killed. The most serious injury was to first squad's Lance Corporal Zumwald, who had taken a laser beam through the shoulder. The planetside navy medical unit didn't have the facilities to regenerate the muscle and bone that were vaporized by the laser, and he had to be evacuated to the *Lance Corporal Keith Lopez* in orbit. Other wounds were lesser, and those Marines could be returned to duty immediately if necessary, in two or three days if there was time for them to recuperate.

Unfortunately, the Coalition forces didn't give the wounded the convalescence time. They launched another attack.

Ensign Charlie Bass listened to the message from Captain Conorado, then spoke into his all-hands circuit, "Third platoon, saddle up! Assemble on your squad leaders. *Now!*" He turned to Staff Sergeant Hyakowa. "Go to the BAS and bring back any of our people who are fit for duty. Bad guys are in the tunnels, and we have to go and kick them out."

"Aye, aye," Hyakowa said, and took off at a run for the battalion aid station, only a couple of hundred meters away in an adjoining tunnel.

"When you've got your people," Bass said into the squad leaders' circuit, "bring them to my location." He busied himself with the schematic of the tunnels, figuring out where to most effectively intercept the rebels and drive them back out.

Only a few of the Marines of third platoon had their helmets on when Bass's all-hands went out, but everyone's helmet was close by, and they all heard the message. They grabbed their gear and weapons and scrambled.

"What's up, Sergeant Ratliff?" Corporal Dean asked when he and Godenov reached their squad leader.

Ratliff didn't look at Dean. "Something. The boss didn't confide in me." He was annoyed that he had to prepare his squad for immediate action and didn't know for what. "Shut up," he said to Corporal Dornhofer when his first fire team leader arrived seconds later.

Dornhofer looked at him, startled; he hadn't said anything. He looked at Dean, who shrugged and shook his head.

Ratliff looked his squad over and wasn't happy with what he saw. Four of his Marines, including one fire team leader, were in sickbay, at the BAS, or back aboard ship. "Dorny," he said to his first fire team leader, "you take Longfellow for now. Dean, you and Izzy stick with me. Let's go." He led the way at a trot to the platoon command post. The two blaster squads and the gun squad arrived within seconds of each other and formed up in front of Bass, who showed no expression when he saw how small his platoon had become in just two actions.

"Stand by," Bass said before anybody could ask any questions. He looked in the direction of the BAS and saw a utility vehicle coming at speed.

The utility vehicle screeched to a stop meters away and Staff Sergeant Hyakowa jumped off, followed by eight other Marines.

Bass shot them a glare and snapped, "Pasquin, Schultz, what are you doing here? The medical officer told me you wouldn't be fit for duty for several days."

Pasquin gave him a crooked grin and said, "I can't let my people go into a fight without papa there to make sure they don't get into trouble."

Schultz merely grunted; he wasn't going to let Corporal Claypoole and Lance Corporal MacIlargie get into a situation where they needed help and not be there to give it to them.

"You two are too badly injured to be here," Bass said harshly. Then his voice eased. "But I'm glad to see you. Take it easy, and don't aggravate your injuries."

"No sweat, boss," Pasquin said as he took his place with first squad.

Ratliff looked relieved at getting back two of his injured men. Lance Corporal Zumwald and PFC Quick, both aboard the *Keith Lopez* for regeneration of bone tissue, were the only Marines of third platoon not present. Ratliff told Longfellow to rejoin his own fire team.

When his Marines were assembled, Bass told them, "Bad guys have gotten into the tunnels. We're going to let them know their presence isn't appreciated." He looked to his left, where he heard the growing noise of a motor, and saw vehicles approaching to pick them up. "I don't have any details yet, not even how many bad guys there are. I'll fill you in when I know more. Now mount up and let's move out."

Third platoon climbed aboard the three utility trucks that had just reached them. The trucks drove them into the unknown.

Ensign Bass listened intently to the information coming over his helmet radio. While Company L had been fighting off the tanks, and both of the battalion's other companies were dealing with armor attacks elsewhere around the perimeter, a brigade-size infantry unit had infiltrated through an area the Marines weren't dealing with and overcome the army "cooks and bakers," rear echelon soldiers, manning that sector of the outer tunnels. More than half the soldiers were dead, wounded, or captured in the fierce fighting, but they'd sold their positions dearly; little less than a battalion of rebel soldiers had made its way into the tunnel complex, and a somewhat smaller number were holding position where the perimeter was breached—presumably to allow follow-on forces to enter the tunnels. More cooks and bakers were fighting a desperate holding action—and losing ground.

The sounds of battle echoed distantly, gradually intruding through the whine of the wheels bearing third platoon to the fight. The sounds got louder as Bass downloaded the latest overlays of where the fighting was, and louder still while he fixed the overlays on his schematic of the tunnels and added routes and symbols to the overlays.

When they were still several hundred meters and a few turns from the fighting, Bass stopped his small convoy and called, "Squad leaders up." He raised an arm and let his sleeve slide down it so his squad leaders could pick him out among the other heat signatures their infras would pick up.

"Receive," Bass said as soon as the three squad leaders, their faces exposed inside their helmets for him to see, arrived, and transmitted the overlays to them. The squad leaders brought up the schematics on their heads-up-displays and examined the overlays with the symbols and routes.

"That's as of five minutes ago," Bass said, transmitting a you-are-here to them. "As you can hear, the intelligence is out of date already." The you-are-here put them a couple of hundred meters closer to the sounds of battle than the overlay showed.

Sergeant Ratliff whistled softly.

Sergeant Linsman said, "They're moving fast."

"No shit, Sherlock," Sergeant Kelly muttered.

"The speed of their advance gives us a major advantage," Bass said, ignoring the remarks. "When a fast-moving object runs into a bigger object moving even faster, it rebounds. Basic physics. We're going here," he sent a signal that made his symbols and routes pulse on the squad leaders' HUDs, "and smack them back so hard they're liable to find themselves back on the surface before they stop rebounding."

The section of schematic the squad leaders examined showed two major corridors. A five-meter-wide corridor made many turns on its inbound journey from the outer tunnel ring; strongpoints had been erected at each turning. The Coalition battalion was advancing along that tunnel. The other major corridor, seven meters wide, that formed an irregular ring inside the outer perimeter, crossed it. Two smaller corridors paralleled the inbound corridor and terminated at the ring-tunnel, only fifty meters to the sides of the intersection. Rooms filled the spaces between the inbound and parallel corridors. There weren't any strongpoints noted on the ring or the smaller tunnels.

The routes and symbols Bass had overlaid on the schematic directed one gun team to set up at a turning of the inbound tunnel where it could fire straight down it past the ring-tunnel. The other gun team went down the left-hand parallel corridor to set up a crossfire along the ring-tunnel. First squad was to set up inside the rooms to the right of the inbound tunnel, and second squad in the rooms to its left. According to still 2-D images Bass had of the tunnel, the rooms had doors into the inbound tunnel that would allow his Marines to fire down the tunnel while retaining a fair amount of cover.

But, as was often the case, the Marines' best protection from enemy fire was the virtual invisibility provided by their chameleon uniforms.

The symbols Bass drew showing where fire teams and the gun teams went didn't indicate which teams went where. He left those decisions up to the squad leaders.

"Any questions?" he asked when he thought the squad leaders had enough time to examine the schematic.

"How many did you say were coming this way?" Kelly asked.

"An understrength battalion."

No one said anything for a moment, then Ratliff softly said, "They're in a tunnel. They won't be able to advance more than two fire teams at a time. Hound, *one* of your guns could hold them up until they ran out of men—or your gun ran out of power."

"Barring lucky hits," Staff Sergeant Hyakowa said, speaking for the first time.

"These tunnel walls are pretty rough cut," Bass added, "there aren't any polished surfaces for lasers to reflect off of."

Kelly glanced at him, then looked at the other two squad leaders. "I'm putting Barber's gun there. You just worry about keeping your people's heads out of his line of fire."

Bass cocked his head, the sounds of fighting were much closer. "Let's do this thing," he said, and snapped his chameleon screen into place. His face vanished.

The sound of pounding footsteps and yells made Lance Corporal Tischler, behind the gun pointed down the inbound tunnel, tense. Next to him, PFC Yi got ready to feed the gun. The whine of laser shots punctuated the noises.

"Easy, easy," Corporal Barber said. "Don't fire until I say to." Listening to the laser fire, he was glad of the lack of reflective surfaces in the tunnel.

The yells, out of sight beyond the bend past the cross tunnel, grew louder, and individual voices became discernible; many of them were screaming.

"Wait for my order." The calmness of Barber's voice didn't show the tenseness he felt.

Suddenly, a running man burst into sight at the bend, seventy-five meters distant.

"Hold it, hold it," Barber murmured.

Tischler's grip tightened on the gun's firing lever.

"Don't shoot! Hold your fire!" Barber said sharply as more running, screaming men turned the bend. "They're ours."

Ensign Bass's voice giving the same command almost drowned Barber out in the helmet radios of first gun team.

Soldiers of the 27th Division, more than half of them weaponless, pelted wide-eyed along the tunnel, fleeing the advancing Coalition rebels. Some of the running soldiers turned right or left onto the ring-tunnel, but most kept going straight.

"Buddha's Balls!" Barber swore—the soldiers were coming straight at his team, and they couldn't see the Marines in their chameleons. "Get out of their way!" He shoved Tischler to his left, to the inside of the bend. The gun fell over with a clatter because Tischler was caught off guard by Barber's shove. Yi barely made it to the wall behind the gunner before the other hit the wall.

Barber swore again and reached for the gun to yank it in close. He wasn't fast enough. The first soldier to reach the bend banked hard off the wall on the outside of the bend, but the second soldier skittered to slow down to take the corner and tripped over the gun, knocking it away from Barber's reaching hand. The third soldier tripped over the spinning weapon and sprawled onto the second. In seconds, an entire squad's worth of soldiers had tripped on the gun, soldiers who had fallen before them, or over Barber, who was trying desparately to get the gun out of the way—one of them kicked Barber's head hard enough to partly dislodge his helmet, dazing him.

None of the soldiers seemed aware of the Marines; they scrambled to their feet as fast as they could and took off again. The last of them almost didn't make it—a laser beam bored through the lower part of the soldier's left calf. He didn't seem to notice the injury.

Other soldiers sped through, but there were fewer of them now, and they were more widely spaced. Barber finally got hold of the gun and passed it to Tischler. Then he scooted forward on his belly to look around the corner.

The bodies of several soldiers littered the tunnel floor; some of the bodies were still moving, and one or two of them were weakly crawling toward the corner where the Marine gun team waited. There was nothing Barber could do for them—maybe the blastermen in the rooms along the corridor could drag them to safety—he had to deal with what he saw beyond the casualties.

Rebel soldiers were advancing along the sides of the tunnel. One man would dash forward, then drop to a prone position with his weapon pointed forward, and another would rise up behind him and dash forward. The enemy soldiers leap-frogged like that on both sides, visible in the middle of the tunnel only at the far end where, one by one, half of them darted across to the opposite wall. The closest of them were almost at the intersection.

"Tischler, get your gun set up next to the corner," he ordered, urgency in his tone. "Fire a burst straight down the wall, then spray the opposite wall beyond the intersection." He could tell by the sounds that Tischler already had the gun back on its tripod and when it was in position.

"What about our people?" Tischler asked.

"Don't worry, they're inside the rooms," Barber said. He shook his head trying to clear it.

"Whatever you say," Tischler replied, and fired a short burst of plasma pulses along the wall.

The invisibility conferred by the chameleons was an optical illusion; Barber couldn't see *through* his gunner and the gun, he had to scoot farther out in order to see to direct the gun's fire.

It looked like the first, short burst had taken out or knocked down every rebel soldier along the near wall, though more were coming around the far bend and returning fire. Barber watched as Tischler shifted his aim to the other side of the tunnel, spraying up and down to get the soldiers who lay prone as well as those who jumped up to dart forward. He got most of them before they reached the cross tunnel and turned into it. Barber didn't worry about them, Corporal Taylor's second gun team was in position to take them out. As though in answer to

Barber's thought, plasma started streaming across his sight from the other gun.

The living rebels still in the tunnel all went prone and spread out to return fire. They may not have been able to see the Marines, but they could see where the plasma bolts were coming from and concentrated their fire on the gun.

"Back!" Barber ordered, scooting backward himself. "Get—" and caught a flash of the most brilliant light he'd ever seen.

If your head's in the line of sight of a laser shot, the beam doesn't need to bounce off a reflective surface to hit you.

Corporal Pasquin had to wonder if he'd made a mistake, leaving the BAS when Staff Sergeant Hyakowa showed up to get any of third platoon's casualties who were ready to return to duty. There'd hardly been enough time for any of the wounds on his back, buttocks, and thighs to begin to heal, and he felt every one of them trying to reopen during the ride to the blocking position in the tunnel, and then the run to the positions where third platoon would stop the invading Coalition troops. But he thought of the alternative, leaving the squad three men short, and told himself he could always go back to the battalion aid station after the fight if he needed to. The bigger problem at the moment was that he and both of his men would have to fire through the same doorway when the bad guys came.

"Shoup, can you fire okay prone?"

"Not a problem, honcho," PFC Shoup replied. Pasquin's infra showed his junior man lying with his head in the doorway and only his left arm and shoulder completely out of it.

"Longfellow, kneel to his left so you can fire over him."

"Got it."

That left the off hand—standing—position for Pasquin. It was a triply awkward position for him to take. He had to straddle Longfellow in order to get close enough to the doorway to lean the back of his left shoulder into it, which had the corner of the doorframe in nearly direct contact with one of his wounds. He winced, but held position. Worse than the pain was the fact that he'd have to fire left-handed. Like all infantry Marines, he had significant practice firing from all positions, and had used all of them in combat. He knew that left-handed off hand was his weakest shooting position. But there was no remedy for it; that was the way he had to fire, any other position possible in his fire team's position would aggravate his injuries even worse than this did.

"Hold your fire," he said, as the broken defenders began running around the corner he could barely see from his angle. "Wait for my command. Remember to keep your fire high enough you don't risk hitting Dorny or Gray." First fire team was in the next room closer to the intersection. "When I tell you, shoot through the crossing passageway, do *not* try to ricochet your shots off the opposite wall. Remember, second squad's over there, let's not shoot our own people."

Then the gun opened fire behind them, sending a stream of plasma bolts down the wide corridor. Flashes of laser beams shot past in the opposite direction. Pasquin leaned out farther. His shoulder wound opened and began to ooze blood. He ignored the pain; he could see the enemy.

"Fire!" he commanded, and his fire team opened up on the enemy.

"What do you want to do, Hammer?" Corporal Claypoole asked when second squad took position in rooms on the other side of the broad corridor from first squad.

Schultz raised his helmet screens and spat. Lowering them, he growled, "Kill."

"Ask a stupid question . . ." Claypoole muttered. He looked at the doorway and wondered how he could bring his fire team's full power to bear on the enemy without exposing them too much—the doorway was less than a meter and a half wide, and three of them had to fit in it. He couldn't remember another time when he'd had to fire jammed that tightly together with other Marines.

He poked his head out for a quick glance at the shouts and running footsteps he heard coming toward them, took a longer look than he'd intended and withdrew his head more slowly. "It's the soldiers," he said. "They look like they had the shit scared out of them. Let them by." Inside his helmet, he shook his head sadly. Then he shook his shoulders and got back to the matter at hand—how to set up in the tight space.

"Hammer, can you fire off hand and leave room for both of us?"

A noise rumbled up from somewhere deep in Schultz's chest; Claypoole took it as a yes.

"All right," Claypoole said, "Wolfman, you go prone. I'll kneel and fire over you. Our own people are in front of us on both sides, be careful you don't shoot them."

Schultz slid his infra screen into place as he turned his head to watch the fleeing soldiers and saw Corporal Barber setting his gun team. "Back," he growled, and shoved Claypoole and MacIlargie out of the doorway, back into the room, seconds before a long burst of fire from the gun streamed down the corridor past their position.

Claypoole yelped when he saw the plasma bolts blur past. "They could have hit us!" he exclaimed.

"What's going on?" MacIlargie yelled. "Barber's too good a gun team leader to make that kind of mistake."

"I don't know," Claypoole snapped. He looked toward Schultz, who stood placidly, watching the plasma bolts from the gun and the laser flashes from the rebels race past. The plasma bolts seemed to be winning, especially when first squad opened up from the other side of the corridor.

Then the gun stopped firing and the laser fire picked up. Schultz was in the doorway firing at the enemy before Claypoole even began to order his men into the tight space to begin fighting.

Even before Lance Corporal Tischler and PFC Yi pulled Corporal Barber's body to safety and resumed firing down the corridor, the rebel advance was stopped by the massive fire put out by the blasters of third platoon. Nearly all of the Coalition troops in the corridor down which the Marines fired were dead or wounded and out of action. Only a few of them, no more than three or four, could fire from the far corner, and their fire was ineffective.

When the rebels fired their lasers, the light beams harmlessly disappeared into the rough surfaces of the tunnel walls. The Marines' plasma bolts sometimes spattered when they hit the walls, spitting sparks of star-stuff in all directions; sometimes they melted tiny rock protrusions and flung the molten metal around. The Marines weren't suffering more casualties, but the rebel troops were getting dinged and worse.

Ensign Charlie Bass did a quick assessment of the situation and raced to first gun team's position, carrying four Straight Arrows. He spared a quick look at Barber, whose helmet had been pulled off by Tischler. Barber's eyes were open, looked surprised, his jaw was slack. Blood trickled from a small hole in his forehead. Bass looked away, expressionless. Barber had been with him for a long time, but he'd have to wait until the battle was over to mourn the Marine.

"Here's what we're going to do . . ." Bass said into his all-hands circuit. When he finished, he waited a moment while the squad and fire team leaders checked to make sure everybody got the word, then stood and trotted along the middle of the tunnel, unslinging one of the Straight Arrows as he went.

"You shouldn't be doing this, Charlie," Staff Sergeant Hyakowa said over the platoon command circuit, "you're the boss."

"I can't ask someone else to do something I won't do myself," Bass replied. The Marines ahead of him were giving him covering fire, firing blasters as fast as they could. They were all using their infras, and as he passed each fire team's position it stopped firing to avoid hitting him.

"You've already done enough," Hyakowa insisted.

"Enough to some, maybe," Bass said when he was halfway to the cross tunnel. He dropped to one knee and sighted the tank killer a few meters short of the end of the wall to the right of the turn. With a bit of luck, the missile would ricochet off the wall and make it around the corner before its warhead exploded. If nothing else, it would send a shockwave and some fragments past the corner.

It was if-nothing-else, and he heard screams from one or two men who were out of sight when the missile exploded when it hit the wall.

Bass was off and running again, his footfalls a counterpoint to the screams. He had another Straight Arrow unlimbered and ready to fire when he reached the cross tunnel. He stepped into the tunnel on the right to get the sharpest angle he could on the corner. He tried too hard for the angle, the missile struck the wall just before the corner and glanced off to impact against the far wall. Its shaped charge sent most of its explosive energy into the stone. Still, it threw out shards of rock in all directions, and there were more screams.

Bass got completely out of the line of fire and ordered the platoon to send everything it had down the tunnel. In an instant, plasma bolts from eighteen blasters and one gun turned the length of the tunnel into a dazzling light show that nothing could live through.

Bass gave it fifteen seconds, then called a cease-fire. He cranked his ears all the way up and listened. He heard a few moans coming from around the corner, and the sound of retreating footfalls.

"First—no, make that second squad, with me," Bass ordered. "Kelly, get both guns to the intersection and be ready to give us covering fire if we have to come back in a hurry."

Bass gave second squad a few seconds to join him, then waited a few seconds more for the two gun teams to reach the intersection, then ordered second squad to wait until he called them up, and pelted down the corridor with a Straight Arrow ready to fire. Halfway to the corner, he stopped and fired his third tank killer. This time, the missile barely missed the corner and exploded where he wanted it to.

"Second squad, move up!" he ordered. He laid the last Straight Arrow down and drew his hand-blaster. When he heard second squad almost on him, he jumped to his feet and dashed forward. He hit the deck and slid the last couple of meters into the corner, turning his head to his left and pointing his hand-blaster in the same direction.

In front of him were the dead and the wounded the Coalition troops left behind. The survivors had already vanished beyond the next bend in the tunnel; their footsteps were growing faint with distance.

"Third platoon, on me!" Bass roared into the command circuit. The enemy was on the run, and he intended to keep them that way.

A short while earlier, the defenders had panicked and run in the face of a powerful assault. Now the earlier victors were panicked and running from a smaller but potent force. Bass stopped the pursuit when third platoon reached the defensive positions from which a battalion of the Confederation Army's 27th Division had been routed. He only stopped there because Captain Conorado said the order to hold came directly from Brigadier Sturgeon.

It was only dumb, bad luck, the kind of unfortunate accident that happens in combat, that put Sergeant Linsman's throat directly in the path of a parting shot that reflected off a mess kit left behind by a fleeing soldier. The laser beam sliced through his throat from the right jugular vein to the left carotid, cutting through his windpipe on its way. He had bled too much to save by the time Doc Hough reached him and put him in a stasis bag.

CHAPTER TWENTY-FIVE

"Grabs, what do you hear on the streets these days?" Cynthia Chang-Sturdevant asked. Covered only by a sheet, she lay faceup on Dr. Karla Grabentao's portable treatment table. Soft music from Grabentao's private collection filled the office. During the last few months, since she had been made aware of the benefits of massage therapy, the President made time for the doctor's visits, no matter how busy her schedule. But she could not spare the time to take massage therapy at Dr. Grabentao's clinic, the Fuller Sports Medicine Clinic (named for her late husband, Dr. Breton Fuller, inventor of the popular Myofascilator glove). So the doctor came to her.

While the President's private office was comfortable in a utilitarian way, it was nothing like the private treatment rooms available at Grabentao's clinic, where her clients relaxed in an atmosphere conducive to massage therapy: soft lighting, soothing music, and the aroma of fragrant herbs. But the doctor did her best to import that atmosphere into Chang-Sturdevant's work environment. The President's staff obeyed the inflexible rule that once a week, during the hour she was under Dr. Grabentao's care, she would not be disturbed.

Dr. Karla Grabentao was not a big woman but she had strong shoulders, arms, and hands, developed over the years as a massage therapist before she obtained her license as an orthopedic surgeon. Now she ran one of the most respected sports-medicine clinics in Fargo. Dr. Grabentao was one of those health-care professionals thoroughly dedicated to practicing the healing arts. She also made house calls and, when she wasn't in surgery, would personally perform massage therapy on certain clients, President Cynthia Chang-Sturdevant being one of them. That had its practical side, because being able to claim the President of the Confederation of Human Worlds as a client was not bad for business.

"Skin is the human body's largest organ," Grabentao had explained during their first session, as she worked on the flexors in Chang-Sturdevant's right arm. "If you could spread it out you could make a rug out of it," she said wryly, "because it covers in all about two square meters and makes up about eighteen percent of your total body weight. Pardon me for talking so much today, but I just think my clients need to know the basics of this type of therapy. How does that feel? Too much pressure?"

"No, no, pretty good, actually." Chang-Sturdevant had complained about soreness in her arm before the session started. She was instructed to let her arm relax completely as Grabentao worked on it and gradually the soreness began to disappear. "I was just thinking about the rug made of human skin when I grimaced."

"Excuse me. I guess that does present a pretty grim image," Grabentao admitted. "But you see how important skin is as an organ? Well, I don't need to tell you how sensitive it is. Did you know there are as many as three million touch receptors in your skin, three thousand alone in one fingertip? So it's very receptive to all kinds of stimulation. A simple touch can reduce your blood pressure, for instance. And during intensive massage therapy that stimulation produces endorphins, pain suppressors. People have known this for thousands of years, since at least as long ago as ancient China." She smiled, but Chang-Sturdevant's eyes were closed as by degrees she began to fall under the spell of Grabentao's therapy. "There is no substitute for the human touch. That's why I don't ordinarily use the Myofascilator glove—you know, the device many chiropractors and therapists use to deliver deep electrical stimulation to the muscles and connective tissues. I use my hands and my arms, as you'll see if we continue these sessions." And they had continued regularly, for months now.

"There's a lot of tension in your shoulders today," Grabentao remarked.

"Matches the tension in the world, I guess," Chang-Sturdevant murmured. She was already beginning to relax as Grabentao's strong hands, using long, relaxing strokes, worked the tension out of her muscles. During most sessions neither woman said a word throughout the entire hour and often by the time Grabentao was finished with her full-body massage treatment, Chang-Sturdevant would be asleep. Other times they would talk the full hour. Today Chang-Sturdevant wanted to talk.

"Are you doing those exercises I recommended for the tendinitis in this shoulder?" Grabentao asked. Chang-Sturdevant winced slightly as Grabentao manipulated her left shoulder.

"Whenever I can, Grabs. Well, dammit, I don't have the time to do them! Think I'll just have you replace the whole shebang."

"Sure, when you have the time," Grabentao laughed. "I just love to cut on people, even when they don't need it, even when the difficulty is caused by their own negligence."

"Touché."

As Grabentao manipulated the President's neck and shoulders, Chang-Sturdevant thought, as she often did during their sessions, how easy it would be for a therapist to murder someone by breaking their neck. Just snap her neck and leave quietly while her victim lay there stone dead. She chided herself for allowing this paranoia to spoil the atmosphere. It just was that she realized there were a lot of people who really would like to break her neck. "I hope you're a member of my party," she murmured. This had become a standard joke with them since these sessions began. Actually, her orthopedic problems were very minor; she valued the therapy because it relaxed her. If she had the time she'd devote an hour a day to this treatment.

"So what do you hear?" Chang-Sturdevant asked again.

Grabentao chuckled. "Madam President, if I tell you, I'll have to double your bill for this session. You know my rate for developing vital intelligence!" Chang-Sturdevant laughed out loud. During the course of Grabentao's day, which was always long, she met all kinds of people, people from all walks of life, and they talked to her, talked about their personal lives, their hopes and fears, their aches and pains, the weather, the economy, and politics. Over the months Chang-Sturdevant had been her client, Karla Grabentao had proved a better source of public opinion than anyone in her cabinet.

"The people I've talked to recently generally oppose your war with the Coalition." Chang-Sturdevant winced at the words "your war," but she let it pass. "The people who've mentioned the war to me don't understand what harm could come to the Confederation if the secessionists are allowed to go their own way. They just don't see the Coalition as a threat to them or anyone else."

"Mmm," Chang-Sturdevant murmured. Grabentao moistened her hands with an aromatic eicosene copolymer petrolatum-based mineral oil crème of her own invention, adjusted the bolster under her client's legs, and started working on her feet. She worked there for several minutes in silence, taking heated pebbles and applying them gently to the bottoms of Chang-Sturdevant's feet. "They're a little dry today, ma'am," she reported, "use the crème at night just before bed, and have a podiatrist look at that callus on the ball of your left foot. I think it's getting bigger." Foot massage was an important phase of the treatment Grabentao offered her clients.

And it was effective; Chang-Sturdevant could literally feel the tension draining from her body. She sighed. "How are things at home?" she asked.

"Fargo is my home now, ma'am. But you mean back on Wanderjahr? I left there before you overthrew the oligarchs," she pronounced the world "oligarchs" sharply. "That was the best thing that ever happened to my people." She started working on Chang-Sturdevant's right lower leg.

"That was because we intervened in your civil war."

"Yes, I know, and we will be eternally grateful to you and your Marines for doing that, ma'am."

"So sometimes interventions in local affairs are justified?" Chang-Sturdevant smiled.

"Yes." The next several minutes passed in silence. Grabentao switched to using her elbow, a technique for deep tissue massage. She finished working on the President's right leg and moved to her left. The silence continued. The music—ancient flute music performed by an ensemble called Los Calchakis—played on. Chang-Sturdevant began to drift off. Normally she'd have given in but not today. "Karla, what do *you* think? What do *you* think about this war?"

Karla Grabentao did not answer immediately. "Ma'am, we really shouldn't talk war and politics during these sessions. That only upsets you and defeats the whole purpose of my visits here."

"Oblige me, please."

Karla sighed. "Ma'am, I am a member of your party. I voted for you and I will vote for you again. I know what it's like to live in a world run by greedy, dishonest politicians, and I thank God for the Confederation of Human Worlds and its president." She spoke with feeling. "But Madam President, my advice to you is don't declare war on the seceding worlds! Call off your armies! Let those people go." She paused. "Now," Dr. Karla Grabentao was back in her role as therapist again, "roll over on to your stomach so I can work your back. And drink more water! You are getting dehydrated."

The Congressional Club at Fargo was a favorite hangout for legislators. For some it offered amenities not available to them on their home worlds, such as a complete athletic facility and interstellar-class gourmet dining, and for all its members it was a home away from home where they could relax and enjoy themselves after a hard day of politicking. In fact, more agreements and coalitions were formed in the private salons at the Congressional Club than in the offices and cloakrooms of the Congress Hall. That was due at least in part to the fact that stimulants flowed more freely at the Club than in the Hall.

Haggl Kutmoi sat in the sauna, a thick towel across his knees, reviewing reports on a portable vid reader. Occasionally he wiped at a rivulet of perspiration from his cheek. Dimly visible through the thick clouds of steam, several other representatives perched in the facility, reading, relaxing, conversing in low voices. Kutmoi had only a nodding acquaintance with the others, but true to the cardinal rule of the Congressional Club sauna, none would engage in conversation with him unless invited to. The image on the vid was a bill he was sponsoring that would give certain benefits to reservists called up for the pending war with the secessionist coalition.

Someone sat down next to him. "Great speech you gave today, Kutie," he said.

Haggl felt a sudden flash of irritation; it was Ubsa Nor. It wasn't enough they were members of opposite parties, but Nor's stubborn opposition to military action against the secessionists had deepened their differences to a chasm. Nor's breach of sauna etiquette was annoying, but another rule of the Congressional Club was that political and personal animosities were left at the door. Haggl quickly switched off his vid. "Ubbie," he nodded casually at Nor.

Ubsa Nor stretched his legs and rearranged his towel. "Going for a swim afterward?" he asked politely.

"Yeah."

"Mmm." Nor wiggled his toes. He was a heavyset man, thick in the chest, as one would expect of a former miner. Compared to Ubbie's life back on his home world, Novo Kongor, life at the Congressional Club was pure luxury, and during his years in the legislature and at the Club's tables, the good living had added kilos to his frame. But Kutmoi couldn't help speculating how he'd fare if they ever came to blows over their politics, which seemed more and more likely as tempers frayed over the war.

"We have to get together," Nor said.

"Over what?"

"This war, Kutie."

"That is just not possible, Ubbie," Haggl said with finality, putting his vid back into its case. He wiped his head with his towel, preparatory to leaving. He couldn't relax with Nor chatting him up.

"Just a moment," Nor laid a hand on Kutmoi's forearm. "We need to have a dialogue, Congressman. Throwing speeches at each other is no way to settle this conflict. We need to join forces and prevail on the president to find a peaceful solution to the secessionist movement. We are about to get a lot of people killed—"

"And lose a lot of money if the embargoes remain in effect. Isn't that what you're really saying?"

Nor shook his head in annoyance. "That is a canard, Kutie, to think all we're interested in is money. We're talking human lives here!"

"We are talking the basic unity of our Confederation, Ubbie! If the Coalition worlds are allowed to break their compact with the Confederation, which I think is illegal under our Constitution—"

"Now hang on there! Don't quote propaganda at me. You know perfectly well that if the Coalition worlds secede that will have absolutely no effect whatever on either the economic or political freedoms of the other members of this Confederation! Those dozen worlds are free agents, Kutie, and when they voluntarily joined our Confederation, the implication was that the union would serve their interests. But now that they believe it no longer does, they have not only a right to dissolve the union, they are obligated as free worlds to withdraw from it."

"Are you Novo Kongorians thinking of joining the rebellion, man? Doesn't it mean anything to you that their forces attacked and are besieging our troops at Fort Seymour? It's they who don't want a peaceful settlement, Ubbie, not us! And you know goddamned well that worlds are voted into the Confederation by a two-thirds majority and they can't opt out unless it's put to a vote; and I guarantee you, it never will be!"

"Well, what do you expect, Kutie? We reinforce the garrison there for no discernible reason except to compel Ravenette by force to remain in the Confederation, and then our troops slaughter dozens of unarmed civilians? Goddamnit, man, how would you react to something like that?"

The two had raised their voices to a level where the other patrons had taken notice. "Gentlemen," one of them cautioned.

"Look, this conversation is not getting anywhere, Ubbie," Kutmoi said in a lower tone of voice. "Let's just drop it, all right?"

"Would you just listen for a moment? I have a compromise I wish to propose. If we can sell the president and your party on this we can share Nobels! Just listen, will ya?"

"So that's it, huh? All this talk about the Constitution and human life is bullshit, Nor! Share a Nobel Prize with you, you bastard? You're a goddamned traitor and you can just go and fuck yourself!" Kutmoi grabbed his vid case and stood up. Although he tried not to show it, standing up so quickly made him dizzy, but Nor was so angry he didn't notice the other man fighting to keep his balance.

"Traitor? You call me a traitor, you goddamned useless flabby-assed piece of shit?" Nor yelled, getting to his own feet. "If you ever had to work for a living instead of sucking off the Confederation teat on your big fat ass all your life, you'd know that it's real people, not fakes like you, who pay the price for your 'Constitutional sanctity' bullshit arguments, you goddamned murdering Nazi swine!"

That was too much. Kutmoi swung his vid case hard against Nor's head. It struck with a sharp *thwack,* flew out of Kutmoi's hand, and skittered into a corner. Nor staggered backward, a hand to the side of his head, eyes wide in astonishment. Horrified at what he'd just done, Kutmoi could only stand there gaping helplessly at the tendril of blood seeping from between Nor's fingers. Nor recovered quickly and delivered a powerful roundhouse blow to the side of Kutmoi's head. Kutmoi went down and Nor pounced on him, screaming inarticulately. Pounding, grasping, panting, and screaming curses, the two, divested of their fragile dignities as congresspersons, rolled naked off the bench and onto the floor. Because of their own perspiration and the condensation in the sauna the other patrons had great difficulty prying the two men apart.

"Well, Suelee, the 'Billie Club' has landed at last," Marcus Berentus sighed, using his pet name for Madam Cynthia Chang-Sturdevant, closing the door to Chang-Sturdevant's private apartment behind him.

"Marcus!" she chided Berentus. She kicked off her shoes, unfastened her tunic and flopped exhaustedly on the couch. "General Billie was our best choice to lead the army to Ravenette, so stop making those remarks," she laughed. "Mix us a stiff one, would you?"

Chuckling, Berentus fiddled with the digital bar. "I don't quite share your confidence in our General Jason Billie, Suelee," he replied. He never used her middle name in public, that privilege was reserved only for her family and most intimate friends, and then only in private. "Old Porter wanted to send the Marine commandant, Aguinaldo, which probably would have been the best choice, but I couldn't have permitted that. This is an army operation. Well, Billie and his boys will muddle through." He handed Chang-Sturdevant a bourbon and soda with ice. He'd made himself a scotch on the rocks. "Scotch is an officer's drink, Suelee," he had once explained, "and I hate it, but I was an officer so I've got to keep up the tradition." They toasted each other and sipped their drinks. Chang-Sturdevant stretched her legs out on the sofa and Berentus took a nearby chair.

"Stay here tonight, Marcus."

Berentus raised his eyebrows. "Well, I dunno, ma'am, I have some books back at my apartment begging to be read, some vids I'd like to watch, a cold dinner waiting, and a cold shower before bed." He shrugged. "You know, the things an old bachelor loves to do in the frigid solitude of his monastic cell—"

"Marcus!"

"Well, all right, the couch will do for me."

"Marcus!" They chuckled and sipped their drinks silently. Chang-Sturdevant suddenly laughed outright. "Wasn't that a scene at the Congressional Club this afternoon?"

"What?" Berentus leaned forward, and laughing harder, Chang-Sturdevant described the incident between Haggl Kutmoi and Ubsa Nor. As she talked Berentus began laughing too, and before she was done they were both in tears.

"But Marcus, it really isn't funny," Chang-Sturdevant said after she'd caught her breath, "I mean, with those two at each other's throats like that, how can I expect consensus on how to deal with this rebellion? I mean, even with our slim majority, the crossovers can defeat every legislative move we make to put an end to this business. I'm willing to compromise on the secessionists' demands, but I can't even get the Congress to agree on those measures!"

"Suelee, we tried to compromise with those people. We bent over backward, were willing to give in to just about everything they wanted. But Summers and his party do not want compromise, they'll only settle for full secession. I'm telling you again, as your Minister of War, the only way we can settle this crisis is by force of arms, and the secessionist coalition will fight us to the bitter end."

"Mmm," Chang-Sturdevant replied.

Berentus put his drink aside, wiped his hands on his trousers, and gently ran his fingers through her hair. "I think I see a few more strands of gray in there, Suelee."

"You rascal," she murmured.

"Ummm, your hair smells funky tonight—but good, but good! I like it that way. You've got the hair of a working woman."

"I give you one hour to stop these insults." They lapsed into silence. "Marcus," Suelee said at last, "you're pretty good, but no substitute for Dr. Grabentao."

"I really am jealous of that woman. But," he chuckled, "I am not without my own therapies."

They were silent again for several minutes. "Marcus," Suelee said, sitting up straight suddenly, shaking her hair out and reaching for her drink, "I am afraid we are in for a long, hard war." Her Minister of War remained silent.

CHAPTER TWENTY-SIX

"Bud, if you don't shut yer trap, when this is over I'll kill ya meself 'n I guarantee you'll die real hard," Timor Caloon shouted at last and finally Clabber lapsed into sulking silence. They had been on the road to Bibbsville only thirty minutes and Clabber had been complaining bitterly and threatening the whole time. Since Timor needed him unscathed to carry out his plan, physical abuse was out of the question. Timor had not yet told his companions what that plan was.

The road to Bibbsville was unpaved, dusty when dry, impassable when wet, and traveling its fifty kilometers an all-day ordeal even in good weather. If the residents of Cuylerville could wait, often it was more convenient for them to order the things they needed shipped on the *Figaro*. The thule buyers came out from the county seat in aircraft. They could afford to do that and although Bibbsville did not have a spaceport, it did have an airfield that could accommodate large atmospheric fliers, permitting connections with other regions of the planet. But for the residents of Cuylerville, travel abroad was far cheaper and more convenient on the *Figaro* because they could afford the time.

For his trip, Timor Caloon arranged to take the only ground-effect vehicle in Cuylerville. With it he could negotiate the potholes and detours and it was big enough to carry himself and eight other people. But the ride was extremely slow and rough. For privacy, Donnie and Charlette climbed into the back of the vehicle at the price of absorbing the full effect of every bump in the road.

"Bibbsville was the biggest city I ever seen before I come to Ashburtonville, Charlette. When I left here, about two years ago, they musta been forty-five thousand people in Bibbsville. It's the biggest town in all of Loudon County. I only been up there a few times, but we all know where we're goin', 'n that's to Lugs's place."

"And this Lugs is?"

"Well, he's the man who owns the curing barns and the processing plant for the thule he buys from us, and he has the distribution system for the finished products. And because of that he is probably the richest man in all of Loudon County. It was him, you can be sure of that, who sent those men down here to kill Miz Pickens and put the fear of God into the rest of us." Donnie snorted. "Well, we're gonna put the fear into his ass, I goddamn guarantee. Daddy's got a plan, you can bet on it."

"It'd be kinda nice of Daddy to share that plan with us, don't you think?" Charlette wiped the dust off the barrel of the rifle between her knees. Already she could taste the grit in her mouth, but nobody wanted to close the windows because the car didn't have climate control and it'd be stifling inside the cab.

"He'll tell us when the time is right." Donnie wiped the perspiration from his forehead. His hand came away smeared with a fine coating of mud. "Damn, I sure miss that apartment of ours, back in Ashburtonville." Donnie laughed. "Guess there's a city boy inside every country boy." He was silent for a moment. "See, because of the climate in this part of the world lotsa folks grew tobacco, still do, but it's the thule that gives the cigarettes and cigars their kick, and if you really want to get high you kin smoke uncut thule, which Lugs also processes. And thule is where the money is. Anyways, Lugs has all these curing barns on the outskirts of town where he flue cures the thule and the tobacco in bulk, which he hangs up inside these barns, which is heated by wood fires, and the heat is circulated by flues, which is why it's called 'flue curing.' All kinds of chemical changes takes place during curing which I don't unnerstand. They's other ways to cure the stuff besides flue curing, which maybe old Lugs uses too, I dunno. Then he has plants that turn all that stuff into cigarettes, cigars, chewin' tobacco, all that stuff, even crap you stuff up yer nose," he wrinkled his nose at the thought of taking snuff.

"So we're going to kill this Lugs?" Charlette asked.

"I suppose that's part of the plan."

Charlette wondered silently what it would be like to pull a trigger on someone, even a despicable murderer like this Lugs person. In her training she had been taught many different methods of killing people but she had never had to use any of them. "What's he like, this Lugs?"

Donnie shrugged. "Big, nasty bastard. Last time I seen him was four, five years ago."

"So what do we do, just walk in and start shooting?"

"I guess so. That's why he's got Bud along." At the mention of his name Clabber turned and glared at the pair. "He'll fill us in before we git there."

At noon they stopped to rest.

"Charlette," Timor Caloon said, "you take your rifle and walk Bud down the road a ways. I want to talk to the boys a bit 'n I'll tell you later what I'm plannin', but I don' want Bud to know until it's time. Don't worry about how long it's gonna take us to get to Bibbsville. We're not goin' in there 'til tomorrow anyways. Now take him off down there 'n if he gives you any trouble, shoot 'im."

Charlette flicked the safety on her rifle to off and then checked the loading indicator, to make sure there was a round in the chamber. There was. She put her finger lightly inside the trigger guard. "Hands on top of your head and move," she ordered Clabber.

Shaking his head and smirking, he trudged off back down the road. As soon as Charlette judged they were out of hearing, she ordered him to sit down.

"Girl, you and your friends are in a world of hurt, d'ya know that?" Clabber grinned up at Charlette.

"My name's Charlette."

"Oh, pardon me all to hell! I gotta take all kinds of shit off them others but goddamned if I'll take lip off a stupid cunt like you!" Charlette menaced him with the rifle but Clabber only grinned. "Think you're pretty damn smart? Well, you ain't! I know what you are, girl, you're a goddamned spy! Worked in a laundry, my ass! You shacked up with that idiot Donnie to find out what was going on in Ashburtonville and you got stuck in town when we sieged Fort Seymour. Sheeyit!" he spit on the ground.

"That's not true!" But if the police in Ashburtonville knew her true identity, they'd also know where Donnie was headed when he left the city. And Clabber had the only radio.

"Sheeyit, what do you take me for, girl? Lugs knows it too, and if he don't kill ya, he'll hand you over to the army. When *he's* done with ya."

The sun beat down intensely and the nausea that had been affecting Charlette recently returned suddenly. It was distracting and she felt the urge to urinate as well. Was she really pregnant or was it something she'd eaten, she wondered. She tried to recall how long since she'd missed her period. Maybe these indications were all false. Maybe her hormones were acting up. She really needed to have a doctor examine her.

Okay, she told herself, mind off your uterus and on the business at hand. She passed one hand across her brow and in that instant Clabber shot out a foot and knocked Charlette's left leg out from under her. She fell heavily on her back. Clabber instantly got to his knees, grabbed the rifle, and pulled it by the barrel. Bad move; Charlette's finger was still on the trigger. The rifle discharged with a roar and jumped clear of Charlette's grasp. The next thing she knew someone was helping her to her feet.

"What happened?" someone asked as strong arms lifted her up.

"H-he—" she glanced down at Clabber, who lay on the ground. The charge had struck him under the chin and taken off his entire face.

"Did fer that sucker," someone said and laughed nervously. They all stared down at Clabber's body. These men had known Bud Clabber all their lives. "He wasn't such a bad sort until he got mixed up with Lugs," someone said.

"We all thought it was a good idea at the time, didn't we?" Timor mused. "Now look where it's got us—'n him," he nudged Clabber's body with his foot. Charlette bent over and vomited several times. "That's okay, that's okay," Timor said, "he was useless anyways, Charlette." Someone handed her back the rifle, safety on. "Well, fellas, I guess that screws Plan A."

"What's Plan B, Daddy?" Donnie asked.

"Plan B? Plan B is 'highdiddle diddle, straight up the middle.' Come on, roll old Clabber down into the gully 'n let the blackbirds feed on him. Let's git back on the road, such as it is."

* * *

"If they don't have a breakdown or sumpin', they'll be here in the mornin', Boss. The boys are already at Cuylerville and everything is quiet. There won't be no more trouble from them ones that stayed behind."

Lugs shifted his Clinton Esplendido from the right to the left side of his mouth and squinted up at his lieutenant. His diamond-studded rings sparkled in the fading sunlight as he ran his fat fingers through the thinning hair on his head. "Rosco, tell the boys to take out the rest of that Pickens family, but no more retaliations against the people down there. I just want 'em scared. Same with those goddamned idiots on their way up here. Christ, Rosco, how we gonna get the next crop in if we kill off all the farmers? If that Clabber idiot survives this trip, give him the Pickens's spread; if he don't, we'll give it to someone else to work. What's the word from Ashburtonville?"

"The Confederation's landed reinforcements, boss, lots of 'em."

"Good! Good! Rosco, war is good for business. Uniforms don't mean nuttin' to us, right?"

"Right!"

"Money does," Lugs nodded. "Soldiers got money. And what do soldiers do when they ain't fightin'?"

"Fuck?"

Lugs grimaced and shook his head. "Well, besides that, during that, after that! Geez, Rosco, git yer mind outta the gutter for a minute!"

"Geez, boss, I was only thinkin', we should diversify, go into the flesh business."

"They smoke, lunkhead! They smoke thule, they smoke tobacco, they smoke grospalm leaves if they can't get nuttin' else. We are in the business of supplying people with that sumpthin' else, which is our shit, our good smokes." A long string of saliva trailed from his cigar as he removed it from his mouth. He wiped the spit off his lips with the back of one large hand and then wiped his hand on his trousers. "Howsomever, Rosco, you are thinkin'. The flesh business, I like that, I been thinkin' the same thing. Smokes 'n sex, we get 'em at both ends. But later. Now tomorrow. I want them all alive, as much as possible. The men, send 'em back to Cuylerville under guard. The plantin' season's comin' up. But that young woman and her husband," he shook a massive, hairy forefinger at Rosco, "keep 'em up here. That girl is more than a ditzy cunt. I think we kin use her."

"But do we need her husband, boss?"

Lugs emitted an exasperated sigh. "Yes, we do, if for no other reason than to keep her 'n ol' Timor Caloon happy 'n growin' his thule. Rosco, you know me! I only kill people when there's profit in it. Now git yer ass out there 'n organize a little reception party for our visitors."

Lugs's real name was Luigi Flannigan. He got the nickname "Lugs" from the bottom leaves of the thule plant, an old term for them adopted from the tobacco growers. The sobriquet was appropriate to Flannigan because he always maintained a low business profile. He also maintained a very good intelligence system and good relations with authority, especially law enforcement, such as it was on Ravenette. In Bibbsville, he *was* the law.

Timor and his party spent a very uncomfortable night parked in some scrub on the outskirts of Bibbsville. As they perched huddled inside the car, Charlette asked Timor what his plan was for the morning. "I was gonna git in with Clabber, pretend to be there on business, just drive in peaceable like, kill Lugs, 'n leave same way we come in. But since you went 'n killed old Bud," he grinned, "well, we're here now. When it gits light we'll take a gander at the factory. Take us five minutes to git our act together. Then we go in. We'll have surprise on our side. Now, let's raise the boys up and take a look at things."

In the predawn they lay prone behind some native shrubs covering the top of a small hillock observing the vast system of curing barns, warehouses, and offices spread out below them.

"The day shift will be arriving in a little while," Timor whispered. "We'll join the crowd, kill the guards, drive in through the main gate, hit the headquarters building. Lugs has an apartment in the HQ. We'll kill him if we can find him, kill as many of them as we can."

"Father, won't they follow us when we try to leave?" Charlette asked.

"We ain't leavin'. Not directly, anyway. Either we git ol' Lugs 'n take the head off this animal, or we take as many of them with us as we kin. Charlette, child, I took you along with us for a reason. That reason was to get you and Donnie out of Cuylerville and out of harm's way. I knew if I tole you beforehand you'd never agree. Lissen. All these boys here," he gestured at the other men spread out on the ground beside them, "they know we're out for blood today 'n we're gonna git it. But we ain't livin' like this no more, understand? We don't care if we don't make it outta there."

"But—?"

Timor rolled over and took a fat envelope out of his shirt. "Inside here is enough money to set you 'n Donnie up wherever in this world you want to go, wherever you want to go someplace else, for that matter." He thrust the envelope into Charlette's hands. "Now gimme yer rifle, you too, Donnie. Then you two git on yer feet and walk over to town, it ain't far and nobody'll see you. You get tickets on the first flier outta here. If things go well, I'll send for ya. If not, you git a new life together. Ma agreed to all this, Donnie, 'n if I don't make it she kin take care of herself. When things quiet down, you kin send for her, where you wind up.

"Charlette, we Caloons ain't as dumb as we look 'n act most of the time. Inside that envelope is information on a bank account I set up a while back in Donnie's name. That account ain't here, not on Ravenette. It's in Fargo, back Earth," he grinned. "You two kin live well on that money. Now off with you."

"No," Donnie said.

Timor slapped his son's face so hard it brought tears to his eyes. He grabbed him by the hair and hissed, "Boy, you do what I tell you! That girl's got my grandchild inside her 'n there's no way I'm gonna let that child come to harm. If we fail here, there's no way I'm gonna let you raise that kid back in that shithole Cuylerville. Now you git yer asses on into town. Charlette, you're a soldier. You obey orders. I'm orderin' the two of you to leave us here. Go. Right now. We'll wait until you're well on yer way before we attack."

The airline ticket office was not yet open when the pair reached town. Worse, a big, hand-lettered sign in the window announced, "Due to wartime necessity, Bibbsville airport closed to civilian traffic until further notice."

"Geez, there goes Plan A."

"Now what?" Charlette asked.

"Plan B, which I just thought of: There's a town about three hundred kilometers down the coast. We'll git us a landcar at a Kertz rental later this morning 'n drive out there. We kin catch the *Figaro* there when she comes for a port call. After this morning it'll be too hot for us to stick around here. But right now it's too early. Let's eat."

Their rental broke down ten kilometers outside town and nothing Donnie could do would get it to start up again.

"What's that place over there?" Charlette asked.

Donnie raised up from the engine compartment. "It's a militia base, I think."

"Maybe they can help with the car."

Donnie considered, then closed the engine compartment. They were parked off the road, under a grove of trees in the early morning shade. A path led from the grove toward the camp. "Worth a try," he said, wiping his hands on his trousers.

A military policeman, grinning unabashedly as he sized up Charlette, directed the pair to the camp motor pool where a harassed motor transport officer, Tamle, judging by his nametape, asked them what they wanted then said, "No way! We're leavin' this mornin' for Ashburtonville! The seat of the war!" He sized up the pair. "Why don't you two go over 'n see the recruiting sergeant? We could use a couple more people. We're way under TO and E strength as it is."

Charlette knew what that meant. She was suddenly struck by an idea. Outside she stopped Donnie. "If Daddy doesn't make it, hasn't made it, this place is excellent cover for us. You know that guy and his henchmen will come after us, no matter what, 'n we left a trail a blind man could follow. Let's enlist, Donnie!"

"But they's goin' off to war, honeybun! We could get really fucked up in a war, darling!"

"Naw, Donnie, this is a militia unit. Nobody ever trusts them in the front lines. We can desert anytime. I'm gettin' real good at that," she grimaced. "What do you say?"

All around them soldiers rushed about, loading vehicles; others stood in formation, undergoing last-minute inspections. Sergeants shouted, officers pouted, to Donnie it looked like everyone was enjoying himself. "Well—"

The recruiting sergeant was just cleaning out his desk when the two entered his office. "You want to enlist?" he asked, goggle-eyed. "All right! Sure! Here, fill out the personal data on these papers. Are you two related or something?"

"We're married," Charlette answered proudly.

"Well, I'll be damned! Husband and wife. That's good, that's good. Neither of you will be messing around with the single troopers then. You got yer marriage certificate on you?" Donnie dug inside a cargo pocket and produced the elaborate certificate Clabber had given him. "What do you do for a living?" he asked Donnie.

"Uh, I, uh was a courier over in Ashburtonville—"

"Can you drive?"

"Yessir!"

"It's 'sergeant,' not 'sir,' I'm no officer, I work for a living. Okay, then put down under Occupation, 'driver.' How about you, miss?"

Charlette did not know what motivated her to respond, "I could make a pretty good spy."

"We don't need any of them just now. Kin you cook?"

"Yes, Sergeant!"

"Hmmm, you got a good command voice, lady. Okay, put down 'cook' under 'occupation.' " He shouted for the medical officer in the next room. "Doc," he told the elderly physician, "physical these two, would you? Have them fill out the clinical charts first and then I'll have Captain Carhart come in and give them the oath. We got to hurry! We gotta be on the trucks by noon. Christ, I go all week without a single enlistment and now this!"

"I don't have time for tests or any of that stuff," the doctor told Charlette, "we don't have any of that sophisticated automated stuff like they do in the big recruiting centers. We're just a militia unit, part-time soldiers. You look to me like you're in pretty good health. But let me listen to your insides and thump around on you a bit." He listened to her heart and lungs and asked her brief questions about her medical history. He had her urinate into a glass which he held up to the light and examined closely. "Clear as a bell," he said, making a note on her chart. "How do you feel?"

"Great!"

"Good," he wrote something on her chart. "Yer married to that young fella that was just in here? You aren't pregnant, are you?" the doctor asked.

"Nossir! Chubby, is all! But I hope to get pregnant. Can we do that in the army?"

"Sure, long as you do it off duty. You won't have much time to do that where we're going." He scribbled something more on her clinical chart and handed it back to her. "Give this to the sergeant."

Captain Carhart was an older man, in his fifties, Charlette guessed, blond hair thinning, a huge mustache on his upper lip. The sergeant addressed him as "Tom," which Charlette, a regular soldier, thought bordered on military blasphemy, but then she reflected it was a militia unit after all, not the regular army.

"Well," Captain Carhart told them after they'd taken the oath of enlistment, "welcome to the 441st Transportation Company, Loudon Rifles, the finest regiment in at least six counties. Now at least you got a job for the duration. Jim, get them to personnel and then quartermaster. Whatever training these two need they kin get it in the field. Since they're married, have personnel put them both in the same platoon."

On the way to the Bibbsville airport, Charlette wondered what the penalty would be for desertion to the enemy. Probably death. Well, she reflected, she'd tell her court martial she was only developing sources. Anyway, whatever might happen now, she was heading in the right direction. She rested her head on Donnie's shoulder and whispered, "I wonder what happened to Daddy and the boys."

CHAPTER TWENTY-SEVEN

So it went. The Coalition forces, with or without armor, would threaten or actually achieve a breakthrough, and a platoon, company, or even the entire FIST would be dispatched to kick them back—and hold their position once the rebels were driven away from the main defensive lines. And always, the orders were to drive the enemy away and *hold* in place.

The Marines hated having to hold; failure to pursue a beaten enemy gave that enemy a chance to regroup and attack again.

Brigadier Sturgeon was unhappily glad for Commandant Aguinaldo's foresight in providing him with the Marines for a Whiskey Company. Glad because he *needed* the Whiskey Company Marines as replacements in the infantry battalion; unhappy *because* he needed to replace those Marines. Some of the platoons in 34th FIST's infantry battalion suffered more than 50 percent casualties in the early actions. Granted, most of the casualties were quickly healed and returned to duty, but some of the Marines were more seriously injured, a few even killed.

Brigadier Sturgeon intensely disliked having his Marines injured or killed. He truly *hated* it when he thought the reason for the injuries and deaths was poor decision-making by his superiors.

Moreover, he was certain that, even if his FIST hadn't been able to win the campaign had General Billie not called them back during that initial pursuit following their first action, 34th FIST could nonetheless have caused enough material and morale damage to the Coalition forces that they wouldn't have been able to maintain as much pressure on the perimeter as they did.

That was Sturgeon's frame of mind when he was summoned to yet another commanders' meeting by General Billie.

General Billie, the consummate staff officer, was enamored of meetings. And, as the consummate staff officer finally given a large command of his own, particularly loved *commanders'* meetings.

Billie was delighted by the opportunity to lord it over commanders of lesser rank, though greater command experience than he had himself—commanders who, for the most part, were their roles reversed, would treat him with all the respect due a valued-but-nonetheless second-class citizen.

"Atten-SHUN!" Billie's aide called out to the unit commanders who were assembled in the grandly named Supreme Commander's Briefing Room. The aide, a syncophantic captain whose name Brigadier Sturgeon never bothered to remember, stood at resplendent attention in his pressed and polished Class A uniform.

Major General Koval, the commanding general of the 27th Division, wearily rose to his feet, as did his three brigade commanders. The three brigade commanders of the 3rd followed suit. None of them came fully to attention, nor were any of them in Class A's. Unlike Billie's pet captain, they had all just come from where their men were engaged in sporadic battle, as their uniforms and posture made clear.

Brigadier Sturgeon, in a rumpled but clean garrison utility uniform, didn't exactly snap to attention, nor was the posture he assumed strictly the called-for stance. Not that there was any specific thing a critic could point to and say, "That's not the proper position of attention." Still, there was something about the way Sturgeon stood erect, heels together, feet at a forty-five degree angle, thumbs along the seams of his trousers, stomach in, chest out, shoulders back, head and eyes straight ahead, face expressionless, that quite clearly proclaimed, "You don't deserve to have anyone stand at attention for you."

Billie's aide noticed and a thundercloud formed on his brow. But there was nothing he quite dared to say to this *Marine* who technically outranked him by a couple of notches.

The aide's thundercloud didn't last for even a second; General Billie strode into the briefing room on the heels of the call to attention and the aide stood at rigid attention. Major General Sorca mimicked Billie, a step too far back to properly be a shadow, though his movements were precisely those of his leader. Lieutenant General Cazombi brought up the rear of Billie's parade at a gait accurately called an amble. Cazombi cast a glance at the assembled commanders that was innocuous enough that the captain didn't catch it, but those who knew Cazombi well enough clearly understood it to mean that he was distinctly unhappy about the way Billie was wasting their time.

Billie was fully aware of the effect stars had on lesser personages. So the stars he wore on his collars were a tad larger than specified in army regulations, and ruthlessly polished to the highest possible degree. He stood facing his subordinate commanders, and shifted his shoulders in a practiced movement that reflected the room's lights from his stars into the eyes of everyone standing in front of him—he'd had the room's lights positioned to allow him to do exactly that. A quite unsubtle reminder to all of who was in command.

"Seats!" he said in an imperious tone; the lord of the manor bestowing a boon on the commoners gathered in supplication at his feet. There was a brief clatter of chairs being taken. Billie adjusted his position slightly so his collar stars could catch different lights and reflect them into the eyes of seated commanders. There's no such thing as too many reminders of who's in command.

"The Coalition rebels have made numerous assaults on our lines," he announced, as though every man he was speaking to didn't know about the assaults better than he did. "Our soldiers have successfully repulsed every one of them." Again, nothing nobody didn't know. And they all noticed that he failed to mention that there had been more than one instance where the Coalition forces had broken through the defensive lines, and were only repelled by a powerful counterattack by the Marines.

"I have received communications from the Heptagon. Our hardline holdout will soon end. The 106th Division is due in orbit within a week, standard. At which time we will have a full corps on planet. The 106th will rotate into positions currently held by the 3rd Division. Several days later, the 85th Division will arrive and relieve the 27th Division on the line. These reliefs will allow the 3rd and 27th Divisions to rest and recuperate from their strenuous efforts in holding the line, so they will be ready to go on the offensive when the 54th and 60th Divisions arrive.

"Gentlemen, we only need to hold out for a few more days before major reinforcements begin arriving."

There were a few sounds of uncomfortable movement from the commanders; a couple of them cast quick glances at Sturgeon. They resented the fact that Billie had made no mention of the role 34th FIST had played in the defense of the Bataan redoubts.

Sturgeon didn't shift position; he knew Billie disliked the Marines, and hadn't expected him to give 34th FIST any credit for driving out forces that had achieved breakthroughs, and then holding their positions until fresh army units arrived to relieve them.

"The best intelligence we have," Billie went on, smiling, "indicates that the Coalition forces know that our reinforcements are due shortly, and are preparing for a defensive in depth of their own for when we commence offensive operations, so we should face little opposition before we are ready to take the battle to the enemy."

Sturgeon *did* react to that statement. He reacted so strongly that he broke protocol by standing up and interrupting the Supreme Commander's speech.

"Sir, by your leave!" he said. Without waiting for permission to speak, he went on, "I beg to differ with the general. According to the intelligence developed by Force Recon assets operating behind Coalition lines, while they may be digging in for a defense in depth, they are also preparing a stronger assault against our lines than any they have attempted so far."

Billie curled his lip at Sturgeon. "Yes, *Brigadier,*" he said, in a tone that left no doubt about how he felt about being interrupted—or how much higher ranking an army full general was over a mere Marine brigadier, "I have seen the reports from Force Recon. I don't know in which tavern those prima donnas are gathering their so-called 'intelligence,' but I assure you, I have far better intelligence than anything they can 'develop.'

"Kindly resume your seat."

Major General Koval and three of the brigade commanders looked at Sturgeon with sympathy, the other brigade commanders briefly looked at Billie with expressions of disbelief at his off-hand dismissal of the Force Recon reports. Lieutenant General Cazombi looked blank-faced at Sturgeon and almost imperceptibly shook his head. Sturgeon, who was about to say something more, caught Cazombi's signal and sat down without saying anything more.

Billie smiled at his perceived victory over the Marine. His aide pompously sneered at Sturgeon.

Sturgeon tuned out the rest of Billie's commanders' meeting. Billie had called Force Recon "prima donnas." Force Recon Marines might think they were better and more capable than other Marines, but he'd never known them to be wrong when they developed intelligence. If Force Recon said the Coalition forces were planning a combined airborne and amphibious assault by a reinforced division against the Pohick Bay flank of the defenses, he believed the assault was imminent.

In order to keep 34th FIST available to repel breakthroughs, Billie had assigned it to a section of the line that he felt was least likely to come under assault—the Pohick Bay flank.

Waiting for Billie to finish his meeting, Sturgeon began planning his defense. One Marine FIST against a reinforced division, perhaps twenty-to-one odds in favor of the attackers. Well, Marines had prevailed against such odds in the past. Thirty-fourth FIST would do it again. He just didn't know how.

At length, the supercilious aide called the commanders to attention while Billie marched out of the room. He brought up the rear and trailed after his master like a puppy.

Before Sturgeon could leave to brief his staff and put them to work on battle plans that wouldn't rely on help from the army, Major General Koval stepped in front of him. The brigade commanders hovered nearby.

"Ted," Koval said in a low voice, "that Force Recon report you mentioned. The Supreme Commander didn't deign to share it with me. Could you let me have a copy?"

Sturgeon looked at him, and the brigade commanders politely waiting just out of hearing distance, but couldn't remember Koval's first name. "General," he said, "it will be my pleasure. One of your brigades is on my left flank, and they should know about it as well. There's a major assault coming, centered on my part of the line, so it will affect your division as well."

"Thanks, Ted. I'll see to it that every brigade commander who needs to know about it also gets a copy of the report." Koval turned on his heel and marched out, the brigade commanders followed him, anxious to learn why he'd spoken quietly to Sturgeon, but turned back when Sturgeon offered:

"I'll give you a feed to the string-of-pearls tactical download as well."

"You know, Hammer, when I saw your back when we were chasing those bad guys down the tunnel, I thought for sure I'd be losing you for a long time." Corporal Claypoole looked at Lance Corporal Schultz with unaccustomed concern. "I was afraid of what your front looked like."

Schultz barely grunted in reply, and didn't bother looking at his fire team leader; instead he kept watching out the aperture of the strongpoint overlooking Pohick Bay.

"Yeah, Hammer, you were a mess," Lance Corporal MacIlargie said, with a wary glance at Schultz. "I didn't know how you kept going." He noticed how carefully Schultz rolled his shoulders.

During the fight where third platoon stopped the Coalition pursuit of the defending soldiers, and the subsequent battle when the Marines chased the rebels back out of the tunnel, patches of synthskin on Schultz's back had torn loose and he began bleeding again. By the time the Marines reached the open air, Schultz's back was drenched with blood. Claypoole had worried that the bleeding was from exit wounds, that Schultz had been shot many times and was probably dying.

Doc Hough rushed him back to the battalion aid station before the last shot was fired. Schultz only permitted that because he knew the fight was over and the Marines would have to hold in place.

At the BAS, they began pumping plasma into him while Lieutenant Brauner, the battalion surgeon, and HM1 Horner were stanching the bleeding. After the bleeding was stopped, they applied a fresh layer of synthskin to his back and thighs, then pumped four units of whole blood into him to replace what he'd lost.

Schultz lay naked under a sheet; they'd had to cut his chameleons off to get to his injuries. When the sedative wore off and he was once more fully conscious, he threw the sheet aside and stood up, and demanded his weapons and helmet and a fresh set of chameleons.

"You get back in bed, Marine!" Lieutenant Brauner snapped. "I'm not letting you leave here again before you're healed." He flashed a signal at a corpsman sorting vials into a medical cabinet.

The big man turned a stone-hard gaze on the medical officer and growled, "Weapons. Helmet. Chameleons."

"You heard me, Marine. I said get back in bed. That's an order." Brauner had treated many injured Marines who wanted to return to their units before they were fit for duty and knew the way to deal with them was to speak firmly. Schultz just looked at him and held out a hand for his weapons. Brauner stepped close and put a hand on Schultz's chest to push him back to the bed.

It was like pushing on a flesh-warm marble sculpture.

"Not a good idea, sir," Horner said, cautiously sidling close. To Schultz, he said, "We don't have an extra set of chameleons in your size, Hammer. We'll have to requisition a set from Supply. So just lay back down on your bed and rest for a while, and we'll let you go as soon as the requisition comes in." Schultz turned his gaze on Horner, and the senior corpsman took an involuntary step back.

"Weapons. Helmet," Schultz growled. He lashed out and knocked the shotgun out of the hand of a corpsman who was sneaking up behind him to slap him with a fast-acting sedative. *"Now!"*

Brauner gaped at him. How had the big Marine seen the corpsman behind him and known what he was doing?

Schultz looked around and saw what he was looking for. The doctor managed to jump out of his way in time to keep from being bowled over when Schultz went to the pile of weapons and blood-soaked uniforms cut from the bodies of wounded Marines. It took just seconds for him to find his own. Still naked, but armed and with his helmet tucked under an arm, he headed for the exit from the BAS.

At the door, he paused and looked back. "Where?" he asked, then nodded when Horner pointed in the general direction of third platoon, and set out to rejoin his unit.

"If you start bleeding again, I'm not responsible!" Brauner called after Schultz when he found his voice again.

Schultz ignored him, just as he ignored the pounding footfalls hurrying behind him a moment later.

"Hammer, you can't go back like that," Horner said when he caught up with the big man. "Come on, I'll take you to Supply, and you can get a fresh set of chameleons."

Schultz stopped, and gestured for the corpsman to lead the way.

And that was how he came to be wearing new chameleons when Claypoole said he thought Schultz was dying on him and MacIlargie noticed how carefully the big man rolled his shoulders.

Of course, Schultz was careful when he rolled his shoulders, just as he was careful of how he stood, and sat, or made other movements. He may not have been willing to stay on bed rest in the BAS, but he wasn't willingly going to do anything that would tear his wounds open again.

Brigadier Sturgeon briefed his primary staff and major unit commanders on the important items in Lieutenant General Billie's meeting: when reinforcements would begin arriving; and the Supreme Commander's total disregard for the Force Recon reports. So, he said, 34th FIST had to come up with its own plans to defend against an assault by overwhelming forces.

Commander Daana, the FIST F2, intelligence officer, accented the need for defensive plans when he summarized the latest reports from the FIST's own reconnaissance squad—"someone" had been clearing lanes through the passive defenses along the waterline; disarming mines and prepping underwater obstacles for demolition.

While the others got to work setting their defenses, Sturgeon took Captain Shadeh, the FIST F1, personnel officer, aside to put him to work reassigning Marines from Whiskey Company to the infantry battalion. Sturgeon then notified Commander van Winkle to expect the new Marines and to have his S1 ready to distribute them to the companies.

It was a solemn third platoon that gathered for a platoon meeting following the memorial ceremony. The platoon hadn't lost any men killed or too badly wounded to return to duty since early on the Kingdom campaign, before the Marines learned how to defend against Skink rail guns. That was also the last time they had lost a squad or fire team leader. Sergeant Bladon, who was then the second squad leader, had lost an arm then, and enough time had passed between the injury and when he began undergoing the regeneration process that his arm might not grow back. Even if it did, he would have to go through extensive rehabilitative therapy before he could be returned to duty. Either way, he wasn't there to resume leadership of second squad. First squad's Corporal Goudanis had also been too severely wounded to return to duty, and might never be well enough.

On that occasion, then-Corporal Linsman and then-Lance Corporals Claypoole and Dean were promoted to fill Bladon and Goudanis's positions and the vacancy created by Linsman's promotion. Now Sergeant Linsman was dead, and so was the gun squad's Corporal Barber.

Ensign Charlie Bass didn't look at the three new men who stood together at the rear of the platoon, the only Marines present who were fully visible—the rest of them were in chameleons, with only their heads and hands visible. Staff Sergeant Hyakowa kept close but unobtrusive watch on the new men—he wanted to see how they reacted to the platoon's response to the loss of men and promotions from within.

"No Marine is expendable," Bass told his platoon, "we all know that. But it's also true that no Marine is irreplaceable. Today we have to replace two good Marines. I'm not going to go into how good Sergeant Linsman and Corporal Barber were, I already said that at the memorial service." His voice broke and he had to pause for a moment; both of them had been with him as long as he'd been with the platoon. They were the twelfth and thirteenth Marines who had been with third platoon when he joined it as platoon sergeant who had died or been wounded too badly to return.

He found his voice again and continued. "I've discussed matters with the Skipper, the Top, the Gunny, and Staff Sergeant Hyakowa, as well as Sergeants Ratliff and Kelly. First, we're all in agreement that it's past time that Corporal Kerr became squad leader and got a promotion to Sergeant. Congratulations, Tim."

He paused for a moment to give the members of second squad a chance to add their congratulations, then said, "As you were, people! And remember, nobody who isn't already a sergeant gets to pin the new stripes on Kerr, and then not until *after* he is formally promoted." He paused again as a wave of good-natured laughter ran through the platoon. The laughter raised his spirits; the platoon's morale was already rising.

"Lance Corporal Kindrachuk has been known to get particularly rowdy and barbaric on liberty, but he's a solid gunner who knows his business. He's taking over first gun team." Again, there was a round of congratulations, before Bass quieted the platoon.

"Now we've got a fire team leader slot to fill," he said, and looked innocently at all the expectant lance corporals in the platoon. "This personnel change shouldn't come as a surprise to anybody. Corporal Doyle is taking over as fire team leader."

The announcement was met with dead silence, except for a strangled gasp from Corporal Doyle. The three replacements exchanged nervous glances; they didn't know what the problem was, but they all realized *something* was wrong.

"Come on, people," Bass snapped. "What's your problem? Doyle's already *got* the rank. He's proven himself more willing than most to speak his mind when he knows he's right." That drew loud laughter. "And he's demonstrated that he knows enough, even teaching men junior to him things they need to know. Corporal Doyle has a lot of fear when we go into action, fear that would paralyze anyone not a Marine—and would paralyze a lot of Marines. But he's able to overcome it and function through his fear. And he's got leadership experience from when he was the company chief clerk.

"Maybe *you* haven't been paying attention, but I've been watching Doyle ever since he was on that patrol with me on Elneal. I've seen him grow since then, and even more since he joined the platoon. Everybody involved in making the decision to move him into that slot agrees that Corporal Doyle deserves to be a fire team leader."

Well, not *everybody*. First Sergeant Myer had roared with outrage when Bass nominated Doyle for the slot and Hyakowa seconded the nomination. The Top still wanted Doyle court-martialed for insubordination for forcing his hand during the Avionia deployment. It didn't matter to Myer that the operation wouldn't have succeeded in its final, successful, step had Doyle not gotten his way; he'd been insubordinate!

When Top Myer wouldn't calm down, Captain Conorado had ordered everybody out of the company command bunker and closed the blastdoor behind them. The company clerks went with the others.

Closed blastdoor or not, the Marines waiting outside the bunker could hear the fireworks that went on for some time between the company commander and his top dog.

Then there was a couple minutes of silence, during which the Marines waiting outside fought cases of the fidgets, and began wondering how much blood they'd see spattered on the bunker walls when the blastdoor finally reopened.

None, as it turned out. Top Myer sat at his field desk, not quite glaring, not quite expressionless. Captain Conorado sat serene with a hip perched on a corner of his field desk.

"Palmer," Myer growled at the company's chief clerk when Conorado looked at him, "adjust the company roster to show Kerr, Kindrachuk, and Doyle in their new positions." He turned to Staff Sergeant Hyakowa and growled, "Let me know where you plug the new men in, and any other changes you make in the platoon roster." He turned to his console and made busy.

Bass and Hyakowa left the company office bunker and returned to the platoon for the memorial service.

"So," Bass said, looking at the new men for the first time, "I'm Ensign Charlie Bass, and this is my platoon. Who the hell are you?"

The three were PFCs John Three McGinty, Emilio Delagarza, and Lary Smedley. Thirty-fourth FIST was the first assignment for each of them, and third platoon was their first operational unit. Delagarza had gun training and became the assistant gunner in second gun team.

"I don't know about you other two, though," Bass said. "We really only have one open slot. PFC Quick has a shattered arm, but we expect him to come back shortly, which means one of you will be an extra man when he does.

"Corporal Doyle!"

Doyle jerked and jumped to his feet. "Y-yessir!"

"You're good with new men. Which one do you want?"

"S-sir?" Doyle squeaked.

"You heard me, Doyle. Which of these new men do you want in your fire team? Speak up quickly, now. Don't make me think I was wrong about you."

"Ah, yessir. I-I'll take—" he looked at the new men and couldn't see any difference between them on which to base a choice. He flipped a mental coin. "—I-I'll take Smedley, sir."

"Good choice, Doyle. If he's half the Marine another Smedley was, he'll make you a better fire team leader."

"Sir," Smedley blurted, "Smedley was General Butler's first name, sir. Smedley's my *last* name."

Bass turned his gaze on Smedley and said slowly, "I'm fully aware of that, PFC. But it's a famous name, and you had best get used to it."

Smedley gulped and tried to turn invisible, which was tough to do in garrison utilities. "Aye aye, sir," he said.

Bass studied him for a brief moment, nodded curtly, and said, "That means Corporal Dean gets McGinty. Be gentle on him, Dean, he's just a loaner."

Everybody laughed except Dean, who scowled, and McGinty, who wasn't sure it was a joke.

CHAPTER TWENTY-EIGHT

General Jason Billie sat comfortably in a private room just off his command bunker entertaining his chief of staff, Major General Sorca. "I want to have a little private talk with you, Balca, before we meet with the rest of the staff and the commanders to hash out our battle plan."

Brigadier General Balca Sorca nodded. "I saw some of them already out there in the operations center when I came in here. Cazombi and Sturgeon are there, gabbing in a corner like a couple of old women. They should be ready in a few minutes."

Billie snorted derisively. "Let them wait, Balca. They serve at my pleasure now. I'll go out and call the council to order when I'm damned good and ready." His face reddened as he remembered the run-in he'd had with Brigadier Sturgeon. Marines attack, they don't defend—what bullshit! That damned infantry jock was incapable of seeing the Big Picture! He reached into a drawer and withdrew a cigar humidor. "These Clintons are excellent smokes and, if you'll join me, let's light up." Billie offered Sorca his travel humidor. Nodding his appreciation, Sorca took one of the cigars, clipped the end, and licked it lovingly. Billie offered him a light and then lit his own cigar. They sucked in the acrid smoke and exhaled.

"De-lightful!" Sorca sighed. "Haven't had a good smoke since, um, before all this mess got started." Immediately the smoke from the two cigars began to fill the small room. That deep inside the complex the ventilation was very poor and, of course, nobody in his right mind would dare expose himself to chance a smoke in the open. From far above them came a series of heavy thumps as if to accentuate the danger of exposure topside.

"Incoming," Balca muttered. Billie had not been there long enough to tell the difference between enemy artillery and their own. Truth be told, he had never been under enemy artillery fire before.

"These are forty-five-minute cigars, Balca. But let's go slow on them," Billie suggested, "keep the smoke down, keep the others waiting, show them their place in this army. Besides, we have a lot to discuss." He reached back into the drawer and took out a brown bottle. "Old Widow bourbon," he smiled, holding the bottle out to Sorca, who raised his eyebrows in admiration. "I brought a lot of stuff with me from orbit, Balca. No reason why the commanding general—and his chief of staff!—should live like the troops, is there?" They both laughed as Billie poured two healthy shots into clean glasses. "Here's sham rocks to my real friends and real rocks to my sham friends," Billie toasted. "You're looking a trifle thin, Balca," Billie observed over the rim of his glass.

"We've been on reduced rations for a while, Jason." The two had been on a first-name basis for years, in private, that is.

"No more! You eat at my table from now on. I brought enough class-A rations in with me to operate my own mess down here and by God, I will *not* dine like a sodden infantryman! R-H-I-P is my motto and 'privileges' is the operative word, Balca. Don't forget that in your rise to the stars, which I am going to see is rapid. This campaign is the making of both of us."

The two smoked and sipped in silence. "As my chief of staff, Balca, you will oversee the day-to-day running of this entire army and that means the Marine contingent. Cazombi as my deputy commander will not interfere. I'll keep him off your back. My plans for him are to store him away so he will no longer be in the way."

"And if anything were to happen to you, Jason?"

Billie laughed. "Nothing's going to happen to me! I'm the commanding general! Generals don't lead troops anymore, despite what that idiot Cazombi and that madman Sturgeon think! Generals stay safe and run the army and that's what we'll do, you and me."

"Cazombi's responsible for this mess," Sorca said. "If he hadn't bled off my engineers and his own troops to prepare this complex, I could've stopped the rebels cold and held on to Fort Seymour indefinitely! I should have stuck him in a back room as soon as I got here, but no, military protocol dictated that I take the damned fool seriously and show him deference as the ranking officer here, although I had the authority to override him. That was my big mistake, Jason! Now we're stuck in this sewer."

"Balca, as soon as the situation stabilizes, as soon as we break out and get the enemy on the run, Cazombi's out of here. My recommendation for your promotion to Lieutenant General has already been forwarded to the Combined Chiefs and I expect the President and the Congress to approve it without debate. But Cazombi doesn't worry me, Balca, it's that Marine, Sturgeon. We are going to have to keep them on a short rein, Balca. That fiasco with Hill 140 the other day could have spelled disaster for the entire command." His face reddened again as he remembered the way Sturgeon had treated him in his command post that day. "Marines have their own chain of command and their own voice in the Commandant and I happen to know that the President likes General Aguinaldo. She likes Marines."

"So does Cazombi," Sorca muttered. Billie threw him a questioning glance. "Yes, it's true. He oversaw a mission that a company from 34th FIST conducted on a restricted world. The officer commanding that company was court-martialed as the result of a complaint filed by a scientist conducting surveillance on that world. Cazombi appeared as a witness for the defense. And you know about his run-in with the chairman over the quarantine policy we've had in effect on the Marines of 34th FIST. I don't know all the reasons why the quarantine was imposed, highly classified stuff, but the word is out that Cazombi's kissin' cousins with the Marines, and him an army man at that."

They sipped the bourbon and puffed on their cigars for a long while. "All these Marines are 'warriors,' " Billie mused at last. "You know the difference between 'warrior' and 'soldier,' don't you, Balca?"

"Yes, a 'warrior' is a guy who likes to fight, raises his sword, and off he goes at the enemy, but a 'soldier' uses discipline and brains to win fights."

"Well, that's Cazombi and Sturgeon, Balca, 'warriors.' Now, we're soldiers, you and me. We got where we are because we used our heads.

We are too precious to our armies to get ourselves killed. So we're going to use these 'warriors' to our advantage. These fools will be our battering rams and if they're used up in the process, all the better."

Sorca grinned and toasted Billie. "How are we going to do that, Jason?"

Billie smiled cryptically. "In time, Balca, in time. All will turn our way in time."

Suddenly someone was knocking on the door. "Are you all right, sir?" It was Billie's aide, Captain Woo. "Are you all right, sir?" he asked again, his voice tinged with anxiety, "There's dirty smoke coming out from under the door!"

Lieutenant General Alistair Cazombi and Brigadier Theodosius Sturgeon sat in a corner of the busy command post sipping gingerly at cups of ersatz coffee. "I apologize for not bringing some of the real stuff in with me," Sturgeon was saying, "but we came combat loaded, ready to fight."

"That is only what we expected, Ted," Cazombi replied. "Tonight, get hold of Captain Conorado and bring him to my quarters, would you? We'll sit around and lie about old times."

"Yessir." Sturgeon sipped his kafe silently for a moment. "You worked a miracle, holding out this long," he said at last, looking around at the gaunt figures in the CP going about their business.

"Not me, not me. These men and women," he gestured at the staff officers around them, "they've taken a beating and are still full of fight. We really had our asses kicked at Fort Seymour, Ted. If we hadn't had this redoubt to fall back on we'd have been overrun the first day."

"I hear that was your doing, sir. And because you held out so long you denied the enemy a bunch of prisoners to use as negotiating chips."

"Well—" Cazombi shrugged, "he's holding out for more 'chips.' But you're probably right. If they'd captured the entire garrison at the beginning, the Confederation probably would've already granted them their demands. But now you're here and there are more coming." He brightened. "But I've gotta admit something else, Ted. That enemy over there, he's smart. He's flexible in his tactics and he won't be easy to beat. We've always considered these people rubes but by damn, they're fighters and they're well led. Since he failed to get us all, now he wants us reinforced so he can win a stunning victory by wiping us all out or bagging our entire force. That is probably the main reason we're still here; we're the magnet he wants to draw more troops into the trap."

Sturgeon nodded. "That, sir, will be his undoing. What can you tell me about our commander? Is he up to a breakout? How much influence do you have on his planning? You're his deputy after all."

"You're going to find out all about General Jason Billie in good time. As for me in this army, I'm going to be kept on a short leash, Ted. It's Sorca who'll be running things around here, carrying out Billie's decisions. They're both politicians and staff officers, not fighters. But Sorca's a goddamned coward. I admit, he was essentially without a command when what was left of it retreated into here, but I had to take over command of the troops myself. He's been no help to me whatsoever. But with him being a big buddy of Billie's, I expect as soon as there's a lull I'll be packed off and Sorca will then take over as both deputy commander and chief of staff and you know how powerful those positions can be in any military command."

"Ugh, Al, this kafe is terrible!" Sturgeon grinned.

"Don't ask me what's in it. Now Billie, his aide, Captain Woo told me, brought in some fine stuff, but it'll be a cold day on Arsenault before we ever get any of it. That tells you a lot about how he views the role of commander of this army, doesn't it?"

"So what do we do, sir?"

"We'll both be in the war council coming up in a while, along with the other unit commanders and the staff. Let's see what the great military genius in there has come up with in the way of a plan. You and I both know we've got to get out of here and maneuver. That's what you Marines do best. But I am going to tell you something now, Ted, that it pains me to say. In all the years I've been a soldier I never thought I'd come to this. I'm through in this army. If I get out of this mess I'm retiring. I'm never going any higher in rank than I now have and I am never again going to serve under an officer like this Billie. If at any time during the campaign that's coming you feel your men are being used as cannon fodder," here Cazombi caught his breath, "you would be well advised to make a report to your commandant. Make regular reports to him anyway via backchannels. Document everything that's about to happen. I know, saying that is disloyalty on my part as an army officer but I'm no longer loyal to that sonofabitch," he nodded toward the closed door to Billie's private office, where Captain Woo was pounding on it excitedly, "so expect fireworks from me at this council."

"Who is that guy at Billie's door?" Sturgeon asked, nodding at the source of all the noise.

"Captain Chester Woo, Billie's aide-de-camp. His fat little ass is Billie's personal fortune cookie." The pounding became louder and as the two watched, thin tendrils of smoke began creeping out from beneath the door.

Sturgeon glanced questioningly at Cazombi and laughed, "Maybe they've managed to immolate themselves in there."

"This army should be so lucky," Cazombi grunted.

CHAPTER TWENTY-NINE

More reports from the Force Recon teams operating behind the Coalition lines came in to FIST headquarters, where they were taken seriously even though General Billie continued to dismiss them as unverified and therefore irrelevant. Unlike the Supreme Commander, Major General Koval took the reports seriously enough that he paid a daily visit to FIST HQ to see the updates.

They were far from irrelevant; it seemed ever more likely to Sturgeon and Koval—and their staffs and subordinate commanders as well—that the reports indicated imminent attack by a reinforced division on the section of the perimeter centered on 34th FIST. The reports indicated that section, the easiest to defend, was selected because General Lyons felt it was held by the least capable units in the Confederation force.

"Not only is he dead wrong, we know he's coming," Koval murmured when he saw that report.

"Between us, General," Sturgeon said, "we're going to give General Lyons the biggest surprise of his military career."

They grinned warrior's grins at each other, all teeth and just enough grin to make 'em visible.

There was only one thing that could foul up their preparations. That was in the next reports Sturgeon got from Force Recon.

When Koval read it, he asked the Marine commander, "What are you going to do if His Royal Supremeness orders you to reinforce the main line of resistance?"

Sturgeon only shook his head, he wondered that himself.

The generals and their subordinate commanders weren't the only ones preparing to defend against a major assault; the preparations went all the way down to the newest and most junior men in every unit.

PFC McGinty wasn't sure of his position in the fire team, not after what Ensign Bass had said when he assigned him to first squad's third fire team. And the way Corporal Dean acted didn't inspire him to begin feeling like he was someplace where he belonged. Not that Corporal Dean was treating him like an interloper; McGinty thought his fire team leader was treating him just about exactly the way a fire team leader *should* treat a new man—introducing him to everybody in the squad and telling him something about every one of them, making sure he knew where to get chow and water, where his position and field of fire were if they were attacked, how to call for medical assistance or ammunition if needed.

But Corporal Dean was so *impersonal* about it. And he hadn't sounded like he really meant it when he said, "Welcome aboard, McGinty. Glad to have you."

Lance Corporal Godenov was warmer in his welcome, but McGinty was a bit put off when Godenov said, "Everybody calls me 'Izzy,' but you don't get to. You haven't been around long enough to remember when that was a question."

Now, what was that all about? Was it a play on his name, "Izzy" Godenov? Why would there have been a question? McGinty wasn't sure he wanted to know.

And they both looked so *hard*.

At least he knew where to get water, what there was of it, and food—and ammo and medical assistance if needed. And if the rebels came, he knew where his position and field of fire were.

PFC Smedley wasn't having a much better time of it. Sure, Corporal Doyle and PFC Summers welcomed him warmly enough. But Smedley couldn't help but feel that a big part of Summers's warmth was because he finally had someone junior to himself in the fire team. And Corporal Doyle seemed so damned *uncertain* about everything. It wasn't that he didn't know things. Not only did Corporal Doyle tell Smedley where to find water and chow, ammunition and the corpsman, and where the battalion aid station was, but drilled him so he actually *knew* those things. The fire team leader even put him through drills so he could automatically hit his designated fighting position and field of fire if they were attacked, and how to react if the platoon was called to plug a hole in the lines somewhere else.

Maybe it was just that this was Corporal Doyle's first day as a fire team leader. But he hadn't just been promoted like the squad leader—Sergeant Kerr, was that his name? or he would be Sergeant Kerr as soon as the promotion warrant came through—and that gun team leader with the strange name. So how had a corporal been filling a lance corporal's billet? Had he been a fire team leader before and did something to lose the job? That would explain why he seemed so unsure of himself. But what Ensign Bass said about him didn't sound like he'd already been a fire team leader. Had he done something heroic and gotten a promotion instead of a medal? If that was the case, why did everybody else in the platoon act like he wasn't a very good Marine?

Smedley had a lot of questions, more questions, and not the kind of questions he'd expected to have when he finally joined a platoon. But Corporal Doyle didn't give him time to dwell on them too much.

"Summers, Smedley," Doyle said as he came in from an NCOs' meeting, "heads up! The word is the bad guys are coming in force through us." He didn't stop to look at his men, but went straight to the aperture to look out over the beach below them. Summers and Smedley joined him.

The beach, two hundred meters distant, was sand and pebbles studded with boulders. A rocky shelf rose a quarter of the way in from the waterline, and the ground rose gently from there, though still scattered with jagged rocks and boulders. A glacis was built in front of the aperture to deflect projectiles up and over.

To Smedley, it looked like a killing ground that nobody would be fool enough to attack across. He looked to his left and was surprised to see Corporal Doyle trembling and Summers looking nervous.

"I-I know what you're th-thinking, Smedley," Doyle croaked. "You think this is an easy position to defend. But l-look at it again." His voice suddenly became stronger. "If their landing craft make it to the waterline, they've got all those boulders to use as cover while they advance by fire and maneuver. Then they can group up under the cover of the lip of the shelf down there, then fire and maneuver again with boulders for cover. They won't have cover when they reach the glacis, but there it's a straight run up to us."

"I can see that," Smedley said, not seeing what Doyle was so concerned about.

Doyle turned hollow eyes on him. "There's not many more than four hundred Marines on this line. They're sending a reinforced division through us. More than twenty thousand soldiers. That's better than fifty to one odds. Do *you* think you can take out fifty of them before they reach you?

"That's not all," Doyle continued. "They aren't going to be bunched up, a whole company right in front of us so we can't miss. Do you know how far apart our positions are? Fifty meters, that's how far. Three Marines have to cover a front more than fifty meters wide. That's why your field of fire extends so far to the right, so that your fire can interlock with the next Marine over."

Doyle looked back out at the beach. "And that damn army general in command doesn't believe they're coming, so we don't get any help from the army," he murmured.

Smedley gaped at him. The world seemed to close in on him and he barely heard Summers mutter, "Something tells me we're screwed, blued, and tattooed."

Elsewhere on the Marine line it was much the same.

Corporal Pasquin hobbled back from the NCOs' meeting, taking very careful steps to avoid stressing the wounds on his gluteus maximi. He looked more somber than Lance Corporal Longfellow and PFC Shoup had ever seen him, and neither thought it was soreness from his healing wounds that made him look that way. He went slowly to the aperture and looked out. Softly, he brought them up to date. Longfellow closed his eyes and moved his lips in silent prayer. Shoup just stared at the beach.

* * *

Corporal Claypoole began briefing Lance Corporals MacIlargie and Schultz as soon as he reached the entrance to their bunker. MacIlargie's face showed increasing disbelief as Claypoole briefed them. Schultz lay on his side on a makeshift pallet. He rolled onto his stomach and pulled his arms and legs under him to lift himself up, then stood gingerly and stepped to lean on the aperture.

When Claypoole finished, Schultz said, "Martac."

"Yeah, what about Martac?" Claypoole answered.

"Bass, Shabeli. Remember?"

"Yeah, I remember. Gu—Ensign Bass, he was a staff sergeant then," Claypoole said in an aside to MacIlargie, "took on Shabeli in a knife fight. And killed him. What's that got to do with us here and now?"

"Remember what I said?"

Claypoole thought back to that horrible day when the eight Marines on the Bass patrol had thought they were all dead, and remembered. "You said he was showing us how to die."

"We're going to show the army how Marines die."

If *Hammer Schultz* thought they were going to die . . .

Brigadier Sturgeon was examining the real-time downloads from the string-of-pearls when the order he didn't want came down from the Supreme Commander's HQ.

According to the visuals shown from the ring of satellites, the assault against the MLR was fierce but shallow, as predicted by Force Recon, and the army brigades in position wouldn't have to hold for long before the assault ran out of steam and the attacking forces withdrew. Of far more immediate concern to Sturgeon was the mass of amphibious vessels gathered on Pohick Bay, and the flights of tactical air carriers swinging inland from over the bay.

Sturgeon grimaced when he read the orders, and told Captain Shadeh to get General Billie on comm for him. It took a minute or so, and Billie was obviously very annoyed about the call.

"What's the problem, General?" Billie snapped.

"Sir, has the General seen the string-of-pearls downloads?" Sturgeon asked, ignoring the wrong rank by which Billie addressed him.

"Yes, I've seen them. They show what I already know—a massive attack against the MLR! I need your Marines there *now* to reinforce that line."

"Sir, I respectfully request the General take another look. The string-of-pearls shows a shallow assault against the MLR and a massive amphibious and air assault about to launch over the beach on the northern defenses—just as Force Recon said was happening."

Billie snorted. "There you go with Force Recon again! That 'massive' air-sea force off the north shore is an obvious feint—and your prima donnas fell for it. I need your FIST at the MLR, and I need it there *now*!"

There wasn't anything Sturgeon could say in reply, because Billie broke the connection. He slowly lowered the comm and stood musing for a moment, while Colonel Ramadan and Commander Usner, his operations officer, looked on, waiting for him to confirm what they suspected Billie had said—and what he was going to do about it. Sturgeon finished thinking and looked up at them.

"Gentlemen," he said in a voice loud enough for everyone in the operations center to hear, "the Supreme Commander has declared that the invasion force," he glanced at the string-of-pearls display, "that is now headed for our positions is a feint, and the assault against the MLR is the main thrust. He has ordered me to move the FIST to reinforce the MLR and help beat back the main assault," he looked again at the display, "which already shows signs of stalling.

"General Billie has four stars to my one nova, I have no choice but to obey. Therefore," he looked levelly at Usner, "I want you to draft an order to Commander van Winkle, instructing him to move his battalion with all due speed to the MLR. When the order is drafted, you will submit it to Colonel Ramadan for approval. Should Colonel Ramadan find any deficiencies in the order, he will inform you so and you will revise the orders as needed, then resubmit them to Colonel Ramadan. You will repeat until such time as Colonel Ramadan deems the orders ready for my perusal. Once I find them acceptable, you will send the orders by runner—use an ambulatory wounded from the FIST aid station as runner—to Commander van Winkle.

"Is that understood?"

Ramadan and Usner grinned at Sturgeon. "Yessir," they said.

"I will begin immediately, sir," Usner said, and looked around. "The very minute I find a stylus to write with, sir."

"Thank you, Three. And while you're looking for that stylus, pass the word to infantry to stand by to repel boarders. Also, request air to thin out those tactical troop carriers, and to artillery to take out some of the amphibious craft."

"Aye aye, sir," Usner said, and got on the comm to infantry, air, and artillery with the orders.

Ramadan leaned close and murmured, "Well, Ted, it certainly seems as though you are following the Supreme Commander's orders to the letter."

Sturgeon merely nodded, and returned his attention to the string-of-pearls display. He looked up again. "Inform General Koval."

"Aye aye." Ramadan turned away to contact the 27th Division commander.

Sergeant Kerr absently rubbed his left deltoid as he stood at an aperture, looking out at the sky and bay—Sergeant Kelly had been a little too enthusiastic at "pinning on" Kerr's sergeant's stripes, and his shoulder was lightly bruised from the trio of punches the gun squad leader had given him. He knew what was coming from the NCOs' meeting, and had his helmet on, looking through the magnifier screen.

A distant roaring drew Kerr's attention to a blank patch of sky. Automatically, he adjusted for the time lag of sound and looked lower. He saw the sparkles of Raptors diving on targets he could barely see at that distance. Streams of plasma were squirting almost straight down from the Raptors. Here and there, a gnatlike target bloomed into a crimson and gold ball as it was shredded by the plasma. But there were so many of the gnats and so few Raptors, Kerr knew their numbers wouldn't be greatly reduced by the time they arrived on top of the Marines' positions.

There was a monstrous *CRACK!* just overhead, and the stench of ozone flooded through the bunker's aperture, flooding out from the streak of plasma fired by one of the artillery battery's big guns, set on top of the ridge the bunkers were dug into. The magnifier automatically adjusted its polarization so the dazzling brilliance of the plasma ball that shot overhead wouldn't blind him. He followed the plasma ball to the water spout where the ball hit. Looking around from there, he saw speckles on the water—the amphibious force coming at the Marines. He couldn't tell if that first shot hit one of the boats, but the second strike did. But the artillery was like the Raptors, so few firing at so many.

Kerr looked into the sky again, then back at the water. The combined air-sea invasion force was big, and it was moving fast. No matter the absolute numbers of troop carriers or amphibious landing craft the Raptors and artillery knocked out, the vast majority of a reinforced division would shortly land on one Marine infantry battalion.

He repressed a shiver, and spoke into the squad circuit, "The bad guys are coming. Hold your fire until you have a walking, breathing target."

CHAPTER THIRTY

The landing craft came in waves, hundreds of them at high speed over the water. They didn't maneuver to throw off the aim of the artillery on the ridge above the bunkers, but relied on speed to reach the beach. Although nearly every shot fired by the artillery scored, killing one of the amphibious craft, there were simply too many of them for the six guns of the FIST's battery to reduce their numbers significantly in the ten minutes or so it took them to move from horizon to waterline. Especially when the artillery had to withdraw in the face of the approaching aerial troop carriers. The airborne force was smaller than the seaborne, and suffered more, but still the vast majority of the troop carriers touched down on the ridgetop at the same moment the first landing craft reached the waterline and began disgorging troops.

The heavy guns of each company's assault platoon opened fire when the landing craft were still a kilometer out, the guns of the assault squads of the blaster platoons opened fire shortly after. The eighteen guns and eighteen heavy guns put out a hellacious amount of fire, but they were firing at hundreds upon hundreds of craft, and had only a minute to do their worst damage before they had to shift their aim to soldiers who were splashing through the surf.

The enemy quickly set up crew-served weapons—lasers powerful enough to chew through plasteel, and fléchette guns that spewed five thousand darts a minute. The crews hunkered down, aiming their weapons through cams so the men didn't have to expose themselves to the fire coming at them from the Marine strongpoints. Their riflemen began dashing from boulder to boulder, closing on their objective. The Marines shot at them as fast as they saw them move, but more rebel soldiers were in movement at any time than there were Marines firing at them.

And some of the Marines had to concentrate on the crew-served weapons that were more immediately dangerous than the maneuvering soldiers.

Corporal Dean dropped; he'd seen a fléchette gun turning his way just in time to shout a warning to his men and drop to cover. The air in the bunker *r i i i ppod* with the passage of a thousand fléchettes through the aperture. A thousand more hit around the edges of the aperture, with a sound like the hail storm at the end of the universe. Fléchettes *whapped* against the inside walls of the bunker, chipping plasteel and throwing chips about. Dean's back was pelted, but he didn't think any had penetrated his chameleons, much less his skin.

When he heard the fléchette gun's fire move on, he groped for a Straight Arrow, found one, and rose to aim it through the aperture at the gun's position. He found it just as it began swinging back his way and fired.

He didn't see his rocket hit; a concussion wave slammed into him from behind, tried to blow him through the wall. Thunder to deafen the gods pummeled his ears and knocked him insensate. He wasn't aware of it when Lance Corporal Godenov rolled him onto his back and over and over again to smother the flames building on the back of his chameleons.

"Let that be a lesson to you, new guy," Godenov said on the fire team circuit. He didn't know whether PFC McGinty heard him—he couldn't hear his own voice, and didn't know if that was because his comm was out, or if he'd been deafened by the roar of the Straight Arrow's backblast. He had still been down, curled in a corner of the bunker, when Dean fired the tank killer, so he wasn't hurt as badly as his fire team leader. He was pretty sure McGinty was curled up in the other corner and figured he should be all right as well.

Satisfied that Dean's uniform wasn't burning any longer and that his fire team leader was still alive, he looked for the new man and saw him on his feet, firing his blaster out through the aperture. He joined him. The fléchette gun Dean had fired at was a piece of twisted wreckage, and the boulder its crew had hidden behind was fractured. But most of the riflemen had reached the shelter of the shelf, and only the crew-served weapons still fired at the ridge. Godenov began aiming and firing at those parts of the weapons he could see, hoping to put some of them out of action. He did his best not to notice that the fire from the Marines seemed to be less than it had been.

Sergeant Kerr coldly and methodically fired ten times while the soldiers were maneuvering to the shelf, and every time he fired, a soldier dropped with a hole burned through him. Kerr would have fired many more times, but he'd had to drop down and scramble away from the aperture once when a heavy laser found it and began chewing a hole through its lip. Then again when a fléchette gun sent a multithousand burst onto and through the enlarged aperture, and a third time when another laser further enlarged the opening. When the soldiers reached the cover of the shelf, he began trying to take out the crew-served weapons that were chewing up the fronts of the bunkers, reaching inside them and killing or wounding Marines.

His shooting, ducking, and dodging were all automatic; Kerr was experienced enough he didn't have to think about how to fight outnumbered from a fixed position. While his body functioned on automatic, and temporarily took out a heavy laser by hitting its muzzle at exactly the right angle to crack the barrel lens, his mind worked on the irony of his current position.

Kerr had been a fire team leader when he was nearly killed on Elneal. Since then, Corporal Ratliff was promoted to Sergeant and became a squad leader when then–Gunnery Sergeant Bass was made Platoon Commander and Sergeant Hyakowa was promoted to Staff Sergeant and made Platoon Sergeant. Corporals Leach, Saleski, and Keto were killed before Kerr rejoined 34th FIST and third platoon two years later. Sergeant Linsman, who wasn't even with the platoon when Kerr was nearly killed, was a fire team leader when Kerr returned, and was promoted to squad leader over Kerr.

Now Kerr was squad leader. Corporal Dornhofer was the only fire team leader left from the peace-making deployment to Elneal. Sergeant Eagle's Cry was dead, killed on Diamunde, and Sergeant Bladon still hadn't returned from Rehab after losing an arm on Kingdom. Both of the gun team leaders had been killed in action since Kerr had *almost* been killed.

Only five of the eleven sergeants and corporals who had been with the platoon those years ago were still alive and fighting. Kerr couldn't help but wonder how many would still be alive at the end of the day's fight.

Kerr was finally a squad leader, though it had taken too many deaths to get him there. And there he was, in his first action as a squad leader, and the positions his squad held left him stuck being merely an extra blaster in Corporal Chan's fire team.

Whistles pierced the din of battle, and masses of men surged over the lip of the shelf, scrambling for cover behind the boulders on the gently rising ground before the glacis. Kerr began picking them off.

Major General Koval grinned tightly when he got Brigadier Sturgeon's message. "That fox," he murmured, then began snapping out orders. Satisfied that the bustling of his staff was meaningful, he turned his attention to the string-of-pearls feed that Sturgeon had so generously provided to him. *Damn that Billie,* he thought. *There's no good reason he has to keep the string-of-pearls feed to himself so that I have to piggyback on the Marines.*

The string-of-pearls display of the bay to the north made it clear why Sturgeon was complying in the most obstructionist manner possible with the Supreme Commander's orders—and equally clear that Billie was absolutely incompetent as a commander. Koval had suspected before, but now he knew beyond reasonable doubt that Billie had gotten his promotions and his command because of political maneuvering and not through any merit as a soldier.

He heard the distant screams of the Marine Raptors as they dove on the Coalition airborne troop carriers, and the monstrously loud *cracking* of the Marine artillery on top of the ridge. But he could see on the display how many targets the Raptors and artillery pieces had, and he knew how few Raptors and artillery pieces a FIST had.

He snapped out another order to his artillery regiment commander.

Will this be a first? he wondered.

"T-take your time," Corporal Doyle said into his comm. "Aim your s-shots, m-make them c-count." Despite the stutter, his voice was calm, and his aim was steady, nearly every shot he took struck home on a scrambling soldier.

"Yeah, sure," PFC Summers muttered. He was firing as fast as he could, moving the muzzle of his blaster with each press of the firing lever. He wasn't hitting with each shot, but he wasn't missing by much, either, and the rebels he just missed tended to stay behind cover longer than they should have.

"Take my time," PFC Smedley repeated. "Make every shot count. Aye aye." He didn't stutter, but his voice was the highest pitched and most anxious of the three—it was his first combat, and he didn't see how any of the Marines in the FIST could possibly survive the assault. His aim wasn't good, he was trembling too hard for accuracy, and most of his shots missed.

"St-steady," Doyle said as he fired another bolt and decked another rebel soldier. "M-make your sh-shots count." He stuttered, but if any part of his mind had been able to sit back and assess the situation, he would have realized that he was less frightened than in any previous battles in which he'd fought.

This time, other Marines' lives depended on his leadership; he didn't have any time or energy to spare on fear.

"St-steady. Make e-every shot c-count."

"What's the matter with you, Sturgeon!" General Billie roared into his comm. "Why haven't you moved your FIST yet?"

"Sir," Sturgeon replied laconically, "Thirty-fourth FIST is unable to move. We are fully engaged with a reinforced division that has our positions under assault."

Billie spat out the cigar he had clenched in the corner of his mouth. "*What?*" he squawked.

"Thirty-fourth FIST is fully engaged. Check your string-of-pearls download."

Snarling in disbelief, muttering that he was going to relieve that insubordinate Marine, Billie looked at his string-of-pearls display. What he saw shocked him so much that if he hadn't already spat out his cigar, he might have swallowed it. The visual display clearly showed a three-brigade beachhead engulfing 34th FIST's position and overlapping onto the army battalions on the FIST's flanks. Two more brigades were on top of the ridge, trying to fight their way into the tunnel system from the rear. He stared at the display for long moments before he realized that the main assault—at least, what he still believed was the main assault—had stalled in its advance. Just because he couldn't see the follow-on forces that would exploit whatever breakthrough the initial assault forces made didn't mean they weren't there, they were just too well hidden for him to see. Of course.

"That—!" his voice twisted and whatever imprecation he made was lost in an inarticulate squeal. He switched his comm to a different circuit and snarled, "Sorca, move your reserve brigade to reinforce the MLR. The damn Marines are pinned down by a diversionary attack." Then to a third circuit. "Koval," brusquely, "move a brigade to the MLR right now! Prepare the rest of your division to act if the Marines can't hold against that diversion." He clicked off each time before either division commander could even acknowledge the orders.

"Sturgeon," he snapped, back into the original circuit, "what is your situation? How long will it take for you to drive off that diversionary attack? I need your FIST at the MLR to defeat the main assault."

"General, *this* is the main assault, the assault against the MLR is the diversion. Now if you'll excuse me, I have a major battle to fight." Sturgeon didn't wait for the Supreme Commander, but broke the connection himself.

General Billie's jaws clamped so tightly he nearly cracked a tooth.

When the artillery pulled off the top of the ridge, they withdrew into the three entrances to the tunnel complex on the back side of the ridge. The guns would be worthless there, because they had to be rolled out of the access tunnels to fire—if they were fired inside the enclosed spaces, they would cook their crews and their own electronics. Coalition forces poured down the backside of the ridge top and headed for the access tunnels. But there were only three tunnels, and the artillerymen were waiting with blasters ready for the attackers, sending far more firepower out than the attackers were able to answer. The rebels couldn't get any of their crew-served weapons set up to fire into the access tunnels. They gave up trying after losing a dozen of them to the defenders' fire.

The attack on the reverse slope stalled.

Corporal Claypoole could hardly believe his eyes when an entire company surged up in front of his fire team's bunker and began flooding across the fifty meters of glacis straight at him.

"*Fire! Fire! Fire!*" he shrilled, shooting each time he yelled "fire." The troops in front of him were so densely packed, he couldn't miss unless he fired over their heads, and he wasn't about to do that.

On Claypoole's left, Lance Corporal MacIlargie fired as rapidly as he did, opening a hole in the charging company with every plasma bolt. To Claypoole's right, Lance Corporal Schultz fired so rapidly his blaster almost sounded like a gun. None of his shots missed, either.

But there were so many of them, and they had so short a distance to go before reaching the front of the bunker, there was simply no way to stop the attack. Even if the three Marines managed to wipe out the entire company charging their position, there was another company charging the defensive wall to either side, between their bunker and the bunkers of the fire teams on their flanks.

It was a hopeless situation, and that part of Claypoole's mind that wasn't occupied with fighting the desperate battle resigned itself to death—and resolved to take as many enemy soldiers with him as possible.

"Teach them to beat *me*!" he shouted.

Then an explosion threw him back from the aperture and knocked the blaster from his hands. A roaring followed the explosion. Then more roaring and more and more until it sounded like it would never end. The ground shook in beat with the roaring, rolling Claypoole around the floor of the bunker, flattening him everytime he tried to gain control of himself.

Finally, the roaring stopped. Dazed, he rolled over and struggled to rise to hands and feet. He shook his head, and coughed, choking on the suddenly smoke-filled air in the bunker. Almost unconsciously, he remembered the air filters on his helmet and turned them on. He coughed a few more times, but breathing became easier. Still groggy, he slid his infra into place and looked around. He saw two large, moving blobs—Schultz and MacIlargie struggling to their feet; neither had been hit as directly by whatever it was that slammed into Claypoole. He looked at the floor, closer to himself, and found his blaster by the glow from its barrel. He scrabblingly picked it up and made his way to the aperture, expecting that any second a fléchette rifle or laser rifle would poke through and kill him.

But no such thing happened, and he reached the aperture without incident. Schultz and MacIlargie were there before him. Neither was firing. Claypoole looked out and gasped in stunned disbelief.

Bodies and pieces of bodies were flung all about the glacis, covering it in meat and gore. The survivors were staggering across the rising land between the glacis and the shelf, bumping into boulders, tripping on bodies and rocks, picking themselves back up if they could, or crawling to the waterline when their legs would no longer hold them up. Nobody was shooting at them, the defenders were allowing them to depart without further abuse.

"Allah's pointed teeth," Claypoole said softly when he found his voice. "What happened?"

Neither Schultz nor MacIlargie answered, neither had any better idea than he did.

Claypoole raised Sergeant Kerr on the helmet comm. Kerr was trying to find out himself, and would let him know when he did.

It took another ten minutes, but word finally filtered down to the fire teams. Guided by the datastream from the string-of-pearls, Major General Koval had deployed the heavy weapons and artillery of the 27th Division and swept the attackers off the glacis. The foot soldiers of the division had counterattacked the two brigades stalled at the tunnel complex on the reverse side of the ridge and taken most of them prisoner.

"Sonofabitch," Claypoole said when Ensign Bass informed third platoon on the all-hands circuit. "The Marines have ridden to the army's rescue often enough. Anybody ever hear of the army coming to rescue the Marines?"

Nobody in third platoon replied in the affirmative.

* * *

When Major General Koval saw how effective his counterattack had been, he smiled. He wasn't sure it was the first time the army had ever ridden to the rescue of Marines, but he was more than willing to claim that singular honor for himself and the 27th Infantry Division.

CHAPTER THIRTY-ONE

"Why is that unit familiar to me?" General Lyons asked Admiral Porter de Gauss, his operations officer. They were in the general's mobile command trailer, embedded in some ruins on the outskirts of Ashburtonville. On the trid screen was a detailed blowup of an orbital surveillance of the coast between Phelps, Ashburtonville's port, and Pohick Bay, where the Confederation forces were trapped.

"They're from Lannoy, Davis," de Gauss replied, through a cloud of cigar smoke, using the general's first name, a privilege the admiral had when they were alone and relaxed. "They're known informally as the 'Vigilante Battalion,' probably because they have a bad reputation as a very undisciplined military unit."

"Umpf," Lyons puffed on his cigar and nodded that de Gauss should continue.

"The 4th Division, where they were assigned to begin with, is a composite unit made up of all the ash and trash that wouldn't fit in anywhere else, but its commander, Major General Barksdale Sneed, has done wonders shaping it into a viable combat unit that has been providing security in our rear. This area of the coast is also within his tactical area of responsibility."

"I know Sneed," Lyons nodded, "good soldier. I've been to Lannoy, too, did you know that Porter? It was a long time ago. Rough place, Lannoy, typical frontier settlement, little law and no respect for what they do have out there. I remember one night in a bar in one of the bigger cities, I can't remember which one now, it was in the northern hemisphere, there was this fight over," he shrugged, "something, nobody knew what, and these two guys almost killed each other. Instead of stopping them the other patrons placed bets on who'd win." He shook his head.

"How'd it end?"

"Oh, they both collapsed from loss of blood."

De Gauss puffed on his cigar for a moment. "Well, Lannoy is not a lot different from some of the other worlds in our Coalition, General," he laughed. "To some degree we all wipe our asses with sandpaper, don't we? Or we like to think we do."

Lyons laughed. "Well, that's what the rest of the Confederation of Human Worlds thinks we do. But you know, Porter, even so, we do obey a code of honor among ourselves, don't we? We don't just disrespect each other on general principles, do we? Now what was old Sneed's beef with this MP battalion?"

"They were deployed initially here, between Phelps and Ashburtonville, here, along the main supply route from the port to protect our supply lines from infiltrators but damn, they kept running amok among the civilians down there, abusing the women, taking things without paying, and fighting among themselves all the time. General Sneed said he had to form six general courts-martial boards in the first week they were there! Unbelievable! So he took the whole outfit and put them here." He toggled a switch and the image on the trid screen zoomed in on a portion of the coast. "It's very desolate out there," de Gauss explained.

"I know, I know, steep cliffs, high surf, high tides. But a whole battalion to watch this stretch of coast? That's diverting a lot of manpower just to get them out of the way. You know damned well, Porter, I've been calling in ash and trash from all over to reinforce our position. We're going to need every man jack when the big push comes. Why not just relieve the battalion commander and his subordinate officers, get some firebrands in there and shape those boys up into real soldiers? Besides, Porter, that coast is so rough nobody in his right mind would attempt a landing there. If Sneed wants someone to keep an eye on the area, send out some watchers and mine the beaches."

"Well, sir," de Gauss switched to a more formal form of address because he saw an argument coming, "General Sneed thinks we're vulnerable in that area. And it *is* within his Tactical Area of Operations," he added, diplomatically.

General Lyons puffed on his cigar. "Hell's bells, Porter, we're vulnerable to sabotage everywhere. Billie's long-range recon people have been snooping and pooping all over the place, but they're hardly capable of causing strategic mayhem. Well," he added quickly, "I respect Barksdale's judgment on how to deploy his troops, but no," Lyons shook his head, "there won't be any landings on that coast," he said with finality.

"Well, sir," de Gauss began as diplomatically as he could, "I think it's a good idea to keep an eye on that stretch of the coast out there. You've said yourself many times it's a bad idea to underestimate your enemy, and you know your history better than I do: How many times has a force been defeated because its commanders thought certain routes of attack were impracticable to a determined enemy?"

Lyons was silent for a long moment, regarding his cigar thoughtfully. "Porter, you're right, I do know my history. More important than anything else in war is that you should know your opponent. Once you get inside your enemy's head you've got him by the gonads, Porter. And I have Jason Billie right where I want him. He won't try an end-run. He's going to come straight at us. That's the way his mind works. I've known that guy for years, and the only original thoughts he's ever had were how to get himself promoted by backstabbing officers who were better leaders than he is. No, no, no, Porter, that area is secure," he gestured at the trid and puffed on his cigar. "Besides," he continued after a moment, "suppose they do put a force ashore there. Hell, three nuns and a boy could stop them by throwing rocks down the cliffs! And it's not that far away from our main force, Porter. If by some miracle a force was able to get ashore out there intact, we could rush in reinforcements and destroy them before they ever got off the beaches."

"So you think the Seventh MPs are sufficient to secure that area?" de Gauss asked carefully.

"Yes, Porter, and I'm thinking of telling Barksdale to withdraw all but a company. We'll put them to patrolling the streets here, keep the troops out of the wine cellars," Lyons laughed.

"If you can keep the MPs out of the wine cellars." They both laughed. "Well, sir, there is one more thing about this issue and I feel compelled to advise you on it."

"And that is, Porter?" Lyons squinted at his operations officer through the cigar smoke wreathing his head.

"Billie has a Confederation Marine contingent with his force. Now the Marines, as you know, are specially trained to make difficult landings, either from space or from land-based points. Remember how they landed on Diamunde during the war there? Straight in over the sea and right smack into the enemy's positions at Oppalia. I was with the fleet when the landing force was launched. They didn't expect us there either. Sir," he leaned forward eagerly, "let's put a reconnaissance company out there, back them up with air and artillery and some of those armored fighting vehicles we still have—they're good artillery platforms when dug in properly—designate some units from our reserve force to reinforce them if the enemy tries to establish a beachhead. Just a precaution, sir. It'd let me sleep better."

Lyons had not participated in the Diamundian campaign. He waved smoke away from his face with a hand before making a reply. "Porter, if it was anybody else over there but Jason Billie, I'd be worried, yes, I would. But we need those troops here for when Billie's big push comes. And Marines? He doesn't have many, and believe me, those he does he'll misuse. They had a good thing going with that attempted breakout the day the Marines arrived, that made me very nervous, Porter, I have to admit, but Billie called them back. No, no, no, Porter, there will be no seaborne invasion on that coastline. Now tell Sneed to withdraw the Seventh MPs, all but a company. I'll make it a personal priority to see that those rascals shape up. And Porter? You're my operations officer, *you* don't get any sleep," he laughed.

"Yessir." Admiral Porter smiled and stood up, saluted his commander and turned to go. He had given in to the inevitable, he'd done his best as a staff officer to apprise his commander of what he thought was a dangerous condition. But the decision had been made and it would be carried out. Besides, General Lyons was probably right. Still, as he made his way back to the underground bunker that served as the army's tactical operations center, he could not shake the feeling that General Lyons had just made a serious mistake.

CHAPTER THIRTY-TWO

There are three age-old maxims about military life that every soldier learns by heart:

"In the Beginning Was the Word—and It Was Changed."

"Hurry Up and Wait."

And finally, if not heeded, the one that leads young soldiers inevitably into irreversible disaster, "Never Volunteer."

Now even in the best organized and led armies, these maxims apply to some degree at some time. Unfortunately for Donnie and Charlette Caloon, the 441st Transportation Company of the Loudon Rifles, Loudon County Militia, was not one of the best organized or led units in the Coalition armed forces.

The convoy had only proceeded a short way toward the Bibbsville aerial port when it stopped without warning and the vehicles, which stretched along the road for more than three kilometers, just sat there in the sweltering heat. The minutes ticked by into an hour and the troops in Donnie's bus became restless. A sergeant got out and walked toward the head of the convoy, to see what the delay was, but nobody he could reach knew.

"Hurry up and wait!" some wag shouted and everyone laughed. Charlette had heard that before but she wasn't about to let on that she'd had prior service on the enemy side.

At last Captain Carhart stepped up into their bus, perspiration dripping from the ends of his mustache. "Listen up!" he announced. Instead of silence his words were met with a hubbub of voices and catcalls. "Goddamnit! Clean the crap out of your ears and shut your traps!" he shouted, obviously in a very ill humor. That brought silence. He passed a hand across his forehead to catch the sweat. "Get your asses out of this vehicle and into that field over yonder! The colonel wants to talk to everyone." The troops groaned and groused and obeyed reluctantly. "Come on! Come on, get a move on! You want to stay in here and fry, that's all right with me," he said over his shoulder, turning disgustedly and stepping off the bus. When the whole company had dismounted from their vehicles, Captain Carhart led them into the field, where the rest of the regiment was forming a huge circle.

"Must be the regimental commander is going to talk to us," Charlette whispered.

"I don't even know what he looks like," Donnie whispered back, "hell's bells, I never even *seen* a colonel before!"

The commander of the Loudon Rifles stood on a ration box inside the circle formed by his troops. He was an older man with a pot belly and a disheveled uniform. His forehead ran with sweat that dribbled down over his nose and chin as he spoke. His voice was high-pitched and penetrating. "This here is the first time this whole regiment has been together at the same time," he began, "so some of you new troops prob'ly ain't never seen me before. I am Colonel Cosiatani Francis, your regimental commander, so take a good look at me and remember this handsome face." As he looked around at the men staring up at him the sweat on his uniform was visible as little dark spots.

"We just got a advisory from the Bibbsville Aerial Port that no flights, repeat, no flights to Ashburtonville are available at this time." A huge groan rose from the assembled troops. "That's due to their diversion to higher-priority commitments, and the fact that the enemy has air superiority in certain areas in and around the seat of the war, which makes flying in there hazardous to life and limb." This information was greeted with silence. Until then, most of the troops had not thought very seriously about the fact that there was a real war in progress and they were headed into it.

"Now," Colonel Francis continued, "I also got a priority message from Gen'rel Lyons's chief of staff that they want us at Ashburtonville as soon as possible, and we are going to obey that order. This poses a dilemma, don't it? Goddamn, men, what this army don't screw up it shits on."

"Ain't that the truth," someone muttered loudly.

"Now how do you suppose we're gonna comply with this order, huh?" Colonel Francis shouted, narrowing his eyes and searching in the crowd for the man who had made the insolent remark. Everyone just stared back at him innocently. "Well, how'dye 'spose, you Mr. Wiseass?" Colonel Francis demanded.

"Gonna swim over, Colonel?" someone asked. Everyone laughed.

"Goddamn, boy, you is either gonna be a goddamn gen'rel someday or remain a buck-assed private forever, I ain't decided yet," Colonel Francis shouted, "but you guessed it! We're going by ship! Now, it's going to take me a while to scare up the transport, so battalion and independent company commanders, break out your tentage and set up by units in this here field. Company commanders, see to your training schedules, 'cause I suspect we'll be here a spell. Well, okay, don't just stand there scratching yer behinds, get to it! Captain Carhart, you come with me!" He stepped down from the ration box shaking his head in disgust and motioned for his operations officer to join him, and shouldering his way through the troops, he headed for his command car. The last anyone saw of him for a long time, he was driving off in the direction of Bibbsville.

"Geez," Donnie muttered, "this is bad news, Charlette. Damn, we thought we'd be quit of this place! Now what if that damn Flannigan finds out we're here? Damn!"

"Don't worry, Donnie," Charlette smiled, gesturing at the troops dispersing to set up their tents, "we're surrounded by a whole regiment of men trained to kill."

"Yeah," Donnie groaned, "that's just what bothers me, 'cause from what I seen of this screwed up outfit, it's hard to figure out just who they are gonna kill!"

After only a few minutes into their first meeting, Lionel C. Ifrit, captain of the containership *Bullwhip,* began thinking of killing his visitor, powering up his vessel, and steaming off into parts unknown, cargo or no cargo. "You, my dear chap, are going to ruin the merchants of Loudon County, you know that, don't you?" he seethed.

"I don't give a flying fuck about the merchants of Loudon County, Cap'n. For Chrissakes, *I'm* a goddamn merchant! But I am commandeering this ship, you are loading my men and equipment on her, and we're proceeding under full power north to Phelps where you'll unload us and we shall proceed direct to Ashburtonville and join Gen'rel Lyons's army. You'll be compensated by the Coalition."

The *Bullwhip* had only been in port a few days when Colonel Francis stormed aboard with his men and demanded of her captain that she be turned over to the service of the Coalition and set sail for the war zone. For weeks before her arrival the merchants of Loudon County had been bringing their crops and goods to the port, and the warehouses were full. "You will have a revolution on your hands, Colonel, when the businessmen of this region discover you are preventing them from shipping their crops and goods to market," Captain Ifrit said.

"We'll deal with them when the war is over, Captain. Now, tomorrow, at three hours sharp, my troops will begin arriving and you will load them and their equipment on board this ship. To be sure of yer cooperation, I am leaving a squad of my men on her until then. If you try to pull any funny stuff you'll be shot, and your first officer will be promoted to captain of this vessel."

Captain Ifrit blanched and puffed out his cheeks. "The men who own this shipping line will not be pleased at this—this—act of piracy, Colonel! You know there's a good chance we'll be attacked and sunk on the way to Phelps, don't you?"

Colonel Francis sighed and nodded his head wearily. Then he straightened up and pointed his finger at Captain Ifrit and said, "Cap'n, you send a message to the owners of this tub and tell them you bin drafted into the service of the Coalition. And don't feel so bad about maybe being sunk. If this scow goes down, I'll be standing there right next to you and we can sing 'Nearer My God to Thee' together as the waves roll over us. See you in the morning."

Since the *Bullwhip* was not designed to carry passengers, the accommodations for Colonel Francis's troops were makeshift at best, but because the weather was good and the seas calm at that season, they spent most of their time topside. Donnie and Charlette, as a married couple, were assigned a tiny stateroom for the voyage, but since they had not yet been fully integrated into their company's roster, they spent their waking hours in the ship's galley. "Don't worry," Lieutenant Tamle had told them jovially, "KP builds men, as we say in the army."

Their "stateroom" was actually the tiny quarters belonging to the ship's engineer, a man known to the crew as "Gabby," probably because he seldom spoke to anyone and then only to insult them with nasty vulgarities. The only exceptions were the captain and the first mate, but otherwise everyone was subject to his outbursts, particularly the unwelcome military personnel and especially Donnie and Charlette for evicting him from his quarters per Colonel Francis's orders and over Captain Ifrit's objections. Gabby went out of his way to harass the couple when they were on duty in the galley. He even came by their stateroom at night, pretending to be looking for things he'd left behind when he moved into a bunk in the crew's compartment. His favorite greeting was "Gettin' any yet?"

Kitchen police was grueling duty, but Donnie and Charlette soon fell into the routine of the scut work in a ship's galley feeding a crew of twenty and the 661 troopers of the Loudon Rifles. They were too tired when off duty to complain about the work. Besides, it took Charlette's mind off what she was going to do once they arrived in Ashburtonville, where she would be forced further into her role as a reluctant traitor. At any event, the bouts of morning sickness subsided during the voyage. Maybe it was the salt air or maybe, she prayed, they were due to a false pregnancy.

Within ten days of her departure, the *Bullwhip*'s powerful turbines had brought her to within sight of the coast about a hundred kilometers south of Phelps. That put her well within range of the subatmospheric fighter-bombers supporting the Coalition forces on Pohick Bay, and Colonel Francis therefore ordered everyone below decks during daylight hours. All efforts were taken to disguise the fact that the vessel was transporting military personnel and equipment.

On the eleventh day at sea, just at dawn, Donnie and Charlette were at their posts in the ship's galley, Donnie setting up the mess line and Charlette already cleaning pots and pans the cooks had used to prepare breakfast. The troops ate their meals in three shifts because the galley was too small to accommodate them all at one time, but the *Bullwhip*'s crew ate first and that was the worst time of the day for the military KPs because the civilians resented the army's having taken over their vessel.

"Hey, Donnie, you screwed your wife yet today?" Gabby bellowed that morning, as he did every morning when he was waiting for the serving line to begin. The routine was beginning to wear thin on Donnie, but Gabby was a big, burly man whom no one felt moved to challenge. His arms were decorated with big tattoos of naked dancing girls. By flexing his biceps he could make their private parts seem to move and he enjoyed teasing Donnie with the display whenever he could.

But that morning Donnie decided he'd had enough of Gabby's teasing. When the big man appeared in front of him in the serving line, holding out his tray for the scrambled eggs, he flexed his biceps and said, "When you gonna give me some of that quail, boy?" Donnie seized a long aluminum serving fork and thrust it straight into Gabby's face. One hand clapped to his cheek, Gabby dropped his tray in astonishment and was about to climb over the serving line when the first plasma bolt from a Confederation fighter-bomber ripped through the galley. The last thing Donnie Caloon saw of Gabby replayed over and over again in his mind afterward in slow motion: the naked dancing girl on his left bicep seemed to flex her hips up and down as the bolt sizzled through Gabby's left elbow and cut him in two just below the ribs. It continued on down the serving line, killing three more men before burning its way through the bulkhead and out onto the deck. The following aircraft put its fire just below the *Bullwhip*'s waterline.

Charlette stood frozen at the sink staring in horror at the steaming mess all over the galley deck. Donnie seized her by an arm. "We gotta get outta here!" he shouted, dragging her toward a hatch leading onto the port side of the ship. The air all about them was filled with screaming and explosions as the ship suddenly lurched forward and then stopped dead in the water, its power plant out of commission. It seemed like only seconds before the two fighters made their second pass on the stalled vessel, raking her with high-energy cannon fire fore and aft. The deck under their feet began slowly tilting to port as the galley filled with choking black smoke.

Most of the regiment had been caught below decks when the attack commenced. As the survivors began making their way topside they were horrified to see the crewmen abandoning ship! Since the *Bullwhip* was a commercial vessel not rated to carry passengers, she only had escape gear for her crew. A riot was in full swing between the soldiers and the crewmen for control of the ship's two lifeboats when the *Bullwhip* rolled to port and capsized. She lay there upside down for less than a minute before going down by her stern.

No one ever knew if Colonel Francis and Captain Ifrit got to sing "Nearer My God to Thee" before descending with the *Bullwhip* to the bottom of the sea. For days after she sank bodies mixed with wreckage washed ashore. But some of those who drifted onto the beaches were not dead.

Even in the most disciplined armies, especially in wartime, when commanders' attentions are focused elsewhere, individuals, occasionally whole units, will get out of hand. Such a unit was the 7th Independent Military Police Battalion from Lannoy, a world on the fringes of the Coalition's quadrant of Human Space. The 7th was known informally as the "Vigilante Battalion." Lannoy, a world only recently settled, was typical of the frontiers of space, wild places where wild men and women gathered, generally to avoid prosecutions awaiting them in more civilized places. The commander of the division to which the 7th Independent MP Battalion was assigned when war broke out on Ravenette soon determined he could do without them, so the unit was assigned "coast watch" duty to get them out of the way and put them in some sparsely populated, remote location where the only trouble they could cause anybody would be to themselves.

Nothing ever happened along that stretch of the coast and the men of the 7th soon became bored with their duty and turned to their favorite pastimes: drinking, gambling, and fighting with each other. Occasionally someone would glance out to sea or make a report to higher headquarters, but usually the men of the 7th, when not sleeping off a drunk, wandered the beaches conducting desultory "patrols." Donnie and Charlette had the great misfortune to be "rescued" by one of those patrols.

* * *

"Come on, admit it," the lieutenant was saying to Donnie Caloon, "you're an invasion force. We found dead bodies all over the beach down there. They aren't dressed in any kind of uniform we recognize. Tell us what you know and we'll go easy on ya." The lieutenant hadn't bothered to shave in days and his breath reeked of stale whiskey.

"We were part of the 441st Transportation Company of the Loudon County militia, going to Ashburtonville when enemy planes sunk our ship."

"Yeah? Who's the bitch?"

"My wife, gawdammit!"

The lieutenant turned to his disheveled sergeant and grinned. "Sure. Man and wife in the fuckin' army! How cozy! You oughta know she's confessed everything. Now tell us your mission or I'm gonna have to get rough with ya."

"The hell you say, you lyin' sack o'—" Donnie shouted straining at the ropes that held him in his chair.

"Okay," the lieutenant sighed, "hook 'im up, Sarge. Give 'im a little juice. He'll talk." He turned and left the room. Down the hall he entered the small chamber where Charlette was being held, securely bound and gagged. "It's all over, sweetie," he announced as he closed the door behind him. "Your boyfriend has told us everything." He grinned as Donnie's screams echoed throughout the tiny building. "That's muh boys, havin' a little postinterrogation fun." He grinned. Donnie's screams rose to a crescendo and then stopped abruptly. The lieutenant shrugged, "We got what we need from him. He's told us everythin'. I jus' need you to fill in some details. Now it's yer turn to talk, sweet buns. Oh, don't worry, lovely, I'm not gonna turn the juice on you, not yet, not till we get to know each other a lot better. 'N who knows, I find I like you, maybe we won't need to juice you up." Grinning, slowly he began to unfasten his belt.

Charlette lay there helplessly. She'd been warned in training that things like this might happen if she ever became a prisoner of war. There was no way she could resist what was coming now. She closed her eyes and wished she were a man. Finally she had really sunk to the lowest circle of hell. If she ever managed to get out of this how would she ever explain to anyone what had happened to her? The old expression, "Out of the frying pan, into the fire" occurred to her and for some reason she found that highly amusing.

Charlette Caloon, lately Sergeant Charlette Odinloc, Third Division G2, Confederation Army, began to laugh.

The lieutenant paused. "What, are you fuckin' crazy?" he muttered. He stood there uncertainly. Then his face turned red. She was laughing at him because—quickly he pulled up his trousers in embarrassment. "Are you waterlogged, bitch? What the hell's so fuckin' funny?" he said because he had to say something in a situation like this. Charlette couldn't answer because of the gag in her mouth but she laughed all the harder when she saw the expression on the lieutenant's face. "Well, fuck yew," he muttered, "Go ahead, enjoy yerself, ya crazy fuck! I'll be back!" He slammed the door behind him and stomped off down the corridor.

Charlette lay there and laughed until the tears ran down her cheeks.

CHAPTER THIRTY-THREE

Lieutenant General Alistair Cazombi was disgusted, as he always was whenever General Billie called a staff meeting. It wasn't that Billie simply failed to admit any error on his part regarding the major assault 34th FIST had just fought off with assistance from the 27th Division. No, that morning Cazombi was more disgusted than usual as he and Brigadier Sturgeon sat there listening to Billie as he and his chief of staff, Balca Sorca, smoked fine cigars. Not that cigar smoke annoyed Cazombi, he loved a fine cigar himself, but neither officer had bothered to offer him or Sturgeon a smoke. It was one of the nastiest snubs in a long line of them Billie had inflicted on Cazombi, so to even up the score, he was making this "conference" a tough one by disagreeing forcefully with everything Billie proposed. He'd have disagreed even if he and Billie were old friends: General Jason Billie didn't know his rear end from his elbow when it came to battlefield tactics. Brigadier Ted Sturgeon lent his support to the army three-star.

"General Sturgeon, I did not invite the other commanders to this conference because they already have their orders for the breakout. But I wanted to talk to you personally since your Marines are going to play a vital role in cracking the enemy's siege of our positions. I feel that you need, well," he shrugged, "last-minute clarification of your role in the coming battle." Sturgeon bristled. What Billie meant was he needed a "pep" talk.

"Sir," Cazombi broke in, "with the fact that reinforcements are due to arrive here shortly, I recommend you delay any action until then. Brigadier Sturgeon and I have discussed another option at some length and we think—"

"Gentlemen, this war will be won right here," Billie pointed to the floor, "not by some wild-assed end-run behind the enemy's lines! I know that's what you'd prefer to do. We are going to break Lyons's siege right here, thrust a dagger deep inside his lines, drive a wedge between his besieging forces and defeat him in detail." He paused to catch his breath. "Alistair, I don't see why you two are insisting so determinedly on mounting this foolhardy seaborne attack on the coast! Besides, the reinforcements will be fresh, full of fight, and I plan to use them to exploit our breakthrough. As you both know, once they get here we'll be like sardines in this place and we just don't have space for all those men and their equipment. We've been over this before—"

"Sir, if I may?" Sturgeon interrupted. "As I've said before, we Marines are not trained in defensive warfare. We're best when employed in attack and maneuver. Now we have the troops to land a reinforced FIST on that coast and push inland. We'll—"

"It won't work!" Sorca interjected. "Look at the physical conditions along that coastline up there!" He zoomed the trid screen in on the seacoast just south of Phelps. "Look. Cliffs a hundred meters high in some places! At low tide the beaches are only seventy-five to one hundred meters wide! At high tide the water's up over the rocks! How the hell do you expect any attacking force, even your vaunted Marines, to land and deploy under such conditions?"

"It won't be easy, nobody's saying that," Cazombi insisted. "But because it's so difficult that part of the coast is very lightly defended. Force Recon reveals only a small enemy force deployed along that fifty-kilometer stretch of coastline, with no heavy weapons to back it up and, as far as we can tell, no substantial forces in position to reinforce it. I'm telling you, General, that place is Lyons's blind spot, but he isn't going to be blind to it for long. We have an opportunity here and we've got to take advantage of it."

"You're dreaming, Alistair," Billie growled. "You saw what happened yesterday. The rebels attempted an assault on what they thought was a lightly defended flank and got their heads handed to them." Another reason he did not want to wait for the reinforcements, one he'd never admit, was that a Marine lieutenant general would be among them and if that officer were as hard-nosed as Sturgeon, he'd never be able to execute his breakthrough plan.

"Sir, that flanking assault failed because one," Sturgeon raised a finger, "we knew they were coming; two," another finger, "they were attacking a highly experienced Marine FIST, and three," yet another finger for each point, "reinforcements were in place to assist at the point of attack. We will succeed because they *won't* know we're coming, that area is defended by a reserve military police company, and," he clenched his fist, "they don't have any units in position to reinforce when we attack.

"As for the cliffs, we can get infantry on top of those cliffs using our own hoppers. The heavy stuff we can offload on the beaches and get up the cliffs by using what you army guys call Shithooks." Those were heavy-duty hoppers the army used to transport artillery and large vehicles, so called because they carried their loads suspended beneath them by a series of hooks attached to cables. "Look here, sir," Sturgeon hurried on, "we have the tide tables for the next week. There's one day when the tide's maximum recession occurs just at first light, the ideal time to attack."

"Sir," Cazombi interjected, "that coast is undefended because the enemy thinks it's not vulnerable. By the time he reacts to a landing we can have the entire FIST over the cliffs and headed straight for Phelps. Then Lyons will have to divert troops from his lines to oppose them and that's when you launch your breakout from here. It's risky, but we think it'll work. It's been done before, sir, and you both know it." Cazombi sat back and folded his arms across his chest. He glanced over at Sorca, who was keeping his face expressionless. Billie pursed his lips as if in deep thought. That gave Sturgeon, who did not know Billie that well, the impetus to continue his pitch under the misapprehension the general was seriously considering their plan.

"It's a 'hammer-and-anvil' tactic, sir. My Marines will be your hammer and your troops will be the anvil. Once we penetrate their rear, nobody, not even Lyons, can hold his army together."

"Gentlemen," Billie began slowly, "I appreciate your work on this alternative plan," he smiled weakly and nodded at Cazombi, "but I have considered the alternatives very carefully, very carefully, I assure you, and I do not need a lecture on what the commanders in past eras have done in similar situations. Our position here is unique, gentlemen."

General Cazombi could sense that Billie was at the end of his patience so he decided to push him further because that would be the only satisfaction he'd ever get while serving under the popinjay. "Sir, you know from your days at the academy that an attacking force must outnumber the defenders three to one in order to achieve victory, and that only with high casualties. We simply do not have the forces to achieve that ratio. If the attack fails, the enemy will counterattack, break into our defenses, and you will lose this entire army. Have you thought about life as a prisoner of war, sir?" Not that Billie would ever let himself fall into the enemy's hands, Cazombi thought. He'd take the first shuttle out if the defenses ever started to collapse, leaving men like himself and Sturgeon behind to surrender the army.

Billie stared at Cazombi popeyed with incipient anger as his face began to redden. "This attitude of defeatism is unacceptable, General," he almost shouted; officers and NCOs in other parts of the command post turned their heads at the outburst but quickly went back to their work, smiling surreptitiously but every ear turned now to the conversation. Soldiers love it when senior officers have a falling out. "You have always opposed my command, General, and it's time that stopped and you and General Sturgeon—"

"Excuse me, sir, but my rank is 'Brigadier,' " Sturgeon interjected quietly.

"All right, goddamnit!" Billie shouted, banging his palm on the table. An operations NCO, his back turned to the conference table, grinned. Five minutes after these discussions were over every word would be repeated throughout the Peninsula. "Now look, Sturgeon, your Marines are the knife blade," Billie continued, controlling his anger with effort. "You will punch through the enemy's lines and my infantry will exploit that breakthrough. None of this waltzing around a hundred kilometers down the coast bullshit, clear?"

"Sir, my Marines, you will recall, did just that when we first made planetfall, and you called us back. If you'd exploited that breakthrough then, we might have attained the objective you're insisting on now. But it's too late now, General. The enemy won't let that happen again. We caught him off guard that time. You send my Marines back in there again, and they'll be slaughtered and goddamnit, General, I won't stand for that!" Now it was Sturgeon's turn to slap the tabletop.

Billie started at the outburst, then leaned across the table and thrust his finger into Sturgeon's face. "General, you get this through that thick jarhead of yours! You follow my orders or you get your ass on the next shuttle back to the fleet, because you will follow my plan of attack, your Marines will lead it and they will achieve the breakthrough, and if it doesn't work, you'd better be left out there as a casualty because I don't want you back in here with your tail between your legs! Clear?"

"Get your finger out of my face, General," Sturgeon answered quietly.

"Or what? You'll bite it off?" Billie snorted, his voice dripping with contempt. "Hell, General, you've been nipping at my heels since you first arrived here. You have my orders, you know my battle plan, and you will prepare to execute it on my orders. That is all, gentlemen."

Both Cazombi and Sturgeon rose to go. "I'll tell you this now, General Billie," Sturgeon said, "I formally protest this decision."

"I protest as well," Cazombi added.

"Shit, General, you've started thinking like this Marine!" Billie snorted.

"I consider that a compliment, sir," Cazombi smiled and bowed from the waist.

After the two had departed Billie sat at the table, his hands shaking. "What is said in here, stays in here," he shouted at his staff. He drummed his fingers nervously on the tabletop. "Both of them are finished," he muttered, "finished, Balca, finished! I have never encountered such insubordination from a subordinate! Unconscionable conduct on the part of a flag officer. And goddamnit, Balca, where were you when I needed your support?"

General Sorca shrugged, "Jason, I added my two credits' worth, but I just didn't see the need to jump in when you had everything under control. In the final analysis, they will follow your plan and it will work. That's a given." But Sorca, who any day now expected to be promoted to Lieutenant General and was thinking of his postwar career, was thinking to himself that maybe he had hitched onto the wrong star after all.

Billie growled and stuck his cigar back into his mouth. He frowned. "Goddamned thing's out. Give me a light, Balca."

ABOUT THE AUTHORS

DAVID SHERMAN is a former U.S. Marine and the author of eight novels about Marines in Vietnam, where he served as an infantryman and as a member of a Combined Action Platoon. He is also the author of the military fantasy series Demontech. Visit the author's website at www.novelier.com.

DAN CRAGG enlisted in the U.S. Army in 1958 and retired with the rank of sergeant major twenty years later. He is the author of *Inside the VC and the NVA* (with Michael Lee Lanning), *Top Sergeant* (with William G. Bainbridge), and a Vietnam War novel, *The Soldier's Prize*. He has recently retired as an analyst for the Department of Defense.

ABOUT THE TYPE

This book was set in ITC Berkeley Oldstyle, designed in 1983 by Tony Stan. It is a variation of the University of California Old Style, which was created by Frederick Goudy. While capturing the feel and traits of its predecessor, ITC Berkeley Old Style shows influences from Kennerly, Goudy Old Style, Deepdene, and Booklet Oldstyle, all of which were also designed by Goudy. It is characterized by its calligraphic weight stress, and its x-height, now described as classic, is smaller than most other ITC designs of the day. The generous ascenders and descenders provide variations in text color, easy legibility, and an overall inviting appearance.